Chrysalis – The Awakening

BOOK ONE

By
M.L. Lacy

authorHOUSE®

AuthorHouse™
1663 Liberty Drive, Suite 200
Bloomington, IN 47403
www.authorhouse.com
Phone: 1-800-839-8640

First published by AuthorHouse 4/6/2009

ISBN: 978-1-4389-5984-9 (e)
ISBN: 978-1-4389-5985-6 (sc)

Library of Congress Control Number: 2009903280

Printed in the United States of America
Bloomington, Indiana

This book is printed on acid-free paper.

CHAPTER I

LATE 1400's

The man stood quietly in front of the slate board. He rubbed the pagan medallion that hung around his neck. A habit he had developed over the many years he had translated these old writings. His long wavy brown hair and his smooth skin gave no indication of his age. His eyes moved rapidly over the scroll; his concern was evident and the distraction of the writing implement annoyed him.

∽

The fine-grained white limestone stick, that wrote the symbols on the board, as the man read from the scroll, grew impatient. It just hung there in the quiet of the room as the man mumbled to himself. These words were not directed at the writing tool, so it had nothing to do and it grew restless.

The writing stick started to quietly entertain itself by drawing little stick figures on the slate. All was going well until the writing tool slanted its angle a little too much, causing it to make a screeching sound as it moved across the slate. In its horror the stick froze, and it slowly turned to face the man.

The man just shifted in his stance and ignored the disturbance.

The stick began to look over its artwork as boredom was setting in. It had a job to do and it figured the man had had enough time to look over the scroll. Now it was time to get back to work.

The white chalky stick began to tap on the black slate; maybe that would draw the man's attention back to their task. When that didn't work, its taps became louder, miniscule pieces of limestone flew in the air as the writing tool assaulted the board. It had succeeded in drawing the man's attention to it.

The annoyance of the sound crept into the man's thoughts. The man lowered the scroll and gave a sigh. "Give me a minute," he mumbled under his breath and then went back to his reading.

When the man had finished his reading, he looked back at the board. A smile lined his lips and he rolled his eyes as he noticed the calcite stone playing a game with x's and o's. He waved his hand and a soft gray brush wiped the doodles way. "I don't have time for your games now. Behave yourself and maybe I'll play you a game later," the man muttered to the stick.

He started speaking again in the ancient dialect and the chalk continued with its duty, drawing the emblems on the slate that spoke of the prophecy of the last Chosen One.

❧

The door to the linguistics' room opened and the man at the slate board turned from his readings to see who belonged to the footfalls he heard. He gave a slight chuckle, "Max," he said in a friendly tone, "what's brought you down here? Curiosity?"

Maxwell Stone walked briskly to the front of the room. One hand thrust into the pocket of the gray wool robes he wore, his other swung with his stride. "Ah, Samuel, you know me, this has always interested me. The way your group unravels the prophecies, rewrites them, so even the common can understand." He picked up a book that sat on the long table and looked at its cover then returned it to its original spot. His eyes turned serious and he motioned toward the young steward who was busy turning on the ancient orbs that illuminated the room.

Samuel understood and sent his steward on an errand, "Kenny, that's fine. Why don't you go and round up the scribes, tell them they have five minutes left of their break."

Samuel turned back to the slate and viewed the writings, checking it against the scroll, waiting on the door behind him to close. He ignored his friend until he heard the soft click, "Okay Max, what's the problem?" He spoke without looking at him.

"No problem, I just wanted to sit in on this session, that's all."

Samuel laughed. He rolled up the scroll and tossed it on his desk, shook his head at his friend then walked along the long table and snapped his fingers, making the writing tablets, ink and quills appear. "Come on, you expect me to believe you had me send my steward away so you could ask

3

if you could sit in?" He angled his chin at his old friend. "Spill it."

Max looked at him; a smile creased his lips. "Nervous?" he questioned.

Sam gave him a confused look, "What, over this? Hell no. It's what I do, I'm a linguist; I translate the old languages. I have twenty of the best working for me. We'll get it right. This one's not any different than the ones that came before it," he spoke confidently to his old friend.

"But this one's important." Max drew nearer to him, the concern in his voice apparent. "All the others were simple really. We knew the stories about the twenty-four Chosen Ones being born to protect us from ourselves." He gave a nervous chuckle. "But this one's about the last Chosen One, and damn, it's got to make you nervous. Have you translated it yet?"

Sam exhaled very slowly, "Yeah, I have. The Chosen One that lives this life is going to have a very heavy task. I want this team to verify my findings, but if I'm correct, this last Chosen One...if she lives...will be our Queen. She will sit on the Elder's throne." Sam looked toward the closed oak doors, his thoughts wandered, "We haven't even found the Elder's throne room so..." he let his thought trail off. With a shrug of his shoulders, he looked back at his friend and continued, "Anyway, she will guide our world with her sisters that still exist. We know from the earlier accounts not all of the Chosen Ones lived, so those that remain will help her...somehow. She will rule in a place called the New World and she will right the wrongs of many paths. Many attempts will be made on her life, and if she lives," Sam stopped what he was doing and looked back at his

4

old friend, "she'll bond to a member of the Fourth House. She'll strengthen his clan, and he'll strengthen her, *after* she has crossed into the Magical realm. I have no idea what this Fourth House is or when it will come into existence or how he, this...guy, could even strengthen her. The prophecy says she will be more powerful than any that walked before her. She will only be allowed seven companions and their hue will be made known to her their presence." Sam gave a chuckle and continued with his task of placing the needed items on the tables, "I guess being Queen doesn't give you all the privileges, but it goes on to say she will be loved by many; she'll be fair and she'll have many enemies. It ended with 'to live, she must transform; to lead, she must transform; for corrupt Houses to fall, she must transform. Only then, can she be bitten.'"

Max watched as Sam finish snapping his fingers at the last station, "What, in all of creation, are you doing? Why are you still using these archaic writing devices? Where's your imagination?" Max snapped his fingers and a very sleek, futuristic machine appeared on the table. He pressed a button on the top of the machine and the lid slowly opened, a musical tone played and a sexy woman's voice sounded, "Good Morning Max." Max had a big grin on his face as he looked at Sam and flexed his eyebrows, "Look, why don't you just use this?"

Sam smiled, looked at his friend and snapped his fingers and made the machine disappear. "Max, you know the rules; we use nothing in this world before the mortals have invented it. Besides, I like to translate in the old fashion. I think better this way, and nothing has been invented in this world that beats a quill and parchment – yet!"

"I know, I know. The Alliance has kept on us to be careful, the prophecy was very clear when things could be invented here. You know, out of all the worlds we could have picked to go to, this is one of the slowest races! It is going to take forever to bring this world up to speed with all the other worlds we've lived on."

"I remember that prophecy. Damn, took us nearly three years to translate it all. That was the only prophecy from that seer too but he's called everything right so far." Sam laughed back at his old friend. "Look Max, you worry about inventing things in this world, let me worry about the prophecies." He looked toward the doors as they opened and his crew entered, then back at his old friend, "Stay a while and watch, this should be interesting."

❧

Samuel stood at the front of the room. He greeted a few of his team as they found their seats in the front. Max found a seat off in the corner at the back and listened to him give out the instructions.

"Okay, settle down everyone." Sam patted the air, motioning for silence. "Today, we have a very important task. This is a very ancient prophecy." He motioned toward the slate board. "And it's very important we get it right. So, instead of us breaking into teams and working on separate projects, I want us all focusing on this one. I'll give you about ten minutes to look it over and form your thoughts, and then we'll begin."

"Sir?" a young woman in the back spoke up.

"Yes, ah...Rachel is it?" His forehead wrinkled as he really wasn't sure of her name, he was very sure she was pretty, and he always became tongue-tied around pretty women.

Max grinned as he watched his friend struggle with his emotions.

"Have you translated it?" She smiled a bright smile to him.

"Ah, yes...yes I have. I...because this is such an important prophecy, I want to ensure my findings are correct," he said to everyone.

Nothing more needed to be said. They picked up their quills and began their translation of the old text.

಄

Several of the quills, dipped themselves in the ink, and began writing while their owners looked at the board, lost in deep concentration.

A few held theirs motionless and brushed their chins with the quill feathers while they decided where to begin.

And a few wrote in the old fashioned way. With quill in hand, they dipped it in the ink, gently tapped the excess off and began to write their words across the parchment as they made their notes. Some changed their minds and tore the parchment up and began again.

಄

After the allotted time had past, Sam cleared his throat and stood before them again. "Okay, thoughts?" He waited, his arms spread, beckoning input. "Anyone?"

That same young woman slowly raised her hand, "Sir?"

Sam looked toward the back of the room with encouragement, "Yes, Rachel."

She smiled as he said her name. "There are no rhymes to this one."

A smile creased Sam's lips, "Go on."

"Well, it tells of the birth of the last Chosen One…"

ᴄ⁊

Max sat back and listened as the linguistic team worked through the process of translating the ancient words. He smiled as he began to realize his friend had successfully translated the old text, but his smile soon turned to concern as he heard the words of warning.

If this Chosen One failed to transform or failed in her path, the mortal and the Magical world would cease to exist. Max sat stone still and began to struggle with his thoughts, *complete annihilation! The gateway that brought us here will not appear again to take us to another world! I can't even begin to envision this!* He gave a silent prayer, *I hope to all that is powerful…this Chosen One never has to be born!*

CHAPTER 2

On a rocky outcrop on the Dakota Prairie
- Mid-October 1975

Darkness loomed over the Dakota prairie; the sky covered by heavy clouds left a void of stars and moonlight.

The messenger made his way along the animal trail toward the rocky ledge he had visited many times in the past. He carefully walked the switchbacks, eyes and ears on constant alert.

Her protectors may be aware of the sisters, he thought quietly to himself as he silently continued forward. The walk was longer than he remembered. *Must be getting old, whew!* He wiped the perspiration with the back of his hand. *One more turn.* He quietly pushed himself forward.

Several small stones from above slid down the hill in his path and he paused. His eyes darted quickly toward the sky searching for any shadow, but it was too dark and no shadows would be seen. *Damn, must be one of the sisters...I hope anyway,* he silently prayed to himself.

Sure footed, he continued forward into the darkness. Cautiously, his hand felt along the side of the hill, the path was narrow and he needed to steady himself. *Almost there,* he comforted himself, *almost.*

৵৹

The messenger stopped at the end of the trail and faced the smooth wall of stone the stood closed before him. "Damn, why is it closed? I thought they were expecting me," he whispered to the night.

He sat on a large boulder, letting his breathing calm. He looked out over the expanse; he could only imagine the view. He had never been here in the daylight, the sisters slept then. He had only made this journey at night and this night was so very dark.

He hated it, he wasn't allowed a light to see by, he could only feel his way up the slope, and he truly hated it.

His ears were pressed to hear any sound, but there were no night sounds. Then he heard it, the quiet rain of dirt giving way, rocks trickled down the hill again! His head jerked in the direction his ears told him.

Silence again, except for his rushed breathing. He pressed himself into the hill, trying to fold into the darkness and he waited. "Where the hell are they?" he murmured ever so quietly.

"I'm right here you idiot," the old woman said in a low tone, causing the messenger to jump at his surprise. Her cackle rang in the stillness of the night.

The owl that stood vigil in the trees took flight. She watched the owl, she could see in this void. She whispered words under her breath and the owl fell to the ground, dead. "Dinner," she said. She held her hand out and the dead owl floated to her. "Owl stew," she turned to the messenger who still stood very quietly, pressed to the wall of the hill. "Ever had it?" she questioned.

Nervously he answered, "No ma'am."

✑

By the sound of her voice, he knew this was Isadora. She was a fat, squatty little woman. She always wore her gray hair in a tight bun on her head; round rim glasses precariously perched on the tip of her nose. Isadora was a champion of the Chosen Ones. She was thrilled whenever one was born, whenever a Chosen One succeeded in stopping the evil from progressing and taking hold in the Magical and mortal world, unlike her twin sister, Esadora who was opposed to them. She was happiest when a Chosen One was defeated in attempts to rid either worlds of the evil, or when a Chosen One was captured and held against her will.

Isadora and Esadora were identical twins and the only way you could tell them apart was by the mole on their face. Isadora's mole was on the right cheek and Esadora's was on the left.

Their older sister Lenora was a tall willowy, pencil faced woman. She was neither pro nor con. The prophecies were the prophecies and she took them in stride. It was what it was; it is what it is.

All three women had their druthers, but none of them would interfere with a prophecy and they were none too partial to those who tampered with them. They could be very ruthless in their assaults to those that did, and that's why he didn't trust them, or like them. He truly feared them.

He had heard the stories, seen the human bones scattered about the outside of their prairie dwelling. At least when his Queen Esmeralda was unhappy, she just killed you, she didn't eat you. He feared these three sisters more than he feared his Queen and that said a lot.

∽

"Pity, it's very good," she smiled. He could only guess she was smiling, he couldn't see in this black. But he heard the smile in her voice. Then just as quick her voice turned harsh, "Why have you come?"

"I've come to check...the progress. Has the child been... born?" he stammered.

"Oh," she laughed a deep, low hiss. "Oh, yes, she has been born. She will be powerful. The Elders are deep rooted with her. Her intended's love will be very strong. She will have many loves but his; oh my...his is a love that runs deep into her soul and hers in him." She sensed his fear, "Yes, you should fear this one!"

"Is there any chance we can destroy her before she crosses? Before she transforms to the Magical world?" he asked, hoping to take back to his Queen any information that might save his neck.

"There is always a chance, but I pity the eternal soul of any Magical that harms the child before her time. Oh, yes, I pity your soul," she whispered the words, eyeing him warily.

He felt her press her fat finger against his chest. He hoped she was trying to make a point and not seeing how tender he might be. The Messenger swallowed hard, "What of this 'chance'?"

"We have seen three humans do her great harm. It was very cloudy whether they will succeed or not, many paths lead to an end. You need to view all from our crystals, come inside and see," she spoke these words softly. He did not want to go but he needed the information. She began her message to him in the rhymes he had grown to hate over these many years of his visits here.

"Come inside and see; things are not always as they seem. This Chosen One is strong, should you doubt her, you'd be wrong." She laughed a sinister laugh as she continued in her childlike rhyme and the messenger froze in his place. "Come with me, take my hand, and let me show you what I can. Your eyes will see, you will learn, this Chosen One will be stern. You will see when said and done, the power of this Chosen One."

Her laugh echoed into the night, as he started to follow her deep into her prairie dwelling. He didn't want to obey but he had no choice. She coaxed him toward her lodgings with her singsong voice. "Come with me little man, learn what you can! Then run and tell your self imposed Queen," she laughed a very wicked laugh. "Tell her, it is as it was written, the last and strongest Chosen One has risen."

"Does this Chosen One...has she been named?" he called softly after her. Was he pressing his luck to ask another question?

"Yessss," she hissed. "It's a sweet name, but a strong name. Aubrey Marie," her voice echoed in the blackness.

The messenger tentatively stepped forward in the darkness. He slowly stepped with each stroke of her voice. He truly hated this, but he went with her and he listened to her singsong voice as it led him deeper into the earth.

October 1975

The messenger sat in a poorly lit room of the castle, waiting for his Queen, Esmeralda to arrive. He shivered and drew his cloak around him. The room was cool, but not enough to make him shiver, he was nervous. The messenger stood and paced, his footsteps echoed through the hall.

He had the information his Queen needed and he knew she would not be happy. He didn't want to be the one to tell her the child had been born; but that was his job, to keep her informed.

He didn't want to anger his Queen. He didn't want to end up like the last messenger, dead, because she didn't like the message. So he paced and he thought how he should tell her the last Chosen One had been born. And she would be more powerful than Esmeralda, have more followers than Esmeralda, and this Chosen One would indeed be loved by many more than Esmeralda.

The child's parents were very old and everyone thought the mother and child would die in childbirth. That didn't happen. The mother was indeed old, the birth was a stubborn one, but they'd both survived.

He would tell her the child was born free of magic to the Coven, from the United House of Three, during the blood moon phase when the earthly world and the spirit world were at their thinnest. The family lineage was of Merlin and the Druid was strong within her. This child would be very powerful, just as it was written in the prophecy. *Simple enough*, he thought, *she shouldn't get angry with that.*

He would remind Esmeralda, the child's family would take great measures to ensure her safety, and it would be difficult to harm her. The child's transformation from mortal to Magical might kill her, but should the child live, she would be a tremendous threat to Esmeralda's plans. He chastised himself. *Our plans, I must keep that thought in my head, OUR PLANS.*

He took out his handkerchief and wiped his forehead. His hands shook, his mouth was dry. *I must not let my thoughts betray me. Esmeralda is cunning, she is an expert when it comes to reading others minds. She will most certainly snoop through mine and if I appear weak, it could be my end,* he thought.

He calmed himself, his pacing slowed as he continued to go over in his mind the message he needed to convey to her.

He would tell her the seers saw the child dying during the transformation as a probable scenario. The child would be weakened by events in her life, but the seers were unable to tell him what those events were.

He would tell her of the plans they had laid out. Since the child couldn't be harmed by anyone in the Magical world until the age of twenty-five, nor could she know anything about this world until that time, they were planning to use mortals to kill her.

They had used mortals before to aide their causes and the seers had seen three new faces that do great harm to her. *This should surely please her; she can then say she had no hand in the death of the Chosen One. Esmeralda can even mourn publicly. She is such a good actress. Everyone will believe she is truly upset by the death of the Chosen One. She may even gain more followers,* he thought.

A soft hiss brought the servant back into the present.

"My Lady," he cleared his throat, "I didn't hear you enter. I was lost in thought of...our plan. Please forgive me," he tried his best to keep his voice calm.

"What news do you have for me?" Esmeralda questioned. She spoke in a relaxed, dispassionate manner as she sat in one of the leather wingback chairs. She crossed her legs, exposing her thigh through the slit in her gown. Her arm rested on the chair, she leaned to the side; her low cut dress gave him a perfect view of her ample breasts. Her strawberry blond hair hung in long soft curls over her shoulders and back. Her angelic face, with bright violet eyes, gave you a false sense of security, because this face could turn from angelic to horrifyingly scary in only a fraction of a second if she didn't like what she heard. She smiled at the messenger, and then waved her hand as she asked, "Has the child been born?"

"Yes, the child, a girl, has been born to the family. She is powerless and plain, totally human, as it is written."

"So, an ugly baby then?" Esmeralda asked. She continued to smile at the messenger making him feel uncomfortable.

"Aren't all babies odd looking, my Lady?" Perspiration peppered his forehead. "She is no different than any other baby. I'm told she has small features and that she is a very quiet child, she doesn't cry much. Her eyes are brown." He did his best to voice his answers with a strong even tone.

"All the Chosen Ones have brown eyes," Esmeralda said. "Let's see if we can make this quiet child cry." She raised her eyebrows as she spoke. Her mind formed a plan of her own to cause this child pain, great pain. "Does *it* have a name?"

"Yes, my Lady, her name is Aubrey Marie," he supplied the information.

"Odd name for a Chosen One, don't you think?" She wasn't looking for his answer; she picked a small piece of lint off the arm of the chair. "Not a very royal sounding name." She looked straight at the messenger. "No matter, she will never sit the throne, she will never sit the Council, and she will never lead."

She continued to watch the messenger, reading his body language. Her lips slowly curled into a snarl, her brow ceased. Her beautiful features turned hard, "Does the Fourth House know yet?"

"Not yet, but soon. The man will be made aware and he will play a part in her protection. The three males of the clan, along with the male of her family, make formidable opponents, just as it was written," the messenger answered. "The seers say the man's love for her would be strong."

"I want her dead. You do understand that, don't you?" she hissed. Lightening flashed and her violet eyes brightened with the sudden burst of light in the room.

"Yes, my Lady, perfectly."

"Good, I'm sure her family is fawning over their precious little joy. Let them, their misery when she is dead, will make my victory that must sweeter." She examined her fingernails as she pouted her thoughts. The news of the child's birth seeped into her reality; this was something she now had to deal with, slowing her plans to dominate her own world.

The messenger started breathing a little easier, a little more confidence in his voice as he continued to speak of their plans. "We have several plans in the making. Our best people are watching her and her family. We did have a stroke of luck; her grandfather has already been killed. He developed a potion to help her through the transformation. We will never know if it would have prevented her death, all his notes and the potion were destroyed in the blast."

"Just as well, she is the last Chosen One, the one who is supposed to set the balance of our world and the mortal world right again," Esmeralda sulked. "Tell me how they can expect one child, one simple plain child, to do this?"

The low roll of thunder sounded in the distance.

"She is most certainly plain, my Lady. She could never match your beauty." The messenger knew Esmeralda was vain and he hoped she favored his compliment.

Esmeralda sat in her chair, and leaned on her elbow. She stroked her lips with her finger as she looked at the messenger, her eyes washed over his body. There was nothing special about him, he was average in height, and his body was well toned. He was bald, his eyes were like polished emeralds though, and she lingered on his eyes, *beautiful*. His mustache hid his lips, but she guessed his lips were soft, she could only imagine. *Maybe I should just see for myself how soft they are.* She smiled at her thoughts. "Tell me of the plans," she whispered and inhaled deeply as she watched him. *I'm making him uncomfortable*, she mused, *good; they are more pleasurable to me this way; so eager to please.*

He cleared his throat, and made a conscious effort to avert his eyes from her breasts. "We have been given three names; the seers have seen her fall to them. We will cultivate them; they will do our bidding in the end. The child can't be harmed by our kind until after she comes of age, but she can be harmed by her own race at any time," the messenger said, hoping this bit of information pleased her. "They can kill her for us, my Lady; no blood will be on your hands. Her family will fall after that. Many will fall after that."

"Who will train them? Can the Red Guard be used?" she asked.

"No, not the Guard, but we can use those that are no longer with them. There are those that are agreeable to your campaign. They favor your leadership, your want to rid our race of the weak, the filth, and even the mortals. They too want this world for our kind. You have those that are loyal to you, my Lady," he assured her.

Esmeralda stood and began to pace. Her cape billowed from her pressed gait. She turned to the messenger, her beautiful violet eyes darkened into an angry sea of hate, "Do not kill the child yet; let her grow into a young woman. I want them to know who the stronger one is, who is more powerful. Give her a false sense of security, but make her life miserable and as painful as possible, *without* killing her.

Let her know her intended, let them even fall in love, and then take him away from her. Let her know fear, let that become her childhood friend." She smiled at this idea and moved closer to the messenger. "Would that not make you miserable, to know your true love and then have them taken from you?"

She ran her fingertips along his jawline and smiled at him. "Yes, I do want her miserable; I want her to feel pain. I want her family to think they are protecting her. I want them to suffer too for their insolence. When their precious little bundle of joy is dead, they will mourn, and I will be merciful," she smiled a sneer, "I will end their lives quickly."

She laughed her witchy cackle and turned to pace again as she spoke, "Then I want her brought here, I want to watch this Chosen One die before me. I want her to see just whom they thought they could beat! I want her to beg!" She turned to face the messenger, raised her finger, "Do you understand?"

She tipped her head to the side with an afterthought, not giving him a chance to answer. "Oh, should the humans succeed in killing her, so be it. I'll take that. However, if they do not, I want her brought here when she comes of age, to die in the dungeons, away from her family. She will weaken, she will not transform." She paused and looked at the messenger and raised her finger again pointing at him, her eyes remained dark and intense. "She must not transform under any circumstances. Do you understand?" He nodded and she continued, "Once she is gone, and we have destroyed her family, I will reign." She calmed and smiled to herself; proud she arrived at the conclusion of her glorious plan.

"My Lady, we can't harm the man; his House will seek retribution," the messenger said nervously.

"I know that you fool. I didn't say harm the man; I said the family. Leave the man of the Fourth House. He will find another, maybe he might want to join us." As she thought of that comment, a thin smile crossed her lips. "No," she laughed, "he will end his own life. Such a pity and such a waste of a firm body! No, there will be no retribution from his House." She thought for a moment, "I would like more assurance on this. Just incase complications arise.

Working with mortals is unstable at best; they don't follow instructions well. They have a tendency to improvise, such an immature race. I want my own clan of vampires. I have heard of a very strong clan, led by Thomas Halsing. Do you know of this clan?"

"Yes, my Lady, but why would you align yourself with such a...from all the stories I have heard, he is a very ruthless..." he searched for the right word to use, "creature."

"Precisely why I want him, a vampire's bite is deadly to this Chosen One. If things get out of hand I want her life ended quickly." She scoffed, "With any luck maybe one of her lovers will slip and in their passion for her will administer a fatal bite." She smiled at the thought of this Chosen One dying accidentally by the hands of one of her lovers. Her eyes focused back on the messenger, "I heard he could be bought for a price, and I am willing to pay that price. Now leave me and find him; bring him here. I will handle the rest." She kissed her finger and touched it to the lips of the messenger. "Hurry back." She smiled and disappeared from the room.

Elsewhere in the castle

"John, the child has been born. She will need our protection. I have seen her future," she spoke softly to him as they lay together. Her eyes were moist as she fought to hide her tears from her lover.

"Celia, we will be ready, she is our last hope. Her family is strong, the Fourth is strong." He wrapped her tightly in his arms, desperately trying to keep her fears at bay. He kissed her gently on the lips, "My darling we will be together, our future is together. When she has gained her powers, everything will be put right. You have to trust, in me, in her family, in her clan, and in her."

"Our future is in jeopardy, John. You have not seen the visions I have seen, the unhappiness that will be in her life. She must cross to our world John. So much rides on this one," Celia whispered.

"Our future is only in jeopardy if we give up hope. I am not giving up nor should you. Your sister is strong; she will cross. She has brown eyes like yours." John kissed Celia's eyes, then her cheeks, making his way to her lips.

"The House of Went does not yet know; her intended is unaware. She will need him, there is so much uncertainty surrounding her, I fear for her John. Her birth was not as strong as it should have been. Her life will be a lonely one, she may not bond with her intended, and she may not even survive the crossing. Her enemies are already planning and I've seen glimpses into her future. I'm concern I won't be able to help her."

As Celia dwelled over the Chosen Ones plight, John drew her close, giving her soft kisses until her tension eased. She replied to those kisses with her own passion, and quietly they loved.

Ft Worth, TX

"Martha, are you tired, my sweet?" Warren asked.

"No, Warren, I'm not tired; I'm too happy to be tired. We finally have a daughter and she is perfect, she's beautiful. Ten little fingers and ten little toes. The Elders have smiled on us."

"We are sure her enemies are aware of her birth, but we have woven our spells. She will be safe within our homes and within our presence. None can harm her. William has gone to tell the Fourth House and soon the House will ask for an audience with us. The prophecy will be fulfilled."

"I worry for our daughter's future, Warren. What if he doesn't love her? What then, Warren? To be with your mate and not be loved, that would be a horrible fate." Martha spoke her fears to her husband as her fingertips outlined the infant's face.

"How could he not? Look at her; she is beautiful. We will raise her right; she will not be spoiled. He will desire her and they will bond. The prophecy says this clearly," Warren said softly to his wife, trying to ease the fear that grew in her heart.

"I know, but I still worry for her future, I have a strong feeling she will be tested beyond measure. She is beautiful though, isn't she Warren?" Martha held her newborn daughter close to her breast.

"Yes, indeed she is Martha. The name you have given her is a strong name."

"Yes it is. Aubrey, Aubrey Marie Campbell," Martha smiled, and Warren tenderly kissed his wife, then his daughter's forehead.

∽

The child slept peacefully, unaware of the trials she would face, the pain she would bear or the love she would have when she bonded with the member of the Fourth House.

CHAPTER 3

PRESENT DAY

September 2007 - 32 Years later,

Yellowstone Lake Lodge Cabins

Four tall individuals stood vigilant outside a cabin at Yellowstone Lake. Their eyes scanned the sky and the tree line. Four pair of ears perked, ready for any sound outside the normal night sounds.

One individual struck a match to light his cigar. Three pair of eyes glowed in the dark from the tiny amount of light.

The cigar smoker chuckled, "Pretty cool the way your eyes do that."

In the darkness another man spoke, "Patience William, your eyes will do that soon enough."

William took another puff on his cigar, "Brad, I think patience isn't the issue here. If anything, we have all been very patient. How are you holding up Steven?" He placed his hand on Steven's shoulder, giving him a little shake.

"I hate this waiting, you should just introduce us now Bill," Steven said to William. Why do we have to wait until October?" Steven knew the answer but he had to speak the question.

"You know why, Steven. She isn't back to herself yet. Those two attempts on her life took their toll. Gran's worried, Doc Craig said she didn't bounce back as quickly as he had hoped after the car wreck. He didn't know if it was because of the accident or her mental state. However, he told Gran every time he mentioned Nick's name to her, he saw a hell of a lot of fear in her eyes. Damn, I should have stepped in sooner." He kicked the ground causing dust to rise, took another puff on the cigar, their eyes watched him.

"Don't be so hard on yourself, Bill. You need to give Bree a little more credit; she's a fighter. By October, she'll be as good as new. Then, Steven, you can be with her," another man said as he lit his cigar, the smoke curled around his head. The tiny puffs he took to start the cigar caused the glow in his eyes to pulse as they caught the light.

"I don't know, Rick, she's much quieter now," Bill said softly, keeping his eyes on the cabin. "She doesn't trust anymore. I've watched her sleep, you know, when Gina has stayed with her. It's not peaceful; she curls up in a tight ball. Gran thinks it has more to do with the transformation than the accident, but I don't know. We asked if she wanted Timmy staying with her in her cabin while we're here; at least she wouldn't hear any noises with someone in there with her. But she said no, she'd be fine. She's trying to put on a brave face, but I know she's scared."

⁂

Bill was still angry with Aubrey's parents for letting all of this happen to her. Bree was special to Bill; she was his favorite little cousin, and he ached with her pain. Nothing was going to stop him from getting Bree and Steven together. Once this happened, everything would be put right again.

However, until that time, he had to stay vigilant. They all had to stay vigilant and keep her safe from those that wished her harm.

⁂

They stood still as Bree's cabin door opened. "Hey Half Pint, whatcha need?" Bill asked.

Startled, Bree looked into the shadows, letting her eyes adjust to the low light. "Oh, Billy, it's you; dang you startled me. I thought I would walk to the Lodge for a drink. Can't sleep, so I thought maybe a drink might help. What are you doing out here?"

Bill raised his hand showing his cigar.

"Ah, and it appears you have some smoking buddies. Well, don't stay up too late; we have an early day tomorrow."

"No, I won't, but I don't want you out here by yourself. I'll go with you, I could use a drink." He turned to his friends, "I'll catch you guys later," then walked toward her and steered her away from his three companions. With his arm around her, they walked down the dark road toward the Lodge.

⁂

His friends stayed in the shadows and kept their cigars away from their faces as they watched the two of them.

Brad smiled as he gave encouragement to Steven, "October is not that far off. Soon you will be with her again, and then you two can go for a nighttime drink."

Steven kept his gaze on Bree, "Bill's right, she doesn't sleep well these nights. I've watched her. She curls into a ball, and pulls the covers tight. She cries in her sleep now, not as much as in the beginning, but every so often, she cries. There's nothing I can do, I can't hold her to calm her fears. All I can do is watch. I hate what they did to her."

"Don't worry, Steven. Once she knows and understands all of this, she'll be fine. We'll keep her safe. They'll never touch her again. We promise you that," Rick said firmly, confidently.

"Why don't we go for a drink too?" Brad smiled, as he placed his hand on Steven's shoulder. "You can be close to her for a little while anyway, hell, we can all be close to her again." With a well-placed thought to Bill, the three of them started down the road. Their appearances changed as they walked.

∽

Bill and Bree sat in the double rocker next to the large stone hearth fireplace in the Lodge. Bill's feet planted firmly on the floor, slowly moving the rocker back and forth. Bree tried placing her feet on the floor to help move the rocker, but with the deep seat of the chair, she had to be satisfied using the tips of her toes. "You are so short Half Pint."

"Not my fault, you guys got all the height."

"What would you like to drink? I better go get it; they may make you show your ID." Bill messed with her hair as they laughed.

"Oh, I don't know something to help me sleep. Maybe a warm brandy."

❧

Bree watched as her cousin headed to the bar to get their drinks, her hands laid softly folded in her lap, the tips of her toes ballerina balanced on the floor to keep the rocker moving. Her shoulders relaxed as she listened to the crackling fire next to her. There was just something about a crackling fire on a cool night that comforted to her.

❧

Bree watched as three men entered the Lodge; faces concealed by beards, hair long, disheveled, and clothes dirty. She envisioned they had been out hiking for several days, living in a tent, and finally came back to civilization for a nightcap before retiring for the night. The three hikers made their way to the bar to order their drinks. The red bearded man said something to Bill causing him to laugh.

"Damn Bill, could you make us look any less appealing?" Steven asked as he looked at his reflection in the mirror behind the bar. "A red beard, Bree hates beards."

"I know," Bill laughed. "I don't want her paying any attention to the three of you." He picked up the drinks and headed back toward the fire, still laughing.

❧

Bill smiled down at Bree and handed her the brandy, "This will help you sleep, and I'll probably have to carry you back."

"Ah, no Billy, I don't think you will."

"So, any more thought on going with Gran to Vegas?" he asked as he sat next to her.

"Oh, Billy, I don't care for Vegas. Too many people, I don't gamble. What would I do with myself for seven days? Really, I don't see much point in going. Mom's really pushing me to go though, says Gran has some very good friends there. She keeps telling me I'll meet some great people, and that may be but..." her voice trailed off as she took a drink, the brandy soothed her throat. She felt the warmth and it calmed her. "I just think it would be best not to go."

"You don't have to meet all of Gran's friends, ya know. Besides, I think she would just enjoy your company. You're her only granddaughter and she likes having you around. We haven't had much time with you. Well, you know, while you were married you stayed away a lot. We've missed that and you and Gran used to do a lot together."

"I know, and I will make all that up, but it's over Halloween and you know how much I enjoy Halloween. No, I don't think I'll go this time. Maybe next year." She took another drink. More people entered the Lodge drawing her attention toward the door.

"Well, I do know they have a Halloween party at the reunion. What better place to see all the strange people than in Vegas, especially on Halloween. Think about it, all the costumes. Gina and I might even attend the party. You don't have to gamble. You could go to a few shows," he suggested.

"Oh gees, Billy, I don't want Gran to have to baby-sit me. She'll be there with her friends. I don't want to be the pathetic granddaughter being taken to shows like a little girl. No, maybe next year."

He continued to try to persuade her, "Gran sees these people every year. She's proud of you and wants to show you off."

"What's this reunion about anyway? I never really asked."

"She gets together with all her friends. They go to shows, play cards, party. It's just a way for them to keep in touch. It's really a social gathering; they just call it a reunion. It's grown over the years and now they have a committee that plans the big meeting. It's one big party where they get caught up on what's going on in everyone's life, and she has wanted to share that with you for the longest time."

"I don't know Billy, what could I possibly have in common with Gran's friends?" She finished her drink and rolled the empty glass between her hands, looking at nothing, but seeing everything in the Lodge.

"Well, you won't know until you go. Hell, I might even drop by and take you to a show." He smiled and watched her, he felt her heavy heart, and it worried him. "Tired yet, or can I get you one more drink?"

"One more would be lovely."

❧

When Bill left to get them another drink, a park ranger came and sat across from her. She hadn't noticed him in the Lodge. He looked at her and smiled; she smiled back, not wanting to engage in conversation, but not wanting to be rude either.

"Hi, enjoying your visit?

"Yes, I am thank you." She kept her answer short, hoping he would get the hint she didn't want to talk.

"First time here?"

"No, I've been here many times," she said, as she watched Billy at the bar.

"Boyfriend?" he asked motioning toward Bill.

"No."

"Ah, husband."

"Cousin."

"Ah," he nodded his head he understood. "I've not seen you down here before. First night here?"

"Yes, we just arrived today."

"Since you've been here before, I assume you have your trip all planned out. Going to do any hiking?"

"Probably," Bree said. Her short answers were not dissuading him and she was starting to get an uneasy feeling in her stomach. Nick started out this way, kept talking with her. She hadn't been able to dissuade him either. Her instincts were starting to kick in again. She started to twist her fingers together as her hands rested on her lap.

"Ever hiked to Heart Lake?"

"No, every time I've been here it's been closed due to bears," she answered, her eyes were alert, hands no longer relaxed, her finger started to tap her leg.

"I could take you back. I'm a ranger, and I take hikers back all the time," he offered.

One of the three bearded hikers came to the magazine stand next to the rocker and started looking at the selection. The ranger looked at him, then back at Bree. "I could take you if you like," he offered again.

"No, I don't think so."

The ranger and the hiker exchanged a glance, and then the hiker turned his gaze back to the magazines. The ranger shifted in his seat, he was becoming uncomfortable as he glanced around the room. He spied the other two hikers sitting across the Lodge, watching him. "Well, if you change your mind, I'll be happy to take you." He smiled and left just as Bill was coming back to the fire.

"What did he want?" Bill's voice was tense. The hiker that was examining the magazine rack selected a magazine and left.

"He wanted to know if he could take me to Heart Lake. I declined. That's all, nothing more. You don't need to kill him. He was being very polite."

Bill glanced toward the hikers. There was only one sitting there now. Bree hadn't noticed where the other two went. Bill handed Bree her drink, "Here ya go Half Pint, this should do it for you, and I promise you'll sleep like a baby."

"One could only hope."

∞

Bill walked Bree back to her cabin. "Now stay inside and go to sleep. I don't want you wandering around out here in the dark. Understand?"

"Yes, Billy I promise. I will stay inside with the door locked," she laughed as she started to enter her cabin.

"Hellooo, you forgot something Half Pint."

She giggled his name as she turned back to him, "Oh Billy, honestly, such the papa bear you are." Nevertheless, she leaned close to give him a soft kiss goodnight on the cheek, then entered her cabin and closed the door.

Bill waited until he heard the click of the lock then walked back to the shadows where his friends were waiting. "Well?"

"Couldn't find him. Hell, he disappeared soon as he got outside, but he knows we're here now. I'm sure he's reported back. They didn't do their recon very well; he should have sensed us right off when he came in the Lodge. Must be a new recruit, thought they would be better at this," Rick said. "We'll be out here all night, don't worry. She'll be safe Papa Bear."

"Hey, what can I say? She gives soft kisses."

"Yes, I'm sure she does," Rick smiled.

"Don't let your guard down, maybe that's what they want," Bill stated. "I can stay out here with you guys if you need me to."

"William, go inside and get some rest. You need to be with her all day tomorrow, we will be fine. If we need you, we will call you," Brad said sternly.

"I'll stay inside with her. She'll not see or sense me, but I'm not leaving her in there by herself," Steven said. "So don't try to talk me out of it." Not giving them any time to protest, he disappeared.

Rick laughed, "Well shit, he left before we could even attempt to talk him out of it."

"We better plan a hunt soon, Rick. I don't think he'll last until October," Brad laughed.

∽

Steven wrapped his cloak around him to stay hidden in the shadows of Bree's room. He watched as she came out of the bathroom. She was all ready for bed, dressed in her sweats and slippers that looked like bear paws on her feet. They were a gift from her littlest cousin, Timmy. A smile creased Steven's lips as he watched the nightly routine unfold.

Bree checked the lock on the door, then walked back to the bed and fluffed the pillows, and took the extra pillows from the other bed for added protection. Pleased they looked comfortable enough; she walked back to the door and double-checked the lock. Satisfied, she took her slippers off and placed them on the extra bed. She sat on the edge of her bed looking around. Steven was sure she would get up and check the lock again, but she just looked at the door, decided it was fine, and got into bed.

He watched her as she mound the pillows around her, pulled her blankets up for added protection and patted them around her.

She tried to read, but her heart wasn't in it. She reached up, turned the light off, and lay there, trying to get settled. The room was quiet, too quiet. Bree reached and turned the light back on and then settled down to sleep. Finally, with her fortress of pillows and blankets, she curled into her ball and fell asleep.

Steven watched as Bree's slumber turned restless. Clinging to the pillow, small cries escaped her lips and she hugged the pillow tighter. Steven moved slowly toward the bed. He saw the tears, her brow frowned, and her jaw tightened. He touched her hand; she flinched. He stroked her hair, gently, tenderly. "Don't worry Princess; I'm here now; nothing will ever harm you again," softly he whispered in her ear and kissed her cheek. Bree started to relax and uncurled from her protective ball. Her grip on the pillow lessened, her cries subsided, and her breathing became even again.

Steven sat on the floor by the bed and rested his head next to her pillow. "Sleep Princess, I will keep you safe.

Please come to Vegas, Princess, please," he pleaded to her heart. He reached and turned the light off, allowing the moonlight to filter though the small opening in the curtains. His hand found hers in the darkness, slowly their fingers interlaced. Soon the only sounds in the cabin were Bree's relaxed breathing and Steven's tone of contentment. The Chosen One slept peacefully for the first time in a very long time.

October 2007 – DFW Airport

The plane sat at its gate waiting for departure. Bree looked out the window and watched the rain splash against the pane. It was still dark, her grandmother hadn't been joking when she'd said she wanted to get an early start. Harried passengers were still filing on the plane, trying to stuff their over packed carry-on's into the overhead bins, pushing and shoving to make them fit. Most were getting away for the weekend and they didn't want to waste time waiting for their luggage in baggage claim.

Bree looked over at her grandmother who was reading the Dallas Morning News, and not paying any attention to the chaos around them.

Her grandmother took her eyes off her paper long enough to assure her granddaughter she would have a wonderful time in Las Vegas.

"Now Bree, you just wait, I'll introduce you to some very interesting people. That is, if we ever get there." She tapped a nervous finger on the armrest.

Bree had joked with her as they hurried to the ticket counter when they got there this morning.

"What's with you? Got a hot date or something?"

"Something like that," Gran replied.

"Gran, what have you done? Tell me you don't have anything planned for me. You haven't fixed me up with someone have you? I really don't think I'd be good company for anyone right now. Let me get this divorce behind me first." It came out sounding more like a plea than a firm statement.

"You just need to get out and meet the right kind of people. I have some very charming friends there. You'll have a good time. I haven't fixed you up with anyone. That's completely in your ballpark."

Bree's grandmother looked at her granddaughter and smiled, "Bree, relax and read your book or take a nap. You know, a nap may just do you some good." She patted her granddaughter's hand, giving her the assurance she had her best interests at heart and went back to reading her paper.

⁊

Sleep would be good, if only it were that simple. Bree had problems sleeping ever since she could remember. She always heard voices and sounds in the night. They were not the normal sounds children said they heard when the house creaked at night, just the settling or cooling from the heat of the day. Those sounds could be explained, but Bree heard her name being called in the darkness, heard laughing in the shadows, objects being dragged along the floor next to her bed. Those sounds couldn't be explained, so she never slept in a room by herself when it was dark.

When she was younger, she was able to seek refuge in her parent's bed. She was safe there, the voices and the sounds never followed. As she grew older, she didn't have that luxury. So she would stay up all night with the lights on studying, the lights kept the sounds away. She would catch her rest during the daylight hours once she got home from school or on the weekends. She became a creature of the night and she adjusted. She'd made the changes needed to maintain her sanity.

That was just the way it was for this Chosen One. If only she knew. If only they could have told her then. However, she couldn't know about the Magical world, or her path, until she had lived a quarter of her life as a human.

They didn't tell her when she had turned of age. She was married to the mortal then and she would have been in more danger. Her divorce to the mortal would be final soon, her father had seen to that.

Eight years had passed since she turned of age. She should have been told about this life. Eight years had passed, not allowing her to be prepared for her life in the Magical world. Now, she was of the age for her transformation into this world. Sometime within this year she will make the critical change from mortal to Magical. Then the prophecy would be fulfilled. But now she needed to know her path, to meet Steven, her true intended, and take her place in his life, with his clan. Again, she would have to adjust; she would have to make the changes needed to survive. Eight years was a long time and she had never been prepared for what was to come.

Bree continued looking out the window. Her headache had returned, not as strong, just a dull ache in the front of her head.

❧

Martha, Bree's mother, really wanted her to go with her grandmother to Vegas. Her mother knew she had made a mistake keeping Bree apart from Steven. Martha did everything that was asked of her by the Council to keep her daughter safe.

Before Bree went to college, her parents were given an ultimatum from the factions that wanted her dead. Her family was told she could attend college free of fear from those that wished her harm on one condition; Steven stayed away until she turned of age. They gave in to the ultimatum; they made Steven stay away, and their daughter suffered for it.

Her parents felt responsible for Bree marrying the mortal; they felt responsible for all the misery in her life. Her mother indeed wanted her to go on this trip, to set her path right. So she had begged, and pushed, and told Bree she needed to meet other people. Maybe she would meet someone special, someone who would treat her right.

"Bree, you're just being stubborn. Go to Vegas with your grandmother. It won't kill you and it may do you some good. You need to meet other people and Gran has some very good connections with her group. You might just meet someone special," Martha pleaded.

"Mom, I am meeting people. I travel, I go places, and I do things. I'm not looking to meet anyone 'special' as you keep putting it, not right now anyway, not until this divorce is over with, maybe never," Bree answered.

"Bree, give it a chance; you're just like your father, so doggone stubborn."

She finally agreed to go, if for no other reason than to get her mother off her back. "Okay, okay, I'll go, and I'm not being stubborn. I just don't see the point. But to please you, I will go. Maybe I'll take in a show or two. I suppose I could go out to the desert and take some pictures while Gran is at her reunion. I've wanted to experiment with this new lens anyway."

☙

Bree hadn't been to Vegas since...well, since she had gotten married, and that didn't go well. She'd be happy when it was all behind her. Nick was the biggest mistake she had made in her life.

She met him at a party when she was twenty-three. She wasn't interested in him, but that didn't stop him. He kept calling, sending her flowers and little gifts. She would politely thank him for calling but would refuse the flowers and gifts.

Nick was at every party she was at, always wanting to dance, or sit by her at dinner. At the last party, she had hit her limit, but Nick brought her a drink. "Okay, I'll leave you alone but the least you could do is drink the drink I have just brought you. I mean you return my flowers and my gifts. I'm starting to get a complex here. I'm really not a bad guy."

Several of her friends agreed she should cut him some slack. "Come on Bree, give the guy a break. He's wearing his heart on his sleeve here."

So she gave the guy a break, she drank his drink, and by the end of the evening she had agreed to go to dinner with him. Five months later, they were married.

Her marriage to him was brutal. She had only just told her mom, dad, and grandmother everything he had done to her from the beginning of their marriage until that last episode with the car accident. They were furious, at her for not telling them, at themselves for letting it happen, and at Nick. They did quite a bit of crying and yelling that night. Her dad did the yelling and her mom did the crying. She just sat there listening. Hell, she'd lived it.

Bree asked them to let her be the one to tell her cousin Bill. Despite their age differences, they were close. Until she came back married to Nick, they had always gotten along.

She closed her eyes tight, trying to blur out the look she saw on Bill's face when she returned home after marrying Nick. He showed up at the house with some of his friends. Bill had never been angry with Bree before, but this night she saw his anger. He had looked at Bree's parents. They had accepted the marriage, and they would not interfere with their daughter's decision, and told him, he must do the same.

But he wasn't going to stand by and let Bree ruin her life. He'd started toward Nick, but Bree's father stood in his way. Not one word was spoken, they just stared at one another for the longest time, and then Bill abandoned his threats. His friends stayed back as well. Bree hadn't understood the change in her cousin that night.

Nick smiled at them. They looked defeated. Nick finally told her to get in the car, but she didn't move quickly enough, so he shoved her along. That was too much for Bill. He'd made one last move and pulled Bree into his arms, keeping her from harm. That was the intent anyway. He whispered in her ear as he held her, "We have just screwed everything up. This is all wrong. It wasn't supposed to be him." Nick grabbed her out of Bill's embrace and practically threw her toward the car. Bill drew his fists back as if he'd wanted to pummel the life out of Nick, but Bree's father gave a quiet warning and Bill stopped.

Bree saw the hurt in his eyes, and it absolutely tore her heart apart. Telling him wasn't going to be easy. He hated Nick, and when she did tell him all of this, he would absolutely want to kill him.

လ

Bree quietly drew her arms around herself as she remembered those times Nick would force himself on her and slapped her face or punched her sides. His threats grew worse near the end of their relationship. He kept saying he knew all about her family, what they were. He'd destroy them if she ever left him.

She had no idea what he was talking about, but somehow she knew he would make good on this threats. Bree wasn't going to let her family suffer, or be destroyed, because of her stupidity.

When Nick would go out of town, he always made Bree visit with his friends Fred and Jared, and he was gone a lot. God she hated them. Fred always put his hands on her and Jared would just leer at her and blow kisses when his wife wasn't around.

She would take long showers, trying to wash away their touches. She hadn't felt clean since she had been married. No amount of showering could wash it away. She had finally decided she would never truly be clean again.

No, her marriage was a mistake. Nothing but broken bones, bruises, a miscarriage, and a car accident. She'd not make that mistake again anytime soon. Bree reached up and turned her vent on her, letting the cool air wash over her, cooling her body. She closed her eyes and listened to the sounds around her. The occasional thump of luggage being loaded, a child in the back crying, occasionally someone coughed. The soft sound of the engines lulled her to sleep. It was peaceful.

ᴄᴈ

Council Building October 2007

Esmeralda sat in her office. She tapped her fingers on her desk as she waited for her associate to arrive. She sipped her sherry and her impatience grew. The hour was very late when he finally arrived. She quieted her anger before she spoke, "Thomas, tell me you bring me good news for a change."

Thomas walked to the bar and poured his whiskey, his back still to Esmeralda. She watched him. His long coal black hair glistened from the light of the fire. He was a tall, broad shouldered man with strong arms and Esmeralda's thoughts quickly envisioned his arms around her. Her anger ebbed, just a little. She knew she would have him tonight.

He tossed his head back as he downed his drink and poured another. The whiskey didn't lessen the bad taste he had for the position he now found himself in. He knew he needed to play this right. He knew he had put more at stake than he had intended. But he had been drawn into this fight. He'd pledged his loyalty to it, all these years now ending. He kept the emotion out of his voice as he spoke, "The child will be at the reunion, she will learn of her heritage. She will know her intended. They will protect her. She will be a very strong Chosen One, my Lady."

He turned to face Esmeralda. "Tell me, is that what you wanted to hear?"

"Yes, yes it is, Thomas." Her eyes widened with her excitement. "It's time we knew just how strong this child has become. She has eluded all the attempts those stupid mortals have made. Your task Thomas, is to meet her, but do not kill her. You need to resist that temptation for the time being. Play with her, make her feel stronger than she truly is. Her clan will loosen their protection once they feel she can take care of herself. Then we will pounce." She smiled at Thomas, "Oh, why so glum my sweet?" She moved to him and ran her hand tenderly along his jaw. "You should be rejoicing, soon your clan will feast upon a Chosen One. You will taste her blood, and this should make you happy."

Thomas gave a low deep laugh, "Nothing is simple, and you should understand that by now. Her clan will not lessen their protection. Oh, Essie, the games you play."

She laughed a very wicked laugh, "She will appear before me on the last day of the reunion; I will end this game there. Her life will be mine; I just want you to test her. Play with the child, Thomas. Have some fun with her. I will keep her alive long enough for you to know her if you like." Esmeralda smiled as she pressed against him, pulling his face to her, "Would you like to know her Thomas?" she whispered softly, her lips barely touching his.

"Yes, Essie, yes I would like that." He pressed his lips to hers, her hands pulling at his hair. Thomas wrapped his arms around her slender waist, as he kissed her harder. Esmeralda found her prize hard. Her hands freed it from its prison of cloth. She slid slowly down his chest, tenderly kissing until her mouth found what she was seeking. The warmth of her lips sent a spasm of elation through Thomas. Her moans filled his thoughts, his hands held tight to the bar, knuckles much whiter than normal, as his wave of pleasure increased and crashed with such explosion. Tiny beads of iced sweat lined his forehead as he fought to claim the breath in his lungs.

She smiled as she came back to him. Her conquest complete, she took his glass of whiskey and drank it. The back of her hand wiped a small drop of the amber liquid from her lips. "Come now Thomas, we have much planning to do, I will make all of this worth your while."

CHAPTER 4

Bree's Story, Saturday Morning, Las Vegas

Our plane landed three hours later. The terminal was awash of people as they came and went during the early hours. One-arm bandits were everywhere. Someone stood or sat at them, gleefully pulling on the arm of the cold steel machine as it gobbled up their money. People waiting for their plane couldn't resist the last temptation to get rich, one more quarter, one more dollar, but the machines kept their riches and made them poorer. Then there were the new arrivals that couldn't wait to get to the casino to lose their money.

Ah, Las Vegas, party central!

We made our way to baggage claim and waited with everyone else for the buzzer to sound. Then one by one, your bag, you hoped, would appear unscathed sliding down the chute and onto the conveyer belt, circling around waiting on its owner to claim it.

I watched as an older couple struggled to gain control of an uncooperative bag that refused to break free of the belt. A very handsome young man stepped to the rescue. He easily lifted the bag and sat it beside them. The older woman was very appreciative. She kissed his cheek and quickly asked if he would collect her other two bags, which he did. Ours finally came into view, and thankfully, I was able to collect them without any trouble.

Gran led the way to ground transportation. I assumed we had a rental car, and was hoping she would do the driving since she had been here so many times. When we stepped outside, I saw two large charter buses waiting to take us to our destination.

The air outside was dry, and it felt good against my skin. I closed my eyes and relaxed as I leaned against the wall, letting the dry air soothe my headache away. My body was warm again and my headache was still with me. The smell of the diesel from the buses wasn't helping either.

"Bree, dear, are you okay? Does your head hurt that badly?" Gran asked. Her concerned was evident on her face.

I didn't want to worry her. "Gran I'm fine. I'm doing what you keep telling me to do - I'm relaxing. Really, I'm fine. What's all this anyway?" I spread my arms indicating the buses.

"Oh dear, Bree, I thought you realized I was bringing you to my reunion?"

"Yes, I did but what's with the chartered buses?"

"This is how they pick us up. For heaven sakes, you didn't think we would drive to the casino, did you? This is much easier and you can get a head start visiting with everyone instead of driving through all this traffic." She waved her hands in the air as if I could see all the traffic before us. "Just try to relax dear. I'm sure you'll meet some good people. Try to have some fun for heaven sakes. You really need to start living. You don't know what or who you might be missing." As she said this, her blue eyes widened and she smiled broadly at me.

I hadn't forgotten about the reunion, I just never thought about how she got around once she got here. I assumed she would have a rental car. She drove everywhere at home so I just thought she would do the same here.

Now, I started thinking about the reunion. Why I didn't think of this sooner, I'll never know, but the thought of a large group of people, Gran's age, coming here to gamble, came into my mind. Probably bringing their grandchildren, or worse their children here, to meet other children from the group. My nerves were starting to engage, *if I act quickly, I could make it back to the terminal and catch the next flight home. This is not going to be good.*

As everyone started accumulating at the bus area, I was pleasantly surprised to find this not to be the case. There were people of all ages waiting to board the coaches and good God - they all seemed to know Gran.

"Millie, good to see you again. One year between visits is just too long," said one particularly distinguished looking gentleman. He kissed her cheek as he greeted her.

Gran just giggled like a schoolgirl, "George, it's good to see you too! Oh, this is my granddaughter, Bree."

"Well, she's just as beautiful as you, Millie dear." He extended his hand to me, "I'm glad to finally meet you Bree, we have heard so much about you. It's about time she brought you."

"It's good to meet you too, ah, George is it?" He looked to be Gran's age, maybe just a little older. He was tall and heavyset. He had a round, clean-shaven face. His blue eyes were warm and friendly, as was his smile. He kept his arm protectively around my grandmother's waist as she greeted their other friends. I knew I was going to be on my own this week and that was just fine with me.

I had worried about spending seven days with my grandmother. We always got along, but this was different. Gran was with her friends, and I always felt uncomfortable around people I didn't know. No, I would be happy to be on my own, nobody here needed to know my past. Vegas was always up, always open. I would be fine.

"Bree, leave your bags here next to mine. This is our bus, we'll collect them at the hotel," Gran instructed me.

I watched as people milled around one another, saying their greetings like old school chums. Free of my suitcase, and with my purse hung over my shoulder, I was able to stand back and watch everyone. I don't think I had ever heard so many people being as polite as they were being. They hugged one another. Kisses on the cheeks were given freely.

A very good-looking young man approached me to introduce himself. He stood very close to me, that caught me off guard, and I stepped back. He stepped closer not realizing his closeness was bothering me. This brought back memories of Nick. He always got close to me before he would strike me. I instinctively stepped back again, and again the young man intruded in my space. He was too close. I didn't like it but I also didn't want make a scene. I took a deep breath, trying to keep the panic that had started to stir in the pit of my stomach under control. I reminded myself this wasn't Nick, but my shoulders started to tingle with tension.

My grandmother came up behind me. "Jeffery, how good to see you. This is my granddaughter Bree, Bree this is Jeffery Fairgate. He's a friend of your cousin Bill."

I noticed a hint of recognition in his eyes.

"Oh, yes, well it was good meeting you," and he left as quickly as he came.

∽

The lights were bright inside the bus as we boarded and Gran sat next to George, which left me to a seat by myself across the isle. I wasn't alone for very long before I had my own seatmate. A man about my age, maybe just a little older, asked politely if he could share my seat.

His hair was very thick, dark brown peppered with gray, and it tossed back and forth as he spoke. His full bushy beard showed some gray as well. His arms were thick with hair, and I could tell, by the tuft of hair at his collar, that his chest was just as hairy. No doubt, his back was too. He had entirely too much hair for me, some women like hairy men; I, for one, did not. With all his dark hair and his dark tanned skin, I imagined if he were to stand away from the light, he could blend into the shadows.

Well, that is if it wasn't for all the gold he was wearing. Several gold medallions hung around his neck and the gold Rolex watch looked like a beacon on his dark arm. His smile was friendly, and I was relaxed in his presence. I smiled in acknowledgment that he could share my seat and he immediately sat and introduced himself.

"Hello, my name is Harry, Harry Schmidt. And you are?" he extended his hand for me to shake and he smiled. He had such a beautiful smile.

"I'm Aubrey, but please, call me Bree. I'm here with Millie." I motioned to the seat across the isle indicating the giggling white haired woman. I had to laugh, the name 'Harry' did seem fitting.

He looked over at her, "Mildred, it's good to see you again, and you too George. You brought a guest with you this time."

"Well, Harry, glad you could come. Yes, I brought Bree, my granddaughter. Remember I told you about her last year."

Embarrassment flushed in my cheeks. *Great, thanks Gran. Does everyone need to know I'm your granddaughter?*

Harry continued speaking as he waved a hello at others as they passed by our seat, "I'm glad I was able to make it too. I have to leave Wednesday you understand, but I'll be back in time for the party on Thursday. So this is that Bree," he said as he turned to me. "Well, this is great. I was hoping I would get to meet you sometime." He turned back to my grandmother to speak about something else.

I happened to look up, during this exchange between the isle, and caught sight of a ruggedly handsome looking man. His eyes were dark, as was his hair. His skin was lightly tanned and he had just the right amount of stubble on his face. He was wearing a long sleeve red flannel shirt, with a white tee shirt underneath. He reminded me of someone who was comfortable camping and hunting. He smiled and I smiled back in acknowledgment. He watched me for a moment before he moved on. I watched him until my seat began to block my view. Then he turned back to look at me, and he smiled again, and so did I. My seat finally blocked my view completely, and I wasn't going to strain my neck like a prairie dog looking out its hole to see where he went. No, I had no interest of meeting anyone.

With everyone seated, the lights dimmed and our bus pulled away from the terminal. A smile came to my thoughts, *if he had just gotten on the bus before Harry, I'm sure he would have asked to sit with me, I'm sure I would have enjoyed his company.*

Harry asked me a question, bringing me back to reality.

"I'm sorry, what did you ask?" He was hoping we could meet at the reception and maybe have dinner together. I was noncommittal as I wasn't sure what Gran's plans were, although by the look of things with her and George, I wasn't in them. Harry assured me we would have plenty of time together. I remained uncommitted but that didn't detour him, but he was polite about it, so I wasn't bothered by his request. We talked all the way to the hotel. He must have tried to get my whole life's story. As we got off the bus, he shook my hand and said he would catch up with me later, and then called out to one of his friends and was gone.

Gran and I collected our bags and checked in. As we stood waiting at the elevators, and I began taking in the view.

There he was again, standing with a group I assumed to be his friends. He faced my direction talking and laughing very causally with them. I watched him. His dark hair was a little un-tame, a little wild in the front. He wore faded blue jeans and his shirt wasn't tucked. He had rolled his sleeves midway up his arm. His shirt was unbuttoned and his white tee shirt was tight on his chest. He was wearing hiking boots. Maybe my earlier assessment was correct, and he was the outdoor type. Had I seen him before? He did appear familiar to me but I just couldn't place him. I felt I should be standing next to him. That's where I belonged, by his side. The way he moved his hands as he talked, his laugh, was all very familiar to me, but I just couldn't place it. I wondered if he was married or if he had a date he was waiting on. I had no idea why he fascinated me. I wasn't interested in meeting anyone, I reminded myself again.

There were five of them standing there, three men and two women. The taller male of the group was a little huskier. His hair was light brown, with streaks of gray, clean-shaven. He was dressed similarly in a green flannel shirt with darker blue jeans, and tennis shoes. His voice was deep. I could feel it in my bones where I was standing. I couldn't hear him but I felt it. The woman holding his arm was a little shorter than him. She had long thick bouncy blond hair, an hourglass figure, and her skin was lightly tanned. She too was dressed in blue jeans, but more fashionable. Her white blouse was tucked and her collar turned up. She wore a blue turquoise necklace and earrings to match.

The other couple looked a bit more reserved. He was about the same height as the one in the red flannel shirt. He was also wearing blue jeans, his light blue shirt was tucked, and he had on a sports jacket with the brown patches on the sleeves. He had black hair. The woman standing with him was wearing dark blue slacks with a white blouse tucked in. She held her jacket over her arm. She was shorter than him but not by much. Her companion had his arm draped around her shoulders.

Our elevator had arrived, and as I started to turn, the man in the red flannel shirt looked at me, straight at me, and smiled. My eyes widened and so did his smile. Embarrassment flushed my face, and he continued to smile. How rude to be staring at someone like that. I knew better, but I just couldn't take my eyes away from his smile. I stepped into the elevator with my grandmother. My mind was still busy chastising me when the elevator doors opened to our floor. Gran was out the door and moving down the hall and I had to make my "excuse me, pardon me please" to get out the door with her.

"Hurry up and unpack dear. Get some rest, we have loads to do tonight," she said as she started to enter her room.

"Gran, wait," I caught her just in time. "What are you wearing tonight? I don't even know where we are going."

"Wear whatever you want. You said you were more comfortable in blue jeans. Wear them. Nobody cares what you are wearing dear. You can trust me on this. The reception starts at six sharp," and with that she closed the door.

"Okay, comfort it is."

My room was quite spacious. Gran had reserved suites for us. I entered into the dinning area. There was a small round table in the center of the room with place settings for two, and a thin vase holding one single red carnation. A sink, microwave, a mini bar filled with little liquor bottles, beer, with all types of snacks and a small refrigerator were along the far wall. I'd check that out later.

I stepped down four steps into the living area. A large entertainment cabinet housing a flat screen TV, stereo system, and game system was on the wall to my left. A large picture window filled the entire wall in front of me. The view of the city from my window was not what I expected, but it was probably more spectacular at night. The living room had a sofa, love seat and an overstuffed chair. The wall on the right led to the bedroom.

The first thing I saw when I entered the bedroom was the bed. It was enormous. It had a thick white comforter as the bedspread. Varying sizes of pillows filled the head of the bed. I sat down on the edge, and as I suspected, the mattress was firm but I sank into the folds of the comforter. I smiled as I thought how delightful it would be to sleep with all these blankets around me, holding me tight. I only hoped the voices wouldn't come, wouldn't ruin my stay.

I continued my examination of the room. There was a smaller entertainment center to the left as you entered the room and another picture window on the next wall, a sitting area with two comfortable looking chairs in front of the window. On the wall to the right as you entered was a set of dresser drawers, then the door to the bathroom that had a large sunken whirlpool tub and a big walk in shower on one wall. The other wall had an antique style washbasin and an enclosed room for the toilet. Coming back into the bedroom, a full size closet was on the wall opposite the dresser drawers. "Well, it's my home for the next seven days so I might as well unpack and get ready for tonight."

It only took me half an hour to unpack and I didn't want to get ready and just sit around until six o'clock so I decided to check out the hotel. I grabbed my backpack style purse, flung it over my shoulder and set out for my adventure of hotel gift browsing!

CHAPTER 5

I wandered through the lobby, wove my way through the casino, and checked out the coffeehouse and gift shops. I just loved gift shops and this hotel had several, plus an entire floor of stores. I bought a few items, two special postcards, one for my parents, and one for my cousin Billy. I even bought a tee shirt with the hotel logo and the saying, "What happens in Vegas, stays in Vegas" on the back. Not sure why, I'd never wear it. One shop was a complete jewelry store. After paying for a few trinkets, I continued exploring.

The hallway off the left of the reception area led to an escalator that transported me into another world.

At the top were restaurants and more shops. Light poles were strategically placed on the sides of the cobblestone walkways giving the illusion you were walking down a street.

I glanced at the sky; then quickly realized it was the ceiling. It wasn't bright but the soft hue gave you the feeling of being outdoors. Street entertainers were performing for the guests. Halfway down the street, I came to an Irish pub that looked interesting, but I didn't enter. Maybe tonight.

Upon passing the pub, I could hear the football game playing on the big screen over the bar and the pub patrons shouting. I looked through the window and watched as several were standing there, shouting, and cheering at a small figure on the TV screen running down the field being chased by a small mass of players. I wasn't looking at anyone in particular, but there he was with his friends. He hadn't changed yet.

Evidentially the small figure made it to the end zone and high fives were given all around. He noticed me when he turned and he smiled; I smiled back and moved on. I saw other faces from my bus ride here, but my mind kept going back to the man in the red flannel shirt. Why did he fascinate me? This was so unlike me. I was always reserved, always stood back from people. I watched them until I deemed they were safe enough to approach. I hadn't followed my instincts when I dated Nick. My instincts told me to run, but I didn't listen. My judgment was clouded then. And look where that got me. No, I would not let that happen again. I would stand back and observe. It was only seven days.

&

Back in my room, I took a long, hot shower, and dressed in blue jeans and a red oxford tailored shirt, not too tight, I didn't like to wear tight clothes. I liked them a little loose but not baggie, enough room to allow me to breathe. I never understood why women wanted to wear such tight fitting clothing. It always looked so uncomfortable to me.

I had made the right selection on my purchase of the bracelet, ring, and earrings. You couldn't go wrong with blue jeans and silver jewelry.

I looked at myself in the mirror trying to decide whether I should wear makeup or not. I knew I would talk myself out of it, but it was something I always did. My complexion had a slight tan to it, allowing me not to have to wear makeup. Which was good because makeup made my face breakout horribly, it didn't matter if it was hypoallergenic. I couldn't wear any without regretting it later.

My eyes were brown. Billy always told me my eyes were a warm brown. The one big problem, I felt I had, was with my eyelashes. They were very fine, but I hated mascara. It always made my eyes itch, so I just went without.

My hair was short. It had more body when it was short. I only needed to blow it dry and it would fan into my face naturally. I had bangs. I could not live without bangs - I could hide behind them.

There wasn't anything fancy about me. I just saw a plain, down to earth face looking back at me.

As I walked into the living room, the phone on the desk rang, but when I picked the receiver up, I just heard the dial tone. As I placed the receiver back, I noticed a package addressed to me on the desk.

Bree, the healing stone is yours; it belongs to you. Wear it always.

"Mine?" The note wasn't signed so I had no idea who sent it. It could have come from Gran, but that wasn't her handwriting. *Hmmm, maybe it was from Gran and someone else wrote the message. Now that's stupid. Why would Gran have someone else write the message? I'll ask her this evening.*

I looked at the necklace; it was a deep red teardrop shaped stone with veins of black onyx running through it, set in sterling silver, and hung from a long sterling silver chain. I put the necklace on underneath my shirt. It felt warm as it touched my chest and that warmth soothed me. I drew in a deep breath as I felt this calming sensation wash over me. I touched the stone and smiled.

I continued with my dilemma, standing in front of the mirror trying to decide if I should tuck my shirt in or not when someone knocked on the door.

"Room Service."

I hadn't ordered room service, so I peeked through the peephole and sure enough, there stood a young man, in a white smock, holding a vase of flowers. Now this had to be a mistake. I opened the door to correct him, just as he was getting his passkey out.

"I'm sorry but..." he cut me off. Clearly, he was sure he had not made a mistake and with a little testiness asked, "Are you," and he looked again at the card, "Bree Campbell?"

"Yes."

"Then these are for you." He moved past me to place them on the coffee table.

"Thank-you," I said as he made his way to the door. "Don't I need to sign for them?"

"No," and he left.

I read the note, 'I am looking forward to meeting you.' That's it. Nothing more...not a signature even. *Can't anyone sign a name to things anymore?* Maybe they were from Harry, and the florist misunderstood his message. "Well, whoever sent them...thank-you; and red carnations," I drew in the scent of the flowers, "my favorite." I cut the stem, and stuck it into the buttonhole on my shirt pocket. I had totally forgotten what I was thinking about before the flowers had arrived and another knock on the door brought me back to the present. This time it was Gran.

"Are you ready dear? Oh, you look fine. The flower's a nice touch," she teased, giving me the 'okay' sign and a wink as she walked past me into the room.

"They just arrived. Not sure who sent them; the card wasn't signed. They're probably from Harry. What'd you think Gran, in or out?" I stood in front of her motioning with my hands, "The shirt Gran, in or out?"

"Out of course, that's the style isn't it? Besides, you look casual that way, relaxed. I do want you to relax. That may just help those headaches, you know. Oh, I like your taste in jewelry too. Are those new?"

"Yeah, I just bought them at one of the shops, and Gran, I am relaxed. Okay, out it is. Oh, Gran, I also received this necklace. It was here when I came back but that card wasn't signed either, so I have no idea where it came from." I took it off and handed the necklace to her.

♋

Millie looked at the necklace. Yes, she recognized the stone. The Elders had left powerful gems and crystals for each of the Chosen Ones; they helped enhance their powers while they were still mortal. The factions that wanted Bree dead had taken hers, but they had been stolen back by Bree's supporters. Soon all the crystals and gems would be in her possession. Millie could tell this stone had already bonded to Bree. That was the pattern. Once a Chosen One touched these special gems, no other Magical could tap into its power. Bree would continue to be strengthened from them once she crossed. Millie watched as her granddaughter finished getting ready. So much was going to be asked of her and it made Millie worry. She knew her granddaughter was strong, she only prayed she was strong enough!

∾

Millie handed the necklace back, "Pretty, now let's get going – times a wasting," Gran said smiling and pushed me toward the door.

"You mean George is waiting," I teased.

She giggled, "Don't worry about me tonight dear. I'll introduce you to some people and then you go have some fun."

"Gran, this isn't one of those, 'What happens in Vegas, stays in Vegas' things is it?" I groaned.

"Well, again, I guess that all depends on what happens. Now let's go already," she said as she pushed me out the door.

CHAPTER 6

Several people were already inside when we arrived at the reception. George stood by the door, waiting on Gran. I had to admit they did look cute together. I had never seen my grandmother with any other gentleman. I had never known my granddad. I was told he died a few months after I was born.

The ballroom was bright and cheery. There were tables set in rounds of ten. Each had a beautiful candle arrangement with fall foliage, pumpkins, or squashes and a different figurine, either a ghost, a witch, a scarecrow, even a few vampires and werewolves.

Tables filled with appetizers were stationed throughout the room. A band was in the front and several couples were dancing. There was a drink station in each corner of the ballroom. Overstuffed chairs, sofas, and love seats were placed throughout the hall for additional seating.

"Bree let me introduce you to someone close to your age, well close enough. If you get bored later then you can go have fun at the casino."

"Oh, I don't think she'll be bored with who you have in mind, Millie," George said and Millie giggled.

Oh, dear this was a 'fix her up' kind of meeting. I need a rock to crawl under until tonight is over with. Gran was pulling me along - my body was rebelling against the tugs.

She continued to look around the room for someone in particular. Obviously, it wasn't Harry. Otherwise, she would have insisted I have dinner with him when I met him on the bus. From behind us, I heard someone call Gran's name. "Millie dear, how good to see you,"

Gran turned, "Oh Steven, there you are, I knew you would be here early."

Yes, there he was, the mystery man from the bus, lobby, and Pub. He wore blue jeans and a tailored hunter green shirt, un-tucked, with a white tee shirt on underneath. He wasn't dressed excessively fashionable, just comfortable. His eyes were indeed brown and they sparkled when he smiled and with that smile, I saw the cute small dimple in his left cheek. His lips looked very soft, *Oh my goodness, kissable soft, I'm sure!* He'd shaved the stubble and I had to admit, I did like this look much better. He had tennis shoes on instead of the hiking boots. He looked very comfortable and I felt I could crawl into his arms and stay there.

He gave Gran a kiss on the cheek, said hello to George. "This must be Bree, am I correct?" He winked at Gran, she giggled.

"Yes, oh yes, this is my granddaughter. I was finally able to persuade her she needed to come with me this year. She can be so stubborn sometimes. But this year, the time was right, so here she is. Bree, this is Steven Wentworth. Steven this is my only granddaughter, Bree."

The warmth flooded into my face as her introduction put me on display. *Tada! Here she is all the way from Ft. Worth, Texas, Bree Campbell.* My eyes widened as I looked at Gran and then at Steven, but he just smiled and my heart fluttered and I smiled back.

Gran continued as she ignored my embarrassment. "Bree, Steven has wanted to meet you for the longest time dear; he kept asking when I was going to bring you, so now I have and you two can talk, get to know one another." Now it was Steven's turn to blush a little, *maybe he would want to join me under that rock.*

"Steven, where is Rick and his lovely wife Sandy, oh, and aren't Brad and Madalyn here too. I so wanted to make the introductions to them but George and I must run. You understand, don't you dear?" She patted his cheek and smiled.

Oh God, she is going to leave me here for them to baby-sit. I tensed trying to keep the panic from rising in me. *I knew something like this would happen. They still want me watched.*

"Millie, don't worry about it. I'll introduce Bree to everyone. She's in good hands now, you go on, have fun," then he winked at me.

"Oh Steven, you are a dear, yes, you introduce her to your little friends. Now, Bree dear, you have fun and don't wait up for me."

∽

I felt like she should have given me lunch money or something. *Okay, better yet, forget the rock just throw me under a moving bus. This was truly embarrassing. Then to go and call his friends little, gees Gran, what were you thinking? If I remember correctly, they didn't look so little.* I slowly turned back to look at Steven, he smiled. "I am so very sorry about that, she does mean well," as I watched her and George leave, then turned back to Steven again, "At least I think she does. I think she's trying to see if I will die from embarrassment, and ya know, she's pretty close this time." I just knew my face had to be three shades of red by now.

"Now, I can't have that. I've never lost a date yet and I don't intend to now. Don't let it bother you," he was laughing as he put his hands on my shoulders to turn me in the direction of his friends that were approaching. "We're used to Millie; we wouldn't want her any other way. I'll introduce you to my little friends." His four other companions joined us; each held drinks in their hands.

"Hey Steven, how's it going?" said the brown haired man as he handed Steven a large Bloody Mary. His eyes were blue and strong. I felt them try to melt the wall I had placed around my heart as he spoke to me. His face was relaxed. His smile crooked and sexy and I guessed maybe he was older than Steven, but not by that much. His nose was straight with just the smallest bump on the bridge. I couldn't tell if he had ever broken it before but it gave him character. He was tall and muscular, not in an overbearing way, not like a body builder. No, these muscles were strong but gentle, just like my cousin Billy. He handed me a white wine and said, "This is for you," as he made a slight bow.

My face gave away my question. The tall blond next to him handed him his drink and said, "We saw Steven talking with you and Millie. We just assumed you were Millie's granddaughter we have all heard so much about, hence the wine." She wore her hair brushed away from her face. She was comfortable in her own skin and had a friendly way of making you feel comfortable too. Her mannerism was very polished. Her eyes were gray and bright. They were happy eyes. Her makeup was lightly applied, just enough to let the beauty of her skin shine.

"Oh, dear Lord, she's spoken that much about me? That is so embarrassing," I said.

"Oh don't be embarrassed, we really did enjoy hearing your life story," said the brunette woman, but she didn't convince me. She didn't smile when she spoke to me and I got the impression I was being judged. She was not as friendly as the blond. She was much more protective of her friends. I felt tension from her and I had no idea why. Her lips were thin and she was wearing red lipstick, her face was oval and her hair was shoulder length with tight curls. I wasn't comfortable with her and I felt she wasn't comfortable with me either. She reminded me of someone used to getting all the attention and now there was a new person touching her world, her family.

"My life!" I repeated. My voice rose a little in alarm. That slow wave of panic started rising in my stomach again. It was nothing like the panic I felt at the airport, when Jeffery stepped in my space. It was the panic I felt when someone knew things about me. Things I didn't want them to know. What all had Gran told them, what all did they know? Surely, Gran would not have divulged anything private. Surely, I could count on my own grandmother to keep my secrets. These were strangers, yet they said Gran had told them my life story. I was hoping that was just a figure of speech and that my grandmother really didn't tell these people all that much. *Oh damn*, I thought, *what was she thinking and then to bring me here and go off with her boy toy while I'm left here being completely humiliated. I need to go outside now and find that bus.*

The man standing next to the brunette smiled at me. His eyes were hazel and warm. They pierced my armor easily disarming my mind. I smiled and he smiled back putting me at ease. His voice was soft as he spoke to me. "Only the good parts I can assure you."

"Steven," said the blond, "you just might want to make the introductions you promised Millie, before Bree implodes."

"Oh, yeah right. Bree, this is Rick and Sandy Collins," he was motioning to the light brown haired man and the blond, "and this is Brad and Madalyn Silverton."

"I like the flower, red's your color," Rick said and then winked. He extended his hand for me to shake. He had large hands that enveloped mine, but they were soft hands, his touch was cool.

"Hi Bree, glad to meet you," said Brad.

I smiled, said my 'hello' and 'glad to meet you', and didn't try to apologize any more for Gran. It was all out. I'd just have to live with it. I'd never see these people again, so what did it matter? At least I wouldn't have to tell them anything. Hell, they probably knew it all now anyway, the good and the bad, and yes, I was sure with Gran, even the ugly had been told.

"Hey Steven, we're going over to the reception party in the penthouse, you two want to come? I heard Rebecca might be there," Brad said winking at Steven like it was an inside joke. Steven just gave back an, 'I'll get you later' kind of grin.

"Brad, honestly," said Sandy. "Steven, you stay here and enjoy yourself. Rebecca isn't any good for you anyway. Take Bree to dinner. Maybe we'll catch up with you two later."

They left and I turned to Steven, "Could this get any more awkward?"

"I don't know the night is still young. Let's see what happens," he laughed.

"You know you don't have to spend time with me, go with your friends to the party," I offered.

"You heard her, Rebecca isn't any good for me, and besides I think I would enjoy your company more."

"I remember seeing you getting on the motor coach for the ride here," I blurted out awkwardly.

Steven smiled, "Yes, I remember you. You were sitting with Harry wasn't it?

"Yes, he seemed to be a very pleasant fellow, although he did ask a lot of questions."

"He can be very pleasant, but I hear he can also be an animal at times."

Steven took my hand and led me to an empty sofa. "Here we go. Now we can talk and be comfortable. Now without the risk of sounding cliché, tell me about yourself."

"I'm sure Mil...my grandmother, has probably told you everything. God, that's so embarrassing."

"Oh, I'm sure she has, but I think I'd like to hear it from you."

We sat talking about nothing important, drinking our drinks. It was a pleasant, easy conversation. He sat facing me with his arm on the back of the sofa. He would ask me questions and listen to my answer. He didn't shy away from my questions either.

He told me he enjoys hiking and canoeing, he lives in the Bear Tooth Mountains in Montana, has a large log cabin, isn't married, he never has been. Just couldn't seem to find that special someone. (He offered that, I didn't ask.) He's a lawyer, he and Rick are in the same firm, but he also has a degree in architecture and engineering, physics, and forestry, but he really liked being a lawyer. He even told me a few jokes about lawyers.

He was an only child, his parents were long gone, and since they were only children, he had no living relatives. I found that sad, even though I was an only child, I did have cousins. My aunt and uncle on my father's side had three boys and we were close. Since I'm the only girl, I was teased endlessly during my childhood. Even now, they couldn't let a family outing go without teasing me.

Occasionally, Steven would start playing with my hair during the conversation, I didn't mind. He told me he had known my grandmother for ages, he even knew my mom and dad, said they went back a long way. I felt bold, I wasn't sure if the wine had anything to do with it on an empty stomach, but I asked him how old he was. I just had to know.

He smiled, he had a very warm smile, "I like bold, and I'm forty years old."

A small frown creased my forehead, as I suddenly felt very inadequate.

"Does that bother you that I'm forty? It's only a number. I could change it if you like.

"Is that your question?"

"Yes, I think we'll go with this one, I have plenty more," he teased.

"No, it doesn't bother me that you're forty. I'm amazed you have several degrees **and** you're only forty.

I finished my wine but still had questions to ask and I was enjoying myself. This was comfortable. This seemed familiar. Maybe I had met him somewhere else, but surely, I would have remembered him. *Oh yes, I would have remembered him.*

"Would you like another glass of wine or can I take you to dinner?" he asked.

ço

Steven's voice had the sound of hope in it. He didn't want the night to end, he wanted her to stay and talk. He had missed their talks, her smile, and her laugh. He just wanted to hold her in his arms and kiss her until she remembered those times. Bill said she should remember. All he had to do was remind her of a few things. He hoped a kiss would remind her, but there was a little fear in his thoughts. What if it didn't? She should have remembered him when she saw him on the bus earlier, but she didn't. What if she really didn't remember how close they used to be, how very close they had been? Thirteen years was a long time to be apart, a lot happened to her during those years and he feared those memories might indeed be gone.

I hadn't eaten since breakfast and the thought of another glass of wine on an empty stomach was not a good idea. Besides my headache was returning and I started to rub my temples.

"What's wrong?" Steven asked as his fingers twisted a strand of my hair.

"I'm just getting a headache. I think I am probably hungry."

"And when was the last time you ate?" Steven stopped playing with my hair and looked at me protectively.

I didn't have to think long on that question and then laughed, "I'm embarrassed to say at the airport in Dallas," I cringed as I said it.

"Millie said you had to be reminded to eat, I guess she wasn't kidding." Steven finished his drink and placed our empty glasses on the table. "Well, let's get some food in you."

❧

He took my hand to help me up, purposely bringing me close to him. His touch was strong but tender. There he stood, watching me, waiting on what I didn't know. His eyes spoke to me. They were dark, strong eyes. I knew those eyes. They were always gentle, loving when I looked into them. Worry lines wrinkled his forehead, bringing his eyebrows close together. His jaw was fixed. I saw the muscle tense as he watched me. He had a perfectly straight nose except at the tip, which had the slightest upturn. His thin lips pursed together, forcing himself not to speak, not to ask. His hair was thick and full, the front was a little un-tame, yes, just a little wild. I knew him, somehow I knew him but from where, or when?

His smile was intoxicating. His eyes looked at the flower, then back at me, and quietly asked, "You liked the flowers? Well, since you're wearing one I just assumed. Rick's right, red does look good on you."

"You sent them! The card wasn't signed. Yes, I do like them very much. Carnations are my favorite, especially the red ones."

"Yeah, I know," he said grinning.

"Ah, Gran told you."

"No, I just knew," he smiled.

We continued standing close to one another. I didn't make any attempt to step back and that surprised me. He was so close, he was in my space, but yet I didn't feel the need to step back. This time I had to fight the urge to step closer, to press my lips against his. I liked being close to him, I just wanted to reach up, put my arms around his neck and kiss him. The desire to do this was strong and I didn't understand why I felt this way.

My mind blocked all the noise in the room from my thoughts, the only sound I heard was Steven's question, "What would you like? Italian, Mexican, American, French?"

"Mexican sounds good."

"I know just the place," his voice was soft, his smile still intoxicating. He turned and led me through the crowded room. Once outside of the ballroom, he took my arm and wrapped it around his. He continued asking questions, his voice was low but I could hear him clearly. The outside noises didn't interfere with our conversation. We heard each other as if we were the only ones around.

Emotions stirred in me bringing unfocused pictures into my thoughts of a life some time ago. The feelings were familiar, the people weren't. I shook my head, searching through those memories for some answers that were just beyond my reach.

CHAPTER 7

He took me to a Mexican restaurant on the top floor of our hotel. The music was loud but not overbearing. I could still hear Steven ask me if I wanted to sit at a booth or a table. I felt a booth would be what I would choose if I had dated this person, "A booth is fine Steven," and he requested one when the hostess greeted us.

Everything seemed to be in slow motion as I took notice of my surroundings. All the unfamiliar voices and sounds were muffled in my thoughts. Colorful blankets and clay pottery adorned the walls. The tabletops were tiled in deep reds, blues, and bright yellows. The walls were painted in avocado greens, pale yellows, bright orange, and reds. As I was sliding in on my side, a familiar voice came into my thoughts, which caused my mind to play catch up with my surroundings. Gran and George were just on their way out.

"Oh, Bree dear, just chance meeting you two here," Gran said coming up behind Steven.

"George, Millie," Steven said, "how's the party going for you?"

"Couldn't be better," said George. "We should do this more than just once a year."

"Let's discuss it at the open forum tomorrow," Millie voted. She slid into the bench across from me and George followed. Gran motioned for Steven to sit, so he slid in next to me, placed his arm behind me and let his thumb rub against my shoulder. The booth was small so we sat close together. Steven's leg was touching mine; that felt comfortable, this was all comfortable to me.

"We've just eaten so we won't take up much of your time, you kids can eat in peace," George said. He smiled and winked at me. I just knew my face was going to be permanently red from all the embarrassment I was feeling.

They continued talking and Steven continued to rub his thumb along my shoulder. My neck muscles were starting to relax. The headache was fading. Now it was just a small annoyance.

Steven encouraged Gran to bring the idea up tomorrow. I heard him say, "I'll back you, only if you promise to bring Bree with you," then he nudged my arm. Gran was ecstatic. George liked the suggestion as well and Steven just smiled and said, "You know my terms."

The waiter came, delivered chips and salsa, and asked for our drink order. Steven spoke up. "Two iced teas, please," he didn't even look at me when he said, "no alcohol until we get some food in you," and squeezed my shoulder. "Bree, don't you like queso?"

"Yes, I do." *Now how did he know that? Maybe I met him when I was in college. Think! Damn, where do*

I know him? My mind started an urgent search of my thoughts.

"I told you she doesn't eat," Gran began, "she doesn't sleep much either." She said this as she wagged her finger at me, playing as if she was scolding me. "She gets her nose in a book and you can forget food and sleep."

"Gees, Gran I don't think he needs to hear all of this, do you?" just hoping she would take the hint.

"Nonsense, I enjoy it," Steven laughed and put his hand on my shoulder. I could feel his cool touch through my shirt, and it *did* feel good because I was starting to feel very warm. "Millie, George anything?" Steven asked.

"Thanks for the offer Steven, but you two go ahead. We were just on our way to the Luxor to play blackjack with some friends," George said. "Millie can bring this up for a vote tomorrow and we'll wait and see what happens." He got up, helped my grandmother up, and kissed her cheek. She giggled that schoolgirl giggle of hers, and off they went, arms around each other holding on tight for the short time they had at the reunion together.

When we were alone again, Steven asked, "You're not upset are you?"

"About what?"

"My ordering you iced tea."

"Heavens no, I like iced tea."

He gave me time to look over the menu, not speaking, just waiting patiently. I was quick to decide on my standard choice; two soft chicken tacos with a small bowl of sour cream on the side, refried beans, and rice.

"I should have known."

"What are you having?"

"I've eaten, it's you that hasn't." He took the menu and motioned to the waiter.

"Couldn't you just order something small?"

"Okay, I'll have a salad. Better?

"Yes, thank-you"

"Good, I've a question."

"Another question? Hmmm I can't imagine," I laughed

"Yes, and I have many more so just be patient," he nudged my shoulder. "Are you feeling okay?" The waiter arrived with our drinks and queso and then took our order.

I was very explicit in my ordering. "I would like two soft chicken tacos. But please don't put the lettuce, tomatoes and cheese in the taco. If I could get them on a side plate I would prefer that. Oh, and may I have a small side of sour cream?" I used my hands to indicate a small bowl.

The waiter grinned and looked at Steven. "Mine's easier, I'll just have a salad, and house dressing is fine. Oh, and you can put it all in one bowl." Steven and the waiter shared a good laugh. "Also, would you mind bringing us two frozen margaritas, Bree, you want salt on yours?"

"Yes, please." The waiter stood there for a moment to see if I had any special instructions for the bartender, he smiled and left.

"I thought you said I couldn't have any alcohol until after I have eaten," I said, poking him lightly in the ribs.

He laughed and pushed the bowl of chips and queso close to me. "Eat some chips. Now back to my question."

I turned slightly toward him. His eyes were so strong and intense as he looked back at me; they held my gaze. I just couldn't look away from him. *Where have I seen those eyes before?*

"I didn't want to bring it up in front of Millie, but you're pretty hot." He spoke very softly almost hypnotizing

"Thanks," I smiled and raised an eyebrow.

"Okay, I'll rephrase, you feel very warm," he said as he smiled, his dimple showing again.

"Oh, that, yeah well, here lately my body temperature does seem to be running on high. I just assume it has something to do with my metabolism because I've increased my workouts. Nothing to worry about, I'm fine."

"You're sure?" he didn't sound convinced.

"I'm reasonably sure. Yeah, well, I don't have a medical degree or anything like that, so I'm as sure as the next person. No glands are swollen and I really do feel fine, and thanks for not asking with Gran here. Her knowing about the headaches is bad enough." I wrapped my arm around his as I thanked him for not bringing it up.

That felt so familiar to me, I had done that before. I just knew I had sat close to him before. We've always touched as we've talked, just keeping that contact with one another. Where do I know him? My mind was desperately searching through old dusty folders in my brain and coming up empty. A file had been misplaced and I really needed that file.

"Okay," he said, "oh, and you are hot, and I mean that in the way you took it before."

"Thanks," I grinned.

"Would you like me to move to the other side? To give you more room," he asked.

"No," I blurted out. Of course I didn't want him to move! I liked being close to him. "Not unless you want to, I mean, if you're uncomfortable." *Good God how lame!*

"No, I'm not uncomfortable. Are you?" he asked, as he placed his arm around me letting his hand rest on my shoulder.

"No...no, I'm just fine," I reassured him.

We continued asking each other questions until our food arrived. He sat close to me drawing circles with his index finger on my arm as it rested on the table.

As the dinner started, there was a small amount of clumsiness like young kids out on their first date testing the waters, just to see where safe ground was. I started to relax as we talked. I was aware of others in the restaurant, but their voices were muffled. All I could hear was Steven's voice asking the questions and my voice answering him back. He really listened to my answers; he was interested. We were comfortable together and I couldn't explain why. After all, I had just met him. However, here I sat talking to him as if I had known him all my life.

I enjoyed having his arm around me; his touch was soothing. His eyes smiled when he laughed, and we were laughing a lot. I had never felt this way with Nick. Nick was too controlling, everything had to be his way or his temper got the better of him, and then I was the recipient of his anger. To sit and play twenty questions, well, you could forget that too.

The waiter brought our margaritas and the food arrived. He waited to ensure everything was correct and I assured him it was fine. Steven watched me carefully, smiling as I assembled my taco. He picked at his salad but he ate it.

"Okay, you're quiet. What's wrong?" he asked.

"Nothing's wrong, I'm just having a very good time."

"You had doubts?"

"Yeah, I did. Oh no, don't get me wrong, I had doubts I would have a good time here in Vegas, not doubts that I would have a good time with you. Oh dear, that just didn't come out right. I'm having a very good time with you and I...don't understand it," I firmly stammered.

"So what is it you don't understand?"

"I've just met you, but I feel as if I've known you for some time," I said a little shyly.

"Sometimes people just hit it off from the start, maybe that's what we did. I enjoy your company too." His smile was genuine. "How's your taco?"

"It's very good, would you like a bite?"

"Sure," he put his hand on mine as he brought the taco to his mouth, taking a small bite but not taking his eyes off me. His touch was cool, soothing. My heart was doing flips. I thought hard as I looked into his eyes, those very familiar eyes. *I've done this before, think! Damn this was so frustrating!*

We continued our conversation. He asked me what hobbies I had. I told him I was into photography and was thinking of taking some classes this winter. I mentioned I had brought my camera and was going to go to the desert while Gran was busy with her reunion. He suggested I not go there alone, and offered to go with me. I accepted his offer and that surprised me. I didn't even know this person and here I was going to the desert with him, throwing all caution to the wind.

"What?" he smiled.

"I don't know? I just can't put my finger on it. It's like a picture far away and the closer you think you are getting to it, the farther away it is." I shook my head trying to clear the fog. My headache was starting to come back. *Damn, just ask.* "Have we ever met before? You just seem so familiar to me, but I can't place it."

"Maybe you've met me in your dreams," he teased.

"Well, since I really don't sleep much, I doubt that I dream."

"Everyone dreams Bree, you just don't remember. It'll come to you."

When the dinner was over, I was afraid the night would end as well. "Would you like dessert?" Steven asked.

"No, I'm fine thank you." He started to massage my neck. "That feels really good," I said.

"Headache better?"

"It's getting there." He found the right spot on my neck, "Oh my, did I mention how good this feels?"

He leaned close and whispered to me "yes" then kissed my neck sending shivers down my arms, someone had done that many times to me before, and I loved it. Then he whispered again, "Was that awkward?"

"Yes, but I like it."

He rested his head against mine. "Are you ready?"

I cleared my throat. "For what?"

"Okay, I'll rephrase. Are you done eating and are you ready to leave the restaurant?"

"Oh that, yes I'm ready."

"We're going to get along just fine, Bree. Now where can I take you? Have you ever been here, I mean, really been here not just passing through so to speak?"

"No, I was going to check out the main street here at the hotel, you know, where I saw you earlier at the pub."

"Well, come on. Let's take a walk and see where we end up," Steven said.

CHAPTER 8

We left the restaurant and walked down Main Street stopping in front of the Irish pub. Coming toward us were Rick and Sandy.

"Hey kids, what, are you two up to?" asked Rick.

"Nothing, thought you were going to the party?" answered Steven. "Bored?"

"Yeah, pretty much, not sure where Brad and Madalyn ran off to. Haven't seen them for quite some time," Rick said.

"Well, Rick, gees, I'm sure Madalyn wanted some time alone with Brad. Ya know, some times you guys hang together way too much." Sandy smiled and winked at me.

"Nah, I don't think we do. What do you think Steven? Do we hang together too much?" He was clearly teasing her and he and Steven went into the pub leaving Sandy and me on the sidewalk.

"Now that was interesting," Sandy said.

I wrinkled my forehead trying to decide what to do. I mean, do we just stand here or do we follow? Sandy had a shocked look on her face, so obviously this was not something these guys generally did to her. "Huh, well, I suppose if we want to be with them we better go in."

Steven's head popped into the doorway, "Well, you two comin'?" He ran out, grabbed our hands and pulled us toward the doorway. He put his arm behind Sandy to allow her to enter first, and then he wrapped his arm around my waist. "Is this okay with you? If you don't want to spend time with them we can leave, it's no problem."

"You're asking me? This is just fine. I would enjoy spending time with your little friends," I did my best imitation of my grandmother.

Steven laughed, "That was pretty good."

⁓

The main room was filled with varying sizes of tables with green or white tablecloths and small candles lit in the center. The booths all had wall sconces dimly lit. The low lighting throughout the pub gave it a cozy atmosphere. We had a large table in the back, and Steven led me toward it. He pulled my chair out and I sat next to Rick. Sandy was on his other side and Steven was on my right. There were spaces for two more guests.

"Yep," Rick closed his cell phone and made the announcement as we sat down. "They'll be along momentarily." I didn't have to ask who would be joining us, strangely enough, I knew. Steven assumed the position; his arm was on the back of my chair with his thumb tapping my shoulder.

"So, Squirt, are you enjoying yourself?" Rick asked.

The way he said it made me look at him quickly. Someone else used to call me that. I hadn't seen him in a long time. A smile crossed my lips as I remembered a memory but I just couldn't quite get it to focus.

"What?" he gave me a hopeful look.

"Nothing...it's...well...it's nothing, and yes I'm having a very good time for the first night, quite better than I had imagined. I have to say Gran and I have a great time together but in small amounts. I wasn't so sure how seven days was going to work."

"I hear that," said Sandy laughing. "Oh, please don't get me wrong, I love your grandmother, but I know I probably couldn't do it for seven days. For that matter I couldn't stay with my grandmother or my mother for seven days."

Brad was leading Madalyn toward our table, "Well, look who's here, the Three Musketeers back together again," Sandy said.

"Well, I must be improving. I had Brad to myself for a whole two hours. Thank you, I feel honored," she said dryly as if she really didn't even want to be here.

Brad pulled the chair out for her, then he playfully reached over and messed Sandy's hair, ignoring her comment. "Hey there Bree, are you enjoying yourself?" Brad asked.

"You're late," Rick informed him, "I already asked. Yes she is, and very relieved she doesn't have to spend time with her grandmother. Our Steven is keeping her entertained."

"Oh dear, you need to run and run fast. Grab a hold of him and run now, otherwise you'll be sharing Steven with these two," Madalyn said. She tried to sound happy but she wasn't pulling it off.

The pub was starting to get busy and it looked as if the waitress wasn't going to get to us any time soon, so Rick, Brad, and Steven graciously went to get our drinks. This left the three of us to talk because from the looks of the bar it was going to be a while. "Well, Madalyn, why don't you move to Steven's seat, this way you can see what's going on, and you can at least watch Brad," I said pulling Steven's chair out. I tried to show my friendlier side to her.

She thought for a moment then moved over and Sandy moved into Rick's seat. I knew they wanted to start questioning me and I just hated the awkwardness of that so I started the conversation. "Okay, what is it ya want to know about me?"

"That obvious?" Madalyn asked. "We don't have much practice at this. We've all been together for so long and we know everything about one another."

"No, I wouldn't say obvious, just natural. What can I tell you?" My eyes were watching Steven. They were at the bar watching the game, waiting to be served. Occasionally the small figures they were watching would do something to cause them to either cheer or moan.

"Yeah, they are delightfully soft on the old eyes, aren't they?" Sandy said, clearly watching Rick. "Yes, they are," Madalyn and I agreed.

Steven smiled at me as he caught my eye, and I smiled back.

The three of us continued our conversation, and we were laughing and joking by the time Rick, Brad and Steven returned. "Well, glad to see you three are getting along so well," said Brad. "What's so funny?"

"Oh, Brad darling, you really needed to be here. Repeating it now just wouldn't be as humorous," Madalyn said as she took her drink from him, and gave him a kiss. She moved to her chair so Steven could sit by me.

Brad looked at me and I shrugged my shoulders, "Sorry, one girl in a family of many men."

I found out they were all good friends of my cousins Billy, Stanley and Ryan. I thought it odd that as much as they said they were around them, I really didn't recall seeing them at the house. Or maybe I did know Steven from there. I thought as I watched him talk, *I need to have a word with Billy. Why he never introduced me to this very scrumptious looking guy is beyond me.*

Sandy asked if I traveled much, I told them about my trip over the summer to Yellowstone. Sandy assumed I had gone by myself and that surprised her, but I corrected her by letting her know Billy and his family went with me.

The waitress brought us another round of drinks and we continued with our conversation. The music was loud and people were dancing. Friends of theirs would stop by the table to say hello, I was always introduced as Millie's granddaughter and got the familiar nods and smiles. I felt sorry for them all for having been subjected to my grandmother's stories of her only granddaughter.

The waitress brought me a drink. I looked at it and then looked at the waitress.

"It's from the gentleman at the bar," she said.

I looked toward the bar, as did everyone else. "Would you mind pointing him out please?" My voice was a little uneven.

The waitress looked toward the bar, "Well, I don't see him now."

I handed her back the drink and asked her to please dump it out. She had a strange look on her face. Steven and the others were a little puzzled as well. "Sorry, I learned a long time ago not to accept drinks from strangers and especially strangers that don't stick around to acknowledge your acceptance of the drink."

The waitress smiled, "Okay, I'll dump it."

After she left, everyone at the table continued looking at me, "What, you haven't met my cousin Billy?"

Brad laughed, "Yes, Breekins, we have met Bill, and I agree he does look out for you."

Steven stood up and took my hand, "If you guys will excuse us I'm going to go and dance with this lovely lady. We'll be back."

∽

Out on the dance floor a slow song was playing. Our position together was comfortable, familiar. My arms were around his neck; his arms were around my waist. We started out talking as we danced, but then I settled my head on his chest with one arm around his neck. He had one arm around my waist and held my other hand, tucked in close. I felt safe in his arms. There was just something familiar about him.

He smelled great. His voice was soft when he said; "I could hold you like this all night." He kissed me on the side of my head and I nuzzled in. He softly exhaled as he felt me relax in his arms. Our motions slowed to swaying.

"I could stay here all night too," I whispered back to him. And as the bandleader sensed our moods, we continued to dance through two more slow songs.

CHAPTER 9

"So, this is his Bree I've been hearing about," Sandy said as Madalyn and Brad moved into Bree and Steven's seats so they could watch them on the dance floor.

"Yeah," said Rick. "Brad, if they had just left things alone back then, those two would have figured out something. But they had to meddle and left him remembering and miserable and her not remembering and miserable."

"Yeah, I know. Bill tried to make them listen, but damn Rick, what could we do? Her mother was scared and wasn't listening to anyone. Hell, Warren couldn't even make her see how much it was going to hurt Bree. Now look at them, right back where they left off. I hope Steven knows what he's doing," Brad said.

"I don't understand, isn't this what he's wanted? Isn't this what you four have wanted?" Sandy questioned.

"Yeah, it is, but he's moving way too fast. If her memories had come back when she saw him earlier then I wouldn't be worried. But they didn't and he's pressing."

"We even left her on the sidewalk when we came in here. Damn, we used to tease her like that all the time. She'd just run in after us, but she didn't do that," Rick said.

"Is that why you left me standing there?" Sandy quizzed Rick.

"Sorry, that's why I sent Steven to get you. Just in case you were pissed," he laughed.

"Well, stop worrying you two, just let nature take its course," Sandy advised. "I have all the confidence in the world Steven will bring her memories back."

"I'm not worried about him being able to bring her memories back. I'm worried they are getting too close too fast. It's *too* dangerous," Brad explained.

Why's it dangerous? Rick and I had sex when I was human and you and Madalyn did too. You don't think they had sex?" Sandy laughed, "Come on, look at them. They've been very close before and Steven's not dangerous, Brad."

"Sandy, let me paint you a picture. Rick and you are close right?"

"Yes, Bradley, you know we are." She giggled and kissed Rick on the cheek. Rick knew the direction this scenario was heading, so he just sat back with a grin on his face and let Brad set the scene.

"Okay, take that times ten and then...Rick has been away from you for thirteen years. How careful would you be? I doubt either of you would even make it to the bedroom, let alone take care not to hold onto to each for dear life!" Brad laughed.

Rick leaned in close to Sandy and softly nipped at her neck making her shiver as she leaned closer to him. "Now

Sandy, you know how dangerous we *can be*, even one small little nip would kill Bree."

"Oooh, yeah that could be a problem," said Sandy. "No wonder he was so grouchy this morning! I don't know the whole story, so fill me in before they come back."

"We never told you?" Rick asked.

"No, I know little bits, but since I had to stay away for so long until I calmed, I was never told anything."

"I forgot you had to stay away as long as you did, you were a wild little thing." Rick leaned over and nipped at her ear.

"Later darlin'. Right now I want to hear this, so tell me." She gently pushed him back and winked.

"Damn, I would have thought Madalyn or Gina would have filled you in," said Rick. "Okay, settle yourself back and we'll tell it to you. Steven didn't meet Bree until she was what, six months old?" He looked at Brad.

"You're joking?" she laughed.

"No quite serious. Now do you want to hear this or not?" Rick teased.

"Yes, darling, I'll keep quiet," she smiled.

Brad began the story, "We had just gotten back from the spring gathering and Bill wanted us all to come over and meet the little bundle we were all charged with protecting. All four of us went. Bill held her but she wouldn't take her eyes off Steven. He'd get up and walk around with her and she'd stretch and turn to keep Steven in her view. Hell, she was only six months, but something about him caught her eye and that was that."

Brad shook his head as he laughed, "She'd let us hold her, or she'd sit on our laps, but if Steven left the room, her eyes stayed on the door until he came back. When she could walk, she'd get down off of whoever's lap she was on and go find him. I think Gina was the only woman, other than her mother, aunt, or grandmother she would let hold her. Bree watched Madalyn but I don't think she was too sure about her," Brad teased, and Madalyn just gave him a smirk and hissed and bared her needle sharp fangs. Brad's easy-going manner started a slow simmer and Madalyn retracted her pointed canines and sat back.

Rick ignored her little stunt, she wasn't going to gain any points with Brad by doing that, and Rick knew Brad would deal with her attitude, so he continued telling Sandy the story.

"During the early years we were around her as ourselves, but as she got older we had to be around her as kids. They were worried she'd start questioning the age differences. Gina made a comment one day, and I'm sure it made Martha...that's Bree's mother, mad. Gina had teased that she and Bill ought to just raise Bree. I do think that thought had crossed everyone's mind, but it was decided that it would be easier for Bill to protect Bree as her cousin, not her parent. That's why Bill and Gina waited so long to have kids. The family decided on a five-year age difference for Bree and Bill. Then Ryan looked the appropriate age to Bill and Stanley was like three years younger than Bill. They had it all worked out, confusing as all hell, but it seemed to work.

Everything was going fine and we were able to watch over her. When Bill was at the appropriate age to drive, he would take her places and we all went. Her parents were happy, Bill was happy, Steven was happy, hell, we were all happy. Then by junior high, it started to unravel. The Council started calling all the shots," Rick finished.

"How was the Council calling the shots?" Sandy asked.

"The Council wanted to be kept informed of her growth. They wanted to know if she was showing any signs of magic, so her parents had to go more often. And every time they came back, they had more restrictions on her...to keep her safe they said. Shit, they just wanted to make her miserable."

Brad joined the conversation, "The Council said they received ultimatums from a faction that was hell bent on killing Bree. Her family wanted to keep her safe...so they all did as they were told. The rest of us were always after them to leave her alone and just let her be herself. There were enough of us to keep her safe. They wouldn't hear it though." Brad was frowning as he spoke. "When she was real little, there weren't any restrictions, but as she got older...let's just say she wasn't enjoying life very much! Bree didn't understand why she wasn't allowed to do things and they were at a loss on what to tell her, so they never told her anything."

"Martha wouldn't let her go with her friends to the malls, or the movies or really even socialize with anyone, because as long as she was home, she was protected. I felt so sorry for her. Damn, her friends would call and ask her to go with them but her mother always said no. Bree never argued. I have no idea why she didn't, do you Brad?" Rick asked.

"No, no idea. Bree never threw a fit about it. Shit, if Bill hadn't stepped in and taken her places she never would have gotten to go anywhere. That's probably why she was more mature than her friends. She was always around older people," Brad said. "It was bad by the time she was fifteen, Bill was worried about her. She went from at least being able to ride her horse all over the ranch to having to stay indoors. Bill had a long hard talk with her parents. Millie, and Bree's other cousins, Ryan and Stanley, backed him up and they finally gave in and let Bree start doing things."

"Bill made a deal with her parents that we would go to functions disguised as other people, this way Bree could go to football games and school dances, and such. Bill would change our appearance and we could keep an eye on her. Then we'd be out front after the event to take her and her friend Becky home. Becky had the biggest crush on Bill." Rick and Brad started laughing.

"We would sit in the back of Bill's car and Bree would always sit back there with us. Whoever was sitting behind Bill is the lap she would sit on, and then she would stretch her legs across the others. Brad and I took turns sitting behind Bill, which drove Steven nuts!" Rick laughed as he took a drink of his beer.

"Why did she sit behind Bill?" Sandy asked.

"She always rested her hand on his shoulder when he drove. Bill liked that, so she always sat behind him. He always played the big brother roll and would lecture her about boys and such. He'd ask her questions about her night and I'll be damned, she never lied to him. If he asked her about a boy she might have been speaking to, she'd tell him what they talked about. Anyway, he'd get into the big brother roll and she'd sit back there with us listening to him, occasionally she'd roll her eyes or make a face at him. He knew she was doing it, but she always listened to Bill. Well, she really listened to all of us. She'd speak her mind if she disagreed; she'd stand her ground with all of us. She just didn't follow blindly because we were older and we told her what to do. Even when she started dating Steven, she'd still stand her ground if she thought she was right. She wasn't bratty or anything, she could accept being wrong," Brad said.

"Just how do you know she didn't lie, Brad? Honestly, she was a teenager. They all lie about one thing or another. I am finding it a little hard to believe she was this perfect," Madalyn said a little nastier than needed.

"Because we took turns going and talking to her. She didn't know who we were. I thought several times we were going to have to go drag Steven away. Once he would go talk to her, hell, he stayed." Brad looked a little miffed at Madalyn, "That's how we knew she never lied to Bill or us."

"Didn't you go with them on their covert dates with her?" Sandy laughed, trying her best to bring her longtime friend into the conversation.

"No, I usually did a girls night out with Gina and the gang. I never went unless Gina needed to go. I didn't really want to actually," she said shrugging her shoulders.

"So, Rick, you two really went to high school dances?" Sandy laughed.

Rick and Brad both smiled as they remembered those times. "Yeah, we did. We made a promise to keep her safe. That was our duty. Steven wanted her safe; damn he was head over heels for her. He didn't want her to date any mortal, oh holy shit no. He didn't want anyone near her.

He wanted to be her first, wasn't going to take a chance on her dating some mortal and letting them be her first." Rick laughed and tried to take a drink of his beer.

"Well, Madalyn, should we be jealous of her?" Sandy teased. She thought her comment was innocent enough, but she felt a wave of worry when Madalyn snipped her reply.

"I don't know Sandy, looks like Steven isn't the only one under her spell."

"You girls have nothing to worry about; she is and always will be all Steven's. She would joke and tease with us when she was older, but she knew exactly when she needed to be with him and only him," Rick said not paying much attention to her attitude.

"When did she start dating Steven?" Sandy asked.

"Bill was able to introduce the four of us to Bree when she turned sixteen."

"Everything was going fine. Steven was doing his best at keeping the peace with Martha. Bree was only eighteen, just graduated high school, getting ready for college, everyone was happy," Rick said. "Then her parents had to go to the Council and another restriction was put in place. The ultimatum was, Bree could go safely to college, but she had to stop seeing Steven until she turned twenty-five."

Brad continued the story, "Martha begged us all to just stay away until that time. Bill became very vocal, told them she was safer with Steven than with any of them. But her parents accepted the ultimatum and Steven had to go away. Damn, when he left, man...that was hard. They had a date planned that night. Steven asked Martha if he could just take her out one last time, he wanted to tell her he had to leave. Martha wouldn't hear of it, she thought it would be easier if Steven just left and she would wipe Bree's memories herself. Bill got nervous. He didn't want Martha wiping anything from her mind. He was afraid she'd wipe Bill out too. Steven was going to take Bree out to dinner at this very fancy restaurant, Bree came in all ready. Her mother and Bill were arguing and stopped as soon as she entered the room. Bree knew they were discussing her. She sat next to Rick on the sofa, watching her mom and Bill. Steven loves her in red and she wore his favorite dress. She hates to wear dresses, but Steven could always get her to wear one for him. She sat there very quietly waiting on him, watching her mom and cousin, trying to figure out what was going on. Bree always was quiet. She had the sweetest impish grin you could imagine though. You just knew she was up to no good. You never knew what she was thinking until she sprung it on ya." Brad was looking at a distant point on the dance floor.

"Why didn't you just read her thoughts?" Sandy asked.

"Couldn't. Her dad put a spell on her so nobody could do that. Warren didn't want anyone taking trips through her mind until she was able to block it herself. He wanted his little girl to have her private thoughts. Spell's still in place, I've tried since she's been here and I can't get in. I'm surprised, Sandy, you haven't mentioned it," Brad teased.

"Now Bradley, you know it's rude to sneak into someone else's mine." She laughed, "Besides, I have tried. I thought maybe Steven was protecting it."

"Are you kidding? He is chomping at the bit to get in there," Rick said.

99

"From the sounds of it, her dad knew what he was doing," Madalyn snipped.

Brad gave Madalyn a stern look before he continued, "Martha gave in and allowed Bill to wipe her memories, but he didn't wipe them out, he hid them. She was supposed to start remembering once she saw him, and as we now know, it didn't work. Anyway, the doorbell rang, and Bree jumped to get it, she thought it was Steven. Hell, she beat her dad to the door!"

"Oh damn! I forgot about that," said Rick. "Those flowers."

"Yeah, *those* flowers. Damn, you should have seen her face when she came in carrying them. He forgot to cancel the order and if he had seen her face that would have killed him. She was beaming. Martha just looked at Bill, and she and Warren left the room and closed the door. Bree really knew something was up then. She stood there looking at him. Tears filled her eyes and he moved to put his arms around her and she stepped back. I can still hear her voice, she just whispered it, 'It's not supposed to happen this way Billy, please don't do this. Steven wouldn't do anything to hurt me. Why doesn't Mom like him?' Oh man, her voice kept cracking. Damn it broke my heart to listen to her. I had never heard that pain in her voice before that night. He told her Steven wouldn't be coming back, not for a long while. She stood there, looking at him as tears ran down her cheeks. She didn't go into hysterics or anything. She didn't throw anything. It would have been better if she did. We could have handled that type of reaction, but she just got very quiet, ghostly quiet and that scared us," Brad said.

"She wouldn't look at anyone. She turned to leave and Bill grabbed her, handed the vase to Brad, and then just held her close. It was as if she knew what he had to do. Her shoulder slumped and she just held her arms around him. He held her for a long time, swaying back and forth with her, trying to calm her as she cried. He hid her memories, and he promised her she would remember when she was supposed to. When he was through, she told him she was going to bed, kissed him goodnight and said her goodbyes to us. She took one flower out of the vase and went to bed. We took Bill out and got him drunk after that. Steven was there for a short time. Bill told him what he had to do and how Bree had reacted to his leaving. Steven just left, and we didn't see him for a couple of weeks," Rick said.

"I've a feeling this is all contributing to her headaches. Her subconscious is trying to remind her of things, and her conscious mind is fighting it. Steven was going to propose to her the night he had to leave. He would have waited until she finished college before they got married but he could have been with her there. He just wanted to marry her. He would have protected her, hell, we all would have moved to Austin," Brad finished.

"Did they keep their promise; did she have any problems in college?" Sandy asked.

"Yeah, there were some problems," Rick frowned. "Her family tried many times to have the Red Guard protect Bree when she was growing up. They argued it was the responsibility of the Guard to ensure the Chosen Ones stayed safe and since Bree was prophesied to be a Chosen One, she deserved their protection.

We knew that was a long shot. The Guard answers to Esmeralda and there was no way she was going to have Bree that well protected. We've known all along Esmeralda is part of that group that wants Bree gone, but she has a powerbase and Bree doesn't. The Council isn't going to rock the boat on the 'chance' Bree crosses," he made air quotes as he said it. "They won't band together until it's a sure thing. They're nothing but a bunch of...well; not all of them, but the ones with weak spines are keeping Esmeralda in power.

Esmeralda successfully argued that the Guard was for the Chosen Ones and that Bree hadn't made the transformation from mortal to Magical. Since it was only prophesied, she would have to wait until she transformed for their protections. So...we formed our own guard. Her cousin Stanley leads them. We didn't even let her parents know. It was Millie's idea really, and a damn good one. We had teachers at her school, students in her classes at college; even her dorm monitor was in our guard. Someone has always shadowed her when we couldn't be around her. She's even being shadowed here, but I've a feeling Steven isn't going to let her out of his sights now," Rick laughed.

"Since Steven wasn't allowed to be around her, he started dating and made sure he was seen at all the formal functions. He did what he could to keep the attention off of her," Brad said as he took a drink of his beer.

"Well, I always thought it was stupid that he dated, and his choices were not who the women in his clan wanted him to be with. We never said anything, but damn Rick, Rebecca! Why did he have to pick her?" Sandy asked.

"It was all done for show, babe. Remember, Steven was of the Fourth House, and the prophecy puts those two together. If we wanted everyone to believe he was not waiting on Bree, he had to be with women that didn't fit his mold. He wanted them to think he didn't care. He even let it be known there were too many restrictions on her and he didn't want to be bothered by them. He didn't want to draw any attention to her, so he found the complete opposite of her and dated them. That Rebecca was a pushy broad. She did everything to get Steven to commit to her, and Steven used that to his advantage saying he was a confirmed bachelor; he wanted nothing to do with marriage. He got the word out there and he dated others. He hated it and there were many times he'd talk about it when we were out at night. But it was all for show, it was something he had to do. I was beginning to worry the government was going to put bison on the endangered species list with as much hunting as he had to do!"

"Well, what did Steven do when she got married, why didn't Bill and Steven do something then?" Sandy asked.

"Wasn't anything Steven could do, wasn't anything Bill could do. Martha and Warren allowed Nick in her life." Brad tried to temper his anger before he continued.

He looked at Rick, a silent understanding passed between them. He cleared his throat and took a long drink of his beer before he continued. "They made a deal with the devil, well, in a manner of speaking. They knew that piece of scum she married had ties with her enemies and they let it happen. They knew it, but they had hoped that would keep her safe. They were given a choice. Let Bree stay married and don't interfere; don't tell her anything, and they wouldn't send an assassin to kill her. They said no Magical would harm her as long as they didn't interfere with the marriage," Brad said, as he took another drink of his beer. His eyes showed his anger.

cᴖ

None of them could understand how anyone charged with keeping someone safe could allow that to happen and Bree was their charge.

Brad watched everyone on the dance floor, searching through the crowd until his eyes fell on Bree and Steven. A smile creased his lips; he had missed her. This separation had been too long, and it was painful for Steven and for him.

cᴖ

Rick didn't mention to Sandy, how outraged he himself had been. He blocked his mind so no one could read his thoughts. His Bree had been in harms way, married to that mortal and there hadn't been a damn thing he could do. Bree would always belong to Steven. Their love was eternal. However, she held a piece of Rick's heart that no one could touch.

cᴖ

"You could tell she wasn't the same person when she came back married. Like Brad said earlier, she was always quiet but when she came back, she was quiet and withdrawn. She didn't have that sweet grin anymore. The sparkle was gone from her eyes. Bill was pissed. Steven tried to calm himself. In all the years I have know Steven, I have never seen him like that, and I never want to again," Rick said.

Rick tried to clear the lump in his throat, "I still think we should have just taken her. I can't believe they let it happen. To this day, I don't understand it."

"Bree wouldn't talk about any problems she had in her marriage. We knew there were problems, but Bill couldn't get her to open up, and damn he tried. We knew Nick was mean to her, yet we couldn't do anything about it. Bree heals quickly so any proof, any bruises, any broken bones would be gone in a matter of hours. And because Bree heals very fast, her family felt she had a better chance at surviving being married to Nick than not. So they just wouldn't do anything," Brad said as he swallowed his anger.

"At first the problems were small, but in our eyes even the smallest problem wasn't worth it. Bill and Millie did what they could to keep her safe. The guard did what they could, but Millie kept warning us all not to interfere unless necessary. Her family was willing to put up with her discomfort because they were looking at the big picture," said Rick.

"Yeah," continued Brad, "then, Nick started really getting rough. Bree was found at the bottom of the stairs in a pool of blood in February. Bill found out she was pregnant, 'was' being the operative word there. She can't have any children now. That one opened their eyes. Her family started scrambling after that, but Bree became withdrawn and stopped visiting them. She wouldn't let Bill come over. She just stopped talking all together."

"We were going to go and take her. We were going to tell her everything and hide her away if we had to. She had the car wreck before we could get to her. Warren stopped thinking they knew what was best for Bree. It was time for them to take a stand. The Council wasn't going to put any more restrictions on her. Warren broke down, Bree was in the hospital, and he was taking the blame for it. He told Bill and Steven to start making plans for her memories to return. Millie, Bill, and Steven have put this whole meeting together here at the reunion, hoping those two could pick up where they left off. It has to happen naturally, and from the looks of it, I think maybe it has, *again*." Rick finished; he shook his head thinking about all the time that had been wasted.

"Why didn't your guard protect her from his abuse?" Sandy asked.

"Millie warned us not to interfere in anything. If you think about it, we actually formed an illegal military and if they were ever found out, many families and clans would be in danger. We just had to ensure they didn't kill her, and until February, it ran smoothly. We should have acted quicker, but we didn't. Bill was on his way to her house to get her, we were going to meet him there, but she wasn't home when we got there. Bill got a call from the guard member that was shadowing her. It all happened so fast there wasn't anything he could do to stop it. Our main concern was getting her to the hospital, and then we all went on the hunt of those three. They went underground. Bree's enemies were protecting them. Nick showed at the hospital but always had several Red Guards with him. We couldn't do anything to him there. Finally, they knew it was a lost cause. One of us was always in the waiting room. Steven stayed cloaked and was always in the room with her. Her doctor was a good friend of ours, he knew all about Bree and he monitored everything given to her. They kept trying to poison her in there.

"Why didn't Steven just go to her when she finally left Nick?" Sandy asked. "Why wait until now?"

"She had to mend, she was very weak, and all the poison and damage to her body took a heavy toll on her healing abilities. She's still mortal, so her strength wasn't what it should have been. We were afraid to tell her anything. We thought if we told her about all of this, the shock might be too much for her to grasp, so we decided to wait until she was fully recovered. That's why Bill took her back to Yellowstone. She loves it there. Stanley and his guard kept watch over her, made sure no one was following her. We helped. We took over at night, so they could stay sharp during the day," Brad said.

"I never knew you went there," Madalyn said as she gave a low growl, irritated she wasn't involved in any of this.

Rick just looked at her, unfazed by her attitude, "Don't even go there with me Madalyn. It was kept as a need to know, you didn't have a need to know. Pure and simple, the less involved the better." Rick finished his beer as he kept his eyes on her.

"Oh, so sayeth the great protectors," she gave her retort and continued to look at Steven and Bree on the dance floor. Still piqued she wasn't in the loop, "I wonder how she will take it when Steven tells her about us." Her lips curled into a wicked snarl. She covered her mouth so the others wouldn't see.

Brad gave her a warning look, "You let Steven tell her, understand?" She kept looking out at the dance floor. "Bree will handle it, she loves him, and she'll handle it."

"Are you trying to convince me or yourself, darling?" she said curtly as she looked back to the group.

"She," Rick looked hard at Madalyn, "will handle it." He tipped his head toward her but her face remained void of any emotions.

&

Steven and I finished dancing and I had to stifle a yawn, but he saw it. "It's time I get you to bed." The way he said it caused me to smile. "Okay, let me rephrase. It's time I get you to bed so you can sleep." He kissed my hand.

"I understood you the first time, unfortunately I can't argue with you. What time is it anyway? Don't they believe in clocks here?"

"Well, no, and I think it best I don't tell you."

"That bad huh?"

"Not really, it's only two-thirty."

We headed back to the table and Steven told them he was going to walk me back to my room and would catch up with them later. Sandy stood and gave me a hug goodnight. Madalyn just gave me a weak smile. But when Rick and Brad kissed my cheek, a memory stirred in my mind. I smiled at them, stood there for a moment longer, trying to remember that sensation from so long ago, then said goodnight to them and left with Steven.

The closer we got to my room, the slower we seemed to be walking. I was dead on my feet but didn't want this to end and I was sensing the same with him. When we arrived at my door, I pulled my passkey from my back pocket but he took it from me. He leaned against the door, his hand gently rubbing my arm. "Can I meet you for lunch tomorrow? I'd say breakfast but I don't think you'll make that."

"I'd like that; I really had a good time this evening. Thank you."

"I did too, and you're welcome. I'm glad Millie finally brought you. I had decided if she didn't bring you this time, I was going to Texas to meet you." He swiped my card key and opened the door. As he handed me the card, he reached over and kissed me on the cheek. I smiled when he looked at me. He leaned in a little closer, watching my eyes for any indication he was moving too fast. He saw none and he very gently kissed my lips. I raised my hand to the back of his neck, holding him softly. Steven stayed close to me as our kiss finished. He cleared his throat before he was able to speak, "I'll," his voice cracked, he cleared his throat and started again, "I'll call you later this morning, get some rest Princess," and he closed the door after me as I entered the room.

Chapter 10

Sunday morning, very early

I was tired, but I couldn't sleep. The events of the evening kept replaying in my mind. I'd had a good time and he'd seemed to have a good time too. I struggled to find a comfortable spot, but couldn't. I decided I would read a few chapters of the book I had brought, "The Red Chill of the Morning", a good horror book. Daylight would be here soon and then I could sleep. The voices and the sounds never came during the day.

Here lately, I had tried to tone down the horror movies and books. Now that I lived alone, in such a large house, there was nowhere to run for protection. Not that Nick had offered me any protection, but when he'd been home, the voices and the sounds stayed away. Whenever he was gone, I left all the lights on and would find things to keep myself busy.

I switched the light on and made myself comfortable, placed all the pillows around me, protecting me from the night. The clock registered four o'clock. I picked up the book and turned it over so I could read the back cover. There really wasn't anything wrong with my current selection. I thought the cover had looked interesting, so I bought it. I opened the book to the current chapter and began reading.

"*Spiders, worms, and flies crawled over the dead bodies as they lay in the mud with the lightning crashing and thunder pounding all around.*

He stood in the shadows watching her, blood dripping from his mouth. His muscles had ripped through his shirt and it lay tattered against his skin.

The sweat and smell of blood was entirely too much for her, she screamed as he drew near, afraid for her life. She knew him, how could she have loved this, this..."

I heard the bar stool drag across the tile floor in the dining room and sat up in bed wide-awake. "Okay, this book's not that scary, I've read scarier. This is actually lame." Then I heard the sound again. I looked at the clock, four-ten. I wasn't going to let the sounds beat me, so I bravely got up to investigate. I found the chair was still up against the table, it hadn't moved at all. *This is ridiculous; just go to bed.* I tried again, but no luck, my mind kept thinking about my time with Steven and his kiss.

I smiled when I thought of the kiss. My body tingled when our lips had met, I wanted to fold into his arms and just stay there. I had never felt that way with anyone, and especially never with Nick.

I turned my attention back to the book, and then I heard the sound again. "Okay, I'll get dressed and go to the lobby and finish the book. I'll have some breakfast and then catch a few hours of sleep. It will be easier to sleep during the day anyway," I convinced myself.

The lobby was very busy for four forty-five in the morning but then again this was Vegas. I bought an extra large white chocolate mocha, found a comfy chair, curled up, and continued my story.

"She knew him, how could she have loved this, this creature.

He looked at her, begging her to understand. The moon had caused him to turn into this, but it didn't change the love he had for her. These people had meant to do her harm, and that he could not allow. He attacked them for his love of her, she had to understand that, or else his pain would be too great for him to bear.

He so very desperately wanted to take her in his arms, to sweep away her fears, but he knew he could not touch her in his present condition so he ran. He ran away from her love, he ran away from her."

I stopped reading because I felt I was being watched, I slowly lowered my book. Three familiar faces were looking back at me and I shyly smiled, "Morning."

"Bree, what are you doing down here at this hour? I just put you to bed not more than a couple of hours ago," Steven said.

"I couldn't sleep so I came down here to read."

"Why couldn't you read in your room?" He looked at me suspiciously. "Just what are you reading anyway," as he glanced at the book. "You scared yourself, didn't you?" He had a little smile on his lips.

"I take it Gran told you about that too?"

His smile just widened, giving me my answer.

"Well, what are you guys doing, don't you sleep?" I asked.

"Sure, but for this one week we don't sleep much. We only see most of these people once a year so we try to make the most of it. Trust me, tonight I will sleep," Steven said.

"I don't get it, Squirt, you really scared yourself reading a book?" Rick asked. "I didn't think that possible. What's your book about?"

I pulled it close to my chest to hide the cover.

"Ah come on, I won't laugh, I promise." He was already laughing.

"It's about a werewolf that falls in love with a young girl. He kills a few people that meant her harm, she finds out he's a werewolf, she still loves him blah, blah, blah, you get the idea."

"Can't happen," Harry said.

I hadn't noticed Harry in the group. I had forgotten about him and his request to have dinner with me. "Hello, Harry, how ya been? What'd ya mean it couldn't happen?"

"I mean it can't happen. Werewolves can't fall in love with humans, it just isn't done." He was very serious about this and I didn't know if he was pulling my leg or he truly believed in werewolves.

"Okay, granted this may be a little far fetched, but how do you know that a werewolf, if they existed mind you, doesn't retain some glimmer of someone he cares about when he makes the transition from human to werewolf? Would it not be possible for him to go somewhere away from her when the moon is full, so he wouldn't be able to do her harm?"

"I'm just telling you that this can't happen because of who he is. He's a monster, he is driven by the moon to kill people and it doesn't matter who that person is, if they are in his path, then they are dead. End of story, no magical love scene, nothing. She's a goner."

"So, you are convinced that love, true love, couldn't occur between them? That two people can't get past their differences, no matter what those differences are, if they love one another?" Steven was now sitting on the arm of my chair. I hadn't realized I was leaning against him. I didn't even remember him moving, but there he was rubbing my shoulder.

The awkward silence hung there as I looked at Harry trying to figure out what broken love happened in his life to make him so cynical. If anyone should be cynical, I would have thought it would be me. But I was still a romantic at heart, and besides damn it, it's fiction for heaven's sake. Anything can work in fiction.

So I spoke first. "Sorry, Harry, but I choose to believe you can overcome any obstacle life throws at you, and believe me I've had enough thrown at me to last a lifetime. So cheer up. It's just a story."

Harry looked at me and I looked back at him not willing to back down from his gaze. He finally smiled, "Yeah, it's just fiction, those monsters don't exist."

I started laughing, "Well, I wish you would tell that to whatever was making the noise in my room. Monsters don't exist," I laughed.

Steven, who had been rubbing my shoulder throughout this exchange, finally said, "Bree, you're still warm, are you sure you feel okay? Have you had breakfast yet?"

"Steven, I told you earlier I'm fine," and I raised my cup, answering the breakfast question.

"Okay missy, that's it, coffee is not breakfast, we're heading that way now, and you're going to come with us. Sandy, Madalyn, and I think Vicki, will be joining us. Won't she Harry? Brad, come here and feel her head."

I looked up at Steven, "Now why would he want to do that, Steven?"

"Sorry, I didn't tell you he's a doctor and you said you didn't have a medical degree, but he does; several I might add."

"Brad, you don't need to feel my head, I'm fine. I don't even have a headache," I lied.

We didn't have to wait long before the elevator doors opened and out stepped Sandy, Madalyn, and one other who I assumed was Vicki. She was shorter than her companions were but taller than I was. She had shiny, thick brown hair, the kind you see in TV ads where the model can tie it in a knot. Her skin was smooth and much darker than the others were.

Rick met Sandy half way and gave her a big hello kiss, Brad was more reserved and waited until Madalyn came to him then he lightly kissed her on the cheek. Vicki walked directly to Harry. He picked her up in a hug and swung her around. It was a tight hug and it made me wonder how she could breathe; it probably would have been the end of my ribs. Harry put Vicki down but kept an arm around her. He looked at me a little strangely, as if he was still trying to figure me out from our last conversation. Steven pulled me to my feet bringing us close together and he whispered in my ear, "I'm glad you're here," and smiled.

The ballroom, from the night before, had been rearranged for breakfast. The only ones who really seemed to eat though were Harry, Vicki and me. The others ordered fruit and V8. They picked at the fruit but quickly drank the V8 and all five ordered another glass. I could tell from the conversation we were about to have that Rick was the instigator of the group.

Rick was a very tall handsome man, deep voice, crystal blue eyes, and a very sexy smile. I liked him. Yes, he was a bit of a flirt, but I liked him. I was comfortable talking with him. He reminded me of my cousin Billy. I could talk to Billy about anything and I felt the same way about Rick. I had to laugh at myself, how did I know I could talk to him like I did with my cousin? After all, I had only met them all last night. But here I sat, right next to him and yes; I was comfortable with him. My mind was telling me we had been friends before. Now, I knew I was tired! I had just met these people and now my mind was telling me I knew them, I had met them all before! Yes, I was tired, I convinced myself.

"So Bree, you really think a werewolf could fall in love with a human?" Rick was looking down as he asked and I was sure I saw a grin on his face.

"Just can't let it go can ya, Rick?" I said.

"No, I mean I'm curious. What if it were a, oh, I don't know, how about a vampire and a human?"

Steven put his arm on the back of my chair, Brad shifted to gain a better view, and Sandy, Harry and Vicki had a curious look on their faces as they waited on my answer. Madalyn's face was void of any expression.

117

I still had a strip of bacon in my hand. *Okay, game on.* "That's a leap. We were talking about werewolves now you're throwing vampires in."

Vicki almost choked on the food she had just put in her mouth. "What about werewolves?" She managed to ask shooting a look at me.

Madalyn sat a little straighter in her chair, no smile on her face, with Brad's arm draped over her shoulder. I stole a glance at her then quickly looked away toward Steven. Her eyes were focused on him, trying to gage his expression.

Madalyn, reminded me of an older sister, who was told to bring her younger sister with her. She put up with me. I was the younger sibling Madalyn was charged with, and she didn't like it. The younger sibling always got the attention. Everyone was always nice to the younger sibling. Steven paid too much attention to this younger sibling, this person who was new to them. Yes, Madalyn had had all the attention until this new person came and she was struggling to deal with it.

Steven continued to smile at me. He kept his arm around me. He was completely in control watching the scene unfold around him.

"Bree was reading a book about a werewolf falling in love with a human, which she thinks, is a possibility, and that the werewolf would not kill the one he loved if, said woman, was in his path. Now I'm curious if she thinks it is possible for a vampire to fall in love with a human," Rick supplied the explanation. Everyone turned to look at me. Madalyn wanted the answer as well. I felt her eyes bore into me with such intense dislike. I looked down so I wouldn't be tempted to look at her, to draw attention to her treatment of my presence in her little family.

I took another bite of my bacon, and chewed it slowly and continued my jousting with Rick. "Well, Rick, first, I said they would take measures to ensure she was safe when the full moon rose, but yes I do believe, if there were vampires mind you, that yes, it is possible for a vampire to fall in love with a human and not want to kill her and drink her blood. It happens all the time in books and the movies. Gee, Hollywood wouldn't lie to us, would they Rick?" I popped the rest of the bacon in my mouth and grinned.

"Okay, let's take that example, Hollywood. They also show vampires having this mesmerizing ability to seduce their female or male victims with their eyes. How would you know if it was the seduction or real love? I mean they have to look at each other, right? So wouldn't it be better to say he, the vampire, is the one in love but the female is not really IN love with him."

Steven shifted slightly in his seat. His thumb was rubbing my shoulder again. Everyone was watching me, waiting for my comeback. I thought about my answer for a few moments, Rick had a "gotcha" smile on his face.

I poured a little syrup over the rest of my bacon, picked up one and took a bite. Thinking on my answer, I finally spoke, "No, I don't believe all women can be mesmerized by a vampire. If, for instance, let's say they met and let's say he, the vampire, fell in love with her first, I don't think he would try to seduce her that way. I think the love that he felt for her would not let him destroy her. He wouldn't want that, if indeed he loved her. So then I think naturally, if it was meant to be, she would, in turn, fall in love with him."

Steven's hand was now rubbing the back of my neck very gently. It did feel good as my head was pounding. I could feel the muscles in my back relaxing with the gentle pressure he was applying. "Balls in your court, Rick."

That got a chuckle out of Brad. Rick looked at me "Okay, let's take that scenario, what if she didn't return his love, would he destroy her?"

My response was quick and I smiled at Rick and very softly said, "No, not if he truly loved her."

Sandy decided to chime in at this point, "Bree, do you not think all men, human or vampire," she smiled, "are capable of, what was the word you used darling, ah yes, mesmerize, are capable of mesmerizing a woman into making her think he is the one she wants?" Sandy was a confident woman. She sat poised in her chair, never slouching, always sitting straight. I liked her, I liked Madalyn too, but Madalyn was standoffish, Sandy was fun. Sandy was also a flirt, just like Rick.

"Sure, and I also think women are just as capable of the same. But what I was getting at, if they love each other, then they have to accept each other the way they are, no tricks. All the flaws are out there in the open and they accept it and move on. Otherwise I don't think it was really love they shared, they're just hot and heavy for each other and would share a romp or two in the hay and say good bye."

"I hope you remember that," said Madalyn. "Loving someone no matter what their flaws are." She sat there staring at me, twisting her fork in her hand. She suddenly sat straighter and averted her eyes from me. Steven had stopped rubbing my shoulder, I felt him tense. I looked at him, his eyes bore into Madalyn and I quickly looked away. I had intruded into this group and Madalyn was not happy about it. I understood that much, but it was only for seven days. I'm sure Gran asked them to keep me company during my stay. After Friday their lives would go back to normal, I would return to Texas and probably never see them again. Maybe I should just stay in my room and let them have their time here. I didn't want to be a bother, but...I... did want to be with Steven. I felt my necklace warm against my chest and I smiled as I calmed my thoughts, no I needed to be here. I was confident about that.

The awkward silence had reappeared at the table. I hated that sound. No one spoke or cleared their throats. I glanced at Vicki and smiled.

Vicki looked at me and smiled back. She started the conversation again, drawing my attention away from the standoff between Steven and Madalyn. "So you think the same for werewolves as well?"

I began to explain my thoughts on the question Vicki had asked. "I think that if they exist, werewolves, vampires, witches, and whatever other mythical sprits are out there in the world, can fall in love with a human, if that's what they would call us, yes"

"But, what if they do exist?" she asked. Harry put his arm around her, and she realized she said something she shouldn't have said.

Steven's hand started massaging my neck. Brad coughed and started to speak but I could see Rick out of the corner of my eye trying to gage my reactions to Vicki's comment. I sensed Rick was testing me, for what I didn't know, but he was waiting on my response.

"Well, that's just great. I couldn't sleep before and now you expect me to go to my room and sleep? Someone is going to have to check under the bed and in the closets then," as I said this I shook my head and took a drink of my coffee. I glanced at the clock on the wall, "Don't you guys need to be going to your reunion? Oh, and Rick, I'll let you know what happens when I run into a vampire or a werewolf."

"Okay Squirt you do that," and he tapped my nose and smiled, "because I would be very interested in what you think then."

We left the ballroom. I walked with them part way and stopped at the elevator to go to my room. "Would you like me to walk you back to your room? I could check under the bed and in the closets if you like," Steven teased.

"I think I'll be just fine, it's daylight. Everyone knows monsters only come out at night. You go ahead."

"I'll call you later." He kissed me tenderly again on the lips, and looked into my eyes to ensure he was not pressing me too far. I returned his sweet kiss and then got on the elevator.

Once in my room I opened all the curtains, took a hot shower, dressed in my comfortable sweats, called for a wake up call at eleven o'clock and fell asleep on my bed.

꿍

The phone rang my wake up and I stumbled to the bathroom to wash my face and brush my teeth. I had to rewet my hair because I had fallen asleep without drying it. The phone rang again; it was Steven.

"Say, I know we were going to have lunch but I'm going to finish up here. You get some more rest and we'll spend the night together again. You have got to be tired and I don't want you falling asleep half way through the evening," he laughed. "I promise you an elegant dinner to make up for lunch. But to be honest I wouldn't want to come back here after seeing you, it was hard enough to let you leave after breakfast."

I told him to come up when he was done and we would spend the rest of the day together and hung up. I noticed the message light on my phone; I hadn't heard the ring. I picked up the receiver and pressed #7 to retrieve the message.

Your sisters love you very much and our fates rest on your shoulders. Do not speak of us until the time is right. You will know when to tell the others.

That was it. My sisters? I didn't have any sisters. I didn't have any brothers either, only cousins. I figured they must have gotten the wrong room or it was a prank call.

I decided not to lie back down, so I sat on the sofa to watch a little TV. My eyes grew heavy and the next thing I knew someone was knocking on the door. I stumbled to the peephole. *Steven*, a tiny smile crossed my lips.

I opened the door and smiled wide, "Hi," and instinctively raised my arms for a hug. He wrapped his arms around me and picked me up. He closed the door with his foot as he kissed my neck very tenderly and inhaled deeply, "You smell so good." He kissed my neck again. He cleared his throat before he spoke, "I missed you today. Are you ready? I did promise you an elegant dinner."

"Give me a minute and I'll be ready." I went to freshen up in the bathroom. My headache was there just enough to be an annoyance so I took three aspirin, washed my face, and brushed my teeth. I rechecked myself in the mirror, flipped off the light and walked quickly into the living room. "Ready," I announced. Steven wasn't alone. Brad and Rick had stopped by. "Hello guys. What's up?" I asked.

"Hey Squirt - did you get your rest today?" Rick asked as he came over to me and wrapped my arm around his, leading me toward the door.

"Yes, Rick, I did. Thank you for asking. Yet, I ask again, what's up?"

"Well, we're here to see if you and Steven would like to go bowling? Now before you turn your nose up to spending another night with all of us, we would really like to spend some time with you. I know, I know, Steven promised you an elegant quiet dinner, but you don't want to go to a stuffy restaurant. Come on, doesn't pizza and beer sound better? You like to bowl and I know you like pizza, and beer goes with pizza so I know you like beer."

"You know this, do you?" I looked at him suspiciously. They all smiled at me. "Madalyn was right. I should have grabbed Steven and started running. Yes, I do like to bowl and I do like pizza and beer, so let's go."

CHAPTER 11

We met up with the others in the lobby. "I told you Bree, didn't I warn you? You should have listened." Madalyn had a smile on her face. She seemed to be trying to mend fences and I wasn't one to carry a grudge so I accepted her silent apology.

"Yes, you warned me."

We entered the bowling alley, and collected our shoes, selected the balls and went to our lanes. "Now," Brad said, as he draped his arm over my shoulders holding me close to him. I watched him as he spoke. "What should we do here; boys against girls, two guys and a girl against two girls and a guy?" Brad too was handsome, and yes, he was proper and polite. I liked him, I trusted him. His eyes smiled at me, I seemed to fascinate him. For whatever reason I felt I was a challenge to him and he liked it. I don't know why I felt that way, but I put my arm around his waist and looped my thumb in his belt loop. He gave me a light squeeze on my shoulder.

"Brad, I think we should play girls against guys," Rick said with a grin on his face.

"Not fair, you guys are stronger than us, and you play this game more than we do," Sandy pouted.

"You have nothing to worry about, darlin'," Rick said as he wrapped Sandy in his strong arms and kissed her neck. "Bree is a very good bowler; she can probably out bowl us."

I looked at him confused. "Now exactly how do you know this?"

"We know Bill, remember?" Rick said.

"Yeah, well, you know he likes to embellish. We'll go boys against girls, but you can't slack. You can't let us win just because I'm the newbie." Brad kissed the top of my head before he released me.

"Okay, done," said Rick.

Steven and Brad just laughed and shook their heads, "We might as well just sit this out and let those two battle it out." Steven winked at me. My mind was going through the files again, looking and searching. Something was familiar with this setting, but I just couldn't get past the heavy curtain that was hiding a place, a time, where this all seemed to happen once before. I closed my eyes and shook my head, my hands pressed on my temple, a sharp pain shot to my eyes making them water. After a few moments, I opened my eyes. Steven was standing right in front of me, "Are you okay?" His face showed his concern.

"Yes...I'm okay...I think I got entirely too much sleep today, that's all. Let's bowl."

Rick and I went first for our groups. We both bowled strikes the first couple of frames. You could tell the other's hearts just weren't in it. Sandy didn't like sticking her fingers in the holes on the balls because of her nails and Madalyn just didn't like being in shoes other people had worn.

Steven and Brad were very good bowlers but decided to sit out since it wouldn't be fair with three against one. That just left Rick and me, and true to his word he wasn't cutting me any slack. The first ten frames, we were even, the second set I pulled ahead, but not by much, the third and final set Rick beat me. All I had to do was pick up the number one pin, right down the center, that's all I had to do.

"Huh," Rick came up behind me. "You should pick that up with no problem," he assured me. "No sweat; just straight down the middle."

I turned to him and smiled, "Are you trying to rattle me?"

"Nah, not at all. You're a good bowler, I'm just encouraging you."

I looked at him skeptically, "Uh-huh, well, go stand back there." I nodded back toward the table.

He raised his finger to his lips to signal he would be quiet. He crossed his arms over his chest and motioned for me to continue with my shot. I shook my head, gave him a grin then turned back to face the number one pin. *Simple enough. You've done this a thousand times. Yeah, but not with these people watching my every move!* My mind was playing a tug of words with me.

I lined the ball up, and readied myself for my approach. I started to take the first step, just started to lower the ball in my swing, when I heard Rick clear his throat. I stopped, and quickly turned to look at him. My brow creased as I gave him a stern look. He just smiled and with his hand motioned for me to move just a little to the left.

"I've watched you; your throw pulls to the right." He came up behind me, and positioned the ball in my hands, his large hands holding mine firmly on the ball. He was so close to me. I could smell his aftershave. Musk, I liked that on him. "There, now you should hit it!" Then he moved back, crossed his arms again and motioned with his hand I should continue. I saw Steven and Brad fighting to contain a laugh. I turned back, and quickly went through my approach so he couldn't interrupt me again. All three of them came to join me as soon as the ball left my hand. We watched it roll, but this time it veered to the left and missed the pin all together.

I immediately looked at Rick, my hands rested on my hips, my eyes narrowed on him, "My throws pull to the *right?*" I questioned him. I crossed my arms and met his start back at me.

"Huh, I could have sworn they pulled to the right, maybe it was the left. Huh, oh well, I guess that means I won!" He broke out in a laugh and messed my hair. "Let's eat!"

We ate the pizza and drank the beer and bantered back and forth who was better. I wasn't tired, my arms hurt, but I was enjoying myself. Even my headache was gone.

Everyone wanted to go dancing. As we neared the bar, Steven pulled me close, "Are you tired? We don't have to go dancing; we can go for a walk if you want. We could see a show. Hell, we're in Vegas, I'm sure you don't want to spend all your time dancing."

"I get to dance with you and be close to you, right?"

He kissed my forehead, "I hate to tell you this, but I'm sure you will have to dance one or two dances with Brad and Rick. They have really taken to you so just be prepared."

"As long as the majority of my dances will be with you, I don't mind." I have had this conversation before, I remembered having it, but I just couldn't place it.

⁊

We sat at the same table we were at last night, in the same seats and gave our drink order to the waitress. The room was moderately crowded. Several couples were on the dance floor. Brad asked me for a dance and I graciously accepted.

Madalyn watched Steven as he told Brad not to keep me away too long. He stood as I got up and kissed my cheek. I took Brad's hand as he led me to the dance floor. My steps had to quicken to keep up with him and when we reached the dance floor, he gently pulled me around and into his arms. I felt a rush of energy from him as he drew me near and it made me shiver. I hoped he hadn't noticed. He gave no indication that he had. The music was moderate, allowing him to hold me in his arms, but kept us moving on the floor. He talked quietly in my ear, asking me if I was enjoying myself. He was glad I decided to come this year and I assured him I was just as glad I came. We talked freely and I made him laugh.

The music ended and he kissed my hand, his eyes sparkled. "I enjoyed that; you're a very good dancer. May I be so bold to ask for another?"

I smiled at him, "I would love to dance with you again."

The music continued with a much slower song. I thought I would feel a little awkward dancing this close to him, especially the way his wife was acting. But, there was no awkwardness to our movements, his arms held me close to him in such a loving way, I felt I was supposed to be there, tenderly tucked in his arms. When the music ended, he softly whispered a hushed 'Thank you' in my ear. I heard nothing but his words and I smiled back at him.

∽

When we arrived back at the table, Rick was ready to begin teasing me again. "Well, Squirt, how's the arm?" He gently squeezed my upper arm as I sat next to him.

"It's good right now but I'm sure tomorrow it will be sore. It's been awhile since I've bowled," I said.

"She has improved," Steven said.

"Okay, I give. Just how do you know all of this? I'm not buying into this all came from Billy. I know I have never met you before this reunion and I'm around my cousins a lot. I can honestly say I do not remember ever seeing you."

"Simple, you're never there when we are. They do talk a lot about you. For instance, we know about your stuffed toy collection that you have had since you were ten," Rick said. "Also, you had a very special stuffed toy, it was a bear wasn't it, that always sat in the middle of your bed. I think you got that when you were, what eighteen?"

"Seventeen," I corrected, my eyes again narrowed as I looked at him, "and yes he *is* a special bear."

Nick wouldn't let me have them when we were married, but they are all back in my possession now, and that very special bear still sits on my bed. I looked from Rick to Brad and thought, *now that's an odd thing for you to know about.* My hand touched Steven's leg, checking to ensure he was still there. His hand rested on mine giving me a familiar reassurance.

"Who did you get the bear from, Bree?" Sandy asked.

I started looking for that file again that was hidden away somewhere in my brain. "It came from someone I used to date a long time ago," I chuckled, "strange, the name escapes me at the moment. That's a terrible thing to say, I can't even remember his name, but I do remember I didn't want to get rid of the bear so Mom kept it for me. It all was so long ago."

Steven saw the frustration on my face. "I'm going to have a dance with my Princess, so if you will excuse us." He took my hand and led me toward the dance floor.

∽

"Steven," I began as we assumed our natural position. "I can't explain this but I really feel I should know you guys. I just can't place any of it. It's like I've lost years out of my life and I don't know where they went."

"Don't worry about it. You're here now, we can start new memories," Steven whispered to me.

"I feel I need to have the old ones too."

He held me close, I felt very safe in his arms. I never wanted to leave this feeling behind. I nuzzled into his chest and inhaled, "You smell delicious, what is that, Brut?"

"Yes,"

"I like it on you."

"I know."

∽

Back at the table, Brad and Rick were becoming equally frustrated. "We may need to bring Bill in a little sooner, so he can just lift the damn spell instead of her trying to remember on her own. Martha must have added a little something after Bill did his part. He said she should start to remember if we just reminded her of a few things," Rick said.

"Yeah, I'm starting to get a little concerned about those headaches. Bill will be here tomorrow night, let's wait and see what happens then," Brad said as he took a drink of his beer.

"Okay, I don't understand," Sandy started. "Why on earth did you take her bowling? Why don't you just let Steven take her out for a romantic dinner? Just from watching them, it's not going to take that much of a push to put her in his arms. You guys are making this way to complicated!"

"We are, huh? Well, Bill told us to do things with her we used to do, and we used to take her bowling. Steven said he could feel her frustration and when she was little, she would take her frustrations out on the bowling ball. I remember the last time we took her bowling. The high school coach begged her parents to let her play softball, but her parents were too worried Bree might get hurt, and then heal quickly...they couldn't take the chance. Hell, you should have seen her fast pitch. Damn, that was one wicked pitch," he laughed. "Those bowling pins didn't stand a chance."

"Well, Brad darling, there are other ways to get rid of your frustrations!" Sandy reminded him.

"I'm well aware of those *other* ways," he smiled and winked at her, "Steven needs to pace himself. He hasn't been able to hold her for thirteen years, let him calm a little!" Brad and Rick started laughing.

"Maybe I should go and cut in on our Steven," Rick teased.

"Then I'll cut in the next time. That should get him all riled up. Let's just see what he's made of," Brad laughed.

"You two are so bad," Sandy laughed. "That is not going to help him calm Richard! Why do you want to torture him?"

"Because it's what guys do. We can have it, he can't, and it's fun."

"Rick you may want to go throw some cold water on him," Brad laughed.

"I'll be back shortly." He kissed Sandy and made his way to the dance floor.

❧

"Go away Rick," Steven said, "she's all mine now. You have a wife, dance with her."

"Nah, I really want to dance with Bree at the moment, besides Brad needs to talk to you anyway."

We stopped dancing, "Why?"

"He just needs to talk to you. Go on, I promise I will bring Bree back to you, now go on."

Rick slipped my hands into his and started moving me away from Steven. He waved his hand at him telling him to head to the table.

"Bree, are you having a good time?"

"Yes, Rick, I really am having fun. Why?"

"Just checking. Steven's having a good time, and it's been a long time since I've seen him this happy. You're good for him Little One." He held me close to him. This was familiar to me as well. When the dance ended and another one began, "You don't mind do you?" he asked.

"No, I don't mind Richard. Why would you think that?"

"Richard, hmmm, am I in trouble?"

"No silly, why would you ask such a thing?"

"Well, you did use my proper name. We always knew we were in trouble with your grandmother when she used our proper name. I just thought, you, being her grand-daughter, that apple didn't fall far from the tree."

"No, you aren't in any trouble." I could smell his aftershave. I surprised myself when I realized I had never noticed cologne on any of the other men I had dated. I will agree there were few dates, but I never noticed the cologne on Nick or Jared or Fred. I knew they wore it, but I was never attracted to it on them. I could always smell Billy's cologne, he wore Old Spice, and I loved that smell on him. Every time he hugged me, I drank it in. Brad wore Old Spice too, the smell was different on him than it was on Billy, but I liked it. Steven wore Brut and that had always been my favorite; I loved the way Steven smelled. Rick was wearing musk and his smell was delicious. I inhaled deeply. "I like that smell on you." I tensed and I felt Rick give a little chuckle. "Oh my, did I just say that out loud?"

"Yes, you did Little One," he laughed. "I'm glad you like it. I'll make a note to always wear it around you, and you do realize I will have to hold you close so you can get your fill. You won't have a problem with that will you?"

"Now you're teasing me."

"No, I'm not teasing you, I'm very serious. I will pick you up and hold you tight so you can have your fill." The music ended and Rick reluctantly released me from his embrace. He kissed the top of my head. "Thanks Squirt. It was fun dancing with you again."

Again, again, but I've just met him. How could I have danced with him before? I kept searching for that damn file. The answers were there I just needed to find them.

Since I had slept so much during the day, I was able to stay up all night. By five, we headed for breakfast. The time passed quickly and soon, it was time for them to go to their reunion.

~

Steven whispered into my ear "Bree let me walk you up to your room; it'll only take a couple of hours. I don't need to be anywhere but with you now." He smiled and arched an eyebrow.

"I'll be fine, you go on and get this over with and we can spend some more time together. Ya know, we need to get you to bed sometime soon."

"Are you offering?"

My heart started racing, my face became warm. I looked at him, and smiled, "I'm not going to rephrase it."

"Good, I'll see you soon."

The elevator doors opened and out stepped Gran and George. "Oh Bree, I'm so glad I found you!" She wasn't doing a very good job at hiding her concern. She quickly spoke her 'hello' to everyone, "Bree, I need to talk to you about something."

"Okay, Gran. What's up?"

Steven looked at my grandmother, and then leaned in and kissed me on the cheek. "I'll talk to you later." I smiled my goodbye at him.

My grandmother pulled me away from the elevator and over toward the hall that lead to a row of phones. She had a serious expression on her face now and George seemed just as concerned.

Steven, Brad and Rick noticed their tension and were going to stay, but I shook my head and waved them on. I turned back to my grandmother, "Okay, okay what's up? What's got you so upset? Steven has been very gentlemanly, nothing to worry about."

"That's good dear, but I'm not worried about Steven right now I'm worried about you. Now I don't want you to get upset, dear, but he's here," she whispered.

"Who's here, Gran?" I played along.

"Nick!"

My shoulders tensed, I could feel the dread creeping in. "What's he doing here and just how do you know this? Does he know I'm here?"

"We ran into him last night at the casino. And yes, he knows you're here," she informed me.

"Great, I was just starting to enjoy myself."

"I don't know how he knew, but he does and he said he aimed to be talking to you soon. I need you to promise me you'll be careful. He's mean Bree, and he's just getting meaner because of the divorce. I think given the chance, he would kill you," she warned.

"No, I don't think he'll kill me Gran. He may hurt me, but I don't think he will kill me. Well, too bad for him, I'll just make sure he doesn't see me. I'm going to my room now anyway, so you go on and visit with your friends, I'll be fine."

"You have my cell phone number if you need me?"

"Yes, but I'm sure I'll be fine," I assured her. I didn't want her to think I was scared. I didn't want her to tell Steven her concerns. But damn, I was petrified!

I turned and headed back toward the elevators with George and Gran in tow. They stood there with me. I sensed Gran's worry and that just made it worse. I stood there nervously patting my leg, waiting on the elevator doors to open. But when they did, out stepped Nick followed by his friends Fred and Jared. You didn't see one without the other two. They moved to stand slightly in front of Nick, as if they were his bodyguards there to protect him. From what, I wasn't sure. Surely, they didn't think I could hurt Nick. They were all dressed in business suits, so I surmised they were there on business.

I instinctively stepped back out of arms reach. It was more out of habit then anything else. Certainly Nick would not grab me in public! "Hello Nick. What brings you here, business, or pleasure?"

"Both," he said very dryly. The other two gorillas just sneered. All three of them looked more muscular than I remembered. Their suits fit them much tighter. "I take it your GRAN has told you I wanted to see you?"

"Yeah, she mentioned it. I really don't have anything to talk to you about. You know we're supposed to be handling everything through the lawyers. So have your lawyer call mine, if you would please." I started to walk away. I didn't want to make a scene in front of everyone.

"No, I think I will talk to you directly and I think I will talk to you now," and he grabbed my left wrist to pull me back. He twisted my arm behind my back, pressing upward making me walk on my tiptoes. He started to push me in the direction he wanted me to go in, back toward the elevators. Jared had just pushed the button.

I tried to pull my arm back, he twisted harder, I heard a pop, and then pain went from my shoulder down my arm and from my wrist up. The pain met at the elbow and it stung. Tears came quickly as I grabbed my arm and told him to let go, trying to keep my voice down so not to cause a scene.

No one noticed him grab me, or his voice getting louder. People continued to pass by as if nothing serious was happening here, just friends talking.

George came up behind me and put his hand on Nick's hand and my arm. "That will be enough Nick, you will release her *NOW*." His voice was commanding and his eyes looked intensely at Nick, causing him to swallow hard. He quickly released my wrist.

Fred and Jared made a motion to intervene. George looked at them and they stopped cold, all three of them stood stone still. "You will let her pass to her room and you will not follow her. Do I make myself clear?" All three just nodded. I was surprised. I had never seen Nick back down like that in all the years I had known him. "Millie, you go on to meet your group now and do what you need to do. I will make sure Bree gets to her room safely." She walked quickly to the reunion hall.

George cradled my arm in his as he led me to the elevator. My shoulder hurt and I couldn't find a comfortable position to hold my wrist. The wrist and elbow were seriously starting to swell. Nick, Fred, and Jared just stood there facing away from the elevators. When the doors opened, George and I got in. As soon as they started closing, I saw the three of them fall forward a little, then they turned and the doors closed completely.

George was gently rubbing my wrist. I shook as the pain throbbed in my arm. Nick was not someone I wanted to make mad. I realized that during our marriage. This was not the first time he had hurt me, but his assaults were always away from other prying eyes. Never had he done anything like this in public.

Now, here I stood with another altercation under my belt and maybe a broken shoulder or wrist, and the elbow didn't look good either. George was being so kind. I didn't even know him. "Thank you," I was able to manage. "I'm sorry about this; you should go back and meet your friends. I'll be fine, really. I'll call the house doctor when I get in my room." I tried to move my hand; I winced. I swallowed hard for fear I might see my breakfast on the floor. I was able to move my fingers, hopefully that was a good sign, and maybe nothing was broken.

"No, I will feel much better once I get you safely to your room, and I know Millie will feel better too," he said softly. "He really should not have done this. I'll stay with you until the doctor comes to check this out. That way I can take the news back to Millie, I'm sure she's worried sick."

I wasn't sure if I was shaking more from the pain or the fear I tried to hide. I needed this to go away. I didn't want anyone to see me like this. I didn't want anyone to know. I hoped my arm would heal before I saw Steven this evening. I had healed quickly all the other times so I prayed this injury would too.

The elevator doors opened and we stepped out. Two people were waiting at the door to my room, Brad and Steven. *How did they get here so quickly?* Steven did not look happy in the least. He looked at me but I couldn't read his reaction. Brad's concern was genuine as he took my arm from George. I started to reach for my passkey in my back pocket when Steven walked behind me and got it.

"Steven, in my bag you'll find a small blue bag, put some ice in it please," Brad said. "Thanks George, we'll take it from here. Millie's very upset, so you might want to get down there to calm her down. We don't want her temper to get the better of her just yet. She's blaming herself, thinks she should have just ridden the elevator up with her instead of talking to her in the lobby."

"That's nonsense," I said. "Nick would have found me one way or the other. I just don't know what possessed him to do this."

George left and Steven brought the ice bag back. Brad was examining my injury. "Does this hurt?"

I winced, "No."

"Bree, answer honestly," Brad said softly.

"Yes," tears stung my eyes, "so let's not do that." I stole a look at Steven. His jaw was clinched, and his eyes were set on my wrist, not looking at me now. *Oh God, what must he be thinking? He's probably trying to figure a way out of this relationship, if indeed it is a relationship. I'm sure he doesn't want to get involved with someone who has a crazy ex-husband.*

I looked away, not wanting that to happen. I knew he would find a way to get out of calling me later. For the first time in a very long time, I was starting to enjoy myself, and now this.

"Okay, I'm sorry. I'm just checking everything out. Nothing's broken, your wrist and elbow's just dislocated."

Brad reached his hand through the neck of my shirt and placed his hand on my shoulder. He pressed gently, and moved my arm, "It's not dislocated. Your wrist and elbow took the brunt of it." Brad's touch was cool like Steven's and my skin was very hot so it felt good against my shoulder. "Bree, are you feeling okay? You're quite warm."

"I'm fine, I don't know why I'm hot, but I feel fine."

He looked at me and raised my chin so I would look at him, "Are you sure Breekins?"

"Yes, Brad I'm sure."

"Okay," he watched me a few seconds more, then said, "Steven why don't you stand next to her for a minute, this just might hurt a little bit. No, it's probably going to hurt a whole hell of a lot so let me apologize now. We'll do it on three," he said.

I knew what was coming and I didn't want him to do it at all. I started to move my arm away but he held firm, just looked at me, and smiled, "Bree we can do this the easy way and be done with it or the hard way, it's your choice."

"Could you explain to me what the hard way is?"

He smiled, "Steven just hold her." Then he shook his head as he laughed, "It will be over very quickly."

Steven was standing by me, and I knew that he knew what was going to happen too. He put his arm around me and pulled my head to his chest, "Shhh, it's going to be fine. Just don't watch."

All I heard was another pop and the lights went out. I came to and found myself lying on my bed; trying to shake the cobwebs from my head. Brad was wrapping my arm, making it ready for the sling. "Just lay still, I'm almost done," he said in his best bedside manner.

"I didn't even hear a count," I mumbled quietly. "I'm really sorry about this."

"I like to do those types of adjustments by surprise, doesn't give you a chance to tense." He smiled down at me, "What do you have to be sorry about? This is what I do." Then he winked, "all finished." He patted my arm. "Want to tell us what happened?" He and Steven were looking at me. Steven's jaw was a little more relaxed now. He looked more concerned than angry.

"I think I passed out."

Brad laughed, "I know that Bree, I mean downstairs."

"Oh that," I looked up at Steven not really wanting to go into it. I was completely mortified now. I was sure Madalyn would have a field day with this. I would be the laughing stock of their little group. She would tell Steven he needn't get involved with someone who's life is such a mess, and I couldn't blame her...my life was a mess! I started rubbing my feet together; I had just realized my shoes were off. I didn't remember taking them off. My panic was returning. I could feel my pulse start to race. I was going to have to explain things and I didn't want to do that. I wanted to avoid my past like the plague! I looked away from Steven and Brad, and then I heard Steven's voice, and my eyes widened because I didn't hear Steven speak these words out loud. I heard them in my head, or so I thought! *She's starting to panic Brad!* And then I heard Brad, *I know, I know, we need to calm her down!*

Okay, it's starting again. I'm hearing things. Don't look at them. Take deep breaths. You can do this Bree. You're not crazy, you're just stressed right now and you only think you are hearing them! My mind kept up its encouragement.

"Aubrey," Brad's voice was very soft, "look at me. I'm your doctor now, and I want to know what happened. Would you like me to ask Steven to step outside?"

Deep breaths, Bree, deep breaths, I kept telling myself, "No, it's no big deal. I'll handle it, you needn't worry about it." I didn't know if I could do this without crying. I found a distant point on the ceiling and stared at it. I swallowed the fear that was choking me, not allowing me to speak.

Brad moved from the bed and Steven sat down next to me. He had one hand rubbing my swollen arm and the other was across me on the other side. "Bree, please I want to know what happened." His voice was low and soft, no hint of anger, no judgment in his eyes, just a sweet smile on his face.

I'd heard that same voice. Where had I heard his voice before? I knew I could trust them, my mind told me this, but my mind also told me I didn't want others to know about my marriage. I wasn't ready to face my own stupidity for staying with someone like Nick.

"Princess, talk with me." He spoke those words so softly. He moved the few strands of hair that hung over my eyes.

I stayed there looking up at him. I saw Brad behind him; he smiled and winked at me, encouraging me to tell them. I cleared the fear from my throat and began to tell them the story. My voice was weak as I began.

"I'm not supposed to speak directly to Nick. We were supposed to handle all of our communications through our lawyers. Dad doesn't like Nick at all, especially since," I saw Steven flinch at the mention of Nick's name. "Well...believe me, he doesn't like him. Anyway, he didn't care what we were supposed to do. He wanted to talk to me then. With Fred and Jared backing him up, it made me nervous because it didn't look like they were taking me to a public place to have the discussion. Jared had pushed the elevator button and I just got very scared. I didn't want it to happen again." I cleared my throat to keep from crying again.

"Didn't want what to happen again?" Steven asked.

I took a breath and continued with my downstairs story, avoiding that particular question. I watched his face as I told him of the events downstairs and I could see his jaw muscles tighten.

"If I hadn't tried to pull my arm away this wouldn't have happened, I should have gone with him to see what he wanted. I could have asked to go to a public place. I'm sure I would have been fine. You two wouldn't be missing your reunion and I wouldn't have my arm in a bandage. You need to go back to your friends. I'll be fine. I'll stay in my room. I'll not be a bother to anyone."

I took a deep breath. The worst was over. I had told them what had happened. Now I waited for the other shoe to drop. I was angry with myself for all this trouble.

I closed my eyes and listened to the silence, I didn't hear anything out of the ordinary. I was able to let out the breath I had been holding. I was relieved, it was just my imagination, I really hadn't heard them talk in my head! I opened my eyes and Steven was still there, smiling at me.

"Bree, this is not your fault and you're not going to remain captive in your room, and you are most certainly not a bother to anyone!" Steven said. "As far as the reunion goes, we come here every year, we aren't missing anything. Anyway, I should have walked you back to your room in the first place. I don't think George is the one they need to be worrying about, do you Brad? You should have seen our faces when Millie came into the hall. Which reminds me, Brad, you may want to go back and let them know the patient is fine. Otherwise Rick may already be plotting something."

"Oh shit, that's right," Brad had one arm crossed over his chest; his other hand was rubbing his chin as he looked at me. I could swear he was trying to read my mind.

Trust me Brad; you don't want to get in my head! I laughed in my mind.

"I'll be back soon. Here are some pain pills, if the pain starts getting unbearable take one, just one." Brad leaned over and kissed my forehead. "Bree you still feel warm, when I come back I want to run a blood test on you."

"Doctor Brad," I said smiling.

He stopped to look at me, "Doctor Brad, that's good."

"Yes, well...do you always kiss your patients on the forehead?"

"Only the special ones, Bree. Only the special ones," and he left the room.

༄

"Do you hurt?" Steven asked.

"No, not really."

He went to get the blanket that was draped over the chair at the window. "Can you move toward the middle of the bed?" I scooted over. He took his shoes off and lay down beside me, and covered us both with the blanket. He pulled me toward him so my head was resting on his chest and stroked my hair tenderly. "Better?"

I nodded.

"You need to get some sleep. Close your eyes, I'm not going anywhere."

"Steven?"

"What?"

"Did you check under the bed and in the closet?"

He laughed and kissed the top of my head, "What am I going to do with you? I promise - nothing will hurt you with me here."

"Can I take you home with me?" My voice slurred as sleep was coming quickly.

"I would like that," he hugged me tighter and I fell asleep safely in his arms, not a care in the world at that moment.

CHAPTER 12

The Guardians Appear

I slept peacefully. I heard the body next to me breathing and that sound soothed me. I felt him as he held me gently in his arms and I felt protected. My mind wandered.

I saw myself in a mountain meadow sitting on a blanket, surrounded by wild flowers. There was a slight breeze making the ocean of grass sway like tiny waves. I listened to the meadowlarks singing their melody in the morning sun. I could tell it was mid-morning, the sun had not crested the trees, the air was still cool, the grass still wet from the morning dew.

I was alone in the meadow, just the birds and me. Then they appeared out of nothing. I saw them off in the distance, four individuals looking at me, watching me. Three strangers and one I knew, my grandmother. She was talking with them as they looked at me.

I watched them approach. The three were dressed in golden robes with red sashes around their waists, two men and one woman. My grandmother was dressed in her gardening clothes, her large brim hat shielding her eyes from the sun. She was busy taking her gloves off. They sat on my blanket with me and spoke.

"Aubrey, these are friends of mine, and they are friend of yours as well. Do you recognize them?"

"No Gran, I don't," I whispered to her.

"Aubrey, search your mind. We are there, buried deep, but we are there," said one of the men. His hair was the color of winter wheat. His eyes were hazel. His smile was warm and his voice was soft.

"I'm sorry, but my mind seems to be playing tricks on me. My mind keeps telling me I know my new friends too, but I have no memories of them. No sir, I do not know you."

"Aubrey, you do know us, let your mind relax. Let your memories surface," said the woman. Her hair was as blond as gold, and her eyes were violet. I had never seen violet eyes before. Now I knew I was dreaming.

"I'm sorry, but I have never met you."

"You are correct, you have never met us, but you know of us. We are your Guardians. You are a Chosen One. Your mind knows this. Let it surface. Face your fears child."

"Bree," my grandmother placed her hand on mine, "what they are telling you is the truth. It's time you knew your path. Time is short now and I cannot teach you what you must know. Listen to them, listen to what they tell you, and follow their teachings. Odessa," she motioned to the woman, "she is my oldest friend. She will guide you through your path, better than I ever could. But I will always be there if you need to talk to me."

I watched my grandmother stand to leave, she turned to me and smiled, "I love you Bree." I watched her walk away and as she did, she started to fade into the field of grasses until I saw nothing but the field.

I sat quietly as the Guardian spoke to me. The meadowlark continued to sing, the light breeze continued to play with the grass.

"Close your eyes Aubrey, and hear my voice. Let us tell you of your path," the one named Odessa said. "We are here to help you along your journey. Your life was laid out a long time ago, but things happened to you and those things changed your path. Now we must put it right again. But, all of these things made you strong, and you will need to draw on your strength to accomplish what must be done."

"What am I to do?" My eyes were closed but I felt the warm rays of the sun lightly begin to kiss my face. The meadowlark continued to sing and the breeze softly played with my hair. I was content. My breathing was calm. Their voices soothed me as I listened to their words.

"When you were born, you were born a mortal. You were raised as a human as it was written in your prophecy. You were not to be told of this world or your path so your thoughts would not be tainted by our world. Human compassion is a strong emotion and one you need to have. It is strong in you my dear.

You had many trials as a human and you overcame them. They strengthened you, and your resolve is strong. When the time came to tell you of our world, your path had turned. You were married to the mortal and the fear was great within those that guarded you and it was decided not to tell you.

Your path had changed and you needed to win one more battle before you could know of this world. We watched the decisions you made, we watched as your resolve strengthened and we watched as you made your choices. We knew then you would never be taken by the demons."

"I don't understand." I opened my eyes and watched them.

"When the mortal threatened your family, you stood firm in your choice and did not cry for protection. When the mortal threatened young Timothy, you stood firm in your choice and did not run. You could have, you could have run away, into the arms of your family, but you knew the young one would have paid the price. You took the mistreatment of the mortal; you did not run. You viewed your choice as a mistake but it was your path that turned and you needed to take it.

The Elders knew your human side better than any of us. They knew you needed to understand your strength. You still question yourself, why?"

"I don't know, maybe because I don't have all the facts?" I said, a little embarrassed and very confused.

She smiled at me, "Then hear the facts, child. Listen to your path. You are of the age to cross into our world but many challenges still lie in your way.

When we came to this world, there were demons that existed, mortal demons. Our Elders destroyed many but many still exist. Other demons followed us here. Those were demons of our world. They mingled with the mortal demons and became one. They are now very strong. They lead good people, Magical and mortals, to the darker side of life.

Our Elders battled against them, many good mortal leaders battled against them. Not all battles were won.

The Elders stayed with us, teaching us. But they needed to evolve. They were here to start this world and to teach us what we needed to know. Then the time came for us to learn to live on our own. But before they departed, they put procedures in place to ensure the future. They embedded some of their knowledge, strengths and skills into seeds and scattered them among several strong families. When the demons come and the threat to our worlds grows, a Chosen One is to be born to help guard against them. The Elders held one seed to be dominate above all others and only when the threat of annihilation was strongest would that child be born. That child would have *all* the powers, knowledge, and strengths of the Elders. That child would become our leader, our Queen, and she would guide us and keep our paths straight."

I started laughing, "And you think that's me! Oh, my... you spin a very good tale. I am not strong or knowledgeable enough to lead anyone!"

She smiled, "Yes, Aubrey, you are. You are the only one who can touch a demon and not be swayed by their powers. Your mind is strong, you will have others to help you in your path but only you can destroy the demons.

You and your sisters can see the cosmic tears that allow our demons to enter this realm. You must mend that fabric which binds our worlds together. We were late in finding this world; our search was longer than our Elders anticipated. We lived in many worlds as we searched for this one, and our wars destroyed those worlds."

"Tell me what is expected of me."

"There is a great division in our world. They want to dominate and destroy those that will not follow them, mortal and Magicals alike. You must stop them.

You must destroy the demons that take them and you must mend the fabric that binds our worlds.

You will sit on the throne of the Elders; your mind will show you where to find it. You will guide our world and protect the mortal realm. You will be our Queen.

Your path has become harder now, because Esmeralda, your nemesis, has found one of the demons and she is looking for others. She harbors this one, she protects it, but you *must* destroy it. She wants to bring this one to bodily form and she needs what you have to do this. That is why she hunts you. None of the other Chosen Ones are as powerful as you. She needs your spirit, your soul because it is pure, your heart because it is loving and strong and your blood because it is very powerful. She wants to give those gifts to the demon and make him whole. That must not happen, because if it does there is no hope.

Your path will not be easy, but this is what you must do. Nothing can change; harmony cannot be restored as long as the demons survive. Through your guidance you will mend the fractures that exist in our world; make our worlds whole again. If you fail in your quest, both worlds will be destroyed, because that is the purpose of the demons; to destroy all that is good.

This is your path now and this will be the hardest thing for your family to understand."

I laughed. "That's a tall order for one person and I might add one very young person. I know nothing of a Magical world. I know nothing of what you speak. I must be very tired. My mind is playing tricks on me. A throne you say?"

She continued to smile at me, not dissuaded by my refusal to believe what she was telling me, "You are to become a powerful Sorceress. Let your memories surface, everything you need to know was put there long ago. You are indeed very young in body but your mind is old. That knowledge will be there when it is needed. You have seen things and your mind has hidden them. Let them surface. Do not be afraid."

"I'm not afraid, but I don't know what you're talking about. Are you sure you don't have me confused with someone else?" I laughed, "I am surely very tired. A sorceress now, I am to become a sorceress, yes, I'm tired."

"Sleep child, listen to your family. I will be with you always. They fear for you so it might not be wise to let them know of the complexity of your path at this time. You will know when to tell them, but they will struggle. They have protected you for so long; it will not come easy for them to let you venture down this road. Guide them child. Show them you are strong. Love them child, because they love you so very much. They had no control in your directions. Ask your questions, they will answer you truthfully."

"I truly do not know anything," I reminded her as she stood to leave.

"Yes, Aubrey, you do. Let Steven hold you. Let him soothe away all your pain from your past. He loves you greatly, as you love him. You will remember."

Then they too faded into the field of tall grass and were gone.

CHAPTER 13

Late Monday afternoon

I heard the knock on the door, but it sounded so far away. I held on tight to the body lying next to me, still holding me gently in his arms. He didn't move to answer the annoying knock.

There it was again, just a soft tap on the door. "Tell them to go away," I said as I nuzzled into his chest and he held me tighter. Then I realized what I had just said and done. My eyes flew open and I made to jump from his embrace, but he held me tight. "Oh gosh! I'm so sorry. I didn't mean, oh dear Lord, did I say that out loud?"

"Yes, you did," he laughed, "please, don't be sorry about it. I'll tell them to go away if you want. They're just concerned. Did you sleep well?"

"Yes, very. Probably the best in a long time." He released me from his embrace and I was able to sit up. My arm didn't hurt. The wrap was starting to make my arm itch, so I knew I could probably take it off. I knew it had healed, but wasn't sure how they would react to that. Would they think me some kind of freak? *The woman that heals faster than a speeding bullet*, I thought to myself.

He rolled off the bed, "Do you want to see them?"

If I had to be honest, no, I didn't want anyone but Steven here right now. I was feeling selfish; I didn't want to share this time with anyone. *Now why was that? I had only met him two days ago*; I reminded myself I wasn't here to meet anyone. However, I had and now I just wanted to spend my time with him. "I'm a mess, let me go wash my face at least," I looked at my arm.

"I'll let them in and come back to help."

"No, no I'll manage."

"I'll let them in and come back to help," he said one more time with meaning.

"Okay."

He closed the door to the bedroom on his way out. I heard all the greetings as I went toward the bathroom. I stood in front of the mirror and took stock of my appearance. My eyes were puffy from sleep and probably from the tears. My hair was going in all directions, "Lordie, what a mess."

I brushed my teeth, which was the easy part. I let the water run hot as I brushed my hair and then soaked a washcloth under the water. As I was trying to wring the water from the cloth, Steven stood in the doorway. He took the cloth from my hand and wrung out the water then gently washed my face.

"Better?" he asked.

"Yes, who's all out there?"

"Everyone."

"Even Gran?"

"No, but Bill is."

"Billy, my cousin's here?" Billy was my knight, my hero, and my favorite cousin. I don't know what I would do if he wasn't in my life. He was always there for me. He's always clean-shaven; his wife, Gina, did not like beards either. His bright blue eyes always held a smile for me and that smile would charm you right out of your socks if you weren't paying attention! His hair was light brown and thick, with just a touch of gray in it and I always made sure I ran my hands through it when ever he picked me up and hugged me.

"Yeah, he wants to talk to you first, before you go out there."

"Okay," I took a deep breath, "Why?" *Why did he need to speak to me in private?*

"He just wants to talk to you."

"Oh," I know my face showed my confusion.

"Just a sec," I turned to face Steven, "Bree, I just," he paused, "oh, the hell with it" and he took me in his arms and kissed me tenderly. He stopped and looked at me, waiting to see if I would pull away. I didn't. I gave him a shy smile, he kissed me again softly, tenderly working his way to passionate, and I didn't resist. I didn't know what it was, his touch, his smell, the way he held me. It was familiar and I responded to his kiss, just as hungry as he was. My good arm was around his waist, I hooked my thumb into his belt loop. Our kiss ended, our foreheads pressed against one another and he said softly, "I have wanted to do that since your first night here."

"I'm glad you did. I was beginning to worry you were always going to think of me as Billy's little cousin."

Then he kissed me again and said, "Oh, my sweet Bree, you are so much more to me than you realize."

His eyes were soft, familiar, but I just couldn't place him. I remembered someone a long time ago. I was close to him, was this that person? Why can't I remember? He started to move away and I held onto him. My eyes searched his face, his eyes. I needed to know this person. He was familiar, but my mind would not cooperate.

He took my hand in his and kissed it, "I'll let Bill know you're ready," he said and left.

Chapter 14

The Talk

"Hey Half Pint," Billy said as he entered the room. "Feeling better?"

"Yeah, you know me, I'm a quick healer."

"Come sit with me Bree, we need to talk. Brad say's you're to elevate your arm." He took me by my good hand and led me to the sitting area in the bedroom, stopping to pick up the ice pack.

I stood in front of my chair, "Billy, look." I started to take the wrap off. "It's all healed now; see I can move my fingers, and bend my arm. No bruising, nothing."

Billy watched me take off the wrap, his eyes looked up at me and he gave a low sigh, "Sit Bree, we need to have a little chat." He sat on the edge of the opposite chair, leaned toward me with his arms resting on his knees. I couldn't remember ever seeing him this unhappy.

"What Billy, what has you looking so unhappy?" I looked into his blue eyes and I couldn't read his unsettlement. This was not like him. He was always sure, never had I known him to have any doubt, but he did today.

"The truth. Bree, I am not what I appear to be and I am afraid to tell you what I need to tell you. Your new friends, they aren't what they appear to be. Damn, your entire family isn't."

"Okay, Billy, you're not making any sense. We've always been able to talk, just tell me."

"No, Bree, we used to be able to talk, until you married Nick. Then you stopped talking to me. You stopped telling me things. You hid your problems from me and I couldn't help you."

"Those were my problems Billy, I created them. It wasn't for you to fix."

"It almost killed you, my sweet cousin. I will kill that bastard if he ever touches you again." A tear ran down his cheek and I raised my finger to touch it. He took my hand and tenderly kissed it; he held it close to his cheek and closed his eyes.

"Billy, how much do you know?" I whispered as I looked down, I didn't want to look into those blue eyes of his when he opened them again. I didn't want to see how much I had hurt him.

❧

Bill gently pulled Bree from her chair onto his lap. He had held her on his lap many times as a child, but now she was a young woman and he desperately wanted to hold her. He wanted to take all of her pain away. He loved her so very much.

❧

"I know a lot, sweetheart. I know he was mean to you. I know you were pregnant and now you can't have any children." I started to move away and he held me tighter. "I'm not letting you go, not this time." I relaxed, he continued, "I know he had something to do with your auto accident. There's probably a lot I don't know, but what I do know is enough. You don't have all the information, you don't know why he did these things to you, but I do, and I need to tell you everything. I'm just afraid of how you will react. I couldn't bear it if you hated me."

I laid my head on his shoulder and drew my legs up. He wrapped his arms around me tighter and I started to cry. I don't know why, but the tears came and he let me cry and didn't speak. My tears ended and I was able to tell Billy everything that happened in my marriage.

I told him I was going to call the wedding off, but Nick had drugged me and I woke up in Las Vegas, saying the 'I do's'. I told Billy about him raping me in the back seat of the car after that. Nick had broken my arm during that altercation. I told Billy someone else was there but I never saw who it was.

I was going to leave him when I got home, have the marriage annulled, but he threatened my family. He said my parents approved of the marriage. I didn't believe him, but then we returned home and Mom and Dad didn't protest, they told me, "Bree, you need to learn to honor your commitments. After all, you married him didn't you?"

"I was confused, I felt lost, and I didn't even know how I got to where I was. When you and your friends showed up, at first I thought you understood, I thought you were there to help me out of my mistake, but then you became quiet, you too did not protest. So I stayed married to him. I made the mistake, so it was up to me to fix it."

"Nick was never gentle with me. Never. It was not what I wanted in a marriage." I told Billy I had tried to leave him several times, but somehow Nick always knew and he would drug me and hit me. Then he always forced himself on me. I reminded Billy nobody ever saw the bruises because I heal so quickly.

I told him what happened that night in February, when I was found in the pool of blood at the bottom of the stairs. How Nick had passed me to his friends for them to have their turn with me. I told him I didn't know who called the paramedics that night. I had heard a woman crying. I thought I was crying.

Then I told him about the car crash, I told him I was going to leave Nick or die trying. I told him how I had overheard Nick tell his friends that he was going out of town and if they wanted to pay me a visit, he had no problem with it. I told him how I had waited until Nick was gone that night, then I left but I had passed his friends on my way down the road.

My heart was pounding in my chest as I described how they were behind me and Nick was returning home. "They must have called him. I was sandwiched between them, but I had made my mind up, I wasn't going back." I told him how I pressed on the gas and ran off the road and into that tree. I wanted to die; I begged to die.

I told him I remembered hearing Nick yelling and Fred and Jared were laughing. Nick said, "Damn fucking bitch. Is she dead Jared, did we finish the job?" I had felt a hand on my wrist. Blood was everywhere. Jared answered him back, "Yeah, she's not long for this world, let's let her bleed out and we'll let them know. By the time she's found she'll be dead and you'll be in the clear." Then they left. I was still conscious. I didn't know how, but I was. I looked for my cell phone but it wasn't near me and I couldn't move so I just closed my eyes and waited for it to be over."

I told him how I heard a woman crying again. "I would open my eyes but I never saw anyone so I assumed I was in and out of consciousness. I was in pain, so it was probably me crying. I felt drops on my face like it was raining. Then it was quiet."

I told Billy how I remembered hearing him and some other guy. I guessed he was a paramedic. "I remembered being lifted out of the car and put onto a stretcher. Gina was there too, she told you to go with me in the ambulance and she would go get my parents. I remembered just before the paramedic stuck me with the needle looking up at you. You were so white. You wiped the tears from your eyes, and saw I was awake. You asked me what happened. All I could say was I had made a big mistake and had tried to correct it. Then I was asleep."

I told him about the doctor that saved me in ICU. "Every time the nurse put a new medicine bag into the IV, he came by and changed it out. That doctor kept my head from getting fuzzy again. I was able to think and I told him I never wanted Nick back in my room. He told me Dad was in the waiting room. Someone from our family other than Nick was there every day. When Dad came in I told him everything. I don't know what he did, but I started the divorce proceedings before I even left the hospital."

"So, Billy, you see, you didn't know everything. Why Billy? Why did he do these things to me?"

"No sweetheart, I didn't know all of that." He kissed my forehead. "Once you have rested, we will tell you everything my sweet cousin. But now you must sleep."

Billy held me safely in his arms and slowly started swaying. I couldn't make out the words he was saying as he stroked my face, my arms, as he held my hand in his. A kaleidoscope of visions raced past my eyes, deep into my mind, lifting the curtain that hid everything. I heard conversations I had had a long time ago. I saw faces, knew names. Those lost files were resurfacing and I was remembering. My head hurt with a vengeance, and my body felt hot. I held on to him and he wrapped his arms around me tighter. I closed my eyes and slept.

✒

Bill thought back, remembering all the times he spent with her as he held her in his arms. Bree's mother never let her do anything all during her junior high years. If Bill hadn't stepped in, her mother wouldn't have let her do anything during her high school years either.

Bill remembered being in the kitchen with Bree when her dad came in with the mail, "Bree, you got something in the mail today." He handed Bree the square envelope. Bree knew it was an invitation to a party and she knew her parents wouldn't let her go. Bill watched as she turned the envelope over in her hand, not bothering to open it.

"Thanks Dad," she said as he left the room. Then she threw it in the trash. Bill remembered asking her why she did that. "Because Billy, they won't let me go so there's no point in opening it. There's no point in asking."

He remembered the look in her eyes, the tears she tried to hide from him, and he felt her pain.

She was fifteen. All of her friends were dating, going to parties or to the mall on Saturdays to catch a movie. Bree was stuck on the ranch with adults all around. Her life was going to school and coming home. She didn't leave the ranch unless she was with her parents or with him.

Her mother said she wanted Bree to have all the human experiences she could have, but her mother was terrified to let Bree out of her sight and Bree was suffering for it. Her best friend, Becky, used to come out and spend time on the ranch, they would go horseback riding all day, but Becky was growing up too, and she was allowed to do all those things Bree wasn't and Bree couldn't blame Becky for not wanting to come and visit.

Bill watched Bree walk out of the kitchen, out the back door. "Where're you going Half Pint?"

"To the barn, at least in the loft I can see the city lights I can't visit. I can at least dream," she answered.

Her pain tugged at his heartstrings. He loved her so very much, he needed to do something, or this was going to be a very lonely summer for her. Bill watched her leave. She didn't head to the barn as she said she was going to. She took off running and headed toward the woods. He could tell from her speed, she had a lot of anger built up and was desperately trying to release it. Bill vanished from the kitchen but reappeared in the woods as a young teenage boy. He felt he could change his appearance, spend time with her, and still protect her. He would never take advantage of her, but he wanted her to have someone she could spend time with. Someone who could make her feel special. Nobody needed to know. What harm could this do?

He went toward the creek, he knew that's where she was, sitting on the tree branch staring down at the water. Sure enough, he found her, "Hey," he called. She jumped. "Sorry, didn't mean to startle you. Are these your woods?" he asked.

"Yeah, well, they're on our land anyway."

This might just be tougher than Bill thought, "My name is James, Jimmy if you like. What's yours?"

Bree smiled at him, Bill loved her smile. It was shy, but bright, a little orneriness to it. Damn she could be a pistol when she wanted to be. After she married Nick, that smile went away and Bill hated Nick for it.

"Aubrey, but you can call me Bree."

"Bree huh, that's a pretty name. Where do you live?"

"That big house up on the hill there. Where do you live?"

"Down the road a piece, in that new housing area."

"That's pretty far away, how did you get all the way over here?" Bree started down the tree.

"I rode my bike, left it up by the road. Thought I would see if there were any good fishing spots back here. You know of any. Nah," Bill waved his hand at her, "you probably don't like to fish. Most girls don't."

"Well, I don't know about most girls, but I like to fish. My cousin takes me fishing occasionally. We have a big pond back behind these woods we go to. You're welcome to fish there if you like."

Bill looked at her and smiled, "You like to fish huh... maybe we can fish together sometime."

"Maybe," she smiled back. She sat down on a big rock and Bill sat across from her. They continued talking; he was able to get her to laugh. That lightened his heart. The light was starting to fade and Bill knew Bree wasn't to be out after dark so he told her he had a long way to go home but asked if he could visit her tomorrow.

"Sure, I'd like that. Do you ride horses?"

"Sure do," Bill answered her.

"If you can come back tomorrow, we can ride horses. You can ride the one Billy always rides. We can take a picnic lunch and I'll show you around the ranch."

"Consider it a date." He watched her eyes widen. He would be her date and Bree would never know. He'd been riding with her many times. What was the harm?

Bree's parents weren't home when Bill came back as Jimmy. He made sure they were gone. Bree was getting their picnic lunch ready when he tapped on the door. The spring was back in her step. She smiled at him, that bright smile he loved. "Ready?"

"Almost," she put a few more items in the knapsack, wrote a note telling her parents she went horseback riding, "Just in case they come home and I'm not back yet," she explained.

"Do you always tell them where you're going?"

"Yeah," she laughed, "always. My family gets a little excited if they don't know where I am, 'specially Billy," she replied.

"He sounds a little controlling," Bill said.

"No, he's cool, he just really loves me," she smiled. "Come on, let's get going."

Bill spent the summer with Bree, as Bill and as Jimmy. As Bill, he would take her to the movies, out to dinner, to get ice cream. His friends would come over and they would play tag football. Bill took her to baseball games, and to Six Flags.

Bree never mentioned Jimmy to anyone, for fear her mother would end it. Her parents didn't know Jimmy. They didn't know he was spending time with their daughter. That was all part of Bill's plan, to give her a secret she could hold dear. Don't all fifteen year olds deserve to have a secret or two?

Jimmy would always meet Bree in the barn, up in the loft. Never did he come to the house. As Jimmy, they rode horses, fished, explored the woods, Jimmy would sit with her in the loft, and they would play Scrabble, or Yahtzee, or just sit and talk. He loved talking with Bree. To look at life through her eyes was an experience.

Then it happened one day, when they were in the loft. It happened innocently enough. Jimmy was getting ready to leave, and he leaned in and kissed Bree on the cheek. He had done that millions of times as Bill, but not as Jimmy. He just wasn't thinking. He had forgotten about teenage hormones, and Bree was a normal teenager. Bree's smile warmed his heart. He should have stopped there. He knew that. But Bill wasn't thinking as Bill, he was sixteen-year-old teenage Jimmy and Bree's eyes were those soft, warm, brown pools that always made Bill melt. He knew Bree had never been with any boy. She had never been kissed by anyone other than her family. However, those kisses were always given on the cheek, never on the lips. No, Bill should have stopped, but Jimmy leaned in and tenderly kissed her. She responded back to Jimmy. Then she broke away and she apologized. Bill saw her hide her face behind her hair.

He couldn't leave it like that. "Bree, I'm sorry, please don't look away from me. Your lips just looked so damn inviting. I should have asked first. I really do like you."

She looked out the loft, cleared her throat, "You didn't do anything wrong. You probably just really shouldn't get involved with me."

"Why on earth would you say something like that?"

"Jimmy, I don't know if you have noticed, but I'm kind of tied to this ranch. If you haven't noticed, we haven't gone to the woods or fishing lately. They're all off limits to me now. No one will tell me why. This is my last safe haven, this barn and this loft. I have a feeling it too will be off limits to me soon. You'll want to go to the movies and I won't be allowed to go. You'll want to go out to dinner and I won't be able to go with you. So we might as well stop now." That sadness came back into her voice. This was not what Bill had planned.

He moved to sit closer to her. He knew she didn't want to cry in front of him. Right now, he was Jimmy not Bill and he wasn't going to leave her like this. He turned her to him, and moved her hair out of her eyes, those beautiful eyes and he melted. "Bree, I don't care if we stay here all summer, I'm just happy to be with you." He kissed her again and she responded. He leaned her back on the blanket and they kissed. Bill made a conscious effort to keep his hands away from her precious parts and he had to admit that was hard. Her lips were so soft. But he didn't want to take advantage of her; but he played the sixteen year old well and let her be fifteen and awkward. He would help her gain her confidence. Nobody will ever know, not even his wife Gina. It would remain Bill's secret.

Bill was content to be Jimmy the rest of the summer. He had already decided to tell her parents he needed to introduce her to Steven when she turned sixteen. It was time they let their little girl be human and Bree needed to date and it would be safer if Bree was able to date Steven. Jimmy would move away at the end of the summer. It would sting for a short while, but wasn't that part of love? Didn't every one lose their first love? Bree really wouldn't lose her first love, not really. Jimmy wasn't real. Jimmy was Bill and Bree would never lose Bill.

Just as Bree had predicted, her last safe haven was now off limits. The summer wasn't over yet, there were still two weeks left of summer vacation. However, her mother and father sold the horses and told Bree she wasn't allowed in the barn anymore. They never explained it to her. Bill and his friends came over to see if Bree wanted to go and get some ice cream. They were in the living room talking with Martha and Warren. Bill was aware the barn was now off limits to her. Bree came into the living room, "Mom, I left my notebook in the loft, can Billy go with me to the barn so I can get it? I really need it."

"Your father can get it for you dear. I would prefer you didn't go to the barn."

Bill knew Bree didn't leave her notebook there. He had kissed her there for the last time yesterday. It was a very passionate kiss. They were in such dangerous territory yesterday. Bill remembered how hard it was to stop, but he did.

"It's okay Martha; I'll run her out to the barn. She can get her notebook, and then go with us for ice cream. Come on Half Pint, let's go." He left with Bree before her mother could protest. Bree climbed the ladder, Bill followed and watched her take the envelope out of her back pocket and laid it on the blanket, and then he went back down. Bree came down the ladder, a notebook in her hands. She must have hid it under her shirt. Bill put his arm around her and as they left the barn, Bill raised his free hand up over his head and the envelope appeared in his hand. He slipped it into his back pocket and took Bree for ice cream.

After Bill dropped Bree off that night, he read her letter to Jimmy.

ℰ℥

Dear Jimmy,

As I told you it would happen, my last safe haven has been taken from me. The barn is now off limits to me and I am not allowed out after dark. My parents have grown more protective of me and even my friends from school rarely come around.

My parents insist on always being around when my friends are here, which does not give us much privacy. That is not how I want you to spend your time with me so I am going to say goodbye. It isn't fair to you.

I truly enjoyed my summer with you, and I don't know what I will do now. I will miss our talks, your laugh, your hugs, and kisses.

I am a much better person for having known you. Know that any girl you choose will be very lucky. I was very lucky for our short time together.

Love, Bree

Bill answered her letter.

Dear Bree,

I need you to know I would never hurt you, but what I have to tell you may do just that. My father is being transferred to another state.

I loved being with you this summer. You have the softest lips I have ever had the privilege to kiss. You have beautiful brown eyes that make me melt. My heart breaks to say goodbye.

I am jealous to think of your next boyfriend, he will truly be a lucky, lucky person. Thank you for my summer.

Love, Jimmy

လ

Bree never mentioned her summer romance. Bill never mentioned it either. Bill spoke to Bree's parents and got them to understand that Bree needed to meet Steven, she needed to start living her life, and he did this without giving away her secret.

လ

Bill laid Bree gently down on her bed, kissed her forehead. He smiled, and then left the room to talk with the others.

လ

The room was dark when I woke. I was alone in the bedroom. I could hear muffled voices coming from the other room as I got up and went into the bathroom. When I came out, I stood there in the dark and listened to the voices outside my bedroom door. I heard his laugh. I hadn't heard it in such a long time. A smile came to my lips; *Steven.* "My Steven."

Chapter 15

The Explanation

Everyone quieted when I opened the doors from my bedroom. I stood in the entrance, frozen in place, until he turned. His eyes locked onto mine and they welcomed me home. He smiled and I just stared. His smiled turned a little tentative, a little weakened by my quiet. No one spoke for the longest moments. I could feel the energy in the room. It was an amazing sensation. Thoughts came at me from all directions, their thoughts.

Too much time has passed.

What's wrong, why doesn't she say something.

I told you, this was useless.

Madalyn hush!

But look at her.

I said hush!

Is she breathing?

I had no idea how I could hear them, but I could. "Thirteen years," I whispered at him when I found my voice.

He squared his shoulders and faced me. "I know," he whispered back.

"Thirteen years," I whispered again. I walked toward him, I saw no one else and I tuned out the voices. They were a distraction and at this moment, I didn't want any distractions. He stood rooted to the floor, unsure of my approach, but he stayed and steeled himself for whatever my reaction.

I stood at a safe distance, my arm outstretched, not believing what my eyes were showing me. My hand drew to his face, softly touching his jaw, my thumb gently stroking his cheek. My fingers moved across his lips. Familiarizing myself to them, reading them as the veil that had hidden my memories lifted and my eyes could finally see them again. He gently kissed my fingertips, causing me to draw a quick breath as I remembered that touch, that sensation. I swiftly pulled my fingers from those beautiful lips. My eyes could see the tiny charge of energy as I rubbed them together, tiny flashes of blues, greens, and gold. "It's real," I whispered again and drew just a little closer. "You're real." The moisture built in my eyes, blurring my vision, I blinked and a tear fell from the rim of my eye, first one, then another and another, until the banks of my eyes overflowed with the swelling of tears they could no longer hold. "You're real," I cried again.

He quickly pulled me into him, "Yes, yes Princess, I'm real, I'm here!" He buried his head in the crook of my neck, I felt his tears, and his shoulders shook a little, his grip tightened. My eyes were pressed so tight, miniscule black dots started to appear in my vision. Memories of us together so long ago came racing back, sweet moments we shared with one another.

I heard a thought, or someone could have spoken it, I wasn't sure. *We've missed you.* My eyes opened just a fraction. I knew that voice. Rick and Brad were in my line of view, Billy stood behind them. Their faces were worried. I was not ready to release my embrace to my love, so I smiled and I gave them a tiny wave 'hello', their smiles widened.

I timidly moved back pulling Steven's face even with mine; our eyes searched one another, validating this was real. I bit my top lip as I anticipated our next move. The corner of his mouth curled into a slow smile and he moved in a little closer, his cool hands held my face, my hands rested on his waist, my thumbs locked into the belt loops. He smiled, "You always did that."

I smiled back, "I haven't forgotten."

He leaned down to test my lips with his. I rose on my tiptoes. One quick peck, he pulled back letting his eyes ask the question, and mine tried to answer but the threat of tears interfered so my lips smiled my answer. His lips very delicately found their mark again, his tongue lovingly played with mine, just like so long ago.

Once our bodies were comfortable with our reuniting, his delicate kiss, boiled into passion and hunger. He pulled me closer, as if that was even possible, lifting me to him. We finally heard someone clear their throat. I held a finger up asking for a little more time, we weren't done yet, but that clearing brought back awareness that we weren't alone. He set me back down, brushed the hair from my eyes, his thumb gently wiped a tear that hung in my lashes. His body shielded me from their view as I collected my composure. I looked into his eyes one more time, "I love you Aubrey."

My heart leapt to my throat and I breathlessly replied, "I love you too, Steven. My Steven." I smiled.

"Yes, I'm all yours, no one but yours," he replied, and then stepped beside me so I could face the others.

I shyly scratched my eyebrow; I shuffled in my stance trying to conceal my embarrassment.

"You're right, she is very shy," Sandy said to Rick. She watched me as if I was an exhibit and she was just making an observation. *Yes, just an observation here. Everyone take note of the short person. See how easily embarrassed she becomes as friends, she hadn't seen for thirteen years, lavish her with hugs and kisses. Interesting!* I musingly thought.

Rick and Brad gave a quiet chuckle as they stood confidently. My little wave had assured them I was fine. "It's good to have you back, Squirt."

My awareness of them was becoming stronger. I remembered our interactions, how natural it all was. My long lost friends were back and until this moment I didn't realize how much I had missed them. "It's good to finally be back, Richard." I held my arms up to him and he quickly cradled me in his. He easily lifted me off the floor, swung me from side to side in his jubilation. "I have missed you Rick." My voice quivered with my emotions of his touch. My arms tightened around his neck, his tightened gently around my waist.

"Oh damn, I have missed you." He kissed my cheek, his hand held my face close to him. I felt the tiny tremble of his lips. His chest gave a slight heave as he gained his breath. After several minutes and a nudge from Steven, Rick released me from his hold. He messed my hair as he would his kid sister, trying to hide those emotions maybe he shouldn't have. Then he winked, smiled, and moved back next to Sandy, who linked her arm in his and gave him an excited smile.

Brad came up to me next. He cupped my face in his hands and kissed my forehead. His thumbs barely touched my cheeks, but I felt his tender touch. He tenderly ran his thumb across my lips and I kissed it. A tingling sensation surprised me as he touched my lips. I don't know if he felt it or not, but he pulled me into a tight embrace, his emotions shoved past the barriers around my heart, his thoughts pushed into my mind. *Welcome home Little One. You have been so missed.*

How was I feeling and hearing this? Maybe I was imagining it, but I knew it was his emotions I felt, his voice I heard. I knew he didn't speak the words aloud.

Billy cleared his throat. I knew that sound anywhere. Brad stepped back. Steven's arms quickly went back around my shoulders. "I ordered room service, you have got to be starving by now," Billy smiled.

I gave him a little laugh and started to deny my hunger, "Bree, you haven't eaten since breakfast, eat just a little something," Steven requested and I agreed.

Sandy sweetly handed me a plate she had been busy filling. It was piled with fruit and cheeses, crackers, a few carrots and dip. She smiled as she handed it to me, so badly wanting to be included in the welcoming. I smiled my thank-you, and quietly thought to myself, *how am I going to eat all of this?*

I know Billy knew my thoughts. He leaned in and kissed my cheek, "We have a lot to discuss. There is so much to tell you. We need to get started." Then he took a few of my carrots and winked.

"Steven, can I get you a drink? I'm sure you feel drained," Madalyn offered, a little anxiousness in her voice.

"Huh, oh yeah. Bree can I get you a glass of wine?" He didn't answer Madalyn. His attention was directed toward me.

"That would be nice," I answered him back, starting to move with him toward the drink table.

"I'll get it, you two just...sit. Make yourselves comfortable," Madalyn said, her voice a little hard. Maybe she was a little miffed as well. "Bill, while I'm up can I freshen yours?"

Steven directed me toward the sofa, he sat in the corner and I sat closely next to him, my plate balanced on both our legs. He quickly placed his arm around my shoulder, his hand touching me, keeping the contact he had been denied for so many years.

Madalyn brought our drinks, my wine and Steven's Bloody Mary. She handed him his first and smiled at him. He smiled back, gave her a quick thank you and took a long drink, emptying his glass by half. I watched him do this, Madalyn stood with my wine still in her hands, admonishing me with her expression. She waited a little too long, Steven noticed this treatment and reached and took my wine from her hand. "Thank you Madalyn, she's fine now," he chided. She shamelessly acknowledged his look, gave another glance at me, and unapologetically took her seat next to Brad. His arm was resting on the back of her chair. His hand gave her a nudge, but she paid no attention and his hand went back to resting on her chair.

Billy started the conversation, "Well, I take it you now remember," he laughed.

"Yes, I remember them. Unfortunately I have no memory of Sandy though." I gave her a regretful smile. I was sure she and I would have been good friends.

"No, you wouldn't know her, she came along after," his hand washed over his face, "after things changed." His voice was restrained.

I noticed he looked at them all. I felt his anxiousness, the energy in the room changed, from relief to worried and troubled. *How was I feeling this?* My thoughts whispered in my head as I tried to rationalize it all. "Billy, just tell me what you need to tell me. Surely, it can't be all that bad. Tell me what caused Steven to be gone from me for all those years."

"I've a question before we start," Madalyn announced, undaunted by Brad's quick tap on the shoulder. The level of stress in the room grew. Steven's hand stayed firmly on my shoulder. He finished his drink in another long swallow. I watched him do that, he noticed and smiled, and then turned his attention back to Madalyn. His eyes narrowed, but she paid him no attention. Her focus was directed on me. She had a question and was hell bent on its answer. She didn't warrant a smile from me, her attitude was as unfriendly as an ex-girlfriends greeting, but I gave her one anyway and welcomed her question.

"Why are you not angry? Steven...all of us...have been out of your life for thirteen years and yet you accepted us all back without any questions, any anger. I would have been royally pissed. I'd be so angry; I'd want answers before I accepted their hugs and kisses. Are you that insecure you need their acceptance?"

Her words spewed forth with such force, I was astonished! I didn't need to look at Steven to feel his thoughts. His eyes bore into her with such intensity. If they were lasers they would have burnt a hole clean through her and into the wall.

I confidently answered her critical remark with a pleasant response. "Billy told me he had much to tell. He told me everything would be explained. I'm not sure why I'm not angry, but...I feel like I need to wait and listen before I pass any wrong judgment. All I know is that Steven, Rick and Brad would never purposely hurt me. Billy would die before he did that. Their reasons must have been important." My hand softly patted Steven's leg, calming him. I blinked as I saw tiny flashes of, well the only way I can describe it is, electricity, around Rick and Brad. I could feel it in Steven's body; I could see it in Billy's smile. *Oh dear, I am either still seeing things or I'm dreaming and they really aren't here.* I squeezed Steven's leg slightly, *that's solid enough. I'm not dreaming.* I turned back to Billy, my interest was peaked, and I wanted his explanation. *This was going to be a humdinger I was sure!*

Billy looked at the others for support before he began. Considering how long as he had waited to tell me his story, it was not coming easy. "Billy," I quietly commanded, "just tell me."

My smile must have given him the comfort and confidence he needed. "Aubrey, this story goes back to your birth. You're not like me," he motioned to the others, "you're not like them either. There is no easy way to say this. You're human, mortal, and we aren't." He sat there a moment, letting his words sink in before he spoke again. "You're parents aren't either, none of us in your family are."

Okay, did I mention this was going to be a humdinger? Make that a colossal humdinger times three! I blinked, then gave a smile, "Right, uh-huh, not human. Then...what, you're aliens?"

He laughed, "Not quite, Half Pint. I'm a wizard, so are your parents and Gran and my entire family; even Gina, and our boys. We are all Magicals."

I didn't say anything. Not because I couldn't think of anything to say, I could, I just couldn't find my voice. So I sat there and stared at him. I thought about what he said. If it were true, that would certainly explain a lot and just maybe, I wasn't crazy. I had always thought I was. I mean all those things I saw growing up, things floating in the air when my mother was cooking, when she didn't know I was there. She always acted so normal when I entered the kitchen though. And what about that apparition I thought I saw in the barn? And maybe those sounds I heard at night were real, not my imagination. Maybe I did hear Steven and Brad's thoughts earlier! But as I sat there looking at them, I realized this couldn't possibly be true. They didn't look any different than me, although I didn't have any idea what a wizard should look like.

My silence held longer than Billy liked. "Bree, are you okay?" The worry crept back in. I could feel him projecting it toward me. My skin tingled from the tiny charges that hit my senses. I rubbed my fingertips together and watched the colors sparkle from the friction.

What the hell was happening to me? I felt fine, I didn't feel drugged, and besides, Billy would never allow that to happen to me while he was around.

"Aubrey," he called my name a little stronger; Steven's hand gently rubbed my shoulder. Rick nervously watched my reactions, and Brad observed. His hand rubbed at his chin.

I looked at Billy, drew a deep breath, "A wizard, you say. Huh!" Then a smile came to my lips, recognition lit in my eyes. "Right, yeah sure, Rick put you up to this," I quickly looked to Rick for his assurance this was all one big joke. "Didn't you Rick?" My eyes pleaded with him to tell me it was just a joke.

"No, Little One, this isn't a joke. Bill is very serious. He's telling you the truth," Rick confirmed solemnly.

I started rubbing my temple, rethinking everything again, making sure I'd heard correctly. A tray of chocolates appeared on the coffee table in front of me, and again, I just stared at it.

A woman's voice came into my mind. *Aubrey, it's true what William is telling you. You have nothing to fear. Why do you not believe what your eyes show you?*

I answered the voice, *I'm not crazy, and it's real? You're real as well? I thought I was just tired, my mind playing tricks on me. What am I talking about? It could still be playing tricks.*

The voice answered me back. *No my sweet child, it is real. You must listen to them. You are the last Chosen One, our highest-ranking sorceress, and soon you too will join the Magical world. Everything I told you was true. You know me as your Guardian, Odessa. Your grandmother introduced us. Relax and listen.*

I shook just a tiny bit, Steven's hand continued to rub my neck, "Bree, are you all right?" he asked. The fear was back in his voice.

I looked at him, and hesitantly answered, "Yeah...yeah, I'm fine...I think." I looked back at Billy, "I'm not crazy then? Everything I ever saw was real?" Now it was his turn to see the concern in my eyes.

"Oh darlin', you most definitely aren't crazy. Why would you ask such a thing, for that matter how can you think such a thing?"

Those damn waterworks started again, "Because I thought I was," one large drop fell from my eye. I quickly wiped it away and held my shaking hands in my lap. "I thought I was losing my mind. I mean, this explains a lot!"

I wiped the tears from my face. Brad got up and handed me a tissue. I smiled my thank you at him. I started my explanation to Billy, "I mean, I've seen snippets of things at home, at your parent's home, well Billy, I even saw things at Ryan's and your home. I never mentioned them cause, well heck, who would have believed me? The way everyone hovered over me, I was afraid something was wrong with me, you know, seeing things. I made the mistake of telling Mom one time that I saw a ghost in the barn. A few days later, I wasn't allowed to go into the barn. She never allowed me to go anywhere with my friends. I thought it was because you all knew I was crazy and I might have an episode or something in front of other people. I was so sure Mom and Dad thought I was loony." I sat there shaking my head, "Hell, I thought I had a few screws loose. I could have sworn, one time, I even saw your mom and dad appear in our front entryway. I was sure they would have me committed if I said anything, so I kept quiet. I really thought I was going to die on that ranch. Every time they came back from one of their trips, I always had new limits, more constraints.

I was always so careful not to mention the sounds I heard." I didn't know whether to laugh or cry. "I kept making up excuses why I didn't want to sleep in my room. I used to be allowed to go all over the ranch on my horse, but ever so slowly, my range kept getting smaller and smaller. The woods were off limits to me. Damn Billy, the only place I had left was the barn. But when that was off limits too, they even sold the horses so I wouldn't be tempted to sneak out there." I looked at Billy with a worried expression, "Billy, they did sell the horses didn't they?"

Billy's eyes were soft. "Yes, Bree, they sold the horses. Is that why you always accepted your mother's refusals to let you go anywhere? I would have taken you anywhere you wanted to go."

"Billy, why would you want to go to a junior high dance? No, that wouldn't have been fair to you." I laughed and shook my head again, "No, it wouldn't have."

Billy's face showed me a little of his relief, "Bree, I had no idea you thought that way. You could have talked to me."

"And say what Billy? If I was afraid they'd have me committed for seeing things, I was sure I'd be put away if I told anyone. I didn't need you feeling sorry for me."

"So you just suffered in silence," he said flatly.

"Bree, you could have talked to me," Steven said softly. "We talked about everything. Why didn't you confide that to me?"

"I...didn't want you to think you were stuck with a crazy person either. I handled it, I rationalized it the best I could to myself. I told myself it was probably due to sleep deprivation."

"Oh Bree, that's terrible. You should never have been made to feel that way. I don't care what the prophecy said. To let a young child think she's crazy just because she wasn't supposed to know about our world until it was time, that's just horrible," said Sandy, the sympathy for my plight shown in her eyes.

"Prophecy?" I questioned looking at Sandy, then back at Billy, "What prophecy?"

"That's part of what we need to talk about. See, you are...ah, gees." His hand ran through his hair. "Now this is going to sound strange, but it's the truth. You're known in our world as a Chosen One. The last and strongest one to be born into this world so says the prophecy." He smiled, and then cleared his throat when I didn't respond to his little touch of humor. "You were born to set the balance right in our worlds, the mortal and the Magical world. We don't know how you are to do this though, that's something only your kind knows. You're of the Elders. You have their knowledge...they started the Alliance. When the Elders left, the name was changed to the Council Leadership Group. We know you are supposed to be a leader in the Magical world so we think it has something to do with you being on the Council. All of this is supposed to come to light when you finally cross into our world."

I interrupted, "Why did the Elders leave?"

"Well, they didn't leave per say, they evolved into a different life form. The Elders were more than Magicals, much, much more powerful. They left us well protected," he smiled. "They left us with twenty-four Chosen Ones and you."

185

I looked at him, and then slowly looked at all of them, "I don't know how to tell you this, but that's not very comforting! They left a crazy person to lead you!"

"Stop that, you're not crazy, short maybe...but not crazy," Billy smiled. "Anyway, you've come of age now. So sometime during this year you will make that transformation from a mortal to a Magical. Once you have transformed, you will bond to a member of the Fourth House, Steven is your intended. He is supposed to strengthen you beyond anything, but again, we don't know how he could do this. You will be a very powerful sorceress and Steven really can't do any magic, well not like you anyway. So, we don't fully understand this part of the prophecy. All we do know is, you two formed a very powerful link and you will help strength his clan."

My face was void of expression.

"I introduced him to you when you were only six months old. You never took your eyes off him whenever he visited," he laughed.

I just stared wide-eyed. Odessa said I was a Chosen One and that I needed to listen to what was being told so I would understand. But right now, I was as confused as all get-out. "A Chosen One. I'm going to cross from my world into your world sometime this year...okay, how? Do I go through a door or a portal? Do I just step across a line? And what does this have to do with why Steven had to go away? If we formed such a powerful link, why did he have to leave?" Frustration sounded in my voice. I turned to Steven and tried just a little humor, just to see if I was still capable, "It's a good thing I like you then." I smiled and he raised his eyebrows.

"Let me just start at the beginning," Billy said just a little exasperated.

"That's probably best, for a Chosen One she's having a lot of problems following the obvious!" Madalyn spewed. I paid her no attention. Billy followed my example.

"Bree, you had to live twenty-five years as a mortal. You weren't to know anything about this world. That was in the prophecy. We don't know why for sure. The other Chosen Ones could know, but not you. It was said so you could have the human emotions deep rooted into your heart and soul, but it just didn't make any sense. Then at the specified age we should have been able to tell you and start preparing you for this world."

I interrupted, "But I wasn't told at that age."

"No, Half Pint you weren't, you were married to Nick, and we, well, and *our* parents thought it was best to not tell you. You see," he placed his elbows on his knees and leaned toward me, "there is a faction in our world that doesn't want this prophecy to come to term. They want you dead. We have been protecting you all your life. All those restrictions you received when you were younger, they imposed them." He straightened up and looked at Brad, Rick, and then Steven. I watched him do this, so I looked at them too. Their faces showed me their anger.

"Your parents and mine did everything they asked them to do. That group succeeded in making your life miserable and lonely. They told them that in order for you to go to college safely, Steven needed to stay away until you turned of age. Your Mother agreed to it and that is why Steven left. Our parents threatened banishment to all of us, even me, if we didn't comply with those demands. We all wanted to kidnap you and just take you away but Gran talked us all out of that. We formed our own militia. Stanley runs it along with his company. We figured he was better equipped to do this since he heads Campbell International Security. He's got his teams in the mortal *and* Magical worlds, so it made sense to put him in charge. Steven stayed away…sort of?"

"What do you mean sort of?"

"Occasionally, I would change his appearance and we'd be at parties or in a class you were in at college. Hell, even then you gravitated toward him. We made sure he stayed away when your parents visited you though."

I turned to Steven, "Why didn't you just become my boyfriend?"

Everyone paused, in the midst of all the cloak and dagger planning, they had never thought of something so simple. Sandy started laughing, "Leave it to a woman to spout the obvious. That's what I would have suggested! I can't believe Gina didn't make that suggestion."

"She did," they all mumbled.

Sandy laughed, "Honesty, Richard," her voice lovingly scolded him. "Bree, rest easy, you have women watching your back now too!"

"Anyway," Billy quickly started again before Sandy focused on him. "Then you met Nick and we all know what happened then. Again, your parents were told to leave you alone, let you stay married to him and they wouldn't send an assassin to kill you."

"My parents agreed to this?" I asked in horror.

"I'm afraid so. They rationalized, right or wrong, that you heal quickly. Your blood is very, very powerful, that's why you heal as quickly as you do." He noticed the look on my face, "Let me guess, you thought you were a freak." I smiled and he shook his head, "Half Pint, why didn't you talk to me?"

"We covered that." I tried to smile but I failed.

He shook his head again and continued, "They figured you stood a better chance staying with those morons then to have to watch for an assassin. Chances are the assassin would have been a vampire, and you would never have survived a vampire's assault. That is the one thing that could kill you while you are mortal and we could do nothing. Your blood would have healed you from a bullet wound, or a stabbing, even an auto accident, but *not* from a vampire's bite until you have transformed."

Madalyn got up and poured more Bloody Mary's' into everyone's glasses as Billy continued. "That's why these guys have to be careful around you."

I nodded, "Because they're vampires." I slapped my leg as I realized the connection. Madalyn stood in front of me as she poured Steven some more of his drink, and I watched her. She dripped a little of the Bloody Mary mixture down the side of the pitcher it was in. She noticed me watching her, her lips smiled a pout, then she winked at me and she ran her tongue sensually along the side of the pitcher, lapping up the red liquid. Obviously, it wasn't a Bloody Mary mixture, she was pouring into their glasses.

"I think she has the idea Madalyn, sit down," Steven's voice was harsh.

Certainly darling," she sweetly answered him, undaunted by the anger in his voice. I watched her sit next to Brad. He took his arm off the back of the chair and ignored her.

Billy let out the breath he was holding. The tension in the room was undeniable. "Bottom line, your life is in danger until you transform. We are going to help Stanley protect you. Steven is your intended and he is never going to be made to leave you again. You two will bond just as it was prophesied." He leaned back in his chair. "Your parents and mine did you a very big disservice and I don't know if we can ever forgive them for that. We wasted so much time by letting that rogue group in our world dictate how you would live."

"What a bunch of bullshit." Rick's face showed his anger and his voice was strong with it too! "We knew her enemies wouldn't stop just because the families did what was asked. We knew they wanted her dead and would stop at nothing. Her parents almost lost their daughter, a Chosen One to their stupidity. We almost lost you, Bree!"

"We continued to watch over you when Nick came into your life. It became more difficult because you clammed up. I knew you were in over your head, but you just withdrew. We waited, we watched, we even planned to take you away and hide you. That was a dangerous plan we had. Many are counting on the Chosen One. Many are counting on you, Little One. Your father finally came to his senses, but it took you almost dying for this to happen," said Billy.

"Billy," I calmly spoke and that amazed me, but I felt changed somehow in knowing all of this. "I can't even image the fear they must have felt. To have something everyone thinks was so important in your charge, to ensure the safety of this individual because so many hung their hopes on this one person."

"Bree, it was their responsibility to ensure your safety, whether you were a Chosen One or just their daughter. They failed you, they failed to take care of you, and they failed to protect you."

"Yet Billy, here I am. I am still breathing. You waste your energy harboring this anger. We can't change the past, but we can change the future. We need to put this energy toward that. What's done, is done, I am stronger because of my past. You all are stronger because of it. Don't let your anger consume you." I looked at everyone, "If you do, then they have won."

"You are too forgiving, my sweet angel. I will put my anger aside, but I will never forget or forgive," Billy said.

I smiled at him, "One day Billy, one day you will. Now tell me, what of this assassin you mentioned?"

"Like I said, it would have most likely been a vampire. Your enemies wanted your death to be very painful. They wanted to make an example of you, and they would have paid handsomely to get this done. They will still pay to have this done! There are many rogue Traditionals that would like to make a name for themselves," Billy said.

"So this all started at my birth. But how do you know that I am the one the prophecy spoke of?" I felt a strong need to find out all I could.

"A seer visited us the day you were born and confirmed you were the one the stories spoke of. We knew before she came, but your mother wanted confirmation." He said it with a little shake of his head, like only women need confirmation. "The sign, a pentagram with the Celtic Shield Knot in the middle, was burnt onto your house, and another one on your crib. When you went from a crib to a bed, one appeared. Whenever you got a new bed, one would be there the next morning after you slept in it. You have a necklace like that don't you?"

"Yeah I do, it's at home, though, in my jewelry box."

"You need to always wear it, Bree," he whispered. "Anyway, this seer told us there would be many attempts on your life, and to not hand you over to the Council. That one act would surely end your life. We needed to do everything we could to keep you safe. She told us what we needed to look for, as your transformation got closer. She said your transformation would be stubborn," he laughed, "just like you." He spoke softly when he added, "She also told us you may not survive the crossing. I think she said, your head will pain and voices will be heard. Your skin will burn and your blood will boil. We know you are having headaches, so we assume that is what the first part spoke of. You aren't hearing strange voices are you?"

I sat a little straighter. Odessa said not to tell them yet, dang I didn't want to lie, so I skirted the answer, "No, I know every voice!"

"Well, Brad wants to take a sample of your blood, just to run a few tests. Your body seems to be warmer than normal so he just wants to confirm it. Don't worry sweetheart, we are going to be with you every step of the way. Brad's a very good doctor and we will make sure you succeed in crossing into our world." He cleared his throat, "she also told us you will be loved by many, and yet still have many enemies. And she finished by telling us that you are the last of the Chosen Ones. Others came before you but were of lesser strength. To live, you must transform. To lead, you must transform. For corrupt houses to fall, you must transform. Only then, can you be bitten. And that is how we knew it was you." He took another long drink and waited for all this information to sink in.

I was curious, "Billy, when you do magic, do you have to say any words?"

"No, I just have to think of what I want and it appears. There are lesser witches that do have to say spells or use a wand. But my lineage is very strong. Gina's magic is strong too. She's teaching the boys before we send them off to wizard prep. They'll go there and mortal public school."

"So, there are no words needed? You just think about it and it appears and I will be able to do this too?" I asked.

"Yes," he said cautiously, "once you become a witch you will be able to do that and other things not even I can do I'm sure."

"Billy, why you? Why were you the one to protect me, why not Ryan or Stanley?" The room was quiet. Billy had a smile on his face as he looked at me.

"From the moment I first held you, we were connected. Even as a small baby, if I was in the room, I had to hold you. It was neat really. No matter who had you, soon as you heard my voice you would squirm until you were in my arms. I could always hear you call my name, no matter where I was." He started laughing, "Gina thought we should have just raised you and maybe if we had your life would have turned out differently." He smiled at the memories he'd had earlier, "No, I liked growing up with you. We had some good times," he winked at me.

"You say that like you're a lot older than me."

"Ah, yeah, well I am. Let me explain, Half Pint. You remember all the times your parents had you stay with us when they went out of town?"

I nodded.

"Well now, remember, we had to be human around you and it would have been awkward for you if I appeared so much older than you. You thought I was five years older, but I am much older than that."

"How old are you then?"

"I've lived one hundred and seventy-five earth years, but in Magical years I am fifty. I would like to stay fifty. True Magicals, which is what I am, age normally until we come of age at twenty-five. Then we age slowly after that. These guys aren't true Magicals. They are what we call, 'Turners'. They were 'turned' into the Magical world, mortals who became Magicals. Are you following this?"

I nodded.

"Good," he continued, "we had to appear to you in the correct ages you were growing up in. When you were five, I had to look ten so my friends had to look ten," he waved his hands indicating Rick, Brad, and Steven. "When you were ten, I had to appear to be fifteen; you get the idea. I would place the aging spell on these fine creatures and we looked the appropriate age. They always looked different to you. When you were sixteen, that's when I introduced you to a very young Steven, Rick, Brad, and Madalyn. You remember that, right?"

I smiled at him, "Yes I remember it." I felt so relieved that all of those lost files had been restored!

"Just checking. When you were little, you always stayed with my parents. But the older you got, well, it started getting a little tricky. When you were in your late teens, your parents had to keep the Council apprised of your progress. They were requested to appear before them more often. You hated being alone in that big house of yours; but you also hated having to have someone baby-sit you. I think that was the word you used, that's why I introduced you to these guys. You could start dating Steven and stay with us, so it worked. You were always protected and never knew it."

I sat there going over everything he told me. The voice came back to me. *Everything he's told you was true, all of it. Now you need to be prepared for your path and that is what I am here to do.*

Everyone was watching me, waiting on more questions, but I really didn't have any more, not yet. All of this needed to be digested and I felt it would be better to ask as I went along, since I really didn't know what else to ask!

"Anymore questions Half Pint?"

I smiled, "Oh Billy, I'm sure I will have many questions but I just need time to understand this. I'm," I laughed, "I'm a lot calmer now, whew! Let me let it sink in; I'm sure, as we go along, I'll ask more. But right now," I turned and gave a mischievous grin to Rick. "Rick aren't I supposed to tell you when I have met a vampire or a werewolf?"

He was in the process of taking a drink of his precious red liquid, "Yeah, now that you've seen both I'm real interested." He turned to me giving me his full attention.

"Both? Aren't all of you vampires? Who's the werewolf?"

"Harry and Vickie, couldn't you tell? The full moon is in a few days, I thought all that hair on Harry would have

195

given you a clue! You won't recognize him on Thursday; we'll need to reintroduce you," he laughed. "Now, about us vampires..." he smiled a sexy grin. The energy coming from him was powerful. He was my protector, our bond before was tight. I felt Rick would always be straight with me. He would never color the answers he gave me, no matter how painful they were. Yes, his energy was strong.

"Well," I looked at each of them including Steven. "It appears you are more scared of me than I am of you."

They all looked at one another. "Well, I guess in a way we are," said Brad.

"Why?"

"Because, we're afraid you won't want us around. We're afraid you will be afraid of us. We're the lowers. We're beneath your status. We're even beneath Bill. You have nothing to fear from us though, Princess," Steven said as his hand rubbed my arm.

"You know I really hate it when you guys say that 'lowers' shit," Billy said in an icy tone.

"Why wouldn't I want you around? I'm not afraid of you. I enjoy being with you. Rick, have any of you tried to 'mesmerize' me?" Now I was teasing.

"No, Squirt, we haven't. Our love for you is genuine. You and Steven are the real deal. But Bree, other vampires will try. You do need to be aware of that. Right now, you're not all human or all Magical. You're smack dab in the middle, so you are very vulnerable. And because of who and what you are, like Bill said, you're very desirable to those that want to do you harm. Traditionals want you more than they want any other human on this planet. They want your blood, and they will be rewarded handsomely for killing you." His eyes were serious; he didn't take them off me the entire time he spoke.

"Well, I'm not afraid of you...of any of you," I spoke firmly.

"Bree," Billy began again, "I would trust your life with these five, but a vampire's bite or scratch will kill you. Period. Nothing can be done to save you and that has them scared. He paused and took another long drink, letting his words sink into my brain, waiting to see my reaction. "Your blood is powerful, you heal very quickly, and everyone wants it. This clan will die to protect you, make no mistake about that."

"I don't think it will come to that Billy."

"You don't? You know the future Bree? Can you see it now?" His eyes narrowed on me. "Your powers will be great, granted. You will be above us all. But my sweet angel you have not transformed. You can't see the future yet, and they worry. I worry. Our love for you is immense. I do not want to think about living in this world without you in it. Steven won't."

"I can't see the future, Billy, but I can feel it. I will be here a long time and so will all of you. I can't explain it any better than I feel it. I know it. The energy in this room is overwhelming. I can feel the energy deep in my bones. I can see the electricity from each of you. I felt the fear you felt when you needed to talk to me earlier. Steven, Brad and Rick are extremely tense, you have calmed," I nodded toward him. "I pick up the energy in the males stronger than I do the females. That's probably because I have had so many men around me all my life." I sipped my wine as

I watched them drink their Drink, Steven watched me watch them.

I had a confused look on my face. I looked at Rick, and he smiled. "What is it you want to ask Little One?" I smiled as he called me that.

"Rick, tell me about vampires. You guys don't seem to follow the stereotypical rules of them."

"No, we don't. When our ancestors first walked the earth they were, but some of us have evolved!" he laughed. "There are two different types of vampires. The first group is called Traditionals. They are your typical vampires. You know, they attack humans and drink their blood. They do exist, and Bree, they are very dangerous, especially to you. It's important for you to understand, you can never trust a Traditional. They exist to kill. It's easy for them. They feel no remorse for their actions. It becomes a game. Kind of like the way a cat will play with a mouse before it kills it. They can seduce you." Rick smiled and leaned toward me, "They really can do this, Bree. Just like it says in all the books you have read. You are still on the human side so I'm telling you this for your own good. We don't know when your transformation will be complete into our world so you're still at risk. We hope that you being with us will lessen the risk. They will never change their ways, Bree, never; and their numbers are great."

"Are any of them here?"

"Oh, maybe a few. Las Vegas is too much a temptation for them to be here for long periods. Most will probably start arriving on Wednesday for the party on Thursday. You are not to be alone at any time during this party. One of us must always be with you, even to go to the bathroom.

Do you understand?" Rick stopped to look at me for my assurance and I nodded.

Rick smiled, "Bree, I know I'm repeating what we have been telling you, but forgive me for saying you are one stubborn young lady. We really need you to understand this. You are powerless against them."

"So after I make this transformation, I won't be harmed by them?"

"Well, anyone at any time can be harmed by them. They can't put you under a trance when you are Magical, but they could still harm you. It's more likely they won't try to, but I wouldn't rule anything out. Your magic will be much more powerful, so you will be better protected. But accidents do happen," Rick said.

"You must be in the other group, I assume you aren't Traditionals."

"No, Bree we aren't Traditionals," Rick chuckled.

"What is your group called then?"

"Non-Conformists," Billy said, "Non-Coms for short."

"That's a good way of explaining it," Sandy said. "We still drink human blood as you can tell," she raised her glass, "but we get it from special blood banks. The blood is cleansed and then sent to us. We have a very large committee that is always running blood drives, going around to morgues, collecting the blood they drain." She grimaced, "sorry, I wasn't thinking."

I smiled at her, "It's okay, it's something I will need to get used to, I'd imagine." I patted Steven's leg and he pulled me into a hug.

Sandy was actually thrilled to have me in the group. She gave a little squeal of delight causing the males of the group to laugh. "Anyway, we drink a lot more when we are here because there are so many people, so many smells. But when we are at home, we can get by with less. We can function in society without any problems because we get a regular supply. As you can see, our skin is not as pale as a Traditional. Well, I guess you can't see that since you haven't seen a Traditional. But trust me, once you see one you will know what I mean. Our touch is cool, not cold. We can go out in the daylight and it doesn't affect us. There are things we have in common with Traditionals. Our eyes glow," she smiled, "but we wear contacts or glasses when we're out in public or around mortals. Otherwise, we would scare the hell out of them. Mostly we wear the contacts. I just hate to wear glasses."

"Yeah, I've seen the glow," I said.

"You have?" Steven asked. "When? We were always so careful around you."

"Yeah, you were when you were around me. But there were a couple of times I saw you guys before you put those glasses on." I laughed, "That added to my worry about being committed."

Billy chuckled as I said this and shook his head. "Oh my dear Bree, what we have done to your head."

I smiled at him, "My head is fine." Then I turned to Steven, "Your eyes give off the prettiest green tint."

"What? Bree, I don't have a green tint to my eye glow; and technically, it's not even a glow. There's an area behind the retinas of our eyes, and it reflects light back into the eye. By increasing, or rather by bouncing the light that comes into our eyes, we can see more effectively at night. So they really don't glow, it just looks like it," Steven said, proud of his technical knowledge on the subject.

"I prefer to say they glow and yes, you do have a green tint. Watch." I got up and turned the living room lights off and dimmed the dining area. I looked at them and laughed, "Okay, I can't show anyone if you guys don't open your eyes." They all opened their eyes. At first, everything was normal. I asked Billy to give me a flashlight. He snapped his fingers and one appeared in my hand. I smiled at him, "I thought you said you just have to think of something and it appears?"

"I'm just doing that for effect."

I turned the flashlight on and started to aim it toward Steven so his eyes would catch the light. "See, Billy, can you see the green tint?

"No, Half Pint, I can't, just a golden glow."

I moved the light toward Brad and Madalyn. "Brad has a purple tint to his, but I don't see any shading in Madalyn's, just the golden glow." Then I moved the light toward Rick and Sandy. "See, Rick has a blue tint, but Sandy just has the golden glow. Huh, I wonder why that is. Why can I see it but you can't and why only in the men? I'll have to think on that one." I turned the lights back on and sat next to Steven again, "What are some of the other things?"

"We still get the urge to kill," Steven said. "It's just the way it is. We can usually keep it at bay because we get a regular supply of blood. But when it becomes too strong, we hunt wild game. It calms us. We stay away from humans until the urge passes. We hunt as a clan a couple of times a year. It's part of our bonding ritual. We are still just as strong, just as powerful as Traditionals. We just prefer to live in the world with mortals."

"Can the Traditionals go out in the daytime?"

Brad spoke, "Yes, but they prefer the shadows and the night. Have you ever walked down a dark hall or dark street and had the hairs on your arm and neck stand up?"

"Yes."

"There's a reason for that. Most sane people shy away from those places. But for those that continue on, well, they aren't always as fortunate," Brad said. I had a question on my face and didn't know how to ask it. "Go on, you can interrupt."

"Brad, how did you meet Madalyn?"

"We worked together a very long time ago," he simply said.

Madalyn felt the need to explain more and gave Brad a sour look. "Brad and I worked in a hospital. I'm a nurse. It was like an emergency room of sorts. I was seriously injured on my way in to work one night. Steven turned me because I begged him to. Otherwise, I wouldn't be here today. Brad wasn't around and I was dying. I begged Steven not to let me die, not to separate Brad and me, so Steven turned me. I knew what they were. Sandy wasn't even part of our group yet."

I looked at Sandy and she offered her story, "I am much newer to this life. I've known Rick for fifteen years though. Rick had moved to this little town I was living in when we met. I had no clue he was a vampire. I had the same thoughts as you, vampires were creatures of the night but I worked days! I saw him several times with some girl so I thought they were a couple and let it go at that. I worked at the local restaurant and Rick would always come in for coffee on my shift. We talked a lot and I noticed I began hating it whenever he brought her with him. I realized I was jealous. Her name was Pam, I think."

"It was, and you know you don't have to think about it."
Rick smiled, "She can probably still tell you what she looked
like." That brought laughs from the males in the group.

"Yes, I can, Richard. Anyway, Rick came in one morning and told me he was going to be gone a few days, he had
a friend that needed some help. I didn't learn until later,
you were the one he was talking about. I guess the green
eyed-monster in me raised its ugly head,"

"You got that right. Such a human emotion," he teased
her.

"Anyway, I accused him of going away with her. Poor
thing, he didn't know what to think. He waited until I got
off work and walked me home. He'd never thought he had
a chance with me so he didn't try. But since I was jealous,
well that opened the door. Anyway, he promised when he
got back we would work it all out."

"So Rick, gees, I guess it is possible for a vampire to fall
in love with a human. Huh, imagine that," I said laughing. Then I had that 'light came on in my head' look on
my face.

"What?" Sandy asked.

"You said her name was Pam, right?"

"Yeah."

"I do remember a girl by that name being around, well
for a short time anyway. And she was with you Rick."

"Yes, Bree, that was a much younger looking me," he
stated proudly.

"Wow, I remember the fight you two had. Then she left
with you Steven, and you never came back. We had a date
planned that night. Everything changed that night." My
eyes started to water again.

"That wasn't his fault Bree. He didn't want to leave," Billy said quietly, staring at a spot on the floor.

"I know."

Rick was watching me with a confused look on his face, "Bree, how do you know we had a fight? What was it over?"

"Well, duh Rick. It was over another girl, some girl that worked at a coffee house is what she said. I remember Pam said 'she could offer you everything, just tell her what that girl could offer you'. And you did. I didn't hear what you said, but she slapped you hard." I made a face of pain and he put his hand up to his cheek, like he could still feel the sting. "That's when Steven," I turned to Steven, "you, came out of the house. I think you asked if they had any idea where I was. Then, as you got closer you were sucked into their fight. Well, you held her back from hitting Rick again. Boy, she was pissed. Then you offered to make sure she got home and you left. And you never came back. I started college a few weeks later."

"Bree, where were you to have seen and heard all of that?" Rick asked. He tried to think back to the moment, knowing I wasn't around.

"Up in the tree you two were under. Whenever the members of my family were nervous, it generally happened when Mom and Dad went on their trips. I could sense it, and it made me nervous. So, I would climb, the higher the better. So I was up in the tree. I loved climbing in the trees, I always found it comforting somehow. It always seemed to relax me. I have no idea why. I was on my way down when your fight began, but something told me to stay out of sight, so I did. Sandy, when did you become a vampire?"

"A year later, I was attacked by a Traditional that was passing through. Rick was on his way to my house when the attack happened." Sandy looked at Rick and lightly touched his arm. "He killed the Traditional and took me back to his place. That's when I met Brad and Madalyn. He called them to help him help me. I didn't meet Steven until after I became a vampire. Rick and I have been mates ever since."

Steven had been sitting very still, very quiet. I turned to him and asked, "So, just how old are you really?"

"I told you. I'm forty and I'm always going to be forty." His voice gave me the indication he didn't want to talk about it yet, so I let it drop.

But Brad didn't, "Ah," Brad started, "Steven is a very interesting subject."

"I'm not all that interesting, Brad."

"Yes, you are. And it will be a good lesson for you both. Steven is from a very powerful House of vampires. The vampire that transformed Steven was of this House. His story parallels yours.

He had fallen in love with a human that was a Chosen One, like you. She wasn't as strong as you are, but she was strong enough. During her transformation, Lazarus, he was a vampire, thought she was dying. The transformation was going badly you understand, and we really didn't know a lot about them because they were so infrequent.

Lazarus didn't want her to die and she begged him not to let her die, not to separate them. He thought if he bit her, to transform her into a vampire, then they could be together for eternity. She wasn't the one the stories spoke of so he thought he could ease her pain. Just make her a vampire, and not let her transform. That was not the case. She did transform into a vampire but...that didn't go well either. She was in terrible pain. It was a living hell for her. So..." Brad cleared his throat, "She begged Lazarus to end it...and he did."

Brad took a slow drink of his Drink before he continued, "Bree, we've told this to you several times this evening, Steven can never bite you to change you into a vampire to save you during the transformation. Nobody can. You must understand this. If you die during the transformation, that's it. After you cross...then we'll talk." Brad absentmindedly swished the remainder of his Drink in his glass and finished it. He looked at me and smiled, I smiled back.

"Anyway, Steven here was Lazarus' next victim. He turned him to take his place in his House and then Lazarus went away seeking to end his life. Lazarus picked a fight with a clan of vampires, and well...it wasn't pretty. So, in answer to your question Bree, Steven is one hundred fifty years old. Mildred found him and nursed him back to health. Steven and I met at a clan hunt one year. Neither of us wanted to be part of that hunt, but there we were. We met another vampire there who was a mortician. He wasn't hunting with the clans, he was there to take the bodies they didn't drain back to his morgue and there he drained the blood and stored it for his use and his friends. That's how we saw our way out of that life...so to speak. Steven and I have been friends ever since and we have lived this way since then as well."

Rick continued, "The Council will be watching you two very closely. **We** know you have enemies on the Council and your union will be devastating to them...they want you dead. But you do have your supporters on the Council. Your enemies can't hurt Steven. Well...if they succeed in killing you that would devastate him. But he is protected by his House."

"So, right now, right this moment I am unprotected by magic?"

"Yeah, but you still have us," Rick smiled a very bright smile.

"Do you have any other questions about vampires?" Sandy asked.

I watched her finish her Drink. "Probably, but I think for now that's enough. Well I do have one more question for tonight."

"What's that Squirt?"

"Do you ever put any alcohol in it?" I laughed as I watched him finish his Drink.

"Nah, it ruins the taste," Rick said.

"Ah, Bree, there's something else we need to tell you." Billy's voice turned serious. "You remember Becky?" He gave a polite laugh, "Of course you do - you two were inseparable."

Becky was my closest friend, the closest thing I had to a sister. We did everything together since we met in the first grade. I was devastated when she died in the car accident. I was supposed to be with her but I'd had a class I couldn't get out of. Her car crashed into the river, they never recovered her body. I remembered her funeral. My life was shattered. Her parents were devastated. I remembered barely eating or sleeping for weeks. "What about her?"

"She's not dead," he flatly said.

I blinked.

"She was dating this...guy, and,"

I interrupted him, "Becky wasn't dating anyone special. She would have told me. She drowned our senior year of college. Her body was never recovered. Remember, she lost control of her car and they found it in the river. There were witnesses."

"Yeah, that wasn't what happened. From what we could piece together, she started dating this Traditional. She was head over heels for him and he felt the same way. They were...sort of bonded to one another. That's rare but it does happen. She wanted to be with him so they concocted this story. She's a vampire now. I was surprised, I never would have thought of little Becky doing anything like that. She was wild for the longest time, but she's calmed down now," Billy said.

I sat there, dumbfounded. *Damn, if I had known about this life, this world, Becky might still be here with me today.* A tight lump formed in my throat and I had to swallow hard to get past it. "You said that a Traditional was bound to Becky. How does that work?"

"Sometimes, when a vampire bites their victim they connect with that individual. It is rare, but it does happen. They have a bond that can't be broken." Steven shifted a little, I noticed Madalyn watching him. "Even if they love someone else they are drawn to one another and there isn't anything anyone can do to change it. That's what happened to them," Brad explained. His eyes stayed on me. He wanted me to understand this. It was important to him somehow.

"Will I ever see her again?" my voice cracked as I asked.

"Maybe...one day, maybe," Billy answered. "Do you have any other questions or do you want to think on this awhile.

I exhaled, "Yeah, I still have questions. Do you guys sleep?" I looked at Rick and laughed.

"Out of all the questions you could ask, you want to know if they sleep," Billy quipped.

"Yeah, lighten the mood a little."

Rick smiled as he answered me. "Nope, well, we don't sleep in the normal view of sleep. We do meditate, and we can get cranky if we don't get enough meditation in. Just like if you don't get enough sleep. Oh shit, are you tired Bree? I forgot about that."

Steven's hand applied a small amount of pressure on my arm. I knew he wanted to spend time alone, but questions kept popping in my head and I needed them answered. Very gently, I entered his thoughts. I had no idea how I knew how to do this, but there I was, whispering softly in his mind. *Soon Steven, very soon you will hold me in your arms and we will renew ourselves to one another.* I felt his tension relax; he gave me a reassuring rub on the arm. "Tell me, do I look tired? Sorry, you're not getting off that easily; I'll sleep later."

"What's your next question, Bree?" Brad asked shaking his head and laughing.

"Billy I know about my side, right? I mean, you are my cousin, right?"

"Now what do you think? I have been around you all your life. We're Campbell's Bree, you and me. So, stop worrying about that. Stop worrying about our ages. I have known these guys for a very, very long time. You'll give

209

yourself a headache if you keep trying to figure everything out at once. We all live very long lives. Some of us have many degrees. We're wealthy, well-educated Magical beings. Believe me; you can get tired of doing the same thing after a hundred years or so."

I didn't want to have to ask, but I needed to know if we needed to talk about my marriage to Nick. "Billy," I whispered quietly, my eyes squinted as I asked something I really didn't think I wanted the answer to, "did you tell them what I told you earlier, about my marriage? Do they know about it now, or do we need to talk about that?"

He took a deep breath, "I told them Half Pint. They knew most of it but I told them what you told me."

"It doesn't change anything for me Bree. Nothing could make me stop loving you. If we had taken you away, as we had planned, families be damned, that would not have happened to you. I love you very much. He will never get another chance to harm you in any way," Steven said softly.

The words came to me from somewhere deep in my mind. I had no idea how I knew all of this, but I felt confident enough to tell them. "I know it was bad. I know you all hated that my life went in that direction, but it had to happen once the path turned. All of it! My path was laid out a long time ago. I know you don't understand. I'm not so sure I do either, but that's what my mind is telling me. My past can't harm me now. They can't harm me now. I have started to change. I can feel it. I felt it as soon as I woke up a little while ago. I'm not hearing voices, so don't panic, but I am hearing my thoughts, others' thoughts from long ago. As I've sat here, listening to all of this, I've felt an energy surging through me, and I know I'm not explaining

210

this correctly, but I can actually see yours at times. I don't understand it...yet, but I'm not crazy!"

"No, Half Pint, you aren't crazy. When Brad runs his test, we'll know," Billy said.

"Yeah, about that, I don't like needles. Isn't there any other way, maybe a finger prick or something?"

"I promise I won't hurt you Bree," Brad said.

"I know you won't hurt me, I just don't like needles."

"You won't even feel it. You don't have to watch, ya know," Brad offered.

"When do you want to do this?"

"How about in the morning, you can get some rest and we'll start fresh," Brad suggested.

Everyone stood, signaling the end of our question and answer session. "Okay, in the morning then. Billy, will I see you tomorrow?"

"Yes, you will be seeing me a lot," he smiled. "Steven, keep her safe." He kissed me on the top of the head, and then smiled, "Get some rest Half Pint." Then he just disappeared.

That took me by surprise and the shocked look on my face caused Rick to laugh. "Come here Squirt," he said as he hugged me close. I ran my hand through his hair, and he pressed into my hand. I felt his tension ease. I liked being able to feel their emotions now. It somehow drew me closer to them. He gave me a kiss on the cheek. He thought to himself, but I heard it, *I have so missed your touch. I love you darlin' and nobody is going to hurt you again.* He picked Sandy up and they disappeared.

Brad took Madalyn's hand. "Come on Maddie. Let's let these two have some down time. I'll be by in the morning around nine o'clock." Then he and Madalyn disappeared.

Steven and I stood there in silence. He was watching me. Probably trying to figure out what to say.

Chosen One, said Odessa, *talk with him, and show him you are strong. You need to be with him now.*

Odessa, would you please tell Gran I would like a meeting with my parents, alone. I think the air needs to be cleared. If Billy and this group were hurting this much I can only imagine how much my parents are hurting.

Yes, Chosen One I will ask.

Please, Odessa, call me Bree. All my friends call me that.

Very well Bree. I am delighted to be thought of as your friend. Then she was gone.

CHAPTER 16

Steven and I stood there in the quiet, "Well, Steven," I finally said. "We've got a lot of catching up to do. Where would you like to begin?"

He took my hand and walked me to the sofa. We sat down and he put his arm around me. "Do you feel like talking a little longer?"

"Of course, I'll talk as long as you like, if that's what you want." I really *didn't* want to talk, but he seemed to still have things he needed to say.

He smiled at my comment, "Bree," his free hand began playing with my fingers. "I love you deeply. I hate myself for leaving you unprotected. I hate myself for leaving you, period. The anger that's in me now is not directed at you, but at your enemies and those three. I will kill them if they ever touch you again. Bill will not get the chance. Rick and Brad will not get the chance. They took our time together away, and those years were precious to us. We had such plans, and they had to be put on hold because of them."

"Hey, you say that like it's all in the past. Is it over now?" I swallowed hard to get passed the lump in my throat. Maybe that was why he wanted to talk, instead of...well...I'm sure he wanted to tell me too much had happened, too much for us to climb out of and start all over again. But that couldn't be, why else would he go through all of this planning if he just...damn. I may not want to hear this answer.

A sweet smile curled on his lips and his eyes sparkled from the hint of moisture in them, "I have planned for this day for so long and now that it's here I..." he must have read the alarm on my face; he drew my hand to his lips and kissed it. "Bree, when you kissed my mind earlier I thought I had gone to heaven. I can't describe the feeling it gave me. It was so warm. I have been so empty without you. Then your warmth filtered through my body, deep into my soul. I have *never* felt anything like that before. You have saved me from all the despair I have felt over the last thirteen years. I love you and nothing will ever change that, I will not leave you again. I...it's just, now...it's too dangerous to get that close. We were close then, do you remember that?" His brow creased as he searched my face for the remembrance he desperately needed to see in my eyes.

I smiled at him to ease his heart, "Yes, Steven I do remember."

He exhaled softly as he heard my assurance. "It's too dangerous for us to get that intimate again." His voice trembled ever so slightly, "If we had continued the way we were then, before we were separated, we would have been very familiar with each other. You would know how to control my passion. I don't know if I can control it now. I want to pull you inside of me and hold you there. I want to keep all the bad out of your world. I want to be with you so badly, I hurt, but I'm afraid of hurting you. I can't express how much I want to make love to you." He pressed his forehead to mine.

Oh, thank God it's not over! "Steven," I whispered very softly, trying to calm his fears, "I do remember those times. You weren't dangerous then, and I don't think you are dangerous to me now." I moved to sit on his lap facing him and took his face in my hands. "I knew your passion then and I know it now." I gently kissed his lips, I felt the tiniest sparks from our touch. "You need to trust me, Steven. After everything I've been through, how can you now tell me you are too dangerous?"

He spoke his words quietly to me, "I could kill you. Remember, we have very strong animal instincts in us. We like to nip at one another." He ran his hand down my neck, and goose bumps rose on my arms. I shivered. That made him smile and I kissed his neck.

"Our talons are sharp; we like to run them across our mate's bodies as we make love." He ran his fingers gently over my arm, and leaned in and kissed my neck. I shivered again, and again he smiled. I gently nipped at his ear; he shook. A small tremor coursed through his body. He gave me the soft moan I was searching for.

"Our love making can be rough, we are very strong, and our teeth are very sharp, you need to understand that. If I broke your skin, even with a playful nip or my talons, it would kill you. I would need to be so controlled and right now," he swallowed, "I don't know that I can. After you transform I can make a small mistake because it won't af-

215

fect you, you won't die. It will take far more than a simple nip, or a scratch to turn you into one of us or to kill you." He kissed me gently on the neck again. I shivered and he smiled. "Don't be afraid of me Bree, I will control myself." Then he sat back and closed his eyes, back in control, his breathing slowed.

I sat there, on his lap watching him. His eyelids fluttered, his breathing was indeed slow and controlled and I wasn't going to stand for that. "Nice try, Steven!" I smiled. "You can try to scare me all you want, but I'm not afraid of you. I do not fear you. If I recall, our love making was not rough."

He smiled at the memories he had. His breathing quickened again, remembering the times I took him to me, the quiet love we shared. "No, they weren't, they were gentle, but passionate. I haven't forgotten."

"You never mentioned them to Brad?" I teased as I played with his shirt buttons.

"No, those were my memories, and I kept that all to myself," he smiled back at me.

"Steven," our eyes met. "I'm going in there to bed. I remember a time when you were already in my room waiting on me. Now, you can sleep here on the sofa, if you really prefer that, or you can come and join me like you used too."

I pressed my body into his as I leaned in and kissed him lightly on the lips, his cheek, making my way to his ear and down his neck. He didn't resist, he didn't move away. I felt the excitement he tried to hide. I was close to my goal, and I continued. I unbuttoned the first couple of buttons on his shirt and ran my hand through the hairs on his chest. I watched as microscopic flashes of energy followed my fingertips, he drew a very deep breath as he too felt the energy. "Steven wouldn't you be more comfortable out of these clothes?"

"No, I think I'm fine this way," he said weakly, his resolve was waning.

My hands moved to his belt, but I continued to kiss his neck. I unfastened it and started taking it out of the loops. He moved enough for me to pull his belt free and I laid it on the back of the sofa. My lips moved back to his lips as I moved on him, slow rotations, my breathing increasing. I started to unbutton my shirt, "Steven, please don't deny me."

He reached to pull me tighter to him, "Bree, hush, just hush." His kiss was unbreakable as his hands held my hips. We pressed into each other, our breathing increasing, our need to be close growing more desperate. I felt his hardness, his want for me, and my desire for him was undeniable.

"Steven, I love you and I'm not afraid of you. Please, take me to bed." He picked me up and carried me to the bedroom. Our lips locked together, pulling at our clothes, grabbing each other and pulling close if the distance became too great. I lay under the blankets, and he moved in beside me.

His eyes stared into mine. He started to say something, but my finger touched his lips, "Steven, please, it has been too long. I love you and I am not afraid of your touch, just love me tonight. No more talk."

He trembled ever so slightly as he cautiously touched me. His cool hands held my face delicately, his powerful brown eyes searching mine for familiarity. His breathing uneven at times, as his fingertips became reacquainted with my body.

Slowly, his fears calmed, I felt his energy surge with mine and his touches became tender but knowing, his mouth was deliberate and his hunger was undeniable. Our palms pressed together, allowing our fingers, one by one, to entwine. Quiet sounds of enjoyment came as we remembered our times together so long ago.

His kisses moved from my mouth, to my ear, along my neck, causing me to whisper a moan and stretch beneath him. He gave me a low sexy chuckle. He remembered my triggers and he stroked them.

His fingers gently outlined my breast, moving to my waist. His hand rested lightly on my hips, waiting for my consent to venture on. I pressed into him my acceptance, as his hand made its way between my legs and I let his finger enter me. My hands tightened around his shoulders as I sucked in air. I softly sighed with the pleasure he was giving me. Uncontrolled trimmers shook me as his fingers gently preformed their magic.

We moved in slow motion, as we searched for our own pleasure center, quietly remembering our tender moments from so long ago. "Steven, please love me now, I ache for you, and I need you now." I whispered my plea weakly. "Ooh, please don't make me beg."

"I love it when you beg," he whispered through a kiss.

Our movements became comfortable, our rhythm in tune. I worked his hunger beyond his limits, pressing him further than any he had been with. I knew his triggers too.

I nipped softly at his earlobe, traveling down his neck, to his chest. I came back to his cool mouth, his tongue savagely played with mine.

Soft 'oh God's' kept escaping my lips. His thrusts were purposeful as he sought his own pleasure while still giving me mine. Memories returned to us of what each other liked and we were exhausting ourselves with our offerings.

Small beads of perspiration trickled from my forehead as he held my face in his hand, pressing his lips to mine, swallowing me, tasting me, "Oh, Bree...this feels...damn GOOD!"

His thrusts became more direct, more powerful, our end was near and we reached for it, determined to find it together.

I tightened my hold around him, pulling him, holding him to me until we found those wonderful fireworks in our minds and they exploded with such forcefulness, one could only hope the walls to our room were thick!

Our eyes stared into one another. The energy that passed between us was strong. Flashes of gold, blue, yellow and green's danced all around us as we finished with our commitment to one another. We were spent. Our breathing was heavy, hearts still pounding.

I felt the cool air of the room sweep across my forehead and I gave a small shiver. Steven pulled the blankets around me, shielding me from his cool body as he lay beside me, his hand washed over his face. "God how I have missed you," he spoke.

"Shhh, Steven, my parents are just down the hall," I laughed, bringing a memory to our minds.

Steven rolled over and kissed me sweetly, "I forgot about that," he laughed.

We both lay there for a few minutes in silence. As he held me in his arms, I could hear a soft purr coming from him, deep in his chest. I felt the vibration against my ear. It fascinated me, "Steven?"

"I'm just very, very content right now, that's all."

I kissed his chest, the purr continued. He wrapped me in his arms. My ear pressed against him, listening, no other sound in the room, and I drifted off to sleep.

CHAPTER 17

The Dream

Sleep came to me, as did the dream. I'd forgotten the dreams. I'd never spoke of them. I figured they were extensions of the movies I watched or the books I read. They had now returned.

I walked the passage again. The darkness swallowed me but I could still see. My hands felt along the wall; I felt the water as it trickled down in places. The rough stone was familiar. Yes, I had been here before long, long ago.

I heard, no, felt them before I saw them. His laugh was raspy and low. It rattled deep in my bones; the small vibrations shook my chest bringing a small cough to my throat. I pressed my hand to my chest to quiet the tremor.

I stood in the shadows. Her long strawberry blond hair hung down her back, her slick silver gown clung to every curve of her body and shimmered in the low light as she moved.

She held a simple clay bottle tight in her hand and I watched her remove the stopper. Then she set the bottle down and stood back, her chest heaved with her anticipation as the gray cloud swirled up from the wide opening.

She moistened her lips in her longing for its approach to her. Her hand trembled as she moved a strand of hair from her face. She watched the cloud tower over her; her sexual appetite for this entity was undeniable as she reached for it, begging it to her.

Her lips parted, as the mist and the sound entered her and she gasped. Her hands caressed her face. She moaned as her fingers pulled at her hair, and then slowly moved down her cheeks, into her mouth and she gently sucked on her fingers, pulling the mist into her further. She moaned with frustration as her hands reached for nothingness, trying so desperately to hold what wasn't there.

His laughs shook her and she trembled as she moved her hands over her breasts, arousing her nipples. Massaging them for his pleasure, trying to find her own, but this was not his intent. This was for his pleasure, his want, not hers. In her pained cry, she begged for his body, his touch. She needed something to press against, but he could not accommodate. He laughed at her frustration and she shuddered with the vibrations his low hoarse rumble was sending through her.

Her hands explored her body making their way across her belly toward her center. Her eyes were wide, her breath quickened. She needed his body but he would not come, and she continued to beg.

A knock on the chamber door broke her spell. She grabbed hold of the table in front of her. Her grab so violent it shook the bottles of liquids. His laugh left her slowly. She reached for it, trying to keep it at her center; she closed her mouth tight but the mist left, seeping through her pressed lips. She breathed hard as she watched her invisible lover take refuge back in its bottle and reluctantly she corked it. The rumble had left her, leaving her unfulfilled. Her want peaked with nothing to satisfy it.

Again, the knock sounded, she composed herself. She smoothed the slick silver gown she wore; her hands once again ran across her breast, a soft lingering shudder shook her. She ran her fingers through her hair to straighten it. She gently brushed her hand over her lips, down her throat. I could see it in her eyes; she was desperate for his touch. Her eyes showed me her determination. She would stop at nothing to restore this demon to bodily form. Oh yes, she would have him.

Again, the knock sounded. With a heavy sigh, she answered the door.

I watched as the dark figure entered the room, and I saw her desire rise again. He was extremely handsome and tall, long thick coal black hair hung over his broad shoulders; dark piercing eyes set against his alabaster skin gave him a haunting appearance and I immediately recognized him as a Traditional.

He smiled a very sensual smile as he swept past her, "The child is there, and they are protecting her." His voice was low and soothing. I found myself fascinated by his presence. "Soon, she will know her path; she will reunite with her love." He smiled a little wider; he raised his hand to softly stroke her face but withdrew it before he touched her; his eyes lingered on her breast and his smile widened even more as he saw the points pressed against the gown. His tongue slowly caressed his top lip.

I heard his thoughts; I saw his intake of a deep breath. *Good...she is in need...right where I want her.* I heard his chuckle in my mind. She took his hand and pressed it to her cheek, drawing his fingers toward her lips. Slowly she allowed his finger to part her lips and her tongue caressed the tip of his finger. She drank him in as he spoke to her, "Her knowledge grows as does her powers. I don't know how this is possible, she is still human, my Lady," he cooed his words to her in such a tender voice.

She moved around him, pressing her breast into him as she inhaled his scent, so close to his lips as she spoke. "Does her mate still love her?"

"Yes, my Lady. He still pains for her and only her. Soon she will ease his pain."

Her fingers moved along his jawline, so delicately, causing the servant to inhale deeply. "Do you feel she will return his love?" she asked, mesmerized by the feel of his smooth skin.

"Yes, my Lady. She will love him like no other. She and her mate will always be as one. No one can match that love. She has her clan and she will be intimate with them as well, but that will be a different desire. They adore her greatly, and she will return their passion and her clan will be stronger because of their bonds."

She ran her tongue over his ear, down his neck. His eyes rolled back as he stood rigid. Her lips brushed his, his hands flexed - he wanted to hold her but permission had not been granted.

Her hand massaged his hardness. She needed his touch; she needed to press herself to him. Her bodiless lover had left her unfulfilled; she needed to be held and she needed to hold.

He stood stone still as she violated him; a small curl on his lips registered his pleasure.

"We will speak of the child later, Thomas. I have other needs that need attending to at the moment." She pressed her lips to his and he lifted her effortlessly in his arms and carried her out of the room.

I stood alone in the shadows of the chamber. The only light came from the table where candles were placed in the middle, but I could have seen even if this light was not there. Nothing could hide from my sight. *They'll be busy for a while*, so my mind started wandering the room.

Shelves hugged the walls, filled with books and potions and pots with ladles. Skulls lined an entire shelf; another had jars of fingers, toes, tongues, livers and hearts. Each jar was marked human, fairy, elf, dwarf, or giant. One jar, a very large jar, held the male organ. I'm sure she found this one the most precious of her collection. I felt sorry for the ones who donated to the jar and wondered if her current lover would be the next donor. *That had to hurt!*

My mind walked along the table viewing its contents. The bottle sat in view, she did not secure it in her hurry to fill her need.

I bent closer to view it; there was nothing special about this bottle. It was a fat clay bottle with a cork stopper, something so simple to hold something so horrid. The bottle shook as I gazed upon it. A smile lined my lips.

"I know you. My line put you there, and there you will remain. You will never gain what you need to be made whole. I will beat you; I will beat her. Know my strength."

I touched the bottle with my mind's finger; it shook. "I am still human but my magic is strong. When I transform I will be beyond your measure and I will destroy you. Never again will you be made whole to destroy these people. Know me - I am your end," I whispered.

I left the chamber and followed the passage past several cells. This was further than I had ever been. My mind told me to know this place. The passage was dark but I could see. Two cells were on each side of me. The bars were of thick metal, the locks heavy. Each had a stone bench with shackles attached to the walls. Molded straw lay on the floor and the smell of damp earth was strong. My mind saw the torture in these cells. Men had lain prostrate on the cold floor as lashes were given hard across their nakedness. Women had been chained to the walls and raped repeatedly. Screams and cries could be heard. All were left to starve and die if they did not pledge to her. I understood the pain, the fear. I will end this too. I know this place now, I will remember.

I continued up the passage, learning, remembering. My mind showed me the way through the darkness toward the opening. I needed to know this place, it was important. I needed to be shown how to get here, it was important.

☙

The light was bright in my eyes, I was no longer in the passageway; I was in a meadow. This was familiar to me; I had been here many times. The Firehole River ran through the valley.

I was sitting at a picnic table. A Clarks Jay flew from the tree to where I sat. "I'm sorry little one, I have no food today," I spoke to the jay. It tilted its tiny head. "I promise the next time I come I will bring you something."

"You have been here many times," the jay spoke, "I have seen you many times. You have changed. You are a Chosen One. You are whom the stories spoke of. We have waited for you my child."

My eyes widened as the jay spoke to me. "I have gained much knowledge, my mind is very tired, and now a jay speaks to me," I smiled a laugh. "I need to sleep, one night of peaceful sleep. I do not understand all that is happening."

"Do not fear me, my child. We have waited for you for a very long time. You are truly a stubborn one. Do you see the bison?" the Clark's Jay asked.

My head turned to look up the valley of the Nez Perce. I heard the wood flute play a soft melody in my mind. "I see the bison. Why?"

"Is that all you see?"

I looked again, "No, I see a man walking toward me. He's wearing buffalo robes; he's carrying a staff of pine."

"What else do you see?"

"His headdress is that of a wolf." As I spoke I heard the drums, I heard the wood flute, and I heard the song. He continued to walk toward me. I watched; the Clark's Jay did not leave.

"Hello my child," he spoke to me. "We have waited for you. Now you have come and we have much to tell, we have much to show. Walk with me my Chosen One. I will teach you what I can in this short time. You must come back often to learn what you need to know."

I took his hand and followed him; the Clark's Jay stayed on my shoulder. We walked back toward the buffalo.

"Tell me what your eyes show you," he spoke to me.

"I see many bison; I see a large valley, with a river. Hills are off to my right and I see smoke rising to my left. I know this place; I have been here many times."

"Yes, you know this place. You have come here often. It relaxes you. You are in the valley of the Nez Perce of the Yellowstone. I have watched for you. Walk with me."

We went deeper into the valley; the sun was still shining. I saw the wolves as they walked the hills, watching us. "What do you know of the earth? What do you know of the spirits?"

"I am ashamed to say I do not know what I need."

"You are of the earth, its spirits run deep within you. You feel the great oak as it sways with the wind. You are strong like the oak. You have the fire from deep within the earth in your heart. Your heart is strong; it beats strong. I feel it in you." He touched his hand to my chest and smiled. "Fire is your friend Chosen One, know this, you will need it. Even the smallest of flames will protect you. Your blood runs like the river you see. It is hot and powerful. Your blood is strong. It gives you life, as does the water in this valley. Your blood protects. Breathe the air of this valley. It relaxes you. You are of this valley."

"Why do I need to know this?"

"It will be made clear, walk with me. Do you see the wolves that follow us?"

"Yes."

"They are your protectors. The members of your clan are your protectors. Do not fail them. You must make them strong. Their ways are different to you. You must change." He touched my chest with his finger making his point that I needed to change.

We came to a clearing, littered with rocks. "Collect the rocks and form a circle."

I did as he instructed.

"Now sit with me in the circle. Close your eyes my child. What do you hear? Do you hear the wind?"

"Yes."

"What does it say?"

"Strength, it tells me to call upon it for my strength."

"The wind can be a powerful force or it can be as gentle as a lamb. Know this. The wind will tell its story; you must listen.

"Long ago, in this valley a small child came and called to the wind. 'Do you hear me?' cried the child. The wind did not answer and the child went away. A few years passed and the child returned. 'Do you hear me?' cried the child. Again, the wind did not answer and the child went away. More time passed and the child was now a young maiden. Again, she cried into the wind, 'Do you hear me now, I am here, and I will be heard. I am strong and I am here and I will be heard.' Now the wind did answer. 'I have seen you since you were small and I have watched. Your enemies know you well. You must change. Like the wind changes its direction, so must you. You must change or your enemies will know you and know how to destroy you. Their ways are not yours, but his love is strong. Others will love you too. You will always be of the one, but you must take the others too.' Then the wind was gone."

"I do not understand this story," I said.

229

"It will be made clear, very soon to you. Know the wind; know its strength. Know your own strength. Know that you strengthen your clan. Change your direction, hide your emotions." Then he was gone and I was back at the picnic area, the Clark's Jay was on the table. "Know your way, my child. Come back soon." Then it flew away.

I listened to the sound of the river as it flowed past me. The wind blew very gently and I watched the wolves that stood on the hill across the river.

❦

My mind started wandering back to my room. I could see every thing clearly as I wandered through the hotel. I floated through the shopping area, into the pub we had all been spending time in. There they were, sitting at a table in the back. Their faces showed me their concerns, all their worry. I stayed for a while and listened to their conversation realizing it was going to take everything I had to convince them all would be fine.

The ringing brought me back to the present.

CHAPTER 18

Tuesday morning

The phone rang our wake up call at seven a.m. sharp. Steven still held me in his arms, my head rested on his chest; his deep purr and rhythmic breathing had lulled me to sleep.

He reached and lifted the phone on the second ring and gently set it back in its cradle. He snapped the light on low, "Good morning Sunshine," he whispered.

I smiled when I heard his voice; it wasn't a dream. It was real, last night was real. I felt the rise and fall of his chest as he held me in his arms. Even though I felt this, my arms tightened around him, keeping him close to me for fear when I opened my eyes it would be the pillow I was clinging to and not him. "Morning, did you sleep well, or meditate well, with me on your chest all night?"

"Best it's ever been." He gently nudged me to roll on my side. His strong arms pulled me into his chest and protectively he held me to him. His lips brushed my ear as he whispered softly, "It's time for me to get up, but I don't want to leave you."

I giggled and smiled. I rolled to face him and my eyes locked on to his deep brown eyes. His stare was total and he kept my gaze and would not release me. I felt his eyes pulling me inside him. We became seamless as our hearts beat and our lungs breathed in unison.

"Damn, I have missed you," then I draped my leg over him, giving enough pressure to roll him on his back. He placed his hands along my hips and raised me onto him. I felt the tingle of a shiver as he slid slowly inside me and I saw him smile. My hips responded with slow rotations as his hands explored my body, making their way to my breasts.

I was aware of my surroundings even though I was lost in my own mind, finding what I had been denied for so long. The pureness of his love filtered through me with every breath we took. It fed my hunger and satisfied me. I heard his name escape my lips and I felt his hands tighten around my hips as he knew my pleasure was not far and he kept me close, allowing me to crawl and beg for the euphoric bliss I needed. I raised, arched my back until I thought I would snap in two, but I found that perfect little spot, it sent shudders through my body and I then collapsed onto his chest.

Steven rolled over on top of me, keeping his momentum strong. "Come back with me, Princess," he whispered. His slow thrust brought me back with him, back to the spot he needed. His kisses were tender, light, at times barely touching my lips making me reach and want him more. Slow and deliberate thrusts, my hips rotating with him, I closed my eyes as he increased the momentum, his breathing increasing. My legs tightened around him, my hands resting gently on his collarbone.

I opened my eyes; he was watching me. His eyes held mine, pulling me deeper inside him. I felt myself wrapping around his heart, entering his soul. I felt his smile with each elated sound I gave, until finally he came in hard thrusts and my body shook from the exhilaration.

He lowered himself onto me, as he kissed me tenderly.

It was a long few minutes before we spoke, "Damn, what brought that out in us?" I asked.

"I honestly don't know. I have never made love to anyone that totally." Our hearts still beat hard against our chests.

"Well, what ever it was it was great!" I giggled, "I think we have the control part down now." I wrapped my arms tight around him.

"Yeah, that we do." He whispered in my ear, "Bree, I will never allow you to leave – know that. You are all mine. This proved it – we are one, we always have been. Damn, I have wanted you for so long."

"So...I'm your prisoner now, am I?" I jokingly teased. I think I like that."

"I'm a very loving warden – you'll see," he laughed.

"Well, I've no desire to go anywhere, Steven. I will always be with you." I stretched under him, "I don't even need handcuffs – although..." I laughed.

"I'll ask Stanley if he has a pair he can spare."

I giggled, "Don't you dare! Can't we just call today off and stay here?"

"Nope, I have plans for us today. We're spending the day just having fun. No reunion, no Council talk, nothing

233

from the past, just us. I told you I wouldn't leave you and I meant it." He slipped out of our embrace and headed for the bathroom. I heard the shower and thought very deviously about joining him.

The message light was on the phone again. I hadn't heard it ring and that puzzled me. I pressed #7, listened to the familiar 'you have one new message', and listened to the cryptic message.

Stay close to your clan today. It is dangerous for them tonight. The yellow is dangerous; the tooth is better. Your blood is strong and will protect. Of three vials, give the four halves and the loved one whole. Do not forget the pendant and the stone.

Why must they talk in riddles? My thoughts returned to the dreams I had. I remembered dreaming of that passage before but I had never seen anyone. I knew the woman in that dream was a threat to me. I didn't know how I knew that, but she was and I would be dealing with her soon. I had never had the one with the jay. I had no idea what it all meant, or if it wasn't my imagination playing with me. *Why would I have to change?* I tucked my thoughts away as Steven came out of the bathroom, "Sure we need to go out today?" I asked.

He smiled at me as he lifted me into his arms, "Yes, you will not hide in our room. We are going to enjoy the day. And if we should run into your ex-husband, he will know my anger." His eyes were intense and I saw his passion for me in them. If Nick knew what was good for him, he would stay clear of me the rest of his life!

I smiled at him. "I love you Steven. I'll be quick, and then we can go."

∽

Showers always seemed to relax me. I hadn't thought I was stressed, but I felt my muscles unwinding as the water ran through my hair, over my shoulders and down my back. I stood there tilting my head under the spray, rubbing my shoulders; twisting to help the muscles relax. "Okay, enough. Let's get hoppin'," I told myself and reached for the shampoo. "Well damn," I pulled the shower curtain back and sure enough; the shampoo was by the sink. "What is it doing over there?" Soon as the question was asked, the bottle rose in the air and came to me. *Okay, that was new.* I was surprised I wasn't scared. "Okay, if I did that, then that was so cool," I laughed, "and if I didn't, then who the hell is in the bathroom with me?" I looked around the small room and decided to do a test. I thought about the bar of soap, and it floated to me as well. "Okay, really cool!" I smiled.

I finished my shower and dressed. My mind was already making plans to practice this new talent, but I didn't want anyone to know I was able to do this yet. I mean, I was still human; I shouldn't be able to do this. I didn't want to freak anyone out.

Steven already had breakfast set up when I got to the living room, he was watching the sports news and when I entered he turned it off. "Steven you can watch the sports. It's okay."

He thought for just a fraction of a second about turning the TV back on, "Nah, there's plenty of time for that. Come on; let's get some food in you. I've ordered your favorite." He pulled the chair out for me, and then he sat down, "Okay I have something special planned for today."

"Steven, I know what you said but I don't expect you to stop your life because of this. But I'm glad you are staying. I just want to spend the day with you. I don't care if we go anywhere. We could stay locked in here all day just as long as we're together."

I noticed how drawn he was looking and that concerned me. The long separation we'd had, arranging this meeting, all the worry that went with it, it had all taken its toll on him. He was happy but his body needed something more. He needed to hunt to release the bad energy he had stored and replace it with good energy.

"No, that just won't do. We're going traveling; you'll need your camera. I have your cloak on the sofa; it's black not red, I don't want to draw attention to you just yet. Once you transform you can wear a red one, but for now, you'll need to be satisfied with black. Bill sent your hiking boots and a warm pair of socks this morning. Hope you don't mind, I had him go to your house to get them. He also sent your necklace, with a message and I quote, 'wear it'."

"Message received," I smiled at him, "Steven, where on earth are we going around here that I would need warm socks?"

"Not here, we're going to Yellowstone, just the two of us. You've always liked to visit there in the late fall. Your cloak will keep you warm."

"Steven, I can't travel the way you do yet, can I?"

"You can if I wrap my arms around you. You don't have any objections to that, do you? I mean, after last night... and, well...this morning...that was extraordinarily delightful," he smiled. "I want to wake up that way every morning with you. You...will need your rest," he winked.

I excitedly gave him a sweet squeal; "I can't wait to experience you again like that! Trust me; I have no problem in wrapping my arms around you. Speaking of that, I don't remember it being that controlled, that passionate. This was much better."

He smiled, "Yes, I agree it was much better," his lips formed a tiny smile as he watched me. He cleared his throat, "But we do need to discuss a few things anyway."

I felt a twinge of panic, "Like what? You said you didn't want to talk about the past!" I put my fork down and looked at him.

He continued to butter his toast, not looking at me, "I don't, I'm aware of your past Bree. We don't need to discuss it. However, we need to talk about our future. For instance, where do we want to live? I was thinking," he continued, taking a drink of his Drink, "we could buy a new home near Bill and Gina and you could get rid of the house you currently have." He set his knife down, took a bite of his toast, and smiled, very pleased with himself for coming to this conclusion.

I thought for a few minutes, my brow wrinkled, I gave him a little grimace, "Steven, I can't explain this just yet, but for some reason I feel I need to keep that house. I don't know why, but there is just something telling me to hang on to it. We can change out the furniture if you like." I poured syrup over my French toast and bacon.

He wrinkled his nose and his mouth gave a little twitch as he looked at me. "I really don't like you staying in that house. I don't want Nick around, or the others, and as long as his name is on the title he has access to the house and can invite others without your knowledge."

"Nick isn't on it any more. Dad bought him out when I started the divorce. I guess that's why he said I would be safe there. Besides, aren't you going to be with me?"

"Yes, but I still don't like it." He thought about it for a few minutes. "We'll go furniture shopping when we get home. Brad and Madalyn should be by shortly, so finish eating so we can leave soon as he's done." He finished his Drink, and I watched him. He was aware my eyes were on him. He set the glass down, "What?"

"Nothing, you just need another Drink that's all."

"I do? What makes you think that?"

"You'll feel better; you're probably going to need to hunt soon as well," I informed him.

Steven looked away from me when I said that, his shoulders tensed. His smile faded. It was obviously a part of his life he didn't want me to know about. We were right for each other in so many ways; he seemed to want to forget what he was. But, I loved him totally and I realized this was going to take some tender coaching on my part.

"Steven, *our* past has taken a lot out of you. Our long separation, your planning all of this, and all the information I gave Billy...well, it has all caught up with you. I can see it in your eyes, and I can feel it in your energy. You need to recharge. So until you are ready to leave my side and go tackle the wide animals that will recharge you, double up on your Drink; humor me."

"You can feel my energy; really?"

My smile widened, "Oh, yes I can feel it!"

He raised his eyebrows, "Okay, I'll double up because I'm not ready to leave your side."

As I sat there talking with Steven, I was also listening to Odessa.

Bree, you are doing very well, she said. *I must say I am impressed. Your bathroom maneuvers were excellent! You are going to be a challenge to your enemies my dear. Here you sit, having a conversation with me inside your head, and you are still speaking and following an outside conversation. Yes indeed, magnificent! None of your sisters managed that.* I could actually feel her smile. *I've a feeling this next goal I set for you, is going to bother you, but you will need to be able to enter into others minds even if they have you blocked. Currently, your mind is blocked from your family. This confuses them. I thought I would need to teach you how to do this, but you seem capable of doing it all by yourself! The magic is strong in you, my dear. Your family's minds are blocked, not from each other, but from you and your enemies. They are still protecting you, but I don't think you are going to have any trouble getting into their minds. You will need to continue to show them you're strong, and I really don't think they are ready to hear this.* She laughed; *I see many arguments in your future!*

❧

I had just finished my breakfast when we heard a knock on the door. Steven got up, and picked up his Drink. He leaned in and kissed me, licked his lips, "Sweet. I think you've had enough sugar for the day."

"So what...now you're my mother?" I teased back. "It's just the syrup."

He kissed me again, "Well, it tastes good on you," then answered the door.

He said his 'hello' to Brad and Madalyn and offered them a Drink. Madalyn declined for both of them, "We're fine, we've had our breakfast, haven't we darling? It was nice and warm."

I could feel her pressing me with her comments, but I was not going to acknowledge her remarks. I would treat her with respect, after all, she was Brad's mate and I didn't want to cause any waves being new to the clan. She would adjust; I just needed to be patient. I got up from my chair and greeted them.

I ran my hand along their necks, just below the ear along the jugular vein. Brad looked tired this morning; Madalyn looked fine, just angry. I frowned, "No, you aren't. You both need another Drink, and then I looked at Steven, "I think you had better schedule a hunt. Would you mind contacting Rick and Sandy and asking them to come by?"

They just stared at me.

"When did this start?" Brad asked turning to Steven.

"She just started this at breakfast; she told me the same thing."

"She did? Really?"

"Yeah...she was right too!"

"Okay, I'm standing right here!" I laughed causing them to focus their attention back at me. "Look, I know I'm very connected to Steven..." I couldn't hold back my smile as my morning treat came back into my thoughts. Steven seemed to know where my thoughts had taken me. He cleared his throat bringing my attention to him and winked. I stammered in my embarrassment, "and it...would seem... apparently to all of you. Let's just get this out of the way and be done with it, you will all feel so much better."

I got up in Steven's face and gave him a kiss, "Now please, contact Rick and Sandy. I'm going to go brush my teeth and I'll be right back. Madalyn, Brad, please, have another glass of your Drink."

I went to the bathroom to wash my face and brush my teeth.

Bree, Odessa spoke. *You're correct; they need to hunt. We can practice while they are gone.*

Yeah, I know. But Steven was so set on us spending the day together.

Bree, if you don't practice and learn what you need to know you may never get the chance to spend time together. You have so much to learn and understand, she warned.

Okay, I'll do my best.

When I finished in the bathroom, and was on my way back to the living room, I picked up the blood stone necklace. The stone immediately warmed my hand. I turned it over and examined it. I didn't understand how I could feel such warmth from a simple stone. I shrugged my shoulders, *stop trying to figure everything out at once, you'll wear your brain out,* my mind warned me as I put the necklace on under my shirt.

Rick and Sandy had just arrived and were sitting in the love seat. They got up and greeted me the same way as Brad and Madalyn. I could tell by just looking at Rick, the darkness under his eyes was more pronounced this morning, his brow creased a little more than I had seen since I'd been here. He too looked very tired; my past must have taken a toll on him as well as Brad and Steven. I placed my hand on both their necks, the same way I did the others, and asked Steven to pour two more glasses. I sat next to Brad on the sofa; Madalyn stood by the window watching us.

"Okay, that's new," said Sandy as she sat back down and looked at me.

"Well, Squirt, what else can you do, and more important, how can you do this now? You haven't transformed yet, have you?" Rick teasingly asked. "Brad, what did the blood test show?"

"I haven't even had a chance to do it yet; Bree feels we need to hunt." He put his arm around me and pulled me to him. "I think she's just trying to get out of this test!"

I smiled at him, "No I'm not; we'll get around to that, I promise. But I really do think you need to do this and I'll not take 'no' for an answer, you all need to hunt. Look at all of you; I can see the strain on your faces. You should have meditated last night instead of sitting at the pub trying to decide what to do about my enemies."

"How did you know that?" Rick tried to hide his astonishment of my correct assessment of his nightly venture, but I felt his emotion. He was curious about my abilities.

"I saw you there in my mind," I smiled, a little proud of myself.

"You saw us? Right. Okay, who all was there?" he challenged.

"Well, the two of you," I motioned to him and Brad, "and Billy. Steven kept checking in to see what you were deciding. Then my other cousin Stanley came with a friend of his, I think his name was Dirk. They stayed for a short while. Billy went home about five, and you guys left shortly after that. Now, did I pass your test?"

All three just stared at me. Wide eyes and mouths a little ajar! "You saw all of that?" Brad sounded stunned as he asked the question.

I just nodded.

"Damn! You're still a scrawny little human, but able to do that. Huh, will wonders never cease?" Rick's eyes smiled but I knew he was trying to get into my mind. I felt him give a gentle push to get passed the barrier that kept my thoughts silent to them. He most certainly would be fun to play with on this.

I smiled at Rick and watched his eyes. When I saw he had given up on his advance, I continued with my logic, trying to make them see things my way. "Look, my past has been very stressful to you. Last night was stressful to you, it drained you; and I need you all at top strength. I can see and feel your anger and I need you to release it. I am asking you to please go hunt today. Steven..." I held my finger up, "I will be here when you get back, well rested and we can spend the night together. I really need you all to do this for me."

I thought my speech was delivered fairly well. I used, what I thought was the right amount of sternness in my voice, but apparently I was going to need lessons! "Bree, I'm not leaving you alone. What if we split up? Two of us can stay here with you, I don't think I could seriously hunt with you here by yourself," Steven said as he came and sat beside me.

"Yeah, Squirt, we can split up. It's just not safe leaving you unprotected. The Traditionals should start arriving soon, and if by chance they find you're by yourself, well, I'm not comfortable with it either. No, I'm with Steven on this," Rick said.

I thought to Odessa, *you can teach me anywhere, right?*
Yes.

Okay; then plan B. "Steven, do you hunt around your cabin?"

"Yeah; why?"

"Well, I could go with you and stay at your cabin until you're done hunting. I would be safe there wouldn't I?"

"Yeah, and I would be happier with that scenario than leaving you here."

"Steven, weren't you going to Yellowstone?" Sandy asked.

"We were, but Bree's right; we do need to hunt, or I just may have to kill her ex-husband and his two friends." He didn't look at me when he said it, but Rick and Brad agreed.

"I haven't had bison in a long time. Wouldn't she be just as safe there in the Snow Lodge? I mean; no one needs to know where we are. We can all bathe in Yellowstone Lake before we come back to the room," Sandy said.

"Oh, bison does sound good," Madalyn agreed as she made a smacking sound with her lips. She watched me for my reaction to her display. I didn't give her one. I would not allow her to mess with my mind. I would treat her with respect but I'd not allow her childish actions to upset me.

"Okay," Rick said, "Yellowstone it is, we'll get there early enough for some fun first." He looked at me, "It's best if we hunt at night, less likely to be seen."

I nodded, showing I understood his comment, but I wasn't happy with the decision. "Steven, I think I would feel better if we went to your cabin instead."

"Bree, there's nothing to worry about, we've hunted in Yellowstone many times," Brad offered. "You'll be perfectly safe there."

"It's not me I'm worried about," I murmured.

"Oh, for pity sakes, we are all very capable of taking care of ourselves," Madalyn said with a little more frustration than was necessary. "You don't need to worry about us. You need to worry more about yourself." She changed her tone but she wasn't convincing me, her anger was strong and she was projecting it toward me. She could care less how I felt. I saw her eyes dart to Steven, she was playing to him, and I couldn't tell if he was buying it or not.

I spoke to Odessa again, *I have a bad feeling about this, but they aren't going to listen to me. The message on the phone said the yellow is dangerous; the tooth is better. Steven's cabin is in the Bear Tooth Mountains. I think we really need to go there.*

Odessa agreed, *Bree, have Brad take three vials of your blood. He only needs a few drops to run his test, and you want to give them a little more protection. Pour a little of your blood in their Drinks. This will protect them if there is trouble. This is what the message meant. It will also help them understand your strength.*

Do I need to say any magic words when I do this? I asked hopefully.

No, just pour it into their Drinks. Your magic is strong; you don't need any words.

But, could I say a few words if I wanted to? I asked a little wistfully.

Bree, you don't need to, your magic is strong. She realized she was losing the argument. *Oh, very well, if it'll make you happy. When you pour your blood into their Drinks, say these words quietly to yourself. 'Taste my blood and know my strength. I will always be with you'.*

❧

I looked at them as they sat there looking at me, "Brad could you please take three vials of blood?"

"Bree, I only need a few drops. Why do you want me to take three?" He reached over, and tucked a strand of hair behind my ear; his hand came to rest on my shoulder. I felt the snap of electricity when he touched me. His eyes glanced quickly to his fingers, a curious look formed on his face, and then he looked back at me, waiting on his answer.

"Because, I'm asking you to." I shrugged my shoulders as I said it. I knew I couldn't explain the feeling I had so they would understand. I would have to tell them about Odessa and the phone calls and the time just wasn't right for that.

"Why Bree, what do you plan to do with the blood he takes?" Steven asked.

I looked at him and wrinkled my nose, "I'm going to pour it in your Drink and you are then going to drink your Drink!" I smiled, he didn't, so I quickly continued, "Steven, none of you understand how I know things. I just know I need to do this, that's all."

Brad squeezed my shoulder in a reassuring way, set his glass down and got up to get his medical bag. He pulled out some vials, "Which size do you need?"

"You're not seriously going to do this are you?" Steven looked at Brad, confused to why he would agree to this.

"Yeah, I think I am. What could it hurt?" he replied, maybe just as confused as Steven, but he understood it was something I needed done.

I saw the needle and I started feeling warm. *Damn, don't pass out; it's just a needle Bree.* I bit my top lip and looked at Brad who was already watching my reaction.

"You don't need to watch," he smiled. He wrapped the rubber tie around my arm. "Bree, what size do you need?"

I looked at the selection he offered me and picked three midsize tubes. Then he told me to make a fist, "Here's the stick, breathe through your nose, you're doing fine." He filled the three vials, then took a very small vial and put a tiny amount in it. "All done." He placed a cotton ball over the needle as he pulled it out. Madalyn gave him a strip of tape to place over the cotton. She watched me. I could feel her anger. *Why was she acting this way? What did I do to piss her off?*

Brad handed me the three vials. The blood made them hot. My eyes showed my amazement as I noticed a small wisp of steam escaping through the hole in the top of the each rubber stopper. Brad noticed it as well and he looked at me, watching to see how I would respond. I scrunched up my mouth and nose, and Brad hid a laugh. "I've a feeling it's not supposed to do that," I said to him.

"Well, not for a normal person, no." I felt his energy as we sat next to each other. For some reason it was strong today and I felt it swirling deep in my soul.

Everyone watched as he dropped two drops onto a glass slide then slid the glass slide onto the plate of the microscope Madalyn had set up for him. He looked into the eyepiece for a short time, then reached into his bag and pulled out a small bottle of clear liquid. He took an eyedropper and put three drops in the remaining blood left in the vial, and gave it a little shake. Steam escaped, and then a faint wisp of very light green smoke rose from it.

He looked at me and put his hand on mine; I felt a rush of his energy as he touched my hand, making me shiver. "Bree, you're on your way through the process." His grip tightened on my hand; his energy was strong. I sensed he felt it as well. He looked a little taken aback but didn't comment on the sensation, he just smiled at me.

I asked the question that was on everyone's mind, "How much time?"

Brad tried to sound comforting, "Oh, maybe nine months, maybe more."

"Or maybe less," I added for him.

"Yes Bree, maybe less," he said very softly, realizing I wasn't comforted by his assessment.

"Can you take the stoppers out of these for me?" I handed them to him; he removed the stoppers, and handed them to me one by one. I spoke the words Odessa told me to say as I poured half of a vial into Brad's drink. I smiled and winked at him; the other half went into Madalyn's. I did the same thing with the next vial for Rick and Sandy. When I got to Steven's glass, he looked at me as I whispered the words to myself. I looked into his eyes and smiled, winked, and poured an entire vial into his drink.

"Now, if you would please drink your Drink so we can be on our way. Steven, I really should let Gran know I'm going to be gone today. I don't want her to worry, but I don't want her to know exactly where we are going. Would you tell her you are taking me to the desert?"

"Yeah, I'll tell her," and he drank his Drink as they all did. I watched his eyes widen, "WOW! That was... damn," he finished his Drink. I stood there looking a little concerned. Steven noticed my reaction and gave me a very devilish smile. He arched one eyebrow as he asked, "Did it taste sweeter to you guys?"

"Yeah, it did," said Rick, raising his eyebrows and licking his lips. "Bree, I think you should lay off the sugar. Seriously, your blood really did make it taste different; it tasted great!" Rick said. He smiled at me, realizing how his enthusiasm must have sounded to me. "I always said you were a sweet little thing," he laughed, trying to ease my tension.

I watched as one by one their approval crept across their faces. Madalyn ran her finger along the inside of the glass, collecting the remaining red liquid, and then sucked it off her fingers. Not wanting her lusting act to go to waste, she smiled a wicked smile at me, then turned back to look out the window.

That sent a chill through me. *Oh boy! Maybe I shouldn't have given her any!* "Okay, if you could just not keep telling me how good I taste, I would appreciate it," I shuddered.

Steven came up and kissed me on the forehead, "I've spoken to your grandmother and told her we're all going on a picnic in the desert; we'll see her tomorrow." He turned to the others; "We'll meet you guys at the Lodge in a few minutes."

Rick and Sandy finished their Drinks and disappeared. I looked at Brad, "What Aubrey?"

"Will you bring your bag with you?" I made it sound more like a request than a question.

"I never go anywhere without it," then he and Madalyn disappeared.

Steven turned to look at me. He took my hands in his and raised them to his lips, "Care to explain?"

"Will you keep an open mind?"

"Yes." He gently kept kissing the back of my hands.

"I heal quickly, so my blood has some properties in it to help me heal. I'm just not comfortable about tonight and I wanted to give you guys a little more protection. It can't hurt, can it?"

"No Princess, it can't hurt," he smiled, and then wrapped his arms around me and gave me a very tender kiss. "I agree with Rick though, you are a very sweet little thing. Now, are you ready?"

"Do we need to pack anything?"

"Ah, already did."

"You did?" I looked up at him suspiciously. "You packed for me?"

"Yes, I know what you need."

"You do? You got into my drawers and got me everything I needed."

"Yeah, you have a problem with that, missy?" He was smiling. "I have watched you, I know what you like to wear," he had his arms wrapped around me again. "I know you like to listen to your music," he kissed my forehead, "and I know what you like to sleep in." I nipped at his chin; he gave a soft shudder.

"No, no problem at all, it's kind of nice. I could get used to it." I smiled at him.

"Well, that's what I'm counting on." He took my face in his hands and pressed his lips so gently into mine, my heart fluttered. I really had to remind myself to breathe. *Damn, his lips are soft.*

"Be right back, don't go anywhere." He went into the bedroom and came out with our overnight bag and I had to smile as I watched his enthusiasm readying us for our trip.

He fastened my pendant that Billy sent around my neck, then wrapped my cloak around me, and put his own on as well. He had one hand on the bag and his other wrapped around my waist. "Put your arm around my waist. Any questions before we start?"

"Do I need to close my eyes?"

"No; only if you want to. I'm driving so it doesn't matter. Hold on, here we go." The room folded into itself, then the next room folded into us, and it kept going faster and faster. I could feel us turning in the direction we needed to go in, north. At least I assumed we were heading north. Space kept folding into itself faster and faster. I was glad I didn't get motion sickness, because this was an old fashioned E-ticket! The ride only lasted a few seconds and when we started to slow, Steven told me to start walking. We walked right out of nothingness into the light. His expert driving made it look as if we had just gotten out of our car and were heading into the Snow Lodge. "Are you okay?"

I giggled, "That was fun! Can we do it again? Come on, one more time around the block," I teased.

He laughed and tightened his hold on my waist. "No more airplane rides for you; you'll be traveling this way from now on. It's a lot quicker, and for you, a hell of a lot safer."

Rick and Sandy appeared, and a few seconds later Brad and Madalyn arrived. They started into the Lodge, but I stopped and took in a deep breath. I could smell the pine, and the crisp cool mountain air felt good on my skin.

I could hear the low rumble of Old Faithful going off. A bull elk walked through the parking lot into the trees, a few moments later I heard his bugle. The sound he made was heaven to my ears, and it sent shivers down my spine. I loved it, my heart leapt every time I heard it. He was announcing himself to all the females in the area, and his was a bold statement. Then I thought about the reason we were here and I closed my eyes. Steven watched my inner struggle and whispered to me, "We're here for bison, not elk. He will be fine, I promise." I opened my eyes and smiled a thank you.

"Steven, I've a question, who made the reservations?"

"Sandy took care of it; she always takes care of the reservations."

We were all on the same floor and our rooms were right next to each other. Steven opened our room door, told me to stay where I was. He rolled the suitcase in, took the camera out of the case, came back, and took me by the hand. "It's too early to be in our rooms, let's go have some fun. See you guys in a couple of hours," then he disappeared with me to go geyser gaze.

CHAPTER 19

The darkness at Yellowstone

There were very few people out on the boardwalk when Steven and I appeared behind a few trees at Riverside Geyser, "I figured we could work our way back to Old Faithful," he said.

Riverside Geyser had just started its spectacular display. Strong bursts jettisoned the hot water and the cold air caused steam to rise in union with its spray out over the river.

I could feel the power of the eruption course though my body. I felt the earth shudder as the force of the water made its way up through its tubing and through the opening. I had always felt the ground shudder here, but now I was more aware of it. My entire body felt the vibration of the earth. My feet tingled from the sensation.

The wind blew the spray in our direction and I covered my camera with my cloak to protect it. I let the geyser mist sweep over me.

I watched the hill behind the geyser. Mule deer grazed undaunted by the earth's forceful bursts. They didn't watch; they had seen it many times before.

In the copse of trees just off to the left, I watched as a dark cloud moved about. Steven took no notice of the shape. It hovered in the trees and then was gone.

We watched Riverside until it played out; then we continued up the boardwalk, hand in hand, in the direction of Daisy Geyser.

"Now, aren't you glad we came?" Steven spoke softly in my ear, hoping I was a little calmer. The breeze blew lightly. The air was crisp and the smell of pine mixed with the sulfur of the geysers was indeed wonderful. Hearing the wind blowing through the pine was a very relaxing sound to me. I was sure it would rain tonight. The rain would turn to snow by tomorrow. I so loved this time of year.

I wrapped my arm around Steven, pulling myself closer to him. "Steven, you know I love it here; but I still wish we had gone to your cabin." I didn't bother to mention the darkness I was feeling or the dark cloud I was seeing. None of them understood me yet, not really. I didn't understand me either for that matter.

I didn't bother to mention the anger I was feeling from Madalyn. There was a reason for it; I knew that much.

Another elk bugled in the distance; its sound cascaded down the mountain.

❧

We arrived at Daisy Geyser. It hadn't erupted yet but it was starting its pre-actions splashing, so I felt we had enough time to walk the short path to Punch Bowl. When we arrived back at Daisy, Rick and Sandy were sitting on the bench.

"Thought we would catch up with you two here," Rick said.

I smiled and gave him a hug. "Rick, I know Steven told you where we were."

"Damn woman, there is no getting anything past you, is there? Are you enjoying yourself, Squirt? It's not too cold for you is it?" He hugged me back then vigorously rubbed my shoulders trying to warm me up.

I noticed I had my cloak wrapped around me keeping the cold wind out; while Steven, Rick, and Sandy were content to leave theirs open.

"No, I like the cold. Just a habit of wrapping myself up I guess." I sat on the bench next to Sandy. I watched the tree line as they were talking. I was paying attention to the conversation but I was more concerned about the darkness I was experiencing.

The shadow was back, hiding in the trees. I saw it, and I watched it. The others never noticed it.

I felt the slightest tremors in the earth; my feet tingled as I felt the energy build; then the release of the pressure as the hot water shot out of the opening of the geyser. The power I felt behind the rush of force was simply thrilling. I was viewing this land in a totally different light. I was one with the earth and that sensation was amazing!

The breeze blew the steam and water away from us, so I was able to use my camera. I walked up the boardwalk to take my pictures of my three escorts sitting on the bench. When I looked through the lens of the camera, I saw more of the darkness behind them, just inside the trees. I slowly lowered my camera and I continued to watch it until it floated out of sight. A pool of dread started to form in my stomach; I didn't like what I was seeing or feeling. I just wanted this night to be over with.

I heard Steven call to me, "Ready to move on Princess?" They were all standing now; Rick stretched his arms in the air. I clicked off a few pictures, and then hurried to join them.

§

As the four of us made our way up the boardwalk in the direction of Old Faithful, Brad and Madalyn were coming toward us. We were all together again. I stifled a laugh as I remembered Madalyn's comment; maybe I should have grabbed Steven and just made a run for it. But as my eyes swept over all their faces I knew they would have found us. I had to admit to myself, in the short amount of time we had all been together; I too seemed to need them around me. The only ones missing were Billy and Gina. *Maybe next time*, I thought.

After we watched Old Faithful erupt, we all headed back toward the Lodge. Everyone agreed to meet back at the restaurant around three o'clock.

"Bree, you need to eat before we leave," Steven said.

"I can call room service later," I countered.

"Think again sugar," Steven said. "You are not to leave the room or call room service while we're gone. Understood?"

"Yeah, I'm sorry. I didn't think," I answered; but I caught a glimpse of Madalyn rolling her eyes. Maybe I should just ask her what was bothering her. I tried to think if I had said something to upset her, but nothing came to mind. Sandy didn't seem to have a problem with me; I just didn't understand why Madalyn did. *Maybe I was being too sensitive and Madalyn didn't have a problem with me at all.*

Madalyn's thoughts pushed into Sandy's mind and my mind tuned in immediately. I didn't mean to listen in, but with the force she had thrown her thoughts at Sandy, I couldn't help but hear them, so I listened.

Sandy, I need you to stand with me on this.

Maddie, why? What good will this do? Steven belongs to her. You know that!

Sandy, either you stand with me or I tell Rick and Brad you have watched over your parents! You know the rules, once 'turned' the mortal trappings do not belong to you. You are in the Magical Realm and there you will stay! How do you think they will take it if they know you've been paying for your parent's utilities? I'll tell them you go there occasionally and watch them! Don't you know how dangerous that is?

Madalyn, that's harsh, my parents are old. They have no money; we have so much, and they never see me. What does it hurt?

Stand with me, against her, and I will keep your secret!

The winds suddenly blew a cold chill through me and I drew my cloak tighter around me. This was not good, not good at all and I didn't know if I should mention it to Steven or not. I had been out of their lives for a very long time; adjustments were going to be needed. I knew this but to have her dislike me this quickly...no, this was not good!

Steven instinctively placed his arm around my waist, pulling me closer to him to shield me from the bitter winds that blew. If he only knew, my chill was not from these winds but from the bitter thoughts that came briskly from Madalyn, he would understand my shivers.

I looked up at him and we exchanged a smile. I decided at that moment I would not complain to him about her. I would step above her and I would not complain about my mistreatment from her. I would let her be the one to do the complaining, and the explaining. I had known these types before I was not going to stoop to her level.

Okay, Bree, we'll see how long that lasts, my mind chastised me.

❧

Once in our room, I began to unpack our suitcase, just to see what my Steven had brought me to wear. But he had other ideas on how we were going to spend the rest of the afternoon.

Chapter 20

Steven was relaxing on the bed as I came out of the bathroom. His six-foot frame stretched the width of the bed as he lay on his stomach watching me, smiling as I walked around in my underwear. He pulled a pillow up under him as he rested on his elbows. "Hey," he said in a low, hushed, voice, "you know I love you, don't you? Bree Wentworth, Aubrey Wentworth, no, Aubrey Marie Wentworth; yeah I like the sound of that."

He stretched his arm toward me, and I took his hand and sat next to him. He rolled on his side; I could feel the vibration in his chest. I ran my fingers through his chest hairs and watched the electricity spark.

"I don't know Bree, I'm extremely relaxed now; I really don't think I need to go hunt tonight," Steven said. He rolled on his back and pulled me onto him.

I felt his neck along the jugular, I kissed it very softly, and again I saw those tiny flashes of color dance on his skin. He shivered, and I smiled. "Yes Steven, you need to hunt;

then, you need to get back here, understand?" I laughed. "Now what did you bring me to wear for tomorrow? I can't just walk around in my underwear."

"As far as I'm concerned you could," he grinned.

I stuck my tongue out at him, and went to open the suitcase. Steven walked up behind me and wrapped his arms around me. "We don't have to go out tonight ya know." He leaned his head against mine. We slowly rocked back and forth.

"And just what would we do? There's no TV."

"We could just wrap up in the covers and you could let me hold you all night. I could whisper in your ear my eternal love for you and then I would show you repeatedly how much I do love you, just like this morning. We could plan our life together, and we do have a lot to plan, Princess."

"Oh, it does sound very tempting, but...you need to hunt. We can do that after, when you get back," I smiled and reluctantly Steven went to get dressed.

When he closed the bathroom door, I finished dressing, straightened the bedding, and put my headset on. Listening to the soft music, I walked to the window, wrapped my arms around myself, and stared into the trees.

The sun was bright in the sky, but the dark feeling was still with me. I kept watching the trees, not knowing what I was looking for, but I knew something was out there.

I looked around our room, I was comfortable in here; it wasn't fancy. I began to wonder just what I was going to do while Steven was gone. I wasn't joking. There wasn't a TV or a radio, no magazines either. I hadn't brought a book, just the iPod. *I guess I could practice moving objects, just to see how far along my strength is*, I thought to myself. *Or, I could talk with Odessa.*

I turned and looked out the window again. I hadn't heard the bathroom door open, but Steven stood behind me.

"Bree," he said softly, taking my headset off, "sweetie, what are you so worried about? We have hunted these hills and mountains so many times; you don't need to worry about us. Let's get some food in you. Then before we leave we'll go to the gift shop. I know how much you love gift shops," he teased trying to get me to smile. When that did not stop my worry, he wrapped his arms around me and kissed my neck. "You like that, I can tell."

"Oh, I do like it when you kiss me. I have missed that; we have so much lost time to make up. I don't know why I have this feeling of dread Steven. Maybe it's just the thought of the hunt," I said as I turned and placed my hand on his chest. It was still wet from his shower, but I could feel the strong, low, vibration. I smiled and kissed his chest.

"Does that please you, Princess?" He placed his hand over mine.

"Yes, very much so; I am fascinated by it. You all seem to do that, I have felt it in the others too. Why do you do that?"

"We're content. I haven't felt this in a long time; say about thirteen years. Even when I was with others I was never content."

That thought had never entered my mind. Of course, there had been others. I mean, damn, I was married. Steven was still very good looking. His body was muscular, not overbearing. His hair showed no sign of gray and was thick. God, how I loved running my hands through it. Of course, there were others...but there will not be any more. I would see to all of his needs, for all of eternity. My eyes gave my question away; I didn't have to speak it...but I did. "Others?"

"Yeah, there were others Bree. I dated. I wanted to draw attention away from you, so I dated and I was very public about it. I pretended to be content, but I wasn't; not until now." He looked at me a little suspiciously, "You can feel it in the others as well?"

"Yes, I can feel it and hear it too. I feel it more with you guys though. I have to be close to Sandy and Madalyn, but I can feel yours clear across the room, Rick and Brad's too. Why?"

"Mortals are unaware of it, that's all."

"Oh," I whispered, reminded of the timeframe Brad had given me to transform. I knew I would make it. This transformation was not going to get the better of me; I would win. I needed my eternity.

"It's going to be okay, Bree." He pulled me to his chest, and I laid my ear against him and listened to the strong sound. We stayed there for a few minutes until someone knocked softly on the door.

"You go finish dressing, I'll get the door."

"Bree, trust me they have seen me in far less clothes than this."

I just looked at him. "I'll just go get dressed," he smiled, pointing toward the bathroom.

"You do that," I grinned.

I quickly placed the clothes back into the suitcase and answered the door.

Rick gave me a kiss on the cheek as he entered, "What took you so long, Squirt?"

Sandy gave me a hug and I just received a quick brush on my shoulder from Madalyn's hand. Brad was the last to enter. He gave me a kiss and whispered in my ear, "I brought the bag, now stop worrying," then kissed me again. The energy I felt from him now was even stronger than what I had felt this morning.

"Just straightening up, that's all Rick. I thought we were going to meet at the restaurant?" Steven came out of the bathroom.

"Nah," he batted the air. "I missed you." He patted Steven on the back, smiled, and winked at me.

I watched as they greeted each other, it was all very pack-like, very fraternal, and that stood to reason; they were a pack of sorts. I just wasn't sure where they all placed.

Brad was definitely the leader, the Alpha of the pack. They seemed to always run things by him for his approval. I wouldn't say Madalyn was an Alpha though. She could be, but she didn't seem all that strong a leader, more of a follower. Maybe their pack didn't require one.

I rolled my eyes. *Gees, that's really quite stupid Bree; these are people not animals. 'Alpha's' for heaven sakes!*

Rick caught sight of my discussion with myself. "Bree, you okay?"

"Yes, I'm fine, nothing to be concerned about." I saw them all looking at one another, I knew they were trying to gain access into my mind. Laughingly I told them, "Sorry, my thoughts are not open for discussion. Damn, I wish I had known about this talent earlier."

263

"Bree, how did you learn that? Steven, have you been teaching her?" Sandy asked a little miffed.

"Not me, this is new." Steven eyed me wryly. "Bree, what other surprises do you have in store for us?"

Sandy had her hands on her hips and her eyes narrowed as if that would help her squeeze into my mind. I could actually feel her trying to shove passed my barriers. I giggled as I narrowed my eyes back at her and entered her thoughts. *Oh dear, she is going to be a handful. Bill was right; she can be a pistol when she wants. Steven will have his hands full. Well, fuck, we all will have our hands full with this one. Why can't Madalyn just leave well enough alone, she isn't hurting a thing.*

I smiled as I came back from Sandy's thoughts, "I don't know until it happens. Can we eat now?" I placed my hand on the doorknob; satisfied that my abilities were growing.

"That's right, got to keep the little human fed," Rick teased. He grabbed Sandy's hand, pulled her close to him, and nipped at her neck; then he stole a glance at me. I think he thought he could pull me off guard, then sneak in and take a quick look around.

Rick was a very sensual individual. His smile was soft and sexy. His eyes were blue and piercing. He had stolen a piece of my heart. I didn't know when this had happened, but he had and he knew it. And I didn't think he would give it back. I think I might have even stolen a piece of his.

He was my solider, my protector, and my Hercules. I needed to keep my eye on him. He watched me; he cared for me and because of that I felt there was more to our past than I was currently aware of.

He had a smile that could turn you on and he knew it and played to it. I'd watched him with our waitresses since I'd met him. His eyes held their gaze as he spoke to them. He'd smile at them as they looked at him, making them believe they were the only two in the room.

I'd even noticed from time to time he'd tried it on me. The way he held my hands when he placed the bowling ball in the correct position, when we danced, even when he sat next to me, he would brush against me and smile.

I liked having Rick around though. I felt safe with him, but I most certainly did not want him rummaging around in my thoughts.

His tone was loudest of the group, and Sandy's, for a female, was equally as loud. Their sexual appetite for one another was strong.

Brad and Madalyn's purr seemed to match each other well; a proper purr for two very proper individuals.

Brad was sensual in his own way. He had always spoken softly to me. I always felt him watching me, not in a leering way like Nick's friend Jared, but more in an interested way, like I fascinated him. I was his mystery; that puzzle piece that was missing out of the box of five thousand pieces. When I would look up at him, he would always smile; he never turned away from me. Whenever he kissed me on the cheek, it was always slow and intentional. I felt that if I would turn my head just a fraction he would kiss me on the lips and not make any excuse for it.

Madalyn's hugs, when she gave them, were always motherly. Not a strong motherly hug, more like an elder would hug a younger member of the group.

I wasn't in their pack and I didn't know if I ever would be considered a part of it, not really. They'd all been together for so long. They were comfortable communicating with one another in their minds. Their secrets were kept better that way, no one to intrude on their thoughts. And Madalyn viewed me as an intrusion.

⌖

As we sat in our booth waiting for the food to arrive, the sky started to cloud over, making shadows on the ground. Those shadows didn't bother me. It was the shadows only I saw, the dark only I felt that had me concerned. I continued to watch the hills, looking for whatever it was that was out there.

"Bree," Steven said softly. "We'll leave about six-thirty, it'll be dark then. We don't have to go far; the bison are just up the road. We should be back by eight at the latest."

I nodded as the waitress arrived with our meals. Our conversations at the table seemed to be relaxed; but things weren't always what they seemed. Rick sat on one side of me, and Steven on the other.

I could feel the vibration from them. It was an extreme sensation and I had to breathe deeply to calm myself.

Rick's leg rubbed against mine. Even if I moved just a little and lost that contact, it wasn't long before his leg or his arm was against me. Touching, they were always touching. They seemed to need that contact.

I picked at my food. They were watching me; I didn't have to look at them to know. I took a chance to listen into their thoughts. I didn't want to be detected; I didn't want to intrude on the pack, but I was curious. I crept into their minds, and I quietly listened to their war of words.

Steven, honestly, what could possibly be worrying her? She doesn't understand us; I don't think she ever will, Madalyn said. She was frustrated with me. *You're still sure about her Steven? Thirteen years is a long time. I know, I know, the stories put you two together. But with everything that has happened, to you, to her, maybe it was just too much. Mortals are weak, Steven. Don't forget that; she is still mortal. How will she react when she knows about us? Can you tell me that Steven?* Madalyn demanded, an angry growl rattled deep in her chest.

Brad answered her growl with a more threatening one of his own, *Madalyn, I told you, to stop doing that. Steven will handle this. If you continue with this attitude I will send you home. I'm not going to allow you to ruin this,* Brad said. His tone was harsh with her, *She is staying; you need to deal with it! I know you two have a special bond, but that does not give you the right to act like this. You are pushing my patience. You may think she's weak, but that would be a very big mistake on your part.*

It's because we have that bond Brad; I needed to ask. Don't get cross with me. I have a lot at stake here too! I don't want him hurt, not like she has hurt him for the last thirteen years, Madalyn said, reminding them again of the years that had passed.

That wasn't Bree's fault Madalyn, Rick thought. *You and Sandy weren't there, but if you had been, I don't think you would be this uncertain. She can handle it. Let Steven tell her. Damn woman, why are you being so pissy with her? What has she done to you?*

I can understand Madalyn's concern, Rick.

I closed my eyes. Damn! Madalyn's threats had pitted Sandy against me too.

Sandy meekly continued, *You, Brad and Steven are so trusting on the past. She's been through a lot, and now you expect her to fall madly in love with Steven and all is well again. I know it looks like that at times, but maybe she's playing him. Maybe she's playing all of us. Don't you think this is just a little too much, a little too convenient? I mean Steven is very soft on the eyes, and she just came out of a bad marriage. Maybe she just wants a good-looking guy on her arm for a change. I mean, do you really think she is connected to us? She isn't even one of us and we all know she never really will be. She can't, she's a witch, a Druid Priestess, a powerful sorceress; or will be, and we are the undead. Remember? We are beneath her,* Sandy said.

My protector came to my rescue. *Don't you start too Sandy. What happened to 'Bree don't worry. Now you have women watching your back too', can you tell me that. I am so surprised at you. You were so excited and now you say this. She has been nothing but friendly to the both of you. I'm disappointed Sandy, I really am disappointed in you,* Rick said.

She has never thought of us as beneath her and you know it. Steven's thoughts were quiet to them as he reminded them, *Bill has never treated you that way, Millie has never treated you that way, and none of her family has ever treated you that way. Why would you think she would? Madalyn you have nothing to worry about, I will talk to her. She will understand.*

Why did she have us drink her blood? Madalyn spat. *What was that all about? I think this has all gone to her head. We hunt here all the time. What does she have to be concerned about? I think it was foolish and I think you three are acting foolish. What will you do if she doesn't understand, Steven? Will you leave us; will you leave me?* Madalyn asked.

Madalyn, if you continue with your treatment toward her, yes, I will leave. I will not hesitate one second. Know that! Steven's voice turned angry, I felt the energy rise in him and it worried me. This whole setup worried me. Where was this coming from? I was stunned. What had I done that was so terribly wrong? I was deep in thought as I finished my sandwich; my eyes absentmindedly looked through the trees. I stopped listening to them. I didn't want to hear any more. That's what I get for listening to others thoughts, I knew better.

I could feel Brad's vibration now, along with Steven's and Rick's. The sensation was amazing. I closed my eyes and listened to their sounds. I could tell whose was whose and it did fascinate me, I felt very comforted by it. Why was I noticing this? I heard nothing from Madalyn and Sandy's was very, very weak.

"Bree," Steven said breaking my concentration, "ready to go to the gift shop?"

I looked at my watch, five-thirty. I looked back outside, "No, not really, you'll be leaving soon. I think I would like to go back to the room and just relax. I guess I'm more tired than I thought," I smiled at him.

ে৯

He took me back to our room. I wasn't sure where the others went; I didn't hear that conversation. Steven closed the door, and I went to the bathroom to brush my teeth and wash my face. He stood in the doorway and I could see him through the mirror watching me, worry lines around his eyes. He wanted to tell me something, I could sense that much. I was content to wait. I didn't want to go tiptoeing through his mind to find the answers. "So tell me, what can I expect tonight?" I asked as I dried my hands. "Sandy mentioned you could bathe in Yellowstone Lake."

"What do you want me to tell you Bree?" I heard the tension in his voice. It still lingered from his conversation in the restaurant. His nerves were on edge and I didn't want to push to make it any worse.

I made sure I kept any hint of anger, or frustration out of my voice as I spoke and that was hard because I was frustrated. I was frustrated at them *and* at myself. Maybe I was pushing into their lives too quickly. Maybe I needed to slow things down. "I want you to tell me what I can expect. Will you be tired when you get back, or will you need to mediate? Will you be hungry? What can I expect, Steven? That's all I want to know."

"We should all be relaxed. We're all tension right now. People say things when they are stressed Bree. They don't mean them." He was looking for my reaction. There was a soft tap on the door breaking my concentration, but Steven continued to look at me. He wanted to continue our conversation. He wanted me to understand. The thing was - I thought I did understand. I had a long way to go to prove myself. Apparently according to Madalyn, thirteen years worth. There was another tap on the door.

"You need to answer the door. I'm sure everyone is eager to get going. Please be careful." I kissed him, put my headphones on, and listened to my music as I walked to the window and looked into the trees. I heard the door open, then close, and then I was alone. Night was falling and I wrapped my arms around myself, feeling scared but not knowing why. It's out there; I didn't know what 'it' was, but 'it' was there all the same.

❧

"What's wrong, Steven?" Brad asked as Steven stepped into the hall.

"I think she heard our conversation at dinner. I'm sure her feelings are hurt. I should have known better. She has been experiencing changes; trying new things. I should have known she would have tried that."

"But, how could she get into our minds? We have them locked from her for just such an incident."

"I don't know how she knows how to do the things she does; but she does. She can even feel everyone's contentment. She says we purr." That brought a smile to his lips.

"We purr. Never heard it put that way, but I guess I can see it. She can feel it?"

"Yeah, and she can hear it. It fascinates her."

"Wow, she's progressing quicker than I thought she would. Well, I don't know where Madalyn and Sandy came up with those thoughts. It's just not like them. I'm sure Madalyn is afraid of things changing between you two. But, damn...she can hear it, huh...amazing."

"I don't know either, but let's not mention this to either of them. I meant what I said Brad; I will take her away if Madalyn continues this childish game she's playing. Madalyn knew the score from the beginning; I'll not have her treating Bree this way. Shit Brad, I haven't been able to tell her about our situation yet! How do you think she is going to handle it with Madalyn acting like this? We should all just go back home now. Blow the reunion off; we've done what we set out to do. Bree's back with me, with us. Let me take her home, sit her down and tell her everything. Explain to her how we live."

Brad exhaled slowly, "Steven, give Bree a little more time to come to terms with everything. We'll explain the problem you and Madalyn have; we'll explain everything. I'll get a handle on Madalyn or I *will* send her home. Her actions are a concern, I agree, but I have no idea what got into Sandy. Rick's not happy with that little speech she gave at dinner, but he wants to handle it."

"I don't know what's going on in our females' heads. This is getting very complicated and it doesn't need to be! We have planned for this for too long for Madalyn to go and screw it up."

"Let's get this hunt over with and get back. Maybe this will help calm everyone, and then we'll talk with Bree."

⁊

I continued to look out the window; I didn't expect to see them walk out of the Lodge. They probably left from one of the other rooms. I just knew Madalyn and Sandy were content to have the three of them back to themselves. I shivered as I watched the dark shadow move across my window toward the trees.

Are you feeling sorry for yourself? That's not like you at all Bree, Odessa spoke.

Just feeling a little insecure, that's all. I shook my head to clear my thoughts, *Okay, I'm ready; what do you have to teach me?* I sat in the recliner and stared at nothingness. I turned off my music and took the headset off.

Your mind is growing on its own, child. Your magic is strong. Everything I thought I would need to instruct you on, you have mastered. We can practice if you like. I can answer your questions, but my teachings here are not needed. I will say I am impressed with your abilities. You can do more than others I have seen. Does this scare you? Odessa asked.

No, I'm not scared as much as I am confused. What started this? I don't understand. Two days ago I was normal, now I can hear their thoughts, move objects, feel and see their energy, why now Odessa?

Because, you have changed, you are aware of your path, your mind's making up for lost time. Remember you should have known about this life long ago. Mildred would have prepared you for this world. Now, you're learning about it and your abilities are developing at the same time, it must feel like everything is being rushed. It's not though. This is about the time your magic abilities would have started anyway. She laughed, *so it's a good thing you know about this now! Could you imagine how you would have felt if that bottle of shampoo came to your hands and you didn't know anything about this world?* We both started laughing. Odessa became serious again, *you are still human but your Magical side is very power-ful, Bree. All your thoughts and memories are rushing to the surface of your mind. I can only imagine how confusing it is to you. I fear this will cause your enemies to act sooner, once they learn how quickly you are advancing. You can't control it I'm afraid.*

We spoke for a while. She told me there were others like her, they were there to teach and help the Chosen Ones cross. I was curious, so I asked if she knew what I could expect the closer I got to the, well...in my mind, the end of this journey. But she said she didn't know because everyone was different. Some had visions, some had pain and others had absolutely no problems. She tried to help me understand the energy I felt when I was with my friends and Billy. We laughed when Odessa made the comment *their energy is strong in you my dear. Your nectar draws your loves to you, like bees to a flower.* Odessa smiled whimsically. Then she laughed a very robust laugh, *enjoy yourself Bree, good things await you. Trust me on that! Don't write them off just yet. You have a special bond with each of them; you just haven't experienced it yet. Close your eyes child; listen to the flute. Let your mind relax and tell me what you see.*

I settled back in the chair and closed my eyes. I took a few deep breaths as I listened to the melody of the flute. I let the melody take my mind where I needed to be. *I'm standing in a clearing, there are rocks littering the ground before me.*

What does your mind tell you to do?

I need to use the rocks; I need to make a circle with them. I have done this before. I was with a chieftain, no a shaman, I think Nez Perce.

Do that child; make the circle.

I saw myself gathering the rocks and making a circle. There were so many rocks; the circle grew. When I was finished, I felt the breeze on my face, my forehead cool as the perspiration dried. I felt the darkness again. I saw the shadow.

What does your mind tell you to do, child?

I need to be in that circle, I am protected there. I stood in the circle. The dark shadows came closer and my eyes followed them as they circled my stone enclosure. I still could not make them out; they were only faceless shadows moving with the wind. "Fire," I spoke, "I need your protection now, please light the way for me." Fire danced on the rocks I had laid in the circle, and the shadows moved back. I spoke to them, "The Earth is my protector, and I feel its energy. You have no place here; go back from where you came. You have no hold on me. You can't hurt me."

The shadows hissed their warning to me. "Death, we do control your death. Your end will come quickly, he needs to be whole."

"He will not be made whole. You have no place here, go back from where you came and walk this land no more." The shadows left; the music stopped. I stayed in the circle. As the flames extinguished I heard the music again and saw a white vapor move toward me. I was not afraid of this vapor and the words floated on soft whispers to me, "Remember what you have seen here. You need to remember." Then it was gone. I continued to take deep breaths. I continued to feel the breeze.

Alarm suddenly registered in my mind and I sat up straight, eyes wide. I got up and moved to the window. *What is it child, what do you see?*

"Something has happened." I closed my eyes and opened my mind. "It's dark, I can't make it out clearly. I can't see in this dark, but I just feel the fear. Someone is hurt."

I can't see anything Bree. Are you sure?

"Yes," I turned toward the door. "They're back, but they won't come for me. I need to go to them." I grabbed the room key off the desk on my way out, and went directly to Rick and Sandy's room and tapped on the door.

CHAPTER 21

"Bree, go back to the room. It's not safe for you now," Steven said. His voice was angry and I didn't understand why.

I stood there, with my hand on the doorknob and slowly turned the knob, but the door was locked. "Steven, let me in please."

"Bree, I'll not tell you again to go back to the room," he demanded. He was truly angry. That felt very out of place, I had never felt his anger...never. "I am very serious Bree; I don't have time for this," I heard him growl. It was a low deep rattle.

I stood there, I could hear cries of pain; the sound of a wounded animal and it was in great pain in that room. I needed to get in, and in my concern to accomplish this I had let my guard down and Madalyn's voice pushed into my thoughts. I felt her cold look; I sensed the sneer on her lips as she bared her minds fangs at me. Because I had allowed her to slip in, she drew control of my thoughts. Her mind towered over me. I saw the animal hidden inside her face. One minute I was able to make out the eyes of the animal, the next they would be her eyes. And those eyes loomed large in my mind as they flashed with her anger and that anger was being focused at me. Her hissed words flooded my ears. Her voice was ugly and her hoarse sounds echoed in my mind. I could feel her straining to hold back her rage, *Go back to your room child, like you were told. It's your fault she is injured, it's your fault she is in pain! Go away and leave us alone or you will regret this, I promise you that! You have done enough damage. Go away! I don't want you here messing up my world.* Her image quickly left my mind.

I was rattled; there was no denying that. I think the only thing that stopped her from doing me harm was the retaliation she would receive. That was the only thing keeping me alive. But, she *was* right about one thing; it was my fault. I'd told them they needed to hunt.

I heard the cry again. I couldn't stand out here and do nothing. Common sense told me to run, but something else was pulling me into that room, and that pull was greater than my common sense. I didn't understand it and my body struggled with my mind against it. But I knew one thing; I was going into that room one way or another. *Brad, please, I can help.* I sent my plea to him.

Not now Little One, it isn't safe. Sandy was attacked by a Traditional. She is not herself. I'm afraid if you come too close she will attack you. You are much safer in your room.

Bradley, she has my blood in her, she will not harm me. I need to help her, please let me in.

Sandy made a small plea, I heard her call my name. She sounded so weak. The door finally opened and Steven let me in. He grabbed my arm; the surprise was evident on my face. At that moment he realized my shock and his eyes quickly softened, but the damage had been done. I read his thoughts, *Damn it! I should have told her before we came; I should have explained everything. This is all getting out of control.*

Madalyn moved in front of me, drawing my attention to her and her face showed me her anger. Her chest heaved as she drew her breaths. Her struggle was very apparent, she was on the verge of losing control and I could not let that happen.

My mind saw everyone clearly. I watched as her eyes darted to Steven, and then back at me. She didn't move. She wanted to pounce. My mind could see Brad tensing as he held Sandy's shoulders to the bed. Rick stood, I saw my protector flex his shoulders, calculating his moves. I had had enough of this and it was not going to continue. She was not going to scare me into submission and I didn't want Rick to attack her. I had had enough of her treatment and I wasn't going to take it any more! Sandy needed me; I would sort this all out later.

I put my hand on Steven's, "Please let me go; I don't have time for this." My eyes showed him my hurt but my voice remained calm. He took his hand off me and I shoved past Madalyn. She needed to understand I wasn't going to take this treatment from her so I was forceful with my push. She didn't challenge me as I walked past her.

Brad was still holding Sandy down. She was twisting in agony. Her face and body were bloody; her hair was matted and her clothes were torn and wet. Her face was distorted with pain; but she recognized me. She knew; she instinctively knew I could help her. "Please," she mumbled so weakly.

As I walked toward the bed, Madalyn yelled at me, "You can't kill her; I'll not allow you to hurt her. I promise I will hunt you down if you harm her."

"That will be enough Madalyn, you will hush now!" My eyes looked hard at her, my breathing had increased and I needed to regain my composure, I needed to keep control over this situation.

Her panic sent Rick into a panic. He stepped in front of me, guarding his mate from me, "Bree, please don't hurt her; Brad can heal her."

"No, Rick, I can't," Brad said and the hopelessness registered on his face.

I didn't say anything to anyone as I tried to step around Rick to the bed. I finally had to put my hand on Rick's arm. "Richard," I began calmly, "I'm not here to hurt her; if you will move I can help her." My soft touch and manner calmed my Richard. He looked back at Sandy, her hard panting breaths increased, then back at me. "Please Richard, valuable time is being wasted. I promise I will make her better." Tentatively he stepped aside and I sat and held my arm out for Brad to take more blood. "Brad I need you to take another vial please; same size as the last three." My voice was firm and commanding. I had no idea why? I really didn't even recognize this person that was taking charge. I rolled up my sweatshirt sleeve as much as I could.

Brad didn't argue with me. "That will be fine Bree. I just need to get to the vein."

As I sat on the bed by Sandy I felt the tension in the room as she moved toward me. I sensed Rick flexing his hands, Steven moved closer, ready to pull me out of harms way should Sandy attack. But she wasn't going to pounce, she moved closer to me, curled up and begged for my touch. I allowed her to lay her head on my lap.

I placed my hand on her forehead and stroked her hair. I felt her pain start to leave her and enter my fingers. I shook my hand and threw the pain into nothingness. I could hear her soft moan of relief and I immediately placed my hand back on her head, drew more of her pain away and threw it into the air. I spoke the words quickly as they came to my mind. "Your wounds will heal and your soul will mend; I lay my hand upon your head. Your pain will leave and your health will return; in you life will still burn; the blood from me I will give to thee."

My pendant and the healing stone warmed on my chest as I spoke, giving me strength, comforting me. I held my hand over my chest as I felt the warmth. The sensation it gave me soothed my thoughts. I knew I didn't need to say the little verse I had just used, but I felt stronger saying it.

Brad was on the other side of Sandy ready for my nod to insert the needle. Sandy kept her head on my lap; her pain was lessening. I didn't feel the needle but I felt the pressure as Brad slid the vial in.

"All done," he announced as he drew the needle out and handed me the small glass cylinder.

Sandy continued to stay close to me. "Sandy," I spoke softly, "I need you to drink this please. You will heal quicker if you just drink it." Her arm tightened around my waist. I put a drop of blood on my finger and put it to her lips. "Sandy, I am familiar to you, I'll not let them hurt you." She licked the blood off my finger, but would not lessen her grip around my waist, I scooted back just enough so I could lean down and whispered into her ear, "Do you still hurt?"

"A little," she softly spoke to me.

I put another drop on my finger, and Sandy licked the blood, she sucked my finger in her mouth. I leaned back down to her. "Sandy if you will drink this, I promise you will feel much better." Then I gently kissed her neck, as I had seen her and Madalyn greet each other. "Please Sandy."

She smiled at me when I did that, rolled over, raised herself up on her elbow, as I handed the vial to her. She drank it all then curled back up close to me and laid her head on my lap. I continued to stroke her head as she rested. "Are you feeling better?"

"Yes, don't leave." Her arms tightened around me again.

Rick knelt beside me and I draped my arm over him, stroking the side of his face, running my hand through his hair. That seemed to relax him. He pressed against my side as my other hand continued stroking Sandy's wet matted hair. I was comforting them. Taking their pain and fright away. Rick rested his head against me; he put his arm around my waist and held Sandy's arm.

"I'm not going anywhere." I didn't look at Steven or Madalyn. I looked at my arm then at Brad. I smiled as I motioned with my head toward my waist, "I don't think I could move even if I wanted."

He gave me a smile, his eyes moved to the hold my Richard and Sandy had around me, "No, you aren't going anywhere."

"I think I'm getting better at you taking my blood."

He smiled back. "I'm sorry I was short with you. Bree, how did you know your blood would heal her?"

I shrugged my shoulders. "I just put two and two together, I heal quickly and everyone wants my blood because of its properties. That's why I gave it to you all earlier. I had a bad feeling about tonight and that was the only thing I could think to do to protect you. You were all so hell-bent on coming here; you didn't want to be told to do something by a weak human. I think the little bit of blood I gave her earlier bought her a little more time. What happened exactly?" I continued to stroke Sandy's hair and Rick's face; I could feel both of their vibrations again.

Brad recounted the story, "We had just finished our hunt and went to the lake to clean up. Sandy was making up..." he cleared his throat, "she and Rick were getting a little frisky; we were teasing them. Sandy ran off into the shadows wanting Rick to follow as he normally always does." He looked at Rick. "All we heard was the scream. There were three of them; I don't think they expected us to react as quickly as we did. But our answer was swift and we got her back here as quickly as we could. I knew there wasn't anything I could do; damn, I hate that feeling of helplessness."

Everyone remained quiet, "Sandy, are you feeling better?" I asked.

"Yes," she said quietly.

"Would you like to sit up?"

"Not yet."

"Okay, would you like Rick to sit here?" I asked, starting to feel a little awkward.

"Not yet?" she whispered.

"Okay." I continued to stroke her hair. "Your wounds are healing; I don't think there will be any scaring. I'm kind of an authority on that, ya know. You want to talk?"

"My life almost came to an end Bree. If you hadn't been here it would have ended!" She started to cry and held me tighter.

"Okay, you can look at it that way or..." I thought this a good time to teach them about changes in paths. "If I wasn't here, if I hadn't come back into your lives, you wouldn't have been here tonight. You wouldn't have been attacked..." She let go of my waist and quickly tried to pull away from me. Rick still held her arm.

"Don't ever think that. I'm so sorry I thought all of that earlier at dinner. I was so wrong and weak. Please forgive me. I'm glad you're in our lives. I'm glad you're my sister. Our path has been corrected! I can't imagine our clan without you now. You and Steven," I watched her eyes glance at him. "He belongs to you and you him. That's all there is to it. *You* belong here and *you* belong to us and I'll not allow anyone to hurt you." Then she just broke down and cried. They were hard tears; she shook off Rick's hold and wrapped her arms around me, pulling me tight to her. She softly kissed my neck.

I was not prepared for this! I hugged her back and let her cry. It was all I could think to do. I started rocking back and forth. I guess she taught me something too. "It's okay, everyone was tense. People say things they don't mean when they're stressed. I heard that somewhere." I smiled, yes, I had heard it from Steven, but that was not enough to excuse his and Madalyn's actions this evening. "Sandy, Rick really needs to hold you right now and I need to talk to Steven. You're going to be all right. We'll all see to that."

"Bree, how did you know I was hurt?"

"I didn't know it was you. I felt Steven, Rick, and Brad's feelings. I knew someone was hurt, I just didn't know who it was. I felt everyone return, and when I left my room I knew to come here." I unwound her arms from my waist, and she placed my hand on her chest, I could feel the vibration, and I smiled. Sandy had accepted me as a friend and I was happy with that. I still heard nothing from Madalyn.

I started to get up and move away but my Richard had other ideas. He picked me up and hugged me. He buried his head in the crook of my neck and I could feel his tears against my skin. I ran my hand through his hair and hugged him tightly. He set me down and kissed me. "Thank you Bree." He whispered it so very softly. I placed my hand on his chest, felt the strong tone of his purr, and smiled. I kissed his cheek and started to move away and he took my face in his hands. "You're part of this family Bree, understand?" Then he kissed me again. I smiled and went to stand by Steven.

☙

"I assume we have some talking to do," Steven whispered in my ear.

I looked at him for a long minute. "Yes, Steven, you have no idea how much talking we will be doing." I turned back to Rick and Sandy, "Rick, I think you need to take Sandy back and maybe two or three hours meditation should bring both of you back to normal. We'll pack your things and bring them back. Brad, are you and Madalyn okay?"

Brad was watching me. He had a small smile on his face. I looked at him as I tried to read his expressions. He was excited; I could feel that. He'd found his puzzle piece. He looked at Steven, then back at me.

Steven gave him a slight nod then he took my hand and kissed it. I couldn't tell if Steven was happy or relieved but I didn't pull my hand away. I wasn't as mad at Steven as I was hurt, but I knew I wouldn't stay that way with him for long. He would tell me why Madalyn was angry with me and he would explain why he growled at me.

Brad thought into my mind; *we need to talk Little One*. With all the drama I had let my guard down again, a mistake, and one I *would* correct. I should have listened to what he had thought to Steven. I had no idea what he was talking about and I continued to watch him. *I know you heard me*, he smiled and I smiled back. My eyes stayed with him as Steven helped Rick.

Madalyn stood next to Brad. She took his hand, drawing a hard look from him. Madalyn looked back at me, she cowed in her approach toward me, "Bree, I need to apologize to you as well. I thought some awful things earlier and they were unwarranted. You and Steven are meant for each other and I was...wrong. I have no idea why I thought you would hurt Sandy. Would you please forgive me?" She looked at Brad and Steven, and then came to hug me. She was a little unsure of how I would react. Hell, I was unsure how I would react! But...I was beginning to understand what was happening.

I hugged her back, but my anger wasn't subsiding. Madalyn had dropped enough hints. Her actions tonight and her words outside this door were finally registering with me. She and Steven had a special bond. I had even heard her say that.

I glanced at Brad; he was watching my reaction. I tried not to give him one, but I was sure I failed miserably. The numbness had set in; everything seemed to be in slow motion as I patted her back, "Madalyn, don't give it another thought."

Brad hugged me, and then looked at Steven, "I think Madalyn and I can clean up here. I think you two need to talk. Steven, I'll leave it to you to explain. Go back to your room and we'll see you back in Vegas. Maybe we can meet for a late drink." He looked for my approval. I stayed uncommitted, but he kissed my forehead. "We'll see you soon, right Bree?"

"Yeah, soon," I gave him a weak smile and left the room.

CHAPTER 22

Back in our room, Steven quietly spoke, "I don't know what to say, Bree. I'm sorry, doesn't seem to be enough. I love you and I worry about you. It's hard for me to not try to protect you. You don't seem to need it though; not any more, and I'm finding that hard to deal with. That's why I grabbed your arm; I didn't know what Sandy's intentions were. But you seemed to know. You're changing and I want more time with you like this."

I didn't say anything as I started to pack. I stood at the bed and thought about the toiletries I had in the bathroom. One by one, they started floating into the bedroom, past Steven, and each waited until I reached to take it from the air and pack it away.

"Impressive," Steven watched the parade of soap, lotions, and shampoo. He gave a sigh, "When did this start?"

"This morning, when I was taking a shower. The shampoo was by the sink, as soon as I thought about it, the bottle came to my hand. I was practicing while you were hunting.

I was going to put on a demonstration for you when you got back." I looked at Steven and the shampoo bottle waited an appropriate amount of time then softly tapped me on the shoulder. I smiled and packed it away and zipped the suitcase closed. I sat on the edge of the bed, looking around the room, waiting on Steven to continue with his explanation to me.

He remained quiet and that quiet hung between us, and it bothered me. Someone needed to speak so I began.

"Steven, it's not that I don't need you to protect me, I do. But there are going to be times when I need you to trust me. I wish I could explain how I know what I know."

My eyes watered and I blinked to stop them. "We're going to be together a long time, Steven. You really need to believe me." I walked over to him. His arms were folded across his chest. He wouldn't meet my eyes, and I didn't force him to. I got as close to him as I could without touching him. "Steven, I promise you, I'll not put myself in harms way if I know I can't handle the situation. I promise I will listen to you. But when it comes to my family, our family, sometimes I might know best; and you and our families are going to have to accept that."

He dropped his arms to his side. I placed my hand on his chest; the vibration was there but not as strong as before. I moved in closer, "What's wrong?"

"There is so much you need to learn, our ways are not yours and I fear you will reject them. You will be treated differently after tonight in our family." He stood still. I left my hand on his chest, his vibration slowed, and that worried me. Was he not content with me anymore? Did he want Madalyn more than me? What had changed between us in the short time from this morning to cause this?

"Steven, teach me then. Tell me what to expect. I'm not going anywhere, you and I will bond and nothing will change that. You do want to bond with me, don't you?" My voice was starting to rise. "Do you not want me to be your mate? Have I changed that much? Steven, damn it! Please, look at me. Do you prefer Madalyn over me?" I hadn't meant for my insecurity to come out like that, but it did and I couldn't suck the words back in.

His eyes widened in surprise, my heart raced for fear he didn't want me now the way I wanted him. "No, Bree. No, I don't want Madalyn over you. God, put that thought out of your mind. Bree, I am bonded to you now. I want you for my mate now. I would marry you right this second. However, before you accept that, you need to understand *everything* you are getting yourself into. Our ways will seem strange to you, but this is how our kind has lived for hundreds of years. It's a deep instinct in us that no amount of changes in our lives can stop." He wrapped his arms around me and pulled me into his chest. "I love you so much."

"Talk to me then, teach me Steven. You said I would be treated differently after tonight. Will they not want me around anymore? I don't want to be made to leave you again, Steven. Please tell me." My ear rested on his chest, the vibration was almost gone now. If he wanted me, why then was my tone fading? Questions were spilling from my lips and I just wanted his reassurance.

"Bree," he inhaled deeply, "God you smell so delicious. Bree," he exhaled, "We should have told you this last night, but Brad felt you should hear this from me and in private.

He wants you to be comfortable to express yourself." Steven laughed, I wasn't laughing. "I want you to let me tell you everything, I'll give you plenty of opportunity to ask questions, understand?" I nodded. He walked me over to the chair, sat down, and pulled me onto his lap.

"Bree," he held my hand in his, entwined our fingers and rubbed the back of my hand with his thumb. "With your actions this evening, you have become the co-leader in our clan. Clans are connected; we are a tight family. Our family has lacked the female version of a leader, someone to step in when the male counterpart is absent. In your case, you took charge even with Brad present and he allowed it. He was comfortable with your decisions. By all rights, Madalyn should have been a leader with Brad, but she's more of a follower. She couldn't step in if he wasn't around... but you could. Brad has led us all these years without the help of one. Someone he could confide in, work things through with. And as a clan we've lacked the guidance of her. You don't understand how much a clan relies on the female leader. Just as mortal families rely on the mother of the family, we rely on her. I know that may sound a bit odd to you, I mean, Rick and I are self sufficient on our own, but we live and work as a clan. And now, you have now stepped into that role. Whether you wanted it or not, it is you who will attend the summits with Brad when we go to the gatherings." He shifted a little and I sensed something else was coming.

"Steven, I don't see the problem. Okay, so now I have leadership responsibilities. What's the big deal?"

"Bree, you and Brad share more than leadership rolls. You have a bond to him." His eyes stared into mine looking for the recognition to his words. I could feel his hand tighten just a hair as he held my hand.

"Bond? What kind of bond?" My stomach was starting to flutter. Miniature butterflies were starting their dance deep inside me.

Steven cleared his throat, "You are Brad's leader...mate. You share a...you two are...will...Damn, why can't this be simple? You will be as close to Brad as you are with me. You and Brad share an intimate bond. You will attend the summits with Brad as his mate." His words rushed out of his mouth so quickly they took me by complete surprise.

The shocked look on my face must have scared him. "Bree...you will still be my mate." That didn't help my shock! "Say something," he begged.

"No!"

"No, you don't want to say anything?"

"No, I don't want to be Brad's mate, Steven. I want to be yours. Brad is married to Madalyn and I'll not do anything to come between them, she hates me enough as it is. I can only imagine what this will do!"

He cleared is throat again, "Madalyn...has other issues. That's something else I need to explain to you." He released my hands and wrapped his arms around my waist. I knew then I wasn't going to like this explanation. "Bree...Princess," he smiled a reassuring smile at me. "Madalyn and I share a bond too." He strengthened his hold around me.

I froze. "Why?" That was the only word I could push through my clinched teeth.

He looked away; I watched his jaw muscles tighten. I watched his Adam's apple move as he swallowed. He looked back at me, his eyes begging mine to understand. "Because,

I 'turned' her. Remember, Brad wasn't there. Rick and I were supposed to meet him at the hospital he and Madalyn worked at. He wanted to talk with us about something. Brad was late coming in and Madalyn was already there. A delivery wagon ran her down; the horse was spooked, she was walking to work. Anyway, she was smashed between the wagon and a wall. I was there, Brad and Rick weren't. I never really cared all that much for her, but Brad was happy with her. She told me they had been talking about getting married. I figured that's what Brad wanted to talk with us about, and there she was…dying." He released his hold on me; he sensed I wasn't going to run away. His hand washed over his face. "What was I supposed to do, let her die? So, when the attending nurse left the room I…'turned' her. She was the first person I had bitten since I became… a non-com," he laughed at Billy's description of their group. "I moved her out of the exam room and wheeled her down to the morgue and stayed with her until Brad and Rick got there. Brad drained one of the fresher corpses and we fed that to her…"

I must have made a face as he told me this.

"Sorry, but she did have to drink. Anyway, we took her away. We had to keep her away from humans until she calmed. We lived in the mountains up in Canada during that time, slowly reintroducing her around humans, until we were sure she'd be okay. It took the bond about two years to develop between us. Normally it happens immediately, but because she and I weren't close when she was human; Brad thought that had something to do with it. But every year at the four solstices, our bodies burn for one another." He stopped and looked at me.

My eyes were wide with all the knowledge he had just imparted. I kept them wide so the moisture that had built would not overflow the rims of my eyes if I blinked. He could see my breathing had increased, he felt my tension level grow! "Our body's burn, Princess. My heart does not. Madalyn is not someone I care deeply for. Brad knows that." He saw the pain on my face and I guess he figured he might as well tell me everything else. "None of this is simple now."

"Why?" I managed to say, it startled him.

"You weren't supposed to be a leader in our clan for starters."

"Didn't the stories say I would play a major part in your clan?" I reminded him.

"Yes, but we all thought that had to do with my House not our clan."

"Why can't Brad confide in Madalyn? Just because she isn't a strong leader doesn't mean she can't listen, make suggestions, things a spouse would do for her husband!" My voice was a little on edge; I was searching for a solution to this problem. But even if I found a solution to my problem, Steven and Madalyn would still need to be together.

"When it comes to hard decisions, sometimes even life and death decisions, Madalyn would be more of a hindrance than a help," he said dryly. "We all go to the clan gatherings, but Madalyn never attends any of the summits. Madalyn knows she's not a leader and she never wanted that role. Even when she was human, she did exactly what Brad told her to do, no argument. You, on the other hand, push. You've always argued your points with Brad, and hell, even with me. You even argue with Rick and Bill. You make yourself heard. You need that kind of strength in these summits."

"Okay, maybe I'm a little thickheaded here. I will attend as co-leader of our clan; I just don't understand why we have to be...you know...close."

"Bree, leaders in families such as ours are usually mates. They need to be connected to one another. You will understand it better as you and Brad spend more time together. Your bond needs to be tight and by being intimate, being comfortable with one another will strengthen that bond."

I started laughing, "Steven that is the dumbest thing I have ever heard. You don't think Brad and I are connected already? Hell, I am so connected to this group it isn't even funny. Brad and I can be close, intimate as you put it without being, well, intimate. I don't have to go to bed with someone to know or like them. I respect Brad; we can work this part out. Stop worrying about that."

"Bree," he said a little firmer. "I'm not worried about it because it's final. You are Brad's leader-mate, and you two share an intimate bond, Madalyn and I share an intimate bond. End of discussion."

"End of discussion? Excuse me!" My voice even surprised me. "Steven this discussion is far from over." I got off his lap and started pacing. My heart rate increased, those butterflies were now large dragonflies and they were all over the place in my stomach! "I don't think so, not going to happen, nope. I like Brad and everything, just not in that manner. Tell me how you expect me to do this." I was getting mad and my pacing increased. "Tell me how you can accept this. Tell me how you could allow another man to take me to his bed and screw me like you do. Can you tell me that, Steven? What about what you said earlier, huh, what about that?"

He looked at me confused, "What are you talking about?"

"Earlier this morning, you said I belonged to you and only you. Now you're telling me I'm Brad's mate as well. Damn it, this can't be happening. I do not understand this Steven." I started chewing on my fingernails.

He got up from the chair and took my hands in his. "Okay, calm yourself; let me finish explaining the way our kind lives so you *do* understand. We don't view sex the same as mortals."

I didn't think it possible for my eyes to get any wider than they already were, but they did. "Oh really! Well that's just peachy! I view what we have as special Steven, I'm sorry to hear you don't!"

"Aubrey Marie I didn't mean it like that, now stop it and listen to me!" He wrapped his arms around me; damn he was strong! Then continued talking softly to me. "Princess, what you and I share, none can replace. I have never felt that with anyone else. We share an eternal love that is so strong, so deep, so warm, and so very special. It's so much more than sex, and I meant what I said. You are mine, you and I belong together and nobody will ever separate us. When I said we don't view sex the same as mortals I meant...well, shit, I meant just that. We Magicals care deeply for one another and we have a very intense need to show others how much we care for them. We love each member of our clan and there are times we need to show someone just how deeply we care. Would you not agree that is a very special way to show someone how much we care for them?"

"Yes Steven I would. That's why we reserve it for the *one*," I held up one finger, "we love so very much."

"Well, that's a little selfish don't you think?"

My eyes widened yet again! "No Steven, I don't think it's selfish. It's all I have to give to you to show you how special you are to me. That intimate act is shared with only you. No one else! But now you're telling me you have not only been intimate with Madalyn but Sandy too! And..." The wheels in my mind were turning so fast, my eyes grew large with recognition and the thoughts I had scared me. I pushed against him but he held me tight. "Oh, no, no, no! Are you telling me I have to...with...Rick as well!"

"You care for Rick, don't you?"

"Yes..."

He interrupted me before I could complete my thought. "Then why can't you show him?"

"Steven, I care for Rick but I don't want to sleep with him! For that matter I don't want to sleep with Brad! I'll give them a greeting card pouring out my love for them!"

I felt the chuckle he tried to hide, "Princess, I'm afraid that will not suffice with your Richard. For that matter, Brad will not stand for it either." Then he just started laughing, "But I would like to see you try that!" He saw I wasn't laughing and he saw the panic in my eyes.

"Oh, shit, I get it now. I'm sorry, I didn't see this before now. Bree it's hard for you right now because you are still human and you view this as having an affair. You're not having an affair in our eyes. Everything is above board; nothing is done behind anyone's back. We even ask permission of their mates, and we are very discrete about all of this. You will never see any of us fawning over another's mate in their presence."

He started swaying with me; he kissed the top of my head. "I didn't explain this very well, let me try again and I want you to listen. You and I will always be together, make no mistake about that. Let's start with the leaders. Generally the leaders are mates and if you were Brad's mate I could not ask Brad to allow me to spend time with you. That's your call!" He smiled, "I serve at your discretion. But you're not his mate - you're mine. *BUT*, you are still a leader, so by all rights, Rick or any other male member of our family, except for me, can't ask to spend time with you. You have to initiate it. Now, Brad on the other hand is a leader and he does not need to seek my permission to be with you, *BUT*, you do have a say whether you want to allow him his...pleasures," he smiled. "He pretty much needs your blessing, he just can't demand to be with you when he wants to...see that's the dominance you have over him, you being the female..." He searched for his word and I offered, "Alpha." He smiled, "our Alpha...Alpha female... how's that?"

I nodded.

"Okay we'll go with that. You, being the Alpha female, will dominate Brad in that respect. You dominate all of us in that respect, well, except me. Okay, the leaders are out of the way...now lets take Rick as an example. You will find...the more you are around him...your heart will pull you toward him. Sometimes," he watched me, "sometimes I too find my heart being pulled toward Sandy. It doesn't diminish what we have, if anything it strengths us...it strengthens our family bond. We are so close to one another it's natural for us. Now we only do this within the clan. If one of us should stray outside of the clan that is not accepted and it wouldn't bode well for the member that did."

"But you dated, Steven!"

"Yes, because I didn't have a mate. We still date to try to find that special person Bree. We aren't total barbarians, and besides I was trying to keep your enemies attention off of you!"

"So then what would you do if a mate strayed? Divorce them?" I said sarcastically.

"No...we would need to kill them," he said firmly. "When we are as close as we are, when we are intimate with each other, we form a link. Our thoughts are linked and we can't have an ex-member out there able to get into our thoughts. It's drastic, I'll agree, but the safety of the clan trumps all. Bree, I love you and I am willing to leave this clan and only be with you. I am willing to take you away and give you your one mate for all of eternity."

"Wouldn't they need to kill you?" I still had a touch of sarcasm in my voice.

He smiled, "Because of who *you* are, they are willing to make an exception. But I would still have my problem with Madalyn four times a year. We don't know what would happen to either of us if we separated. No one can answer that question; Brad has researched it and researched it. We had hoped that you would accept our ways and this would just be a small inconvenience. Brad would be with you during two of those times and since you are one of the leaders you could choose to be with anyone else if you wished during the others. Or you could be with Brad during all four. I don't want you alone; I know how your mind works. I don't want those little insecurities creeping in when I'm not there." He laughed, "Rick thinks he understands you more than anyone and I will agree he reads you very well, but...I know you." He tipped my chin up to look into my eyes, his mouth enveloped mine, and I melted in his arms.

It was quiet in our room as he calmed my fears. When he felt I had been sufficiently calmed, "Are you ready to go back or do you have more questions? Brad needs to talk with you and Rick and Sandy want to see you. We also have two new members we need to introduce you to. They're still a little wild. We're working with them, but they can't greet you. They've tasted a lot of human flesh so we want to ensure they have totally calmed."

He stood there swaying with me. I was quiet a little longer than he liked, "Ask your questions, Princess."

"What happens at the gatherings?" I closed my eyes as I asked; resigned to the fact this was what it was. I would have to accept it or leave. I didn't want to leave but I didn't know if I could accept this so willingly.

"Clans gather on the spring and fall solstice. In the fall, we select new members into our clan, in the spring they are either accepted or rejected into the clan by all the members. You will go to these summits with Brad as his mate. You will take the list we give you and try to bring them into our clan. They have the right to reject our offers. The rest of us will be there, but we won't be around you very often, we have other duties while we're there and we will socialize with other clans,"

I froze and he felt it."

"Aubrey, I explained that, we will socialize, that's all. This is the only time during the year we do socialize with others, well, except when we come to the reunion. At the spring gathering, if we are accepting the members we picked in the fall gathering, we ready them for the Ceremony of Acceptance. They pledge their loyalties, and all that stuff. Around January we receive notice of those that want to join clans. We review the listing and at the spring gathering you and Brad will make the ones we chose aware we will be watching them over the next couple of months. Then at the fall gathering, we will give you a list of who we want you to extend the tentative offer too. After each gathering ends, our clan goes on a hunt to celebrate and that's when Madalyn and I take care of our little problem."

"Steven, if you were with Madalyn during the year, would that help your 'problem'?"

He continued to sway with me, I felt him softly kiss the top of my head. "I don't...choose to be with her all that often, Princess. I told you I don't feel that deeply for her. If she wasn't in our clan, if she wasn't mated to Brad, I wouldn't...choose her as someone I wanted to be with. It happens, that's why the vetting process is as stringent as it is." He felt me tense again. "Sweetheart, we'll work through this." His arms tightened around me, "Come on; let's get back and everything will work itself out. I promise." He went and got the bag off the bed, and collected the camera bag and our cloaks.

I wrapped my arms around myself and stood at the window, looking out into the blackness. It had started to rain; the weather was matching my mood. The sky was crying with me. I saw my reflection in the window; Steven was behind me. The sadness I felt was in my reflection. The dreams I had, washed away with each drop as it ran down the windowpane.

I understood the dream I'd had, the story the wind told me. *Their ways are not yours but his love is strong. Others will love you too. You will always be of the one, but you must take the others too.* I didn't want Steven to see the tears, the anger, or the hurt I was feeling.

"Please, Bree, don't turn away from me. I can't change any of this. I know it's hard for you to understand, but you have to."

I shook my head, wiped my tears and turned back to look at him. I wasn't mad anymore; I realized if I wanted to be with Steven, I would have to share him with others. I had to accept this way of life or leave and I wasn't sure which I was going to pick. My family values were being tested and I didn't know if I would pass or fail.

"You need to stop looking at this in human terms," he spoke to me softly.

All my bottled up emotions came out. Brad was wise to have him tell me in private. Steven was going to get my reaction! "I am human Steven. How else am I supposed to look at it? I'm not a polygamist. I don't share well. I'm an only child and I don't share well at all, and I'm very jealous. Can you not see this from my side?" I pleaded. "I am trying to deal with all of this as a human, because that's what I am. I haven't lived your life."

"This was the hardest thing I needed to tell you." He tried to judge my temperament from my body language, but my human side was at a loss to him. They had lived so long this way; they had forgotten what it was like to be human.

303

My hand was rubbing my forehead; panic was filling my stomach. What next, what would be asked of me next? I was venturing into a very strange world. None of this was ever brought out in movies. Vampires were supposed to bite you, drink your blood, and leave you spent. Now I had clan issues to deal with, Traditionals who wanted me dead. I needed to transform into a powerful sorceress, and if I lived through that then I would sit on the Council so I could help lead my 'kind', for lack of a better word. And I find out they accept intimacy with one another as a way of showing how much they care! Polygamy, now I'm into polygamy. I took both hands and pressed them against my head. *This just can't be happening. This is just a damn soap opera.*

He put his hands behind me and pulled me to him. His kiss was cool on my lips and it was a very loving kiss; I relaxed in his arms. His vibration was still there. I rested my hand on his chest deciding this was too much to deal with right now. I'd let the future take care of itself. Why was I the only one that had to change, that had to accept? Why couldn't they make some changes? Maybe I would be able to make changes, bring my values, and mix them with their ways. Maybe I could change some of this to make it more comfortable to me.

CHAPTER 23

We arrived back in Vegas and I felt Steven's neck. The hunt had done its job. I felt his strength, his lust to kill subsided; but our conversation in Yellowstone had left him worried. "You need to order your Drink please."

"Okay," he smiled, "Tell me, oh clairvoyant one, do I need one or two?"

I leaned against the counter, "You, Brad, and Madalyn need one; Sandy and Rick will need two. I would like a complete bottle of wine to myself. Steven, you need to get out of those wet clothes, I forgot all about those. I'll let Brad and Madalyn know we're back and order room service. You aren't to bother Sandy and Rick; they still need another hour or so of meditation."

❦

Steven went to shower and change clothes. I needed to talk to Odessa. *Odessa, did you know about this? Nothing. Odessa, I know you're here somewhere. Please, I need to talk to you.*

Yes, Bree, I was aware of what was happening. I couldn't tell you because you would have changed the course. If you knew of this prior, would you have helped Sandy?

Good question, but I smiled. *I would, yes, I would have.*

This needs to happen, Bree. I know it is not your way, but it is your clan's way, and it is your destiny.

How is this my destiny? I questioned.

You must live this life if you want others to follow you. They will listen because they know you live as they do. You will be challenged many times as you travel down this path. Many things will be strange to you. For you to develop you must experience them. Some will be pleasant and some will not be as pleasant. This, at the very least, should be a pleasant experience for you. I felt her smile a comforting smile in my mind.

Others have led; they didn't have to live through all of this. Will Steven and I always be together? The fear I had at being separated from Steven was enormous. We had just come back together and now all of this was happening. I felt that as long as I was with him everything would be fine. At least that was my hope.

You personally know they didn't live through their pain? You know they never had challenges to overcome? They may not have had the same problems you are now facing, but they had their own demons to fight. You needn't worry about Steven, his love for you is as strong as yours is for him. You will always be one. This can never change, she assured me.

My thoughts turned to Brad and Madalyn. *Brad, we're back.*

I know Bree; soon as Maddie is finished changing we'll be up. Bree, are you all right? His thoughts were tight; I could tell he was worried.

Yes…no…I don't know. Just a little stunned I guess; no, make that a lot, not a little. I need to shower and change as well; we'll see you soon. Leave Rick and Sandy alone, they still need their rest.

I ordered room service from the special number Steven always called. I watched him as he came out of the bathroom in his boxers, still drying off his chest. His hair was wet. I stood in the doorway watching him for a short while, trying to understand how all of this was spiraling out of control. I wanted him all to myself. Yes, I was selfish; I didn't want to share. Now I realized he never really was all mine. I'd shared him all along and that brought tears to my eyes. I quickly went to take my shower.

☙

By the time I was done, Brad, Madalyn and room service had arrived. I stood in the doorway of the bedroom watching them. Steven was pouring everyone a Drink. He sensed me and I could tell he sensed the panic in me. I felt his fear, his worry that everything was slipping out of his control too. He handed Madalyn her glass, "Her orders," as he motioned toward me. Madalyn came to greet me. She hugged me this time, but I could feel it was forced. She tried to act normally, but I felt the resentment.

Bree, I heard Odessa, *close your mind to the others for a while, I sense you need to rest.*

Gees, Odessa; ya think?

Brad came to me, and stood in front of me, blocking my view of Steven. Did he feel this would help the situation? If

307

I couldn't see Steven would I accept my roll in the clan, my roll with him? "We need to talk." Then he kissed my lips. It was a tender kiss. My heart did flutter and that caught me off guard, but I didn't let on.

"Have you had your Drink yet?" I was able to ask. My lips trembled slightly and I swallowed back the tears.

"Not yet," he answered and smiled. He sensed my nervousness.

"Then drink your Drink and please let me have mine. I think I'm going to need it. Maybe even something stronger."

He smiled.

Steven handed me a glass of wine, I felt his neck, then his chest. The familiar vibration was still strong. He leaned in and kissed me, *I love you; know this. There is no one I want more than you.* "Madalyn and I are going to meet our newest members. We'll see you downstairs."

The door closed and Brad and I were alone in the room, I suddenly felt very shy. "Care for any more wine?" he asked.

"No, I haven't even touched this one yet. Give me a minute, won't you?"

"Take your time Bree, I know this is a lot for you to grasp all at once. We'll take it slow." He finished his Drink then poured himself a glass of wine. He brought the bottle with him, took me by the hand, and led me to the sofa. He sat there for a few minutes then got up to sit in the chair facing me. "Well, Bree, you never cease to amaze me." Brad was smiling.

"I'm so happy you see the humor." My retort did not upset him.

"Drink your wine, my dear. We have a lot to discuss."

I could feel his vibration where I sat. I pressed my hand to my chest and he quieted his tone, just a fraction. I immediately looked at him and he smiled. "Ah, Steven told you." He raised his eyebrows in answer to my question.

He sat in his chair watching me, observing me. "Our world is strange to you." This wasn't a question; he was making an observation.

"Yes, Bradley, it is."

"Bradley? Am I in trouble?" He charmed me with his smile as he continued to watch me. I continued to drink my wine. The room remained quiet. The clock on the desk was the only sound in the room. He was expecting an answer to his question and was content to wait. So was I and I continued to drink my wine until it was gone. He came, sat beside me, and poured more wine into my glass. With his arm on the back of the sofa, he played with my hair, smiled at me and went back to sit in his chair. I smiled. I felt his energy; it was strong inside me causing the hairs on my arms to rise.

"Bradley," I began, he smiled as I spoke; he had won the silent contest, "you are not in trouble. I fear we are all in trouble, you, me, Steven and Madalyn. Nothing good can come of this."

"Bree, it has worked for years. Why do you think it won't continue?"

"It has worked because you are all vampires, you accept these facts, but now you have the human element, me. That was something you hadn't counted on."

He took a drink of his wine. The quiet was back for a short while, and then, "Yes Bree, I hadn't counted on that.

I don't know why I didn't. I didn't count on you becoming my partner. I have searched for one, but you were right under our noses. Madalyn isn't a strong leader; she knows this. Even as a child you were independent, stubborn." He laughed at his memories. "Or maybe I had counted on it. Did that thought ever occur to you?"

I looked at him and smiled an impish grin, "No Bradley, you had not counted on this."

"You won't be human that much longer, that should make it easier."

"Bradley, the human side of me runs deep. It will always be difficult. I have to retain my human emotions to be able to do what is expected of me. My path is far more complex than you realize. Even more than my family realizes." I patted the cushion next to me, "Please come and sit by me, distance will not change things now." His eyes registered my comment. He came and stiffly sat next to me. I waited and he started to relax. He was finally able to place his arm behind me; his fingers played with my hair.

"Take us into your confidence Bree. I don't think you were meant to walk this path alone. All of this has happened for a reason. We love you too much to let you do this by yourself."

I was relaxing with him, probably with the help of the wine. "Bradley, there is a part of this path none of you can help with; it must be done by me alone."

"You know this how?" he asked.

"When I woke this morning, after Steven and I loved last night, all those memories came flooding back into my mind. Things even you didn't know, my family doesn't know. Some are still hazy, I don't know what they mean or when I will need those particular ones, but they are there now. When I need the knowledge, it will be there. It was a dangerous path when I only had Steven to consider. His love for me will most certainly get in the way. Now, I have our love to consider." I looked at him. "It burns doesn't it? The desire in you burns. Your want is strong, not as strong as Steven's, but strong. You are bonded to me in a similar way Steven is bonded to Madalyn." I felt older somehow as I sat there with him. We were equals and talking with him in this manner was comfortable.

He finished his wine. "Yes, Bree, it does burn. I thought, as I sat here, I could overcome these feelings. I stupidly thought I could control myself, but I do want to be with you in a way *I* was not even prepared for. I knew when you *joined* us; we would spend time together. I knew it wouldn't happen right away. You're special and I knew," he gave me a very sweet smile, "you would need time to accept all of this. But I never realized how much I would hurt wanting you. I've lived a very long time and I have *never* felt this." He watched me as he spoke, and he waited for a few seconds to pass before he asked, "Do you burn Bree, for me I mean?"

I felt my face warm, I lowered my eyes as I took his hands in mine, "Let's say, I'm simmering. My mind and my heart are embattled in a war now. My mind tells me I can do this. I can handle this life. But my heart has different thoughts on the matter. I honestly do not know which will win."

"When did you know?"

"I knew things were different this morning, I didn't know what it was though. I felt our energy and now that

Steven has explained things to me...I understand." My smiled turned shy; he raised my hands to his lips and kissed them. "I wanted to believe I could change all of you to make me more comfortable, but after feeling your desire tonight, I know that will not be possible. When you kissed me on the lips earlier, I felt the rush of your emotions, your need. I see the energy that passes between us; it's very similar to what I have with Steven. Our love is not the same as Madalyn and Steven's; theirs is more a lust. Once it has been cooled, they are fine. But ours is a love and Bradley, the three, well, four, I need to include Billy here, you are all dangerous to me."

"Bree, you know we would never hurt you. Please, you have to know this."

"Bradley, I do know that. The danger is your need to protect. It is so strong in Steven and it is strong in you." I started to laugh, "It is even just as strong in Rick, and we all know how Billy is." I looked at him and smiled. "Your need to protect me will not keep me from what I must do. You must understand that. And that is why, you four, are a danger to me."

"You understand Steven and Madalyn's needs then, how we live in our clan?"

"Yes, Bradley, I understand, but that does not mean I accept. I'm trying but you will need to give me time. The human in me is very strong. It always will be, it gets in the way and always will. I don't know how to change that or even if I can. I don't know how to separate my love for Steven and my...love for you. I have no idea how I could even... Rick...damn this is getting complicated," I said quietly.

"We will take it slow. Richard is a very patient man. You will see. You will feel that pull and that need and he will wait until you are ready. What of us now? How do we handle this?"

"I don't know. I don't have the answers for that," I said; a little saddened I didn't have the answer. I thought I was supposed to have all the answers; I was a Chosen One for heaven's sakes. What good is it to be so damn special and not have all the answers? I couldn't change this. I couldn't say any magical words that would make this all disappear and make it the way I wanted it. Everything packaged neatly, Steven all to myself, and Bradley with his mate, Rick and I just very good friends.

"You have changed Bree, from yesterday to today, there is a change. A maturity has grown in you." He smiled, "I like this change."

"Yes, I'm sure you do." I nudged him. He sat very still just watching me. "It doesn't mean I have all the answers. It doesn't mean I can just fall into the way your lives are. I will go to the gatherings and attend the summits with you, as co-leader and I will lead our clan with you. As for the hunt after the gatherings, well, let's just say that isn't my cup of tea. I have no desire to see Steven and Madalyn together. I will leave that part of our lives to you and our clan. I will return home, I'll not interfere with that."

"You could be with me during those times. I will take things as slow as you need. We can go anywhere you want. We don't need to be there, the hunt is more for the clan than for us." He took my hand and placed it on his chest. His tone had strengthened again. It warmed my heart and strengthened my resolve. "This is my sound for you Bree; it is different than my sound for Madalyn."

"I do like the feel of it." I placed my ear against his chest and smiled. "Yes, Bradley, I do like it." I faced him; he leaned into me and kissed me, and it was a tender, sweet kiss.

"It amazes me how strong my desire for you is at this moment," he said as he cleared his throat. "You don't have a purr, as you like to call it," he gently placed his hand on my breast, "although I can feel your heart pounding." His eyebrows rose as his hand stayed on my chest, feeling the racing beat, waiting on it to quiet.

"Bradley, I can assume Steven filled you in on our conversation he and I had in Yellowstone?"

"Yes, Little One, he did. You're not a polygamist." He smiled at that thought.

"I am one woman with two mates, two husbands; what else would you call me?"

"Lucky," he smiled. "Bree, I am secondary to Steven except when we are leading, when I need you to be with me as my partner. I will never be able to replace him." He raised his eyebrows and leaned in close, "but because of our status, we never need to seek permission either," he smiled and I amazed myself as I smiled back at him. "Now, do you have any questions?"

I stared at him for the longest few seconds, "I have concerns as well as questions. Bradley, since I am your... Alpha, can I assume you will keep my confidence when we talk?"

"Alpha? Huh, I think I like that analogy. You are the Alpha female of the clan. Yes, I like that, and yes you can assume that."

I looked at him and gave him a wary smile.

"Bree, if you do not want me to speak of what we talk about you just need to tell me."

"I don't want you to speak about what I'm going to tell you. How was that?" I smiled.

"That's good," he laughed. "Now what is it you want to tell me?"

"I'm concerned with Madalyn..."

"Leave Madalyn to me..." His voice hardened and his eyes grew angry. Not what I wanted.

I gently cupped his face with my hand, "Bradley, I do not wish her punished. I'm just concerned. She doesn't like me much right now. I'm sure it is just all the uncertainties surrounding us. This will pass. But I am concerned, her temper...needs to be controlled." I decided not to tell him of her treatment in Yellowstone. Maybe once everything had calmed down, so would her anger.

He took my hand and kissed it, "I will counsel her then. I will be tender but firm; we'll start there. But she will understand and give you the respect you've earned."

"Was Sandy an only child?"

"What? No I don't think so. Why do you ask?"

I bit my lip as I decided how best to tell him, without getting her into trouble. "Bradley is it true, when you are 'turned' you must abandon all the mortal trappings?"

"It's wise to do that, it makes the processes easier to deal with. The amount of loss that touches your heart is so great, so, if you turn away from the mortal world, even if it's just for a short while, it makes it easier to adjust. What does this have to do with Sandy?"

"But it's not a demand?"

"No, it's a suggestion. That's all."

"Sandy has been secretly watching over her parents. Apparently, they are old, and they don't have much money. She's been paying their utility bills. Bradley, this next bit of information I'm about to give you is just so you will understand why Sandy spoke against me. Madalyn threatened to tell you and Richard what she was doing. Apparently, they think it's the rule."

He started laughing, "Oh, my sweet Precious Bree."

That took me by surprise, "What? It's the truth. That was what I heard."

"Oh, my darling, I believe you. We are well aware of what Sandy has been doing. Rick even increased her household budget to cover the expense. He didn't want Sandy to do without anything and he knew she would." He saw the look on my face when he spoke of this and laughed again. "Trust me Precious; it's a very large budget. Sandy has very rich tastes. I'll talk to Rick, maybe it's time he eased her heart." He brushed a strand of hair from my face. "What else do we need to talk about?"

I smiled, "What will my role be at these gatherings?" The human side of my mind was yelling out to me, *what are you talking about, who gives a rip about these gatherings?*

"Well, I suppose you mean other than being with me," he smiled and so did I. "We have dinners we need to attend. We socialize with other clan leaders. We review our bylaws, vote on any changes. Nothing earth shattering.

At the Spring Gathering, we either make a formal offer to the ones we selected at the Fall Gatherings or we let them know the clan has rejected them. They can reject our offer if they choose. If they accept us as their family, then they go through the Ceremony of Acceptance and they go through a bonding ritual of sorts after the Gathering is over.

Rick will get a listing of those that are looking for a family around the end of January. They will study that list and give us the names they want us to extend an offer too. We will meet with those at the Spring Gathering to let them know we are considering them. At the Fall Gathering, we will select the ones we were considering. They are watched during the following months. They live with us, socialize with us; they are a part of us; *but* they do not bond with us until after we have accepted them at the Spring Gathering." He nudged me, "Do I need to explain the bonding ritual?"

"No, I have a fairly good idea what happens."

"You do? Okay, just making sure." He looked at me and smiled, apparently Steven spoke with him about my apprehension on this. I would need to talk with Steven to remind him what we talk about stays between us.

He watched my reactions brush across my face. When he decided I had accepted this as fact, he continued, "Let me tell you, those four are very picky. As you can see, we haven't grown. Sometimes they exasperate me. I imagine they really don't want others in the clan, they like our group the way it is."

"Now they can exasperate both of us."

"I like the sound of that." He sat close, his hand played with my hair.

I frowned, "Will I be here, I mean will I be able to...will I be human or a Magical?"

"I'm sure you will still be human in March; you will be a beautiful sorceress by September." He smiled as he brushed my bangs out of my eyes.

"Are there any other clans that are in our predicament?"

"What, the leader's aren't mates?"

"Yeah, not to mention one of them is soon to be a sorceress; if she lives," I chuckled.

He grinned. "Yes, there are a few. None of them have a sorceress, there is one that has a fairy and one that has an elf if I'm not mistaken, but most are all vampires."

"I guess I am a little confused. If a vampire is dangerous to me, you know, one bite and I'm a goner; why would you allow me to go to these gatherings before I have made the transition? I assume Traditionals are there?"

"We will have to revisit that. I may go by myself again this year, come back at night so we can discuss the days events. I don't want you left by yourself. Steven will be with Madalyn during that time and Rick and Bill have other duties. We'll see how this all shakes out the closer we get to that time, but I would so love it if you could go with me. If not, then we will just have to wait until September."

"Billy goes to the gatherings?" I smiled.

"Ah...yeah...so does Gina," he cringed as he told me. "I shouldn't have said that. I told Bill he needed to talk with you, he needed to explain things to you."

"I see...Bradley..."

He took my hand. His touch was cool and I liked the feel of his grip on mine. It was firm but gentle; I had no desire to pull away. "Is this something else you want me to keep to myself?"

"Yes, please...let Billy inform me in his own time."

"I think I'm going to enjoy leading with you. Do you have any other questions?"

"No...not now." I stood and Bradley stood with me. He kissed me one last time, very sensually. He wrapped his arms around me as if I had been gone for such a long time and he hungered for my touch. "Bree," he stopped, trying to decide how to form his request. He tried to start again, he opened his mouth, but no words came out. He smiled at me.

"Ask your question Bradley."

"March is several months away. I would really like to be with you just once, and then I promise I will wait. I can't explain it, but there is just something now that draws me to you. There's this essences about you that attracts me. I've not felt it before this night, but it is most power-ful. I fear if I don't love you soon I will burst from all of you I drink in."

My human side suddenly spoke out, the realization of what was going to be expected of me came rushing back to the front of my mind and I started to panic. "Oh, Bradley, I don't...I don't think...no. I really don't know if I can do this just yet. It's too soon; I need time to absorb all of this. I'm not ready; really, I'm not." I was shaking my head; my nerves were building into tense knots in my shoulders. The human side of my mind was reaching a loud crescendo. I thought my head might explode with all the yelling my mortal mind was doing with my Magical mind. My heart was pounding. My Magical side told me I could handle this, but my heart was breaking; and the human side of me was being stuffed into a tiny box. Tiny little magical fingers were pushing me deeper and deeper into the darkness of that tiny box, then they started wrapping chains around it and finally the large metal lock clicked tight and my human side was quieted. *Damn, please don't lose the key to that box,* I thought.

I turned to move from him; he held me, not willing to let me go. I heard the voice of the wind again in my mind, *you must change child; for you to succeed in your path, you must change, you must accept.*

I turned and looked into his eyes. I knew my path; but was I able to accept? That was the question being batted around in my mind. He was so close. He gave me soft, tender little kisses as he said, "Try. Please try." He wrapped his arm around me, held my face gently in his hand and pressed his lips to mine; his mouth open, his tongue lightly brushing mine. I felt dizzy with want for him, but I started to struggle, one last effort from my human side to free my mind, but he remained gentle. He continued to hold me, his lips were soft, and I started to respond to his touch, his kiss. He held me in his arms so delicately, as if I might break if he pressed too hard. One arm around my back; his other hand held the back of my head. Softly, he kissed me. Tender moans escaping, his want getting stronger, harder. Mine were just as hot, just as passionate, my hands reaching, holding, and pulling him closer to me.

My heart was beating faster. I realized I wanted him as much as he wanted me. I wanted his touches, his kisses. "Please, just this one time. I promise I will wait after this; but damn, my love, I am so in need of you now." I shivered slightly; he knew I was nervous. "Never doubt my love for you."

His kisses caused my body to relax. When I opened my eyes, I was unfamiliar with my surroundings. I looked at him.

"I brought us to the second room in my suite. Put all the others out of your mind. I am being selfish and I want to be the only one in your thoughts."

My mind took control, my heart quieted. I responded to his kisses with a strong desire to be with him, to have him inside me. Each kiss strengthened my resolve. I pressed into him, wanting his touch.

His arms wrapped around me tightly, pulling me to him, pressing into me. Our kisses were passionate and hungry for one another. My hands shook as I started unbuttoning his shirt; he lifted mine over my head. "It's okay, you don't need to be nervous with me," he encouraged. His hands moved over my breasts, softly massaging my nipples until they responded to him. His lips made their way down my neck, toward my breast, as he continued to undress me.

I stood naked before him; his eyes washed over me, smiling his approval. I shivered in the cool room. He wrapped me in his arms and held me close. The cool touch of his hands against the warmth of my skin soothed me. He continued to become acquainted with my body.

I wrapped myself in his arms, my hand running along his waist, finding the snap on his jeans and unsnapping it. He finished the job of unzipping his pants and I found my gift hard, his want was indeed strong. My hand gave soft tender strokes and he responded to my touch. He softly whispered my name, his breathing increased. Soft pleas came with each stroke. "Oh, damn, Bree; damn I want you so badly." As each kiss grew in its intensity, his hands held my face so gently, so tenderly, our hearts pounding. As Bradley rested his forehead against mine, he swallowed hard. "My God I can't believe my need for you."

The room was quiet as we stood in the darkness, swaying quietly in each other's arms. "Bradley, are you all right?" I asked coyly, running my fingers through his hair.

"Just savoring the moment, my darling. I don't want this to end."

I wasn't Bree, the one bonded to Steven, I was Aubrey, Bradley's mate; and I realized I could make love to him as his mate. My mind became older, I felt older. The awkwardness slipped away, as tender loving touches took its place, as I became familiar with his body. At that moment, we were the only two in the world. It was right; it was supposed to be.

"Are we moving too fast?" I kissed his lips softly.

"We are not moving fast enough!" He reacted so quickly, picking me up and pressing his mouth hard to mine as he laid me on the bed and he moved onto me. My leg wrapped over him as he slid ever so gently into me and I arched to accept him. My eyes closed, as I stretched under him and held him close to me. Never had I dreamed of his touch to be so tender, so loving. His kisses continued to be ravenous; he needed to have me; he needed me to be only thinking of him. Slowly, ever so slowly, we moved together, neither of us in a hurry for this to end. The pleasure sent waves through our bodies, slow gentle thrusts, rocking us back and forth.

I whispered his name in his ear; my tongue traced the edges, sending a quiet tremor through him. I gently nipped his earlobe, his pleasure increasing. His voice was soft and breathless as he whispered, "Oh damn."

My legs tightened to control him, "Slower Bradley, not yet." I felt him shudder as he tried to slow his passion. I was controlling this; I kept my legs around him, moving with him. I watched as he closed his eyes and smiled with each rotation of my hips. I gave intense pleasure to his senses and I brought him to the brink and then refused his release. Slowly he would reach his point, and again I would refuse his release. His eyes would smile to me as he quietly begged for more, a teasing laugh escaped my lips and he pressed his lips to mine. "Wicked," he whispered.

I continued to whisper softly to him, my lips so close to his ears, gentling touching them as I whispered, I felt his body tremble.

Our arms tightened around each other and we rolled until I was on top, stretching and crawling; sitting on him to find the bliss I knew was near. He saw the fire burn in my eyes as he watched me. His hands lovingly caressed my body; he smiled as he watched the nipples of my breasts harden at his touch. Just before my euphoria erupted, he brought me to his lips and we rolled. "Oh no beautiful, I can be just as wicked. We will meet this together." His momentum increased and I arched at the anticipation of our journey. He rose enough to watch my eyes roll into my head as I stretched and moved with him. "Oh, damn, please," I moaned so quietly to him. He brought his lips firmly to mine as I held him tight, and we both reached our end to-gether, sending hard shudders though our bodies. This love was strong and intense. The energy that ran through us was hot. I felt the heat from our passion all the way to my toes.

Our hands held tight to each other as he came to rest beside me; our breathing was heavy. "Thank you Aubrey, that one was all mine and oh, damn, I thank you. I have never, in my long life, felt anything like that." He laughed a little wicked laugh, "My dear, you can be truly naughty when you want to be." He whispered in my ear, "I have a strong love for you. March is truly a long way away; it will be very hard for me to keep that promise." Then he kissed my ear sending a ripple of shivers through me.

We laid together for what seemed to be an eternity, but only minutes passed, his hand rubbing gently up and down my arm. "I could stay with you all night, Aubrey. I don't want this to end yet. I have been with humans before, but none can touch you. The craving I have for you is so very strong. I have truly never felt this before. There is something so very special about you." The vibration in his chest was strong and I laid my ear against it as he stroked my hair. "You're not talking. Do you not feel the same way?"

I rose on my elbow to look at him, my hair fell over my eyes, and he tucked it behind my ear and saw the tears. "I do love you Bradley. I just realized my mind won over my heart and I am very confused. I feel as if I have somehow cheated on Steven and I am at a total loss at explaining myself."

"Oh Precious, you haven't cheated on Steven. He has your heart and your love and you have his. Never doubt that. You are his; I have you as my mate for so few times. Our love is different and I like the way it makes me feel. It's so warm; I have never felt that warmth before. It's special; you are so very special to me."

I looked at him and grinned, "Bradley, you are very special to me as well." I giggled an evil little giggle and kissed him again, "I promise I won't be wicked this time, I want to ensure you don't burst!" Our kisses again turned into a yearning we both had, and again I moved on top of him and he loved me.

CHAPTER 24

As we entered the restaurant, Odessa came into my mind.
*I need to make you aware you will be tested again tonight.
There is a Traditional here on her orders. He will try his best
to seduce you. You have nothing to fear; he has no power over
you. No vampire can seduce you Bree, but your families do
not understand this; you must show them. Meet his challenge.
I do need to warn you this will greatly upset the males of your
clan, not to mention Bill; but it is something you must do.
They need to be reminded you have another duty too. Keep
your mind closed. You will learn much tonight for all is not
as it seems.*

My eyes locked onto Steven. He looked at me and
smiled. I knew then that he knew I had been with Brad.
I was one step closer in his mind to accepting this life and
I'm sure Brad felt the same way. Steven rushed to meet
me; his smile reaffirmed my suspicion. Brad squeezed my
hand; "I'll wait for you at the table. Dance your dance with
Steven." He smiled and kissed my cheek.

Steven came up to me and I was just so unsure of how I was supposed to act. I was just with Brad and Steven had no problems with it. This was all so unnatural. I looked at my hands; I just couldn't look into his eyes. His hand slowly lifted my chin to meet his gaze. "Princess, I love you, never, never doubt that. You are becoming one of us and I could not be more pleased." Then he kissed me.

I hugged him and kissed him back hard. "Dance with me Steven."

"Don't you want to meet everyone first?" he chuckled.

"No, I want to be in your arms now; they will keep. I want to dance with you and have you hold me as if we are the only two in the world at this very moment," I pleaded.

"It will get easier, Bree, I promise."

I stopped and pushed back to look at him. "I don't want it to be easy, Steven."

%

We danced two slow dances together. He held me tight; my hand rested on his chest. I needed to familiarize myself to his tone. I took his hand and placed it on my chest. "I have always felt it," he whispered in my ear as the song ended. "Let's go back to the table. Brad is calling us; he's a little annoyed he can't communicate with you. Is your mind closed to us, Bree?"

"For now; I have a lot to sort through. Does this upset you?"

"A little; will you let me in to help you?" He sounded a little hurt.

"Soon; I need to understand it first, but soon."

Everyone was at the table including two new people. Sandy got up to greet me with a hug and a kiss, and I watched Gran and Billy for their reactions. It didn't seem to disturb them in the slightest. Madalyn did not greet me, which was fine. She could continue to be mad if she liked. If that made this better for her, then I was fine with it. I had my own demons to fight now and I didn't know if I was strong enough to take hers on too. Rick came up to me, hugged me, and kissed my cheek. I grinned at him and gave him a kiss on the lips. He whispered a 'thank you' in my ear and told me we have a lot to talk about, then returned to his seat.

My hand rested on Brad's shoulder. I felt his strength rush through me. We were connected. Steven sat, but I continued to stand. Everyone looked at me. "Bree what's wrong?" Steven asked.

"I don't know," I looked at Billy. "What, you can't hug me now?"

Billy looked at me; "I kind of have to be given permission from your clan?"

He wasn't ready to talk to me about his involvement in the clan yet. "Come again?"

"It's protocol, I need permission."

I looked at Brad, then at Steven, then back to Billy, "Excuse me, but that's stupid. You are my cousin and you do not need anyone's permission to hug me. Now get yourself over here or I will make a scene you do not want to see! Hi, Gina sweetie. How are you feeling? Hi Gran, we will be talking soon." My eyes narrowed to her, hoping she would catch my need to speak with her. The tiniest smile lined her lips and she gave a slight nod, she understood.

Brad laughed, "You'd better do it Bill. She generally makes good on her promises."

Billy wiped his mouth on his napkin, came over to me, and gave me a big bear hug. "I've missed you Half Pint. We'll talk later," then he kissed me on the cheek and set me back down.

"Bree, I'm fine," said Gina. "Just another five weeks to go, then you'll have a new little cousin."

"I can't wait." I went over and patted her belly, gave her a kiss, then moved on to Gran. "Where's George?"

"Oh, he had so much to do to get ready for tomorrow; but he wanted me to be here to welcome you back and congratulate you on your new clan." Then she thought into my mind; *your parents will be here tomorrow to talk with you. Thread lightly Bree, they are hurting.*

I thought as much, I would like you to be there too.

If that is your wish, then I will be there.

I noticed the two new members sitting quietly between Madalyn and Sandy, a woman and a man. They were young. If I had to guess I would say they were both in their early twenty's. They were very pale and the dark circles were very noticeable under their eyes. I started to wonder just how long it took to transition from a Traditional to a Non-com. The young woman watched me; the male wouldn't meet my gaze.

I suddenly felt pressure against my chest, against my heart. It was the strangest sensation. It wasn't debilitating, but I was aware of it. The cold sensation squeezed my heart as it pumped my warm blood. I caught my breath. The cold squeezed again. I pressed my hand against my chest. The coldness left. I stood still for a moment. I tried to take a deep breath, but the cold came back and pressed against my lungs. The frigid hand squeezed and made it difficult for my lungs to expand. I touched my pendant and the bloodstone. I felt the warmth of the stone wash over me and the cold touch of the tiny fingers left me. My breathing returned to normal.

Steven watched me. He quickly thought to me, *Princess, are you all right?* He stood and pulled my chair out for me.

Yeah, I think so. I have no idea what that was all about, but it's gone now.

Brad too had noticed my weakness. His hand went immediately to my wrist, checking my pulse as my hand rested on my lap. I felt the men of my clan's concern, and that was not what I wanted. I opened my thoughts and gently kissed their minds. *I'm fine, please stop worrying.* I watched as Rick sat back, his arm still on the table but he smiled with his eyes to me.

I felt his gentle push to gain entry into my mind and I cracked open the door to my thoughts ever so slightly, my mind peeking around the corner to him. *I like the feel of your thoughts Aubrey. I truly have missed your touch.*

My mind smiled back, *I know you have my Richard*, and I gently closed the door again. I felt Billy's unsettlement. I could only hope he would ask me to dance tonight. We had a lot to discuss.

Brad released my wrist when he was satisfied my pulse was strong again, my weakness completely gone. I sat up straight and took a deep breath. "Too much excitement," I offered.

The lounge was starting to get more crowded and much louder. Everyone was laughing and having a good time. And as I hoped, Billy asked me if he could have a dance.

"Well, it took you long enough." I kissed Steven on the cheek and told him I would be back. I thought to Bradley. *Do I need to seek permission?*

Only with outsiders, and I will tell you right now, my answer will be 'no'.

Then why should I ask? I smiled in my mind at him.

Do you feel up to dancing?

Bradley, Billy has carried me many times. If I feel faint again, know I am in good hands, I whispered in his mind.

Billy was behind me, helping me from the table. He asked for a slow dance when we got to the floor so he could talk to me. "Everything okay, Half Pint? You looked a little pale for a while there."

"I feel fine now, not sure what that was all about. But in answer to your other question; no Billy, everything is not okay. Bradley and I share a bond. I am mated to him as well as Steven!" My human emotions escaped from the box that held them and they were bubbling to the front of my mind again.

"Well, yeah I know. That's interesting, didn't see that coming," Billy said.

"Apparently nobody did. Did you see me becoming a leader in the clan?"

"No, didn't see that either. We thought you would play a role in Steven's House, only because he has family on the Council. We really thought that's what it meant," Billy answered, maybe even a little amused.

"You knew about Madalyn and Steven?"

"Yeah, I did. Wasn't sure how you would react, hell none of us were. Steven, shit, you should have seen him when Brad told him he had to be the one to tell you. He didn't want to tell you, but it has been this way for him and Madalyn ever since he made her a vampire. It was only right the news came from him."

"Steven explained *everything*, I can't believe this Billy," I was gently banging my head on his chest. "This giving of themselves, no jealousy, no guilt. This just isn't right. I can't do this."

"Oh, my sweet little Bree, you will understand as you bond with them. You will need that closeness and you will ache when they aren't near. You can't stop Steven and Madalyn, so there is no reason why you can't be with Brad during that time."

"You don't have a problem with it?" I asked, trying to give him an opening. But then I realized my William would not talk with me here about this. He would talk with me when we were alone, when he could have me all to himself.

"No, Bree, sweetie, I really don't. We're Magicals; I understand this way of life. It is so much different from the way you live as a human. We love deeper than humans do; we *need* to bond to one another. We touch and have a need to be touched by others. We have a deep desire to show others how much we love them. I am always holding you, picking you up. That should make sense to you now. Magicals are very sensual, more so than humans. Humans are high strung; you will begin to understand these ways as you live it. Just relax and enjoy yourself. This is our way."

"I feel like I'm cheating," I protested.

"That's a human thought. I know, I know, you are still human; but my sweet angel, it could be worse."

"Oh, please tell me how. What could be worse?"

"You could remain an outsider from the clan and those few times a year he would be with Madalyn, making love to her, being with her, and you couldn't communicate with him at all. It comes up every so often and they have to quench it. What Steven and Madalyn have is nothing but lust, animalistic lust. Steven will not make love to you in that manner. Madalyn will never be able to replace you in his heart, in his soul. You make Steven human; he is tender with you. It will be the same with you and Brad. I see it in the way they treat you now. Neither of them will make love to you like they make love to Madalyn. Vampires are different with their mates. Rough, but that's how they like it."

"How do you know all of this, Billy? I questioned, nudging just a little more.

"Oh, I know this side of them. We are not as bashful as you are, my sweet. That is one of your qualities we find endearing. We males share our thoughts. We have been friends for a very long time and will continue to be. I know the pain Steven has felt for you and I have hurt for him. Brad is there now too. We all love you in our own way."

"I will never understand this life."

"Which do you want? Do you want to be by yourself, unhappy, and hurting during those times Steven is with Madalyn, or be with someone who loves you just as much? Though he could never replace Steven in your soul; maybe he can make you just as happy."

I swayed with Billy. I was quiet and he didn't like that.

"Okay, Bree, with the risk of you going ballistic on me; take the human part of you and shove it aside for just a few minutes." He pulled me away and looked at me, then pulled me back to him. "This will make it easier on Steven. He truly didn't know how you would react to this." I tensed. "Listen to me now, before you fly off the handle. Steven is prepared to walk away from his clan, his life here, everything just to keep you. When he had to leave you that summer, I was very worried about him. I had to remind him repeatedly, he would be with you in the end. I promised that to him. Then Nick came along and again he worried me. He watched you when you would come over." I pulled back to look at him. "You never saw him; nobody knew he was there but me. He loves you that much, but he has a problem and that problem is his bond to Madalyn. Every one of them are worried you won't accept this way of their life and leave. They know Steven will go with you. This will hurt Madalyn greatly, you can't imagine how much. That will hurt Brad, and you leaving, that will hurt Brad too. In the end, it will hurt Steven, and that will hurt you."

"I don't want that," I said, but I knew I didn't want this either. Why was everyone wanting to shove my human emotions into and under things, didn't they understand I needed them.

"I know you don't, but it's your choice. Steven would feel better knowing you too had someone dependent on you. It's really a win for both of you. Is it ideal in your eyes? No. It never will be. You want the one love, one mate for a lifetime. Bree, be honest. That doesn't always happen in the human world. Trust me, I have seen, heard, and even witnessed this. Remember, I am a lawyer and I do have many human clients."

I decided to table this conversation for a while, it was going to take time and I needed to move on to other things.

"Billy, that new woman at the table, she looked very famil iar but I can't place her. The hair color was wrong for her face."

"Keep thinking; it will come to you. Try her as a blonde." The music was ending.

I stopped and looked at Billy. "No, can't be."

"They wanted you to have someone you were familiar with, someone you knew very well."

"I thought they were Traditionals?"

"Well, they were; right now they are Tweeners," he looked at me and I gave him the 'a little more information' look. "Tweeners are the ones in between Traditionals and Non-Coms. Steven and Rick started working on them soon as they were able to locate them. Madalyn and Sandy have been helping them through the transition; they are having a rough go of it though. They're still a little wild. They will not be allowed to greet you for a very long time, but I think your clan is willing to do what is needed to cross them over."

I took Billy's hand and walked back to the table. I looked directly at them. "Becky?"

She looked at me; a small smile crossed her lips, then it was gone. "Yes, Bree, it's me."

I didn't know what to say, I looked at her companion. "Are you going to introduce me?"

She looked at Steven. He nodded. "Bree, this is Ted. Ted, Bree," she motioned with her hands. Her job was done; she continued to look down. I squished my mouth and decided to give up for now. I knew Becky well enough, or did; to know when she clammed up the conversation was over.

I took my seat and Steven assumed the position. How I had missed that - his arm around the back of my chair and his thumb rubbing my shoulder. Soon he would be rubbing my neck. I hadn't had my headaches for a while but I so loved him touching me.

The waiter came and refilled our drinks and Steven ordered chips, salsa, and a bowl of queso, fried zucchini with ranch dressing, chicken fingers, and Buffalo wings. I was finding out more about my clans' relationship with my family. Steven, Rick, Brad, and my cousins played baseball together for The Mystical's. They even played against human teams and I was told that all Magical teams were given strict instructions to play with 'normal' strength when they played against the humans. No one made any move to explain to me what 'normal' meant!

They had been trying to get a football team together. But because of the holiday seasons, mainly Halloween, which is a month long event apparently in the Magical world, it's just a little difficult to get enough people involved. This had not detoured them however; they all got together with a group of others, a few werewolves and some other vampires and witches, for weekend fun.

Everyone was having a good time. Gran was talking with Gina about the baby and Gran's other great grandchildren.

I heard a familiar voice; Billy turned and stood up extending his hand to someone coming up behind me.

"Ry, I was wondering when you would show. Where's Kim?" Billy asked.

Ryan was the oldest of my cousins, and a very stern individual. His wife, Kim, was just as strict. Spending time with the two of them was about as much fun as spending a Friday night at the library. You wouldn't know it by watching them but their kids actually had a great sense of humor, they probably got that from my cousin Stanley. He was just as serious, just as firm, but he did have a fun side, he just never let it show much.

"Hey everyone," Ryan said as he took Billy's hand and gave it a firm shake. "Kim's up in the room unpacking. Thought I would come by and see you all. Bree, sweetie, how are you?" He leaned in and gave me a hello kiss. He looked at Brad, "Sorry, forgot to ask permission."

"Not a problem, Ryan," Brad said. "Bree has made it clear family is family."

Ryan sat down and leaned forward, arms resting on his legs, and informed everyone I would go before the Council on Friday. "I had hoped they would have waited until next year, but several are pushing. Tensions are rising; races are vying for positions. Have you heard about the Elves? They've broken into two factions again, and now there are two leaders and they both want to be on the Council. The newest faction's a very radical group; they have taken to calling themselves Transitionals. Their leader, Broderick, he's relentless in his demands on their government. He and his followers have wanted to change the way they live for a very long time now and the government doesn't want that change. Time will only tell how this will all work out. Elves can be a nasty lot when they don't get their way."

Ryan looked at me and smiled; he put his arm around me and gave me another kiss on the cheek. "Word has gotten out that Bree's here; she's being watched. They know about the headaches and the warming. They know that soon she will become powerful. It's just the fear, the uncertainty, surrounding her."

"You do realize I am sitting right here don't you?" I said as I took a bite of zucchini.

"I am well aware you are here Aubrey," he teased back.

"Should we increase her protection again?" Rick asked. I watched him and Billy. I felt their tension, their shoulder muscles tightened; they sat a little straighter. My bond to them was strengthening.

"Couldn't hurt; the infighting has started on the Council too. Esmeralda's furious; the gems are gone. She's started an investigation, but shit, they weren't hers to begin with. Now the Council wants Bree to appear before them so we can all see for ourselves how far she has progressed." Ryan gave me another reassuring smile, and then looked down at his hands.

I sat quietly and listened to all the information he was feeding my clan, "Tell them it isn't soup yet." I said back to him and smiled.

"Bree, you aren't taking this seriously. We really should talk before Friday's meeting with the Council," Ryan softly scolded me. His eyes were worried, and he was correct, I wasn't taking this seriously.

"Ry, I'm not worried, you shouldn't be either." I smiled back at him and tried to put his heart at ease.

"When it comes to you my dear little cousin, I always worry. You will go before them on Friday afternoon. Some members will press hard for you to go with the Council for your protection. We can't let that happen," he said as he looked around the table at the men of my clan.

"Ry, I've no intentions of going anywhere, so put your mind at rest dear cousin," I said continuing with my calm manner.

"Not that simple. Have you transformed and not told us?" Ryan asked

"No," I smiled.

"Then I will continue to worry," Ryan said.

"Then you're expending energy you don't need to," I countered.

"Stubborn. My hat goes off to your clan." Ryan got up to leave. "I'll talk with you later, Bree."

"I love you, Ry."

"I love you too." Ryan leaned in and kissed me on the cheek again, said goodnight to everyone and left.

Rick asked Steven if he could have a dance with me. I thought that a little odd, he'd never asked Steven before. Why now? Was this the way it would be from now on? They had to ask Steven or Brad's permission to dance with me?

♋

Rick held my hand tight as he swung me around once we got to the dance floor, pulling me into his arms, holding me close as we swayed with the music. I deeply inhaled his scent. "I told you I would hold you tight so you could get your fill," he laughed.

"Rick, stop teasing me; but I do like that on you."

"No, I will never stop teasing you or holding you; so just get used to it," he whispered.

"Rick, I've a question for you. Why did you ask permission to dance with me? I don't remember you ever doing that before?"

"Steven and Brad want to take things slow with you. They don't want us to scare you off," he laughed. "I don't scare you, do I?"

"No, and that's silly. You don't need to ask permission. You can dance with me and hold me any time you like." I closed my eyes remembering all my dances with this very gentle soul. I remembered all the talks he and I had. I could feel his tension ease, but I also could feel he wanted to say more.

"I've missed this, Bree. I shouldn't be telling you that though," he said.

"Why?"

"You have enough on your mind without having to worry about my missing you. That's all."

"Oh, Rick, stop worrying about my mind. It's fine. I like dancing with you and I have missed you. When my memories returned, I felt such longing for all of you. We must have spent a lot of time together. I'm very content now, so I'm telling you to stop worrying."

"This isn't too much for you then? I mean I know how your mind works maybe better than Steven and Brad. I can tell the struggle you're having. Do you want to talk about it?"

My hand tightened around his, "No...I..." I cleared my throat as I thought of the awkwardness of him holding me close and wanting to discuss all of this. "No, Rick, not now," I quietly answered.

"Okay, but I'm always here if you need to talk. Remember that," he whispered to me as the song ended. "Damn, too soon."

∽

I sat next to Steven, he could tell I was tired, but I was enjoying being with everyone. A chill ran down my back and I shivered very slightly, my chest tightened again. Steven felt it and I felt the worry rise in him as he took my hand in his. *Bree, I think you've had enough excitement for one day; I'm calling an early end to tonight,* he advised me.

I smiled and looked at my watch, and then back at him, *two-thirty is not an early night!*

It is for us, my sweet, he teased. "Well, everyone I want a little alone time with my Princess. We've all had a very long day; see you all at breakfast." He stood, took my hand to help me up, and then I heard an unfamiliar voice.

CHAPTER 25

Bree meets a Traditional

"Well, well, look who we've run into," said our newest visitor. I could tell from the description Sandy had given that this was a Traditional vampire, and he had a large number of his clan with him.

Steven pulled me back behind him. Brad, Billy, and Rick stood up. I felt the tension quickly rise at our table and it truly concerned me.

"Relax. I'm not going to do anything here; too public. I like my advances in private." He looked around Steven and directly at me. "Very private," he smiled showing me his pointed canines.

His face registered with me. I remembered the dream I saw him in, I knew this Traditional as Thomas. He was much paler than I remembered but his appearance fascinated me. He was indeed tall and broad shouldered, even in my dream he was a very imposing figure. He wasn't dressed as causally as I remembered. Today he was dressed just as I would have thought a vampire dressed. His black cape, with starched high collar framing the back of his head, clipped together with gold buttons and connected by a gold chain. His crisp white shirt with black suit neatly pressed, the crease in his pant legs was sharp. His shoes polished to a high glossy sheen, long slender fingers wrapped around the silver bat handle on the cane he carried. His long coal black hair was tucked under his cape. Dark sideburns framed his smooth alabaster chiseled face; the dark circles under his eyes and his thin ice smooth lips, all fascinated me.

I heard the heeded words of a member of his clan. *Careful Tom; you've been without your Drink for sometime. Tread lightly.*

I know what I'm doing. His voice had a deep velvet tone to it as he spoke, "Steven, you worry too much." He offered me his hand, his eyes tried to push his will of control to me.

Steven stepped in front of the offered hand and I heard his low rattled growl deep in his chest. I sensed the tension in my men. It raised in strength a few decimals and I felt their rumbles deep inside me.

"Gentlemen, where are your manners? Aren't you going to introduce me to this sweet young thing?" He paused, "My dear, politeness seems to have escaped them. My name is..."

"Thomas," I said just above a whisper.

"Yes," he paused and watched me, "And you are?"

"Aubrey, my name is Aubrey." Brad was behind me. He put his hand on my waist and gave a slight squeeze. Madalyn and Sandy shifted in their seats. Gran stood. "Thomas, what is it you want?"

"Ah, Mildred. Is this the one I have heard so much about? The one who is to save your beloved culture? Why, she is so small to be such a threat to ours. Please, tell me how this creature can save you if she can't even look or talk to me without you all guarding her?" He spread his arms gesturing to them all and smiled at me again.

"She is not your concern at the moment," Steven said.

"You are correct, Steven. For the moment she is not a concern; I wish to keep it that way," he smiled. "Tell me, my dear, have you really seen a true vampire? Oh, not these gentle souls," he sneered, "but one who could make your blood boil from his touch; make you desire him more than life, make your body ache when he is not around? I could show you such a man, my dear," his stare intensified. "You needn't fear me; but you should. Are you afraid to speak with me Aubrey? Are you afraid of what you are feeling now?"

Odessa spoke to me; *Bree, he is baiting you.*

I know, I thought back. *He's trying so hard, I hate to burst his bubble; but everyone is getting nervous. I might as well step in it now.*

"Yes, Thomas, I have," I answered back surprising everyone with my calm manner. "I feel that way about Steven. He is a true vampire Thomas, just the same as you. He just prefers his Drink in a glass!" I smiled, "He and I are strong together; we are one. I feel that way about my clan; they strengthen me. You can never match that Thomas; no matter how hard you try. And no, Thomas, I do not fear you."

Thomas' smile eased a little, and then came back strong. "Now that is sweet. You mistakenly think that what you

343

feel for Steven is the same as I could make you feel." A low deep laugh escaped his lips. "It's easy to feel brave my dear, when you are surrounded by your clan. I dare say you would not be as brave if they were not holding you. Let me hold your hand and see if your desires don't change." Thomas looked at the others. "How can you know if she is strong enough to take on all those who wish her harm if you can't even trust her thoughts and emotions with me?" He was laughing at them now, baiting them. He played this game very well. "You place so much on this transformation, but she is doomed to fail; and you all know that. You are just hiding it from her on a slim hope she will survive. Such foolishness...no matter, I will taste her in the end. My clan will feast upon her dead body."

Okay, that's just gross, I thought.

Odessa spoke softly to me, *I told you; you would need to do this tonight. You must prove yourself to your families. They worry for you so, Bree. Remember, no vampire can control you. Your family does not understand this. You need to show them just how strong you are. I will be here if you should falter; but I do not see that happening. You are changing Bree; you just don't realize how much you have changed already. You will learn much tonight, my dear.*

I started to step out from behind my protectors. Brad gave me a low growl. It came from deep within his chest. He would not let go of my waist. "Just what do you think you are doing, my darling?" he whispered in my ear. I turned to look at him and took his hand, "We spoke of this earlier. Trust me."

Steven turned. "It's time you trusted me too; I'll be fine."

He looked at Brad, waiting for my Alpha mate to step in and make me stop. When Brad didn't speak, Steven understood. I was his charge and he needed to make me stop. "Bree, this is not a book, this is real. You need to sit down now." His voice was stern and I knew I was in for a talking to later; but right now, I had to do this. He needed to understand that. The rest of my family felt the need to voice their concerns.

I continued to move from behind Steven as Billy began to counsel me. "Bree, you've no idea how hard this will be. Listen to Steven and sit down now." His tone was just as harsh.

I didn't say anything back to him; I looked at Rick. "Do you wish to add anything?"

"Bree, please don't do this. I know you think you are strong; but you are not ready for this. Do as Steven and Bill say and please sit down."

"Gran, Madalyn, Sandy, anything? Now's your chance." Our two newest members watched me.

I turned back to Thomas, "I do not fear you, Thomas. You have no control over me, nor will you ever and Esmeralda knows this. My family is nervous. They will soon see my strength, as will you." My voice remained calm. "Would you like to sit or stand for your little experiment?" I extended my hand for him to hold. "Take my hand, Thomas. Know my strength and know you can't claim me," I smiled. My thoughts were taking charge. I wasn't the young mortal; I was confident in my abilities. An 'oldness' came over me and my mind took control. I could sense the Elders deep within my soul. I knew my path and my strengths. My tests were beginning and soon my families would start to understand my strengths.

He smiled and ran his tongue over his teeth, then raised his finger to his lips, "Such a foolish little girl you are. No matter, I will make quick work of you, and leave you wanting more. Standing will work just as well. I will catch you when you fall and hand you gently back to Steven."

"Very well, you may begin when you are ready." My voice was clear and calm. I felt Steven's anger growing.

Thomas took my hand in his. His touch was icy, not cool like Steven's. I smelt his cologne when he raised my hand to his lips to gently kiss it. His eyes looked into mine and he too saw my strength. He weakened a little; I felt his pain, his want. He knew he could not have me but he played along, hoping I would misstep and then he could claim me. I heard his tone deep in his chest and I smiled.

He sensually smiled as he thought into my mind. *Look at me Aubrey and tell me what do you see? Look into my eyes. Do you see us entwined together in an embrace?* I remained quiet; I was looking into his eyes. *That's it Little One, look at me. Do you see me pulling you close? Do you feel me gently kissing your neck, your lips?* His voice was rhythmically soft. He moved closer to me; his lips were so very close to mine. I remained quiet. *It is just the two of us, no other soul around. Fall into my arms, Aubrey. Let me kiss away your fears. Let me show you my love for you. I can make you happy. I have watched you; my love for you is strong. I ache for your touch. Do you not feel mine?* He drew a deep breath and I was suddenly reminded of Bradley's remark. *There is just a scent about you I can't describe; I can't get enough. You pull me toward you and I so desperately want to be with you.* I wasn't sure, who was trying to hypnotize who, at this point! *I can be strong Aubrey, and I can be gentle. I will not be rough with you; I will be tender. I can give you your most desired wish. I would be all yours; I would never mate another. That is your wish is it not, my dear? I can give you that. Just let me show you. My desire is strong and you shall know it.*

That's it! And women fall for this? What am I missing? I thought to Odessa.

I told you he had no power over you. You heard his words normally. A mortal woman would have heard his voice in a soft melody; she would have been hypnotized by that musical tone. A vampire's melody is very beautiful to mortal ears. Hearing it normally, like you just did, it loses that power. I am impressed. He offered you your greatest wish, and you did not take his offer. Maybe you are more accepting of your clan's ways than you are giving yourself credit for. You can end this now. I think the others will be convinced; mad but convinced. You are strong and he is aware, Bree. The danger to you will grow.

I broke from his gaze and smiled softly at him. I took my free hand and gently touched his neck; I felt the weakness in his veins. "Thomas, I'm sorry but I told you; you have no powers over me. Your gaze can't affect me; your voice has no melody to me. Your eyes are not dangerous to me; you have no control here."

His eyes became angry; he didn't speak. "If you are done, may I please have my hand back?" I asked as his eyes stayed with mine as he raised my hand to his lips.

I gave him a sensual smile, "Careful Thomas. She will be very angry with you should you bite. I have seen the jar, she doesn't want me dead just yet, just tested." I thought into his mind, *I leave you wanting more. Know this, Thom-*

as; *I can control you. You like to be controlled, don't you, Thomas?*

That shook him. I saw it in his eyes. He saw the strength in mine; he felt it in my hand. He thought back to me, *is that not your wish, my dear, to be with only one? Don't cast me aside so quickly.* He smiled and kissed my hand. "You do taste delicious. No matter, my time will come." He looked me up and down. *Such a pity, ooh such a waste; I could save you. I could hide you away where no one would find you. I could love you like no other,* then he released my hand.

I thought back to him. *Maybe at one time that was my wish; but Thomas I do so enjoy a challenge and my clan has proven to be one. I will not hide from anyone, Thomas. I will meet my challenges.* Then I spoke aloud, "Thomas, your time will not come. You need to understand that."

"Oh, Little One, you have no idea what is in store for you. You will never transform and we will win."

"I've a fairly good idea what's in store for me, Thomas. She will be angry with you. I fear you play a very dangerous game."

You are learning well my child, Odessa said.

He laughed a deep belly laugh. "Steven, I think you have far more to handle than you realize."

The tightening in my chest was returning. I slowly moved back to my seat and sat back down, trying not to draw attention to my condition. But everyone was watching me, my chest tightened harder; I closed my eyes. "What's wrong, Bree?" Gran's voice rang through my thoughts. I remained quiet; my arms resting on the table, my hands were clinched in fists; my eyes closed but flinched with the pain. Steven sat beside me. Brad had his hand against my back; he could feel my labored breathing, silently taking my pulse.

"Bree what is your mind telling you to do?" Gran asked. She started to guide me through this process, reminding me I already knew what I needed to do. Thomas and his clan sat at the next table and watched. "Do what your mind is telling you, Bree; you know it is right," Gran continued with her guidance.

Very quietly in my mind, I remembered what my strength was and I called upon the wind. I had no idea how it would find me inside, but my mind told me to do this. *I need your strength*; I whispered my thoughts on a breath of air. I felt the smallest breeze kiss my forehead. My body cooled, my hair moved with the gentle breeze and the wood flute played in my head. *Thank you,* I said to the wind.

Everyone at the tables remained quiet. They watched as my hair swirled gently with the invisible wind. My pain lessened, my body relaxed; but I could still feel the cold fingers deep in my chest.

Gran, could you give me a small candle please? I thought to her; my eyes were still closed. My breathing had returned to normal, but I needed protection from this feeling and the only thing that came to my mind was fire. I was sure the hotel would frown upon a circle of fire being started in their restaurant, so the only thing I could think of was a candle.

What color should the candle be?

I shrugged my shoulders, it didn't matter to me what color but that must be an important question or she wouldn't have asked. White seemed to be the color for 'good' in my mind so that is the color I asked for.

A small white candle appeared in front of me. The flame flickered and grew in its intensity. Slowly the flame shrunk until it was a small flicker. Odessa spoke in my mind, *what do you sense, Bree? Let your mind wander. Seek the evil. It can't hide from you now, but it doesn't know this. Find what you seek, my child.*

My eyes were still closed but I could see everyone as if they were open. I could feel the worry from my clan, and oddly enough even from Thomas and a few of his clan. I heard the voice of one of Thomas' clansmen; *the females need to leave, Tom. We can't talk with them here. They need to go!*

I saw dark patches hovering over Ted; a large dark patch was hovering over three members of Thomas' clan. They reminded me of the dark I saw in Yellowstone. The same hate and evil I felt there, I felt here. The only difference was that here it was grabbing my insides. It hadn't touched me in Yellowstone, but I was outside when I had seen it. I had the strength of the wind and the protection of the fire that burned deep underground. I watched as the dark patches enveloped their hosts, and I knew these four needed to leave our table. And apparently, if I wanted to know why Thomas was truly here, the women needed to leave as well. I knew that much, but how was I going to accomplish this? I opened my mind to my grandmother. *Gran, I'm going to ask you to leave the table and you need to take all the women with you. I'm going to ask Bradley to send Becky and Ted away. Thomas has something to tell and they will not do so with you here. I will be fine, I promise, but Gran...I do not want our conversation here heard by anyone else, my powers haven't grown enough to accomplish that.*

I'm not worried about you my dear; I will take care of the concealment spell. However, I don't think your men will be all that accommodating, she answered.

Then I opened my mind to all men present; excluding the women and the ones the dark held.

Brad, I need you to send Becky and Ted away. Send them to their room to meditate. I just need them away from this table.

Why Bree? Why do you want me to do this? I need to know your thoughts before I send members of our group away, when we are in a potentially dangerous situation, Brad said as he watched Thomas.

Bradley, because they are unknown to me. I feel a bad energy at the table and I need you to remove my unknown element.

Brad looked at Rick, Steven, and Billy; he then turned his gaze on Thomas.

Thomas tipped his head. *We are not here to attack you, Bradley,* Thomas assured him.

Brad had Rick send Becky and Ted back to their room for meditation. The sensation lessened, but did not leave; it was still at the table. *Thomas, how many new members of your clan are with you?* I asked.

Why?

Because, I am asking Thomas, I said calmly but commanding, causing Thomas to sit a little straighter.

I have three new members with me, my Lady, Thomas answered.

Are you vetting them properly? I asked.

Yes, my Lady.

Thomas, I am asking you to please send those three away and, so you do not to draw attention to them, please send two of your clansmen away as well. I don't care which two.

My Lady, you are asking me to send five away when you only sent two of yours. You have two very powerful witches at your table. You leave me very vulnerable, Thomas protested.

Very well, Bradley, I am asking you to send Madalyn, Sandy, and Gina away. There Thomas, I matched you five for five.

My Lady, I mean no disrespect, but Mildred and Bill still give you far better supremacy. One of them must go as well, Thomas again protested.

No, Bree, that leaves us very vulnerable. I will not ask all four of them to leave, Brad said firmly.

Yet you expect me to send mine away and accept you will not attack? Thomas railed.

You still will have eight men to our four. I will not allow this, Brad challenged.

Oh, enough, I shouted at them all with my mind. My hand drew to my forehead and I began to massage my temples. The flame from the tiny candle pulsed wildly. *I know this is a foreign subject to all of you, but I am asking you to trust. For the love of God, will you just trust me for once?*

Brad exhaled; he placed his hand on my arm. *Madalyn, Sandy, Gina and yes, Millie, please go upstairs. We will be fine.*

Thomas, please, I am asking you to trust me.

Thomas nodded to his clansman sitting next to him. He selected six members of their clan to leave. Three of these members were their newest members; but I didn't know if the dark was clinging to the new members or the old.

Steven leaned in close to me, he had been very quiet though out this whole process; but I was aware of him the entire time. His leg never lost contact with mine; he sat very still but very close to me. "Are you feeling better now, Princess?"

"Yes, the sensation is subsiding quickly now." I smiled and opened my eyes. "Whew! That's better." I folded my arms on the table and smiled at them.

Billy made a glass of water appear in front of me, "You look thirsty, Bree, and hot. Are you feeling okay?"

"Yes, I'm fine now, a little shaky but fine." I drank the water, blew out the candle, and smiled at them again, *Billy, I need everyone to have a drink of their special liquid. Do you mind? I would like a nice chardonnay and please pour yourself whatever you prefer.* Billy looked at me strangely, *please Billy; I know what I'm doing.*

Eleven tall glasses of their special red liquid appeared on the table, drawing everyone's eyes to them. With the slightest wave of my hand, I moved the glasses toward everyone, "Thomas, you look thirsty and so do your men," I said as the drinks found their way to each of them. I could see Thomas' mouth water; it had been quite some time since he'd had his precious Drink. He did not reach for it and I watched the muscles flex from his men. This was a torture to Thomas and that was not my intent. "Thomas, you have gone long enough, do not torture yourself any further. Drink the Drink I have placed in front of you," I said a little firmer. We continued to stare at each other, "Oh very well,

Richard, please take a drink of Thomas' Drink; show him I mean him no harm."

Thomas took his drink in his hand, "That is not necessary, my Lady." He tipped his head to me, took a long drink and his men did the same.

I watched as they emptied their glasses to quench the thirst that burnt in their veins. I felt their settlement as they placed their empty glasses on the table before them. "Would you like another?" I smiled as I looked at each of them.

"No, my Lady. That was very kind of you, but...we are fine," Thomas said.

I decided to lead this discussion, I already had my foot in hot water with my clan, might as well take a complete bath! "So, tell me Thomas," I gestured toward his remaining clansmen, "how long have they been with you?"

"Gentlemen, watch your manners," Rick warned.

I turned to Rick, a little startled by his words, "Why?"

"Because," the man sitting next to Thomas offered the explanation, "we normally don't discuss matters of importance with females around. We tend to have to watch what we say, what language we use."

Another one of Thomas' clansmen spoke up, "You are a female; maybe you too need to leave, let the men have this discussion."

Rick and the one sitting next to Thomas who just spoke groaned, Steven smiled, and Billy just shook his head.

I looked around Steven at the clansman that stuck his vampire foot in his mouth. He was stocky, broad shouldered, dark hair, dark eyes. His lips were pursed, his jaw tight, his brow creased. His expression told me he didn't like women sitting in on matters of 'importance', let alone to ask a question during a meeting. I was not going to be intimidated; I was already in deep shit with my men. So why get cold feet now? "I don't think so, so get over it. My ears are not delicate; your words will not shock me." I looked back to Thomas, "My answer, please."

"Since before you were born, my Lady," he smiled, suppressing a laugh.

I tipped my head toward him, "Thomas, you are not my slave, please do not call me by that title. My name is Aubrey or you may call me Bree. You are comfortable with them; our conversation will remain between our two clans?"

"How dare you question our loyalty to the head of our clan," demanded another of his clansmen.

I felt Rick and Billy's muscles tense, Steven repositioned himself in his seat, blocking me into the table for my protection, Brad's hand moved to my waist so he was able to grab me and hustle me away if the threat became too great. I watched the same scenario start to play on the other side of the table, Thomas' clan vying for position just in case the threat level rose any higher.

I looked at each of my clan, smiled at Thomas, and then looked at his clansman that had taken offense to my question. He was a tall man, his shirt was tight against his chest and arm muscles, the paleness of his skin gave him a mocha complexion, he wore his hair cut in a tight afro, his brow was creased, his lip twitched. Yes he gave a very menacing appearance. "I meant no disrespect. I merely asked, as I am sure your leader would have asked, if he were in my position. Should the wrong people find out about the conversation we are about to have, it would not bode well for your clan or ours."

"They are extremely loyal to me my...Aubrey," Thomas smiled.

"I want you all to calm yourselves." I spoke at them all, "We are not enemies sitting at this table. Rick, do you have any questions you wish to ask?"

Rick gave me an odd look, and then turned his attention back to Thomas and his clan. "Greg, when did these new members come to your clan? I don't remember you taking any during the gathering."

Evidently Greg was important in this clan since Rick directed his question to him and not Thomas. If he weren't so pale, I would have found him attractive. He was as tall as Rick and muscular, blond hair, clean-shaven. He had a very bright smile, sparkling gray eyes, and a dimple in his chin. I had to remind myself he also wanted my blood, so I would keep my distance.

"We didn't select them at the gathering. They came to us after it, during our hunt. Most unusual, but since we didn't find any at the gathering that suited our taste," he looked at me, and smiled, "we listened to their request. You must agree to make such a request after the appointed time and during our bonding hunt took...some balls." He cleared his throat. I watched as he searched his words before he spoke again, a small smile creased his lips as he carefully spoke so as not to embarrass me. "Their females were most enjoyable during the hunt, they fit in well with us. We are vetting them in the proper manner. Our females are happy with the selection. We can take theirs at any time we wish, as I said, they are fitting in well." His smile broadened, as he looked at me, happy he had accomplished his task, "I hope I didn't embarrass you."

"Not to worry sailor, ya didn't," I smiled. "May I ask a question, or is it forbidden for a woman to speak?" I looked around Steven and at the clansman who thought I should leave.

Brad laughed, "Ask your question Bree."

"What made you accept them? I mean, surely they had some redeeming quality you were looking for other than you found them enjoyable for sex, or were you just surprised they had the gumption to ask and figured they would fit in?"

Thomas laughed, "Aubrey, you are unfamiliar with our ways. We have specific times to select potential members; we would have been within our rights to kill them for interrupting our hunt."

"Yes, Thomas I am unfamiliar with your ways, that's why I asked. Now I will ask, then why didn't you kill them? What stopped you from doing just that?"

"Good point," Rick said, "why didn't you? I know your clan. You don't like to be interrupted during your rituals, and you are protective of your females. I can't imagine you would just let anyone," Rick looked at me and smiled, "enjoy your females without a thorough vetting."

Greg looked at Thomas. It dawned on them, they were at a loss to explain why they accepted them, but they had and now they had realized they had let something into their clan that might prove harmful to them.

"You may not want to let on you are aware of this Thomas," Billy advised. "Sounds to me you have a little witchcraft going on, and we all know who the witch is."

"Why do you say that Billy?"

"Because Half Pint, Thomas' clan is legendary. Unless you had a death wish you wouldn't try to join them the way these did. Greg, I can't imagine you not questioning it, nor you Thomas. Somehow they or someone else worked a spell over you."

"Well, what about you, when did you let those two in?" Greg asked. "You didn't take anyone at the gathering either."

"No, you're correct there, we had been working on them for a while. We knew Bree would be joining us and one of our females thought it would be a good idea to find this particular female. Since she and Bree were close growing up, they thought Bree might be more accepting with some of our," Steven smiled at me before he continued, "issues, if we had someone she was comfortable with."

I looked at Steven, then Rick, I found the use of the word female unsettling. Why did they call them that? It just seemed so derogatory. What's the matter with the word woman, or mate or spouse or just their name for heaven's sake? I wasn't going to point this out; that was something I would do in private. I was out numbered and I wasn't going to get on a soapbox to a group of chauvinists, and all vampires to boot!

"Have you always been with Esmeralda?" I asked. I didn't know this clan. My men seemed to be familiar with them, but they had never spoken to me about them. And I had a strong feeling they were not going to willingly give me their history.

"No, she contacted me the first time, when you were born. I wasn't interested, but then she made me an offer I just couldn't resist." His smile was friendly; his arrogance was gone. I sat quietly. "You want me to tell you what she offered?" He became a little uncomfortable.

"I already know what she offered you Thomas."

"You do?" He eyed me suspiciously.

"Yes, it's not hard to figure out. She wants me dead, but I'm afraid that will not happen by your hand or by any others. It would seem your mistress," I looked at him and smiled, "doesn't trust you. Would you not agree?"

"I have given her no such reason to mistrust me, Aubrey."

"She is not someone to play with Thomas. I said earlier you play a very dangerous game and I meant that."

He tipped his head in acknowledgement. "I appreciate your concern. However, you needn't worry; my clan is strong."

"Thomas, when all is said and done, it doesn't matter how strong a clan is, it's who comes out on top. And my dear Thomas...that will be me!"

I unnerved him with my comment; his men shifted in their chairs as they became uncomfortable with my assessment of their situation.

I smiled a little coyly, "Thomas, your mistress has used you; she does not trust anyone other than herself and her demons. If you thought she would spare you in the end, or spare your clan...you should rethink that. When you go to her tonight, and tell her all that you have seen, she will not believe your story." His clan sat quietly and listened to my words, "Soon Thomas, she will be made to believe and fear me, and that puts you and your clan at great risk. Her decisions will not be thought through, and that will be dangerous to you, because you were sure...you could have avoided this day." I smiled, "Thomas, know you could not have prevented my arrival. I don't want you or your clan to get caught in the middle. She will require much of you soon, because she will begin to panic. My strength grows daily; my will is strong and very soon she will see."

He looked at my clan; maybe a little surprised they were allowing me so much freedom in this meeting. My clan sat confidently by me, none spoke or showed any hint of worry, and *that* worried me. They were too quiet.

"I will continue to play along with your ruse," I added, "to a point. But know I can be just as steadfast in my resolve and my bark will not be worse that my bite. You have stayed too long. I gave you the information she needed, go and give it to her."

Thomas nodded his acknowledgement to me as he stood.

Then I gave him another warning, "Mark my word Thomas, she will replace you. Her dark creatures have reported back to her." I pointed my finger at him, "we are not your enemy. I would not mention to her we had a friendly conversation or that you suspect traitors in your clan. And Thomas, you need to drink more; your body has weakened.

"I'll keep that in mind," he cleared his throat. He smiled as he looked toward the bar and spotted someone heading our way, "Ah, Greg, we may want to head this problem off. We have just had a delightful conversation, why spoil the night."

I looked toward the bar and saw Jared coming toward us. "Surely Greg, you don't let him touch your women?" I smiled the question.

Greg looked at me, and then at the male members of my clan and I got a hint of sadness, "No...ah..."

"You may call me by my name. It's okay."

"No, Aubrey, he's not someone we let close to our women." His eyes gave me pause and I entered his mind as Thomas spoke with him.

Bree will be fine Greg; her clan will not let those creatures near her again. I had hoped to scare her off but she is very strong. She's confident; I'll give her that. Her clan will take care of her, or she them, not sure now which. We have our business to take care of, send Sean to move Jared off. I think ole Sean was even impressed with our Chosen One.

Greg spoke to two of their clansmen who went and intercepted Jared and walked him out of the room.

∽

With Thomas and his clan gone, I now had to face my men. "Well, that turned out better then I thought it would." I smiled; they were not, so I waited for the other shoe to drop...I didn't have to wait long!

"Bree, tell me, what the hell were you thinking?" Billy asked.

"Which time?" I asked and knew immediately I shouldn't have.

"Bree, we are their enemy. Don't you understand that? They are *your* enemy. They want you dead; she wants you dead. Hell, half of the fucking Council wants you dead. We have spent the last thirty-two years keeping you safe and you sit here and tell them we are not their enemy? Well, yes the hell we are." Billy finished, and then started again, "You gave him way too much information. Hell, we didn't even know half of it. What are we going to do with you? Did you not see how many members are in his clan? He comes prepared. It was very possible your entire clan could have been wiped out tonight, just so you could prove he had no powers over you. That sounds just a little selfish don't you think?"

We hadn't talked a lot about my transformation in the many hours that had passed since Brad took my blood and the faint green smoke appeared. This was part of my life too. They were going to have to deal with me doing this if I had to deal with two mates. If I wanted them to believe I had a chance to survive, then I had to take Billy's comments on. I stood up and faced all four of them.

"I know you are going to find this hard to believe, but they are not our enemy. Yes, you have kept me safe for thirty-two years and I do appreciate that fact, but Billy, you have not been keeping me safe from them. I have a feeling you have always been on the same side. I never would have let the others of our clan leave our table if I didn't believe we were on the same side here. I wouldn't put my clan in jeopardy to prove my powers. You should know better than to even suggest that! I gave the appropriate amount of information I intended to give and nothing more. It will get back to the correct person, I'm sure of that. I know things now. I have told you repeatedly I have the knowledge of the old ones, I have their guidance, but you don't hear me."

"Just how do you know it isn't a trick, how do you know you aren't playing into their hands? You are so young and very naive, Bree," Billy scolded.

"He is correct in that point, Bree. It may have been ir-responsible on your part to give away as much as you did,"

Brad pointed out. "How do you know you aren't falling into their trap? You are very new to this life. I fear we gave you too much leeway during that meeting."

Now *that* made me mad. What more was needed to prove I knew what I was doing? "There's a five letter word my clan needs to learn. It's a simple word really, but it requires much courage and I fear my clan does not have the courage to use it. My path is more complex then any of you realize. There is a part of this path that none of you can help me with; it must be done by me alone. I know I will have to go up against Esmeralda..."

"What is your word, Bree?" Brad asked testily.

I answered him calmly, "The word is 'trust' Bradley. Like I said, it's a simple word, but it takes a great amount of courage to use it properly. If I am going to succeed in this, I need you all to trust my judgment. There is more at stake than you know. Billy, I am going to do things that will test your blood pressure, but you are going to have to trust I know what I am doing. That's a big leap of faith for you, for all of you. If you can't let me do what I need to, we might as well stop right now and let the other side win; let those of the dark win. I would like to believe that the people sitting at this table believe in and trust me. I would like to believe that my mate, and my Alpha mate, believes in me. I not only have to be a leader in our clan, but I also have this to deal with. My life didn't stop because I became a leader with you Bradley. Many things have been thrown at me today and I'm handling them. I don't see it on the other side. I would like to believe my families do not think I will fail. Because if they do, then why go through all of this? Why waste your time and mine? If you are just letting me have a good time before the lights go out permanently, then don't. I don't need that kind of help. I will go it alone."

Brad stood up and the other three remained very calm. *Mom and Dad are fighting now children* "You are correct Bree. There is a lot at stake that we don't know about, because you refuse to take us into your confidence. The word 'trust' works both ways." Brad threw his napkin down on the table; his eyes did not leave mine.

"Yes, it does, but I have given you all my trust," I spoke back to him. We were so close I didn't need to shout. All the events of the day today came gushing forth, my human side clearly visible. "I trust everything you told me I needed to do, but I received nothing back from you. You've kept your secrets from me for fear I can't handle it. Giving me information in small pieces, when and what you felt I needed to know. You expect me to trust you and I do. I do what is asked of me and I have not once backed away from that - even when it goes against every fiber of my being. I have not once asked any of you to change."

I turned to leave "Bree, where do you think you're going?" Brad asked tersely.

"It's late, I'm going to bed."

"Well, then we will take you to your room. Sometimes you are such a stubborn child," Brad said.

"Little One, we are just looking out for you." Rick smiled; stupidly he was trying to make this situation better.

I turned and looked at all of them. I was truly angry, but I spoke in as calm a manner I could muster, "I do not wish to be escorted to my room. I am not a child nor am I your Little One. Goodnight." I turned and left.

Chapter 26

The Tongue Lashing

I stood staring out my window at the night skyline. I was right; it looked much better at night. All the flaws you could see during the day were hidden by the night. Even though it was dark, the lights of the city burned my eyes as they watered with the tears. For the first time in the last two days my headache was back, I was burning up, and I was miserable. My neck muscles were tensing, causing my back to hurt. I just wanted this to go away.

I had spoken badly to them. I didn't mean to, but the words just kept coming out of my mouth. I'd told them all to go away and I would do this on my own. I knew I couldn't, but I was getting tired of this whole mess! It just seemed like a cloud was constantly hanging over my head and no matter how hard I tried, I couldn't get it to go away. Something new kept being introduced to me every time I thought I had a handle on things. My instinct to survive was growing stronger but the stronger it seemed to get the more alone I felt.

I had no one I could talk to about the confusion in my head, the feelings I was experiencing, my deep love for Steven and my love for Brad. I couldn't talk with my mother about this. I was certain she would not understand. Maybe I could talk with my grandmother; she said she would help me understand this life. Gina and I were close, but she would feel the need to tell Billy. I didn't have a close friend I could talk with anymore, I truly felt so alone here, and now I had told my clan to leave me alone as well. Damn, I just wanted the whirling in my head to stop. I needed a break, but I knew it would not come. What was I thinking? This had better be worth it. I closed the blinds and left the darkness outside. I went to change my clothes, turning lights on along my way.

The hour was late and I needed to sleep. I let my mind wander. I knew where they were, all of them, including Gran. I watched them. Sandy seemed angry with Rick; he sat quietly, watching Gran as she wagged her finger at Steven and Brad. Both sat with their arms folded across their chests, listening to the point Gran was making. Gina said something to Billy. He looked unhappy, they all looked unhappy. I was making their lives miserable. Madalyn sat between Steven and Brad. That's generally, where I sat. Steven didn't have his arm around her though; that was encouraging. My world was slipping through my fingers and I didn't know how to stop the slide.

Bree, you're starting to feel sorry for yourself again, Odessa's voice came to me on a whisper. It comforted me, made me realize I was not truly alone.

Yeah, I am. I need to rest.

Maybe you should listen to the conversation; I think you may be surprised. It's a conversation, Bree. You're not entering their thoughts. It's a conversation, and I one I think you need to hear.

∽

Gran was busy rebuking the male members of my clan, with Gina and Sandy's help.

"William James, I can't believe you called her selfish. What in blue blazes were you thinking? And you Bradley - calling her a child? My Lord man, could a child take on all she is being asked to do? Richard, there is a time and a place to call her your Little One, and this was neither. Steven, you couldn't even bring yourself to stand up for her. You had all better get your priorities in order, or you just might be without her, and I for one would not blame her in the least. I wouldn't blame her if she were upstairs packing."

I could tell Gran was mad, her face and neck were blotchy. Sandy punched Rick in the arm; she only managed to hurt her hand. Gina wouldn't let Billy put his arm around her and he looked so lost.

My grandmother continued chastising my clan. "Bree has accepted everything you four have told her; and not once, not once, has she walked away from her responsibilities to you or to your clan or to her family. Everything you are telling her goes against everything she has grown up with, but she trusts you four. She knows you wouldn't lie to her. You're worried about leaving your clan vulnerable. I left because I knew, if she was pressed, she would have been able to wipe out his entire clan. You were not in any danger. She doesn't know what she can do yet, but she is stronger than I am."

"Gran, she's still human. She can't possibly be stronger than you yet," Billy disagreed, which was not a wise move on his part. Gina punched Billy's shoulder. He paid no attention to it, I'm sure he didn't feel a thing.

"William," Gran said a little calmer. "You have watched her. You have felt her strength. I am telling you right here and now, if someone she loves was being threatened, I pity the individual in her path. The problem you four are having is that you can't dominate her like you can these three." Gran motioned to Madalyn, Sandy, and Gina. Sandy and Gina smiled, but Madalyn continued to sulk.

She knew that last statement got their attention and she continued. "You have been so long without the female counterpart of Brad, you don't know how to handle it. Now you have one, and a very strong one I might add. You four don't know what a prize you have here, but I can tell you Thomas does." Gran pointed her finger at Steven and Brad, "I can tell you the Council does. Hell, why the do you think everyone wants her dead? Yet, you four sit down here sulking, leaving her alone in her room, treating her like a child."

She looked at each one of them, making them meet her gaze. I started feeling sorry for them. Many times I had been on the other end of her lectures growing up. I knew how uncomfortable they could be.

"I know my granddaughter, and I can tell you right now what's going through her head. She's sure, if she hadn't come here, your lives would be much better off. She wouldn't have upset your apple cart Madalyn." Gran's gaze was piercing. "*You* and Steven could have your times together with no problems. Now you're limited, and that makes *you* mad. *You* can't have both Steven and Bradley to yourself, and Steven, *you* would be free to date whoever you wanted and have them at any time. A carefree life, is that what *you* would like Steven?" Gran didn't wait for an answer. She knew him better than that, but she was making a point. "Bradley, *you* could continue to lead your clan the way *you* want and not have to talk with her about anything, not have to explain yourself." Gran settled herself a little more in her chair. Her eyes were watering. "Richard, you and William would continue being the protectors of the clan. Everyone would continue to do as *you* say, hunt where *you* say, live and work and study where *you* two deem safe. But this little human came along. This short little shit, as you like to call her Richard. And she questions you. She makes you think about things and *none* of you like it."

"Mildred, you know that's not true," Brad said. "We have waited for her to join us. We have planned for this day for so long. Steven has done everything asked of him by her family and he has suffered the most for it. Your judgment of us was unfair."

"Was it? Then why are the four of you sitting here? Why are you punishing her?" Gran asked.

❧

I think I've listened to enough Odessa. I fluffed the pillows on my bed and lay in the center of the bed with the pillows all around me. I was familiar with this. I knew Steven wouldn't be back tonight, not after his tongue-lashing from Gran. Hell, I'd be lucky if he talked to me tomorrow. My room was quiet and I didn't like that. I had gotten used to having everyone around, having Steven lying next to me. But now my room was quiet. I was going to have to get used to the quiet again. So, I just thought about my IPod and I concentrated on it and my IPod came to me. I stayed on my back and stared at the ceiling. With my headset on, I listened to my music as I began to plan for the next day.

CHAPTER 27

A Little History Lesson

The dream came again. I walked the passage toward the magic chamber; I knew this passage now. I could hear them talking and I quickened my pace to hear all I could. It was important; my mind told me I needed to hear this conversation.

She was there and so was Thomas.

"Thomas, what news do you bring me? How strong has she become?" Esmeralda asked as her servant entered the magic chamber. She kept herself busy perusing a large, brown, weather worn, leather book.

"I was unable to seduce her, my Lady. Her powers grow even though she is still human. She is very strong."

"Hmmm, good Thomas," she smiled a very evil smile. "Still human but her magic grows, that's where I need her to be!" Then she laughed, "It doesn't matter, Friday will be her last day with her family. We will bring her here. I

371

have a great need of what she possesses!" She continued browsing her book.

Thomas looked concerned, "What could this child possibly have that you need? How can she help you?" He was digging for more information.

Esmeralda just laughed. Not wanting to give more information, she ignored his questions. "Does she fascinate you?" she asked nonchalantly.

Thomas remained quiet a fraction of a second too long.

"Ah, she does fascinate you. Now I understand; she has you under her spell as well as her clan. Yes, everyone loves Bree, the Chosen One. Sweet, desirable Bree." She slammed her hand down hard on the table and watched him. "I do not love her, Thomas. Do you understand that? I want her dead and if you do not want to bring her to me, I will bring in those that can. Am I making myself clear?" Esmeralda screamed, her paranoia seeping through just a little.

"Yes, my Lady, perfectly," Thomas answered. He was not disturbed in the least by her tone. He stood there completely relaxed, evidentially she had chastised him before. Maybe her bark was worst than her bite.

"Tell me Thomas; was she in any pain this evening?" Esmeralda questioned.

"I noticed just the tiniest amount of discomfort. I think she said she had a headache. Nothing more."

"Really? Nothing more - just a headache? She didn't appear to be in any other pain?" Esmeralda asked again.

Thomas realized she had been informed, so he had to recover quickly, "Well, there were her theatrics. I think she did this so we would even the playing field. You do know I went with a large contingent of my clan? They are a small group, and I think she was trying to even the odds. I can tell you their leader wasn't happy when she requested he send her grandmother away with the rest of the females. No, she probably got a good scolding for that. Her clan will learn not to let females negotiate, especially the inexperienced ones," he said nonchalantly, giving Esmeralda the impression he wasn't hiding anything.

"Theatrics? So you do not think she was in any pain then, it was all theatrics?" Esmeralda asked as nonchalantly as Thomas.

"I was there Essie. Were you?" Thomas asked, raising an eyebrow to her. He didn't answer her question.

"No, Thomas, I was not there. You can rest easy."

"Are you having me followed? Do you no longer trust your loyal servant?" Thomas moved in close to her. "Essie, have I ever given you reason to doubt me?" He nudged her neck with his nose, his tongue licking toward her jugular. "Essie, you should know better." He nipped at her ear, and she shivered with her pleasure. Her anger softened, took his face in her hand, and pressed her lips hard to his.

Their kiss finished, Thomas smiled. Pleased he had reassured his mistress of his loyalty, he continued with his deceit. "Essie, what is all of this? What do you seek, my Lady?"

"Something to make your job a little easier my sweet. We can break her, Thomas. Her human side is strong. She will not take to their ways. She already struggles with it. It will weaken her, then, my Thomas, she will fall to you, and you will bring her to me," she smiled. "I have a great need for some of her...blood. I want her heart beating in my hands when I rip it from her body."

"You promised her blood to my clan."

"I only need a little. I never promised her heart to you though." She laughed with such a hateful sound. "No...I never promised that to you!" She went back to her book, turning the pages, looking for something. Thomas moved along side her. "Tell me what you seek, Essie." He nudged her neck again.

"Oh, just a little spell to help bring her down. They need to bond a little sooner, my love. And this human child will not stand for it. Ah, this looks promising." She ran her finger along the page, and went to collect the needed ingredients. I watched as she mixed and stirred, she whispered the words to herself. Small wisps of smoke rose in the air, making circles as it reached toward the ceiling. She closed the book and smiled, pleased with herself, then turned to Thomas. "I have strengthened the process, they will now need to bond soon, or she will die. We still have time my love. Let the spell work, you will see." Her laugh was shrill. Thomas kissed her neck. She turned to him and gently cupped her hands to his face, pulling him toward her for another kiss. "Now my love, it is time for you to please me."

❧

I turned back the way I had come, past the cells I had visited before. I moved toward the opening, feeling along the walls. My hands became sticky and I looked to see what was on them. Blood. It was seeping down the walls. This was new; I had always felt water before. I looked at my hand again, and the blood was gone. I continued down the passage toward a small pinhole of light in the distance. I needed to know how to gain access to this place. It was important, that much I knew. The passage's twists and turns were being filed in my mind. I could see the pinhole getting larger; I quickened my pace and exited the passage. The air was cold, the sky bright. Prairie lands were before me; mountains were in the distance. It was familiar to me; I had been here before.

∽

The view started to fade. Another place unfolded in my dream, a library. Ceiling to floor built-in oak bookcases, all shelves were filled with books or small sculptures. There was a spiral staircase at the far end of the library taking you to the mezzanine above. There, more bookcases were filled with more books.

On the main floor of the library, four comfortable black leather wingback chairs were placed in the center of the room, and a person sat in each chair. A small table sat next to each of them to hold their drink and ashtray. My vision was blurred so I could not make out the faces. I could smell cigar smoke. The light haze from all of the smoke hung like a low cloud just above them.

In the first chair sat a person in a black robe with a green sash. I heard his voice; I knew his voice. My cousin Ryan was speaking with this group.

"Aubrey is aware of the meeting on Friday. I worry for her; I don't think she fully understands the seriousness of the situation. All of this is new to her and I fear she thinks she can handle it. Her body does warm; I felt it when I kissed her forehead. We knew she was having headaches," Ryan spoke to them all in hushed tones.

"Ryan, do you know if the Guardians have spoken to her; is she hearing voices? Does she speak of anyone assisting her, guiding her?" asked the woman.

"No, Elsa. My brother has told me she specifically said she is not hearing voices, nor has she mentioned anyone helping her. He has removed the spell that hid her memories. He said she handled it well. She was more relieved to know she wasn't crazy. Apparently, she knew more then we had given her credit for."

"Ryan, don't underestimate Aubrey. I have spoken to her; she is a very strong mortal. We have so much riding on her; she will need all the protection we can give," said another man in the group. His face was blurred.

Ryan spoke his concern, "John, I wish the females in her clan were as strong as Aubrey. Sandy is strong, as Bill likes to tell me; but Madalyn can be timid at times. She will be a problem to her."

"Well, Bill should know just how strong Sandy is," John laughed.

"Yes," Ryan laughed, "he should."

"I have heard Esmeralda is looking for a new assassin; Thomas is starting to fall out of favor with his mistress," John advised him.

"I was unaware Thomas was struggling with Esmeralda."

"I don't think Thomas is aware either. Esmeralda plays her cards very close to her ample breast," John smiled as he answered.

"John, really," the woman sitting next to him chastised. "I need to give Bree another gift of the stones. I will watch to see what she will need."

"Well, they are ample; I only speak the truth. Celia, you had better be careful; Esmeralda knows someone on the inside is helping. It will not take her long to turn on her sisters," John said.

"I am not her sister. My true sister lives with a clan of vampires," Celia laughed. "Ryan, how is Bree dealing with her, uh," Celia gave a sincere smile, "well in her mind, problem?"

"I think she is having a hard time. The human part is so strong. She wanted a fairy tale existence, but reality is setting in. She will learn, as she lives a long time, that variety can be a good thing in her life with her mate." Ryan laughed, "So human, so mortal and so very young."

"She will learn. Maybe I should talk with her, I want to ensure she enjoys her future," Celia smiled as she winked at Ryan.

"Let's let her get used to the two she has before you talk with her, my sweet. We need her to take care of the problems at hand first," John teased, "before her mind gets clouded with the want of others."

"I don't know, her clan loves her immensely," Ryan said. "We may be worrying about the wrong group killing her. The four of them may love her to death," Ryan laughed.

"Ah, young love; I remember it well," Elsa laughed. "There's something to be said for older love, too. The older you get the better it is. You youngsters are too impatient. You wait, mark my words, it's true what they say; it's like a fine wine the older you get. She may yet surprise you, Ryan."

"No, Bill tells me she is struggling, and her clan is worried. Her human side is very strong. Let's hope her magic is stronger," Ryan prayed.

The dream changed again. Now, I sat at the picnic table like before, the Clark's Jay flew to greet me. I had a slice of bread in my hand and was tearing it into pieces. "I promised to bring you something the last time I was here," I said.

"Yes, you did, and you have kept your promise. You always keep your promises, don't you, child?"

"I try. I may not always succeed, but I do try."

The Clark's Jay flew to a rock by the water's edge. "Come here child. Look into the water, and tell me what you see."

I went to the river and looked into the clear water of the Firehole River. I saw the rocks in the water; I saw the fish and the moss. Then I saw nothing but a smooth surface and images started to appear. The landscape was foreign to me, but I knew this place. My mind told me I did and I told the jay what I was seeing.

"Yes, child, that place is not here. It is called Zamora; it is where we came from. We did not always walk your earth; this was a parallel world to yours. We came through the cosmic portal many hundreds of years ago. We destroyed that world, and many others, through our wars. What else do you see?" The jay asked.

I looked again. I saw bodies lying disemboweled on the ground; others were dismembered. Those not dead yet, cried in agony.

I watched the battle unfold before me. From high atop a hill, I saw fire bolts fly from the hands of men and women toward the creatures at the bottom of the hill. Spells were being hurled back and forth; screams and cries echoed through the landscape as they fell on their victims. The sky turned grey as clouds formed overhead.

Giants came from the trees, tearing their victims apart. When they caught one, blood spewed, and body parts went in all directions. They picked up large boulders and threw them at their victims smashing them into the soft dirt.

I saw others eating the flesh of their victims and drinking their blood. The wildness of these creatures sent shivers through my body. I knew them to be vampires. I watched them, the blood dripping from their mouths as they gorged themselves on the flesh and blood of the fallen. I watched as they chased the weakened ones. I heard their victims scream as the vampires sank their sharp teeth into them. I watched as they continued eating, while their victims struggled to free themselves from their talons. I watched each victim die a slow and painful death, and I shivered.

I witnessed a group of fair-skinned creatures hurtle their arrows toward the group on the hill, and at the Giants. The arrows bound them in golden ropes and crushed them. This group was fast, they moved with lightening speed through the carnage.

I saw sparkling balls of light move all around and when the light was close to a victim they would fall and die. The pain must have been great, as the screams hurt my ears and I had to cover them to drown it out.

I watched as the lightening in the sky flashed. The sound of thunder was intense and it overwhelmed me. I again, covered my ears and fell to the ground; but I did not take my eyes off the water.

Tears fell down my cheeks as I continued to watch, to learn. I saw the faces of the dead and dying. Their cries tore at my heart. I heard the laughter from these monsters as they continued with their assaults.

Then I watched as the sky split and the group from the hills flew into it. The flesh eaters followed, as did all the others that were still standing and fighting. They all fled to the jagged opening in the sky and then they were gone, and that world exploded into millions of pieces and was no more.

❧

The image in the river vanished and I was looking into the Firehole River again. Then another image appeared. We were now in a valley filled with wild flowers, boulders, and trees; but I saw no one. I waited and slowly one person from each of the groups that had flown through the torn fabric that bound our two worlds together started to appear. They met in the circle of stones on the ground and I listened.

"Zamora is gone, we have destroyed it. Do we dare destroy this new land we have come to?" Asked a grey bearded man. He was very tall, thin, and very old. The beard was well past his waist and he carried a staff adorned with diamonds and emeralds and rubies. The crown of the staff held a purple crystal that sparkled brilliantly. His robes were grey, and he wore a white sash around his waist. "We need to live in peace here. We need to agree to this, today." He pointed his finger at each one of them. "This world is our last hope. It will contain many who are not as we are, but here we must remain. My race does not wish war with you. We need you, each of you; and you need us as well if we are all to survive."

Another man spoke. He too was tall, thin, and pale. He wore a black cloak; his hair was shiny and black. "We wish to be left alone as well. Our numbers are few now. We must grow our clans. We have tasted the blood from this world and it is good. We wish to remain and live in peace. We have no qualms with you, but we took you at your word before, and you have turned on us. You wish to end our existence. Why should we trust any of you now?"

The tallest man of the group spoke. He was a Giant; I was certain of this. "We will go to the far reaches of this world and make our homes in the tallest of mountains. We no longer want to war with you. Through our arrogance, we have destroyed our world. We wish to live in peace."

The tall bearded man spoke again, and I assumed he was a wizard, "We can forge an alliance with each group. This alliance can govern our races to ensure we do not over reach. There is no other world we can go to. We cannot destroy this world as we have done so many times before. There will be many people of this world and we can live among them peacefully." He turned to the vampire, "Take the blood as you need, but do not take the blood of the Magicals. Grow your clans as you need, but not of the Magicals, unless they desire it so."

He looked to the Giant. "Take your people to the mountains, live in peace; but join our alliance. Each group needs to select a member to sit in this alliance; together we will build our world to coexist with the creatures of this world. We will meet again on the next full moon of this world to seal our bond."

Another large man spoke. He had a dark complexion, he stood straight, his hair was long, and he wore little clothing. "The full moon causes my kind problems on this world; our bodies revert to our ancestors' ways. Maybe a crescent moon would allow us to attend as well; unless that is your intent, to keep us out," he questioned suspiciously.

The bearded man smiled, "A crescent moon will suffice."

Then they were gone; the image vanished and the water returned.

❧

I turned to look at the Clark's Jay. "Is this how it began? You were not of this world originally?"

"It is our story, many hundreds of years ago. Now this is our world as well as yours, child. We have coexisted for many years with the mortal world. Others have tried before to overthrow your world, but a Chosen One has always turned them back. Now there are those who lead that want to dominate. They have grown tired of this way of life and want the change. They are few, but their numbers are growing. They must be stopped before they destroy this world. Because in destroying this world, they will also destroy themselves. There is no other world we can escape to. They do not understand this or believe this, but the portal will not come again to allow us to leave. We have used it too many times before. Now it will only allow others to enter. This is how the demons come. We have destroyed many, but many still exist.

This is your path my child. To destroy the cosmic portals, and there are many, and stop the demons from coming. Destroy the demons and again, there are many that cause our leaders and yours to sway to the bad, to the dark, to be evil. She protects a demon. You must start there. Your path is very dangerous, my child. If you fail, this world will end."

The Clark's Jay flew to the trees and I was alone. "I am only one person and I am very young. Why have you put so much on me?" I called to the jay, but received no answer.

Chapter 28

Wednesday morning: The Apology

I stayed very still; I was aware of a presence in my room. I was still surrounded by my pillow fortress. Surprisingly I felt protected and I had no idea why. Very slowly I opened my eyes. My bedroom door was ajar just enough to allow the light from the living room to filter in causing the three tall individual's eyes at the foot of my bed to glow and each set was looking straight at me. I could tell from the tint of those eyes whose was whose; and I could smell the soft scent of Billy's aftershave. I heard my tone in all three of them. That was comforting, but they said nothing.

The eyes with the tint of green walked to the side of the bed as the others left the room and closed the door behind them. Now I was worried. I had totally messed everything up, and this was where Steven was going to end it. Madalyn had been right all along. Thirteen years was a very long time. I was going to be on my own. I was getting what I had asked for, and I had no one to blame but myself.

I continued to stay very still; my eyes followed Steven as he sat on the bed. I could still hear his tone for me in his chest, and that gave me a little encouragement. But the longer he went without speaking, the encouragement lessened. Steven turned his gaze from me and my heart sank. I could see the outline of his face and I feared that would be the last silhouette I would remember him by. I would not hold him to his promise to bond to me. I could not bear that. I would release him from his commitment. I would still have three powerful Houses in my line. I would still be strong. Just one House shy, that's all. I was sure I would never see any of them again after today, and I wondered if that would include Billy as well. Had I even lost my cousin?

He reached and turned the lamp on low and I saw the hurt look on his face and that tugged painfully on my heartstrings and my anxiety rose. My heartbeat increased and my face flushed quickly from the blood as it rushed to my head as I readied myself for his goodbye.

"Bree," he finally spoke, his voice was low, and sad. "I don't want you to leave."

I had braced for the worst, but that hadn't come. I had no idea what he was talking about, and then I remembered Gran's words to them. I had no idea what would have caused him to say this? I was still here in Vegas, a place I really didn't care to be, in my bed. If I remembered correctly, I was sleeping; so what gave him the impression I was leaving? "Steven, I'm not leaving. Why would you say such a thing?"

"Your suitcase is out; it's packed with your clothes," he said, motioning to the suitcase at the foot of the bed. His eyes returned to watch me.

I smiled as I realized what he was referring to, "Ah! Steven, you are correct, it does have my clothes in it, and it still has yours. I haven't unpacked since we got back from the hunting trip. If you remember correctly, I wasn't given the chance. Things happened rather quickly when we returned."

I listened as he exhaled softly; the sound of relief was in that soft flow of air. He smiled, "I forgot. I'm sorry; we have thrown a lot at you lately. Things are being rushed and there doesn't seem to be anything I can do to stop it."

"Steven, I'm right where I want to be, here with you and our clan. I'm going to make missteps along the way. You're going to make them too, as will everyone else in our clan. None of us are perfect, it's what makes us who we are," I said softly.

"Bree, in my mind, you are always going to be here. That's it, permanent. Millie reminded all of us not to take that for granted. I just can't assume you will always be here just because the prophecy said it's so, or just because I want to believe it. I can't assume you will always accept our ways without an explanation. You did nothing wrong. I need to apologize to you; I let you down. I won't do that again. You deserve more from me than that." He looked away. I could feel his muscles tensing, preparing for my response.

"Steven," I removed the fortress of pillows and blankets and crawled toward his lap, "Steven, look at me." He lowered his eyes before he turned to meet mine. I smiled as I ran my hand gently along his jaw. He pressed into my hand and inhaled deeply. "Please, stop beating yourself up. I don't want that. If it makes you feel better, I accept your apology; but know you didn't need to give me one." I ran my hand along his shoulders, up around his neck. He pulled me close to him and kissed me, his passion was still intense. His body trembled; he pushed me back onto the bed and continued his kissing and exploring. Our breathing increased. *My Steven was back*, I thought.

But then he stopped. "Damn, I forgot." He sat up and looked down at me, and smiled that sexy little grin of his. "Bree, the others need to speak with you."

"Can't it wait until the morning?" I looked back, smiling, trying to coax him back into my embrace.

"You don't know how much I wished it could; but they are sitting in our living room and they each want to speak with you," he said sheepishly.

"They're out there now?" I drew in a deep cleansing breath as my body switched gears. "Okay, let me get dressed and I'll be right out."

"Bree, they want to speak with you individually."

"But, Steven if I talk with them all at once, we can get back to the matter at hand more quickly." I pressed the issue, as I walked my fingers up his arm.

"Bree, give them their time. They each need one on one time with you. Then I promise we will have ours." He raised his eyebrows as he spoke his reassurance to me.

"Okay, send them in and I will speak with each one and give them the time they need to put their hearts at rest."

He looked down at me lying there in my nightshirt. He ran his hand along my legs and smiled. "Well, maybe you should get dressed. You needn't look this inviting to the men of your clan."

"Ah, good point, Brad's out there," I said as I rolled to get off the bed, heading to the bathroom.

"As well as Rick and Bill, my love," Steven reminded me.

∽

When I finished in the bathroom and reentered the bedroom, I saw him sitting back in the shadows of the sitting area in the room. He was patiently waiting for me, and when he saw me, I saw his smile. He stood as I neared. "Good morning, big guy." I smiled, gave him a sweet kiss on the cheek and went to sit in the chair across from him. He continued to stand even after I sat. "What's wrong, Rick?"

He walked the few steps to me, extended his hand for me to take, which I did. I thought he wanted to shake my hand for his apology. I thought it a little corny, but hey, Rick was my solider, my protector, and my Hercules. Maybe this was his way of apologizing. A handshake, all was forgiven. 'Move along now, Little One,' he would say, and all would be right with the world. I could live with that.

I took his hand and he effortlessly pulled me to my feet, and led me to his seat and onto his lap. I moved to get up, but his hold was firm, tight but gentle. He was not going to release me from his arms.

"Hush Bree, I need you to sit with me and listen to what I have to say," he said firmly. "Please," he said more softly. I relaxed and readied myself for his speech.

When he was content I wouldn't break from his embrace, he relaxed. His free hand washed over his face, he exhaled, and looked at me. His smile was just as bright as it had always been.

His tone was there, deep in his chest. I heard it clearly. I laid the palm of my hand on his chest, feeling the low vibration it made.

I saw my familiar sparks when my fingers touched his skin and my eyes widened in my surprise. I felt his energy rush through my fingertips.

He took my hand in his and raised it to his lips for a gentle kiss. My face spoke my question.

His voice was low and soft; my eyes followed his lips as he spoke to me. "Bree, I'm not apologizing for calling you 'Little One'. I have always called you that and I always will. I use it as a term of endearment with you because I love you. I have told you how special you are to me."

He still held my hand in his, entwining our fingers. His large hand enveloped mine. His thumb rubbed the back of my hand and I watched the energy flash across the back of my hand with each stroke of his thumb. His touch was cool and I was comforted by it. I wanted him to get all of his feelings out without an interruption from me. This was hard for him and I didn't want to make it any harder; so I remained quiet and hoped it was the correct response.

"My heart tore when you said you weren't my 'Little One', but then I realized you were upset and you didn't understand the love I have for you."

He smiled at me. "We aren't doing a good job of preparing you for this life. We had a meeting tonight and we have all decided we need to be better at it. I need to do a better job. Millie was very upset with us, said we behaved badly. You did nothing wrong in the meeting. And I will say, for your first experience with a Traditional, you handled yourself very well. I could tell Thomas and Greg were very impressed with you," he smiled. "Probably a little jealous of our clan, if truth be told." He looked at me and winked. "You noticed their lead female wasn't present. You wouldn't care for Sylvia. I'm somewhat surprised she's a leader in that clan anyway, but it's their taste, I guess. Anyway, we need to be a little more trusting. It's hard though. Oh, we trust you," he continued, "For God's sakes don't misunderstand that. But, we have protected you for so long; and when you start to walk out from under the umbrella of our protection, it tends to make us a little nervous. We say things maybe we shouldn't, speak before we think. We don't take into account your feelings; they're softer than the other females in our clan," he smiled. "I like that though. I like your softness. Damn, the deeper I get into this, the harder it becomes. I'm finding it hard to explain, to make you understand."

I cupped his face in my hands; my thumbs gently caressed his cheeks. "Try Rick. I really need to understand our relationship. I need to understand you."

He settled himself in the chair, locked his arms around me tenderly. I smiled, not knowing if he was bracing in case I tried to bolt and run or what; but I let my muscles relax and he relaxed.

"Bree, we have protected you all your life and we are not about to start letting others get near you. I know you are aware of our rituals, the way we live. Our need to show our love to others in our family. And I also know you. I know that has made you nervous, it's not how you were raised. This isn't fair to you."

His comment took me by surprise.

He smiled as he watched my face change expression from surprise to embarrassment. "All the Chosen Ones before you were prepared for this life and we have thrown everything at you in two days. Hell, I'm surprised you haven't gone running, but you're a trooper. I'll give you that. I just want you to know I love you Bree. I always have. And...I do want my time with you and I'm willing to wait until you have accepted everything and if...you never get to that point...I can accept that too. I just don't want you to leave."

"I'm not going anywhere Richard," I said very quietly.

"Promise?"

"Yes," I whispered. "Richard, we will find our way. I... don't know what that will entail but...I know I need you in my life. My heart's calm when you are with me. I've felt your energy rush through me at times and..." I felt my face warm, "I liked the thrill it gave me."

"I'm not supposed to ask, but I'm going out on a limb here. May I please kiss you?"

"Richard, you've kissed me before. Why do you feel you need to ask me now?"

"No, Bree, I've greeted you. I've given you quick little pecks on the cheeks and lips, I've not kissed you – there's a difference."

I looked at him skeptically. "There is?" I said dryly.

"Yes and if you will stand I will show you."

Rick had that sexy little grin on his face. He motioned for me to stand, which I did. He stood and took my hand, pulled the footstool over with his foot so I could stand on it, giving me a little more height. He softly held my face in his hands, leaned in for his kiss; and, oh, hot damn, it was one heart-melting kiss. Open mouthed and tongue, pure heat generating kiss. He pulled me tighter to him. That one kiss went on for quite a few minutes; I was most certain. At least I thought it did; I had lost track of time. When he'd had his fill, he held me close. He cleared his throat. "You should know I play dirty," he whispered softly.

All I could say was, "Oh!"

He pulled back from me. "Are you okay?" he teased.

"I'm fine, Rick," I acknowledged. I looked up at him, his eyes held my gaze.

"Are you sure you're okay?" Rick asked again a little more tensely.

"I'm fine," I assured him. "But Rick..." I bit my lip as I looked into his eyes.

"What, Little One?" he asked softly.

"May I have another kiss?" I wrinkled my forehead in anticipation of his answer.

"I thought you would never ask." He smiled and pulled me to him and I felt the urgency of his advance. If he could have swallowed me whole I think he would have.

I pressed my hands to his chest as he held me close. Tiny bursts of energy sparked as my fingertips touched his skin. I ran my hands up behind his neck and held him tight. Soft sounds of delight came from deep within my soul as I hungrily drank in all he was offering me. He pressed himself harder to my lips, his sounds just as urgent. Our hearts raced and thundered against our chests until I thought mine would burst through. His hands pulled my hips into him and I became aware of his desire.

My human emotions had escaped from the tiny box my Magical fingers had shoved them into earlier and began shouting their disapproval of my actions. With each soft moan I gave the shouts became louder until finally they won and I begged for us to stop.

"Oh damn, stop...please...please stop my Richard. I'm sorry," I cried. "That was not my intent. I was going to make a joke!"

"Wh...at?" He was barely able to say. He held my head to his chest. His heart and tone pounded in my ear and I thought I would go deaf. "A joke? Okay."

"You don't understand. I was going to kiss you just as devilish as you had kissed me and then tell you I play just as dirty? I'm sorry...so much for my heart beating calmer when you're near me!" I giggled.

He held me there close to his heart, quietly chuckling and swaying with me. "Aubrey Marie, I'm going to enjoy you. And you should be aware I am going to do everything in my power to convince you to spend time with me," he informed me.

"Consider me made aware," I giggled. My heart was calming and I moved to put my arms around his neck so I could see him. I smiled, "I'm so sorry, that was cruel."

He flexed his eyebrows, "I'm not sorry one bit. You are now very well aware of my love for you. You do hold my heart; and I do love you." He ran his finger over my lips. His eyes told me he wanted to kiss me again; but I knew better and I kissed his finger instead and smiled.

"Get some rest, Squirt, I'll see you later," then he disappeared.

❧

I was sure he spoke to the others, because I soon heard a soft tap on the door and Billy poked his head in. His apology was going to be very painful; I could already tell. Gran must have really laid the law down to him.

I held my hand out to him. "Billy, why so glum? You and I have had harsh words before and we have always made up. We're family Billy. I could never stay mad at you for long; you know that." I did my best to reassure him, but he wasn't listening.

"I have never called you selfish before, Half Pint. Never. I should never have said it this time either. I know you're not selfish." He sat in the chair and I sat across from him, watching him.

His body language showed me he was at a loss as to how to make this better. I walked over to him, pushed him back in the chair, and sat on his lap. "Billy, talk to me; don't leave this hanging or we might never get past it."

He sat quietly, not sure where to begin, so I began for him. "You had so much emotion going through your head. There I was, this person you had protected all her life, this person you had held since she was a tiny baby, talking to a group of people you didn't want her near. These were people in your mind you had protected me from. And there I was throwing away all that protection, all your love. Hell, I would have been mad too. I would have said some things to hurt you too. I know you love me more than anyone does. I promise I will never show disrespect to any of your feelings again. Will you accept my apology, Billy?" I smiled at him.

"Bree, I need to apologize to you; not the other way around," he said quietly. I laughed. He looked at me, shook his head, and laughed as well. "Damn, Bree what am I to do with you? You are entirely too forgiving."

"Billy, just by you coming here to talk with me is apology enough. Dang, I thought I would never see you guys again. I was so scared when I saw the four of you at the foot of my bed; I thought you were all here to say good-bye. I figured Madalyn had made her point and Steven was listening to her. Shoot, I thought you were all listening to that rubbish," I finished, realizing I might have just said more than I intended to.

"Half Pint, you don't have to worry about Steven listening to Madalyn. The only bond they share is the one you are aware of. Nothing more. She has no pull with him, and I know it pisses her off; but that's the facts. Oh, trust me, she thinks she does; but that's all in her head. Brad listens to you when it comes to the clan, and that makes her mad, although I have no idea why. Brad has never asked her opinion when it came to the clan. You let Gina handle her; she'll get Madalyn's head on straight."

"Billy, I appreciate the offer, but you tell Gina to let me handle her. I'm not as timid as I might appear at times. She and I will have our "come to Jesus meeting" one day, but right now is not the time. She has some jealousy issues to work through, that's all. We'll get it sorted out," I advised.

Billy rubbed my arm; my head was resting on his shoulder. "Are we okay, Half Pint? Are we solid?"

I took his hand in mine, raised it to my lips, and very delicately kissed the back of his hand. "Yes Billy, you and I are very solid together." He hugged me tightly.

"Billy, you need to go spend time with Gina; stop worrying about me and go take care of her. I'll see you later today; but right now, I have one more of my precious clan's hearts to ease. Then I need to be with Steven. I don't want to go through another night like tonight so I am making an executive decision. Any more arguing and we talk about it then. No more of these late night therapy sessions." I got up from his lap, but he continued holding my hand.

"You consider me and Gina part of your clan?" Billy asked.

"Yes, sweet William, I do. Got a problem with that?" I asked, giving him another opening to talk with me.

He just smiled. "Nope, no problem at all. And I will never stop worrying about you, so get used to it. I'll see you later." With a hug and a kiss, he was gone.

∽

Brad was my next patient. I had to wonder what he and Steven had talked about all this time. I hadn't heard anything out in the other room; just the soft tap on the door and Brad's head peeking around the corner as it opened. He smiled as he came up to me, taking my hands in his, and pulling me up to him for a quick hug and a kiss. "Okay, missy, I'll make this brief," Brad said. "I'm sorry. You're not a child and I shouldn't have said that. What I should have said was, you are the most stubborn, beautiful young woman I know, and damn, that turns me on." He pressed his lips to mine and I couldn't help but laugh.

"Brad, honestly, what kind of apology is that?" I laughed as I pulled back a little so I could look at him.

"My kind. Like it? You are hot ya know, beautiful and young and you do turn me on so, it works. Bree, you can't stay mad at me. I'll not allow it, so accept my apology. And know, I will probably do or say something in the future that will cause me to have to apologize again." Then he handed me a black satin bag. "Open it," he smiled. Which, of course I did. I mean, what woman in her right mind turns down a gift from someone she loves? Inside was a beautiful silver and gold necklace with two hearts entwined in one another. "That's how I feel. I love you, Precious, and I truly am sorry I called you a child. I know you aren't. You hold my heart in a way no other can. Nothing about your life is going to be simple now; and I don't want you to ever leave us. Don't ever leave me, Bree," then he kissed me tenderly. "Sure I have to keep that stupid promise I made?" he asked.

"Yes, Bradley, just a little while longer. I love you too and I do accept your apology; but just like I have told Steven, Rick, and Billy, you don't need to apologize for anything. I'm just happy you aren't leaving me," I said. "Go get some rest, I'll see you later." I kissed him goodnight, it was a very long kiss. I thought we were going to take root to the floor; but when he smiled before he disappeared, I had to agree it was one damn good apology.

ᕙᕗ

I sat back down in the chair and waited for Steven. He came in with my traveling cloak, his already around his shoulders. "Are we going somewhere?" I asked, suppressing a yawn as I stood.

"Yes, Princess, we are. You haven't seen the sun come up since you've been here and I remember how much you enjoyed that." He wrapped the cloak around me and pulled me to him for a soft kiss. He inhaled and smiled at me.

"What?" I asked.

"I can smell them, each one, that's all."

"What?" I asked again, a little confused.

"Each one of your clan, I can smell them on you," he said causally.

"Do I need to shower or something?" I sniffed my shirt to see what he was talking about.

"No, it's a good scent. It's of us so it doesn't bother me." He kissed me again. "Come on, wrap your arms around me and let me take you to my favorite spot, one that I have been saving for you. We can watch the sun rise over the mountains and then I'll bring you back for some much needed rest."

I wrapped my arms around him and looked up into his eyes; those beautiful, powerful brown eyes I so deeply adored. "Can you kiss and drive at the same time?" I teased.

"Yeah, Bree, I think I can manage that," he whispered, as he pressed his lips to mine. When I opened my eyes again, I felt the fresh morning air kiss my cheeks. The gentle breeze played with my hair. We were high in the mountains with a perfect view of a gorgeous sunrise about to begin.

The sun was still below the next mountain. Golden rays of the early morning light swirled through the purple clouds of the night, making them give way to a brilliant spectacle of colors. Steven stood behind me, his arms wrapped around me, holding my cloak closed to keep the chilled air of the morning from me. His cloaked billowed with the breeze. I felt safe in his arms and I wondered how I could have ever thought this man would leave me? The sun crested the mountain peak, bathing us both in brilliant sunlight. I closed my eyes and leaned back into Steven and let the warmth wash over us.

"I love you Princess, and I will never leave you. Do you accept my apology now?" he whispered.

I turned to him, "Steven, I do so love you. You needn't apologize, but yes. This is the best apology I have ever received." We shared another kiss and were back in our room.

"Time for you to get some rest. I want to take you to a show tonight, so get some sleep. I'll be right here next to you, I promise." He picked me up and laid me on the bed, moving alongside me. I placed my ear to his chest, his arms held me to him, our cloaks wrapped protectively around us as I drifted off to sleep. His tone sounded softly, lulling me to a long awaited rest.

Chapter 29

Folding Space

It was almost ten before I stirred; Steven was still holding me. He was waking from his meditation; his hand started rubbing my arm. "Good morning, sunshine," he whispered.

"Morning," I mumbled. Did you rest well?"

"Yes, I always do with you near me. You needed your rest, and it sounds like you could use some more." His voice was light, his tension gone. My Steven was back to normal, all was right with the world.

"Hungry?" he questioned.

"Famished."

"Good, we'll meet everyone for lunch, then I want to take you shopping. We can take a walk along the strip; get out of this hotel and let you see the sights. How does that sound?"

"Wonderful, but I need to meet with my parents first."

"Why?" he asked. I heard the smallest bit of tension in his voice.

"I asked Gran to have them come here. We need to talk. I have questions, and they have the answers. Well, I hope anyway."

Steven continued rubbing my arm. "What kind of questions?"

"I need to know what they were thinking, what drove them to accept the demands from my enemies." I sat up, "It's funny; when I need to be in control of a situation my mind takes over. I know things; I can talk confidently about things. But when I get that little twinge of uncertainty, when I start feeling self-conscious, the human emotions come back to the front of my mind."

"Bree, don't meet with them yet. Give yourself more time. Let everything sink in just a little longer."

"Why? I'm afraid if I do that, *my* anger will start to build and eventually it will take hold and I won't get past it. I need to move beyond this, I need to understand."

"I think you understand already. You said it yourself - remember? You said, 'you couldn't even imagine the fear they must have felt. To have something everyone thinks is so important in their charge. To ensure the safety of this individual because so many hung their hopes on this one person. And yet here I am, still breathing'. Remember that? You keep telling us not to waste our energy harboring anger. You need to take your own advice. Don't meet with them right now, Princess. Live your life; learn our ways. You're part of me, part of our clan. I'm your protector now, not them. I don't care what the explanation is now. It won't change anything. And if it's not what you want to hear, if they can't explain it now to your satisfaction, then what? I promise, when we go home, if you still need to talk it out with them, I will go with you."

I looked back at him, his arm tucked behind his head, his other hand still rubbing my arm.

"You belong with me now Bree. I'll not be giving you back to your parents, so I don't care what their explanation is. **We** need to move beyond it, because no amount of explaining can change anything. I'll not allow anyone to hurt you again."

"So it's settled then?" I asked.

"My darling, I have learned with you nothing is ever settled. But for now, this is." He pulled me to his lips for a very warm vampire kiss. "Better?"

I exhaled, "I'll do as you request, but you're taking a big risk with my emotions."

"I'll take my chances," he laughed.

❧

Steven went to shower, letting me rest a little longer wrapped tightly in my cloak.

I laid there in the quiet and started thinking about the dreams I'd had the night before. I felt my dreams gave me the advantage and I was not going to let that advantage go to waste. My mind began taking notes on each issue, filing it away for when I needed them.

Esmeralda's plan to make Madalyn and Steven bond sooner than the solstice was not going to work. I was not going let her beat me; I was not going give in to my jealousy. I was aware now of her plan and I was determined to beat her at her own game. I would know what I needed to do when the time came.

I smiled at my memory of Thomas not giving her the information she was looking for. I thought he enjoyed keeping the information from her too. But, it did make me wonder what his game was. Who else did he work for? Was he a double agent? I was getting into this 'cloak and dagger' drama.

My thoughts went back to the conversation I'd overheard in the library. I had been naive when I'd thought they only loved their spouses. If I was going to succeed in this world I would need to put some of my human thoughts out of my head. I guess I had really never looked at it from their perspective. I had been so bent on them looking at everything though my eyes, but I would not be a mortal after I crossed. I would belong to the Magical realm. That would be my world and as I lived in that realm I would need to adjust to their ways. As mortals, we lived short lives compared to the Magical world. But my human side was still strong and still told me how wrong this was. Damn, I wished for once it would just shut up. I didn't want to lose Steven and I did enjoy my time with Brad. No guilt about being with another. Guilt, that was a true human emotion; and apparently one they were not familiar with. They had all lived so long as vampires they had lost their human side. Billy had always been a wizard; he had never experienced human emotions. Time, I needed time to sort through all those feelings. But the dreams had helped. I gave a wicked laugh. *Oh Ryan, I'll not give you the last laugh. I may yet surprise you. I may take to this way better than you think.* I thought I would enjoy talking with Celia.

Then Odessa was in my head again.

How are you this morning?

"I'm fine," I said aloud.

You may want to just talk to me through your thoughts. People might think you're talking to yourself, she laughed.

Odessa, the dream I had last night? Did you come through the...the gateway that opened to our world?

No, child, I'm not that old! She laughed a very robust laugh. *I remember the stories of the wars, the worlds our races destroyed. But when the Magicals came here, this world, this land, calmed them. I know you don't understand all of this, and I hope the dreams help. You seem more receptive to things after you have seen them. You seem to understand the ways of your clan a little better. I have confidence you will be able to embrace them and enjoy yourself. They will never hurt you, Bree. Each Chosen One has been different. Some have embraced this life; some have not. A few have died while trying to fulfill their quest and some did not live up to their potential. They were more content to let others fight the battles. A few have even gone dark. However, you Bree, you are special. You are strong; the strongest I have ever met to be exact. My dear, I can guide you but there is nothing for me to teach. You are learning on your own; your mind is developing all by itself.*

Odessa, can I ask a personal question?

Of course you may.

Do you have a mate, a spouse? Someone you love? I asked just a little embarrassed, but I was curious.

Yes, I have a special love, and I have known many others, she smiled. I could feel her smile in my soul, and it made me feel warm. *Is that your only question child?*

Can you explain to me how they travel? Can you teach me to do it?

No, you haven't transformed. You can't travel that way yet?

Odessa, I stopped and started laughing. *I am doing a lot I shouldn't be able to do. Don't you agree?*

That is true.

Could we at least try?

I can explain the process to you and you can try. Bree, you know you need to continue practicing getting into others thoughts. I can't stress how important that is for you. She is shrewd; you must be prepared. I want you to practice this constantly. You are extremely good at it but the more you practice the stronger you become. You need to practice on your family.

Oh no! That's just not right. That is totally rude, and the last time, well, we both know where that got me, I stammered.

Bree, lives depend on you being able to do this. You need to be able to hold your blocked mind from others, even when you receive information that...unnerves you. Remember how easy it was for Madalyn to gain access to your thoughts in Yellowstone? You let your guard down. You must master that! You will need to be able to break into Esmeralda's mind to be able to find things out. And you can't let her know you can do this. She is very good at doing this and knows when uninvited guests try to enter her mind. You do not need to listen to your family's intimate thoughts. Just start a conversation and listen to those thoughts. Magicals are harder than humans; you need to practice.

Okay, but not on Steven or Brad.

Yes, Bree, even on Steven and Brad. You have an emotional tie to them; they will be your hardest.

Okay, okay, I will practice on them, but later. Right now I want to talk about traveling.

They are correct; you are stubborn. That is to your advantage; don't lose it. Traveling is simple for us really. We place the thought of where we want to be in our minds, and then we fold space toward ourselves. As space starts to fold, we flow into it with our minds and we take our bodies with us. You will move slowly at first. The better you get at it, the faster you will travel. Then it will look like you just vanish into nothingness and appear out of thin air. Let's try a short distance, from here to the living room. Envision the living room in your mind. Now fold yourself to it.

I envisioned the living room. I envisioned me pulling myself to the room. Nothing. *Aren't there any magical words you use?*

No, we just start folding space. Try again. You want to fold space, not pull yourself along as you would with a rope.

I closed my eyes and envisioned the living room, then remembered what it looked like when Steven folded the space on our trip to and from Yellowstone. I envisioned it the same. Then next thing I knew I was flat on my back. I had run into the door.

Excellent, you should not be able to do this yet. You may want to keep your eyes open though, she laughed.

I was rubbing my head as Steven came out of the bathroom. "Bree, are you all right?" He came to help me up. "What happened?"

"Nothing, stupid really. I was thinking about something; not paying attention to where I was walking. Ran smack dab into the door." I smiled. I hadn't lied, I had been thinking of something and I had run into the door. *Odessa, did I really do it? Oh my God, that was so cool!*

Yes, you moved a short distance. She laughed again and was gone.

"Are you sure you're okay?" Steven asked again.

"Yeah, trust me. By the time I'm ready the bruise and bump will be gone. Quick healer, remember?"

"Go take your shower. I'll let everyone know we'll meet at Casey's in thirty minutes."

"Sure you want to go out in public with me? We haven't been outside the hotel, except for Yellowstone, since we've been here. Now you want to take me along the strip. What's gotten into you?"

"Yes, Princess, I'm sure. I can't keep you tucked away forever. Even though I could, but that wouldn't be much fun for you and I don't think you would stand for it. We'll take it slow, but please do me one favor. There are a gazillion people here, so stay close. Don't go wandering off on your own. Got it?"

"Got it. Now let me go get ready so we can eat. I'm starving." I smiled and kissed his cheek and went to get ready.

Chapter 30

Everyone was sitting at the table when we arrived. Steven was very quiet and alert as we walked the short distance to Casey's Bar and Grill. I decided I would like to stay in or visit small communities. There were too many people, too many variables in Vegas. I didn't like it when my clan was tense.

Casey's restaurant looked like an old wrecked pirate's ship. You entered through a large hole in the side. Family seating was on the main floor. All the staff was dressed as pirates or British sailors, or some other seafaring character to help entertain the kids. The second floor was for smokers, drinkers, and gamblers. And the third floor, which was where we were heading, was for smokers, drinkers, gamblers and dancers. The top deck had a retractable ceiling, a bar, no gambling machines or dance floor; but it did have tables. You could sit there and watch the fireworks at night when they had them, or the stars. Of course that was pointless; too many city lights to really see them. But the top deck was always full from what I'd been told.

We had a table on the third floor by a large open window. The breeze felt warm for late October; a hint of rain hung in the air. If you paid attention, you could hear the street sounds. So I stopped paying attention. Casey's was full this time of day and there was a mixture of Magicals and mortals on our floor. *This will be interesting*, I thought. Now that I knew about this world, I wanted to watch and just see for myself how unaware I had been.

Everyone from my clan was present, except for our two newest members. Gina, Madalyn, and Sandy greeted me with a kiss on the cheek and a hug, as did Rick and Billy. Brad greeted me with a kiss on my cheek so close to my ear it made me shiver and him smile. *Bradley, behave*, I thought to him. As I sat, I asked about our missing members. "Where are Becky and Ted?"

"We didn't want them here. We don't want them around you. Not sure what we are going to do with them at this point," Rick said. "They need to leave."

"Well, what can you tell me about them? How long has Ted been a vampire? Where did he come? Can you tell me?"

Brad entered my mind. *Bree, dear, it isn't done this way. If they decide they want the ones selected in the Fall Gathering in the group, they will tell you everything. However, if they decide against a fall selection, they most likely won't tell you anything. It's what they do.* He placed his hand on my leg under the table.

What's the harm in telling me? From the way Rick sounded, they have already made up their minds they don't want them in the clan. And besides they didn't select them at the gathering, remember?

It's just the way it is. They don't have to give us a reason, whether they find them at the gathering or not. His hand moved up my thigh.

Hey, I thought you could wait until the solstice. Now behave...please, I reminded him with a giggle in my thoughts.

I like to touch you. If you want me to wait until the solstice you are going to have to put up with this, my love. Otherwise I will take you to my bed now. Brad smiled a very sensual smile to me with his thoughts.

The waiter brought several appetizers. We all passed them around; I couldn't believe how hungry I was.

"Why do you need to know this?" Billy asked.

"I don't know, curious I guess. I don't see the DC around Becky, just Ted. He seems to be keeping it to himself," I answered.

"DC?" Rick asked, with a grin on his face. "What the hell is a DC?"

"Dark Creature. I gave them a name." I smiled back at him.

"I don't see any problem in telling her," Steven said. "She's not going to let it drop anyway." He gave me a sideglance and smiled.

"Okay, but we have to decide what to do with them and soon." Rick's eyes narrowed on me making his point. "Ted's been a vampire for twenty years now; the last ten years he has been with Becky. He turned when he was twenty-three. Supposedly, he was walking home one night and was attacked. They were interrupted so they didn't kill him. Ted said he was left with the garbage," Rick said and I interrupted him.

"So you don't believe him?"

"Well, Squirt, generally when a group attacks they finish off their victim. If it was a single vampire, then I could see it; but he was very adamant it was a group. Oh, I imagine it's possible, but not probable," Rick said, then continued, "When he woke, he said he didn't understand what had happened. He was hungry and very thirsty. His body burned; that all fits. He said he heard an old drunk stumbling around and that's when he made his first kill." I wrinkled my nose and made a face, Rick smiled. "Do you want me to continue? You haven't eaten yet."

"Yeah, I asked. Please continue, just don't get too graphic!"

"Ted said he hid in the sewers until his strength returned. It took several kills before he could go out into the sunlight. Said he never believed in this stuff when he was alive. He was able to find others like him, and supposedly, that's how he learned about you.

He stayed with a group of vampires, mostly rogues, killing on whims. He got tired of that after a while; found another group and they said they would accept him into their clan if he could prove his worthiness - he had to kill you.

He told us of a couple of times he had tried to kill you, but you always slipped though his fingers. Then he found Becky and, if you believe this, they had some chemistry causing them to bond to one another. We did believe his story at first; everything was checking out. But now that we are rethinking this, we are finding small pinholes in it. It's all too convenient. Ted said he and Becky roamed without any direction for all of those years. I think he had plenty of direction; maybe she was unaware. He told us the group that sent him after you wouldn't let them join them. We've got some people checking this out; and when they get back to us, we'll know how we should continue. If he lied, he's dead."

"No chance for him to explain himself? Just dead, just like that?"

"Yes, Bree, just like that," Steven said.

"What about Becky?"

"Depends on what her role was or is. But she won't be allowed to stay with us either way," Rick said. "You okay with that?"

"I reserve the right to think about it."

"You can think all you like missy; but our judgment will stand. You will need to do a very big song and dance to convince us otherwise," Rick smiled.

I looked at Steven; he smiled at me. "Hungry now?"

"Yeah, surprisingly I still am. I think I'll order a hamburger and fries, something decadent."

Rick motioned for the waiter, and he brought several menus.

Brad entered my mind and laughed, *Feel better?*

Oh, I suppose. How are you today? I asked.

I'm just fine. Oh, I could use a little one on one with you again but I won't press.

Bradley, what's wrong with Madalyn? She doesn't look very happy with me right now. I feel so much tension at this table. Rick looks worried; Billy's been very quiet too. Surely it's not because of Ted.

I thought I would practice holding two conversations at once.

"Steven, what would you like to order?" My chin was on his shoulder.

"Don't know yet. Why?"

"You could share mine with me if you like?"

"No, you like your meat well done; I like mine rare, very rare," he smiled.

Brad continued talking in my head. *Maddie isn't doing well. I've spoken to her but she sees how tight you and Steven are; she's scared. I've told her she has nothing to worry about. Not sure what's up with Rick or Bill.*

Hmm, I'm sure her knowing you and I spent time together isn't helping.

Yeah, about that. I didn't tell her!

I couldn't keep the shocked look off my face and turned quickly to look at him. He was looking at the menu, not paying me any attention, but the corners of his mouth curled into a mischievous grin. I quickly looked away.

"Rick what are you having?" I asked trying to recover.

"I thought I would have the shrimp, Squirt. Why?"

"Just asking."

I answered my thoughts back to Brad. *What do you mean you didn't tell her?*

Just that, I didn't tell her.

Why not?

Bree, my sweet, being the leaders, we have no rules. By all rights, we can have each other any time we wish, or we can have anyone else in the clan any time we wish. We don't have to ask! Now, can we discuss this later? I heard the amusement in his voice.

Oh, you better believe we will be discussing this!

You're a little feisty today, he laughed.

The waiter took our drink order and suggested a cranberry spiced rum drink for me. "No thanks, I'll have water please."

"Oh, I think you would really enjoy the cranberry drink. It's a very festive drink," he tried again.

"No, I'll stick with water, but thank you," I said a little stronger.

He smiled and left. Steven looked at me. "What was that all about?"

"Don't know; but I hate it when people try to get me to drink things I don't want," I answered.

They all looked at one another.

ও

I listened to Rick and Bill's thoughts as they gave out instructions. *Keep your minds open. I think we have some guests. Off Steven's right shoulder, see them Bill? They've been keeping an eye on Bree since she walked in.*

Not to worry, they're discussing a show. The one with the baseball cap on is wondering where their mates are. Evidentially they are late and he is getting just a wee bit mad, Sandy informed them.

We have a group of three sitting two tables back from you Rick, and they are discussing Bree. Nothing bad. They've recognized her. They're just watching her, nothing to alert on just yet, Billy said.

ও

Steven told me to take his water and not to drink the one the waiter gave me. "No problem." I kissed his neck and entered his mind. *I love you.*

415

I love you, too. What are you doing?

Nothing. Just nothing.

Uh-huh, like I believe that, little missy. Sometimes you can be just a little naughty.

Just a little?

His smile answered my question.

❧

I seemed to be able to carry on conversations and talk to others with my mind and even listen to others thoughts all at the same time. That was so easy! Gees, three-way communication. Now who would have thought I would be doing that? I really could have used that talent growing up! I figured I could practice on other Magicals and use my family only as a last resort or when I needed to know something they were hiding.

At the table next to us sat an elderly couple. They were talking about the visits they had been having and everyone they had missed during the year. They agreed to keep better tabs on their friends. Nothing interesting in that, just empty promises they would make to themselves and break after a few tries. So I went into the mind of the gentleman sitting closest to Steven. *That waitress has the nicest breasts I have seen in a while,* and the woman he was with was thinking, *Oh my, I'd like to get that between the sheets. I'm sure he's good.* She was fanning herself with her menu.

I put my hand to my head, closed my eyes, and gave a small chuckle. *My God, is that all Magicals think about?*

"Bree, you okay?" Brad asked. His hand immediately started rubbing my back as he had yesterday, thinking I was having another chest pain.

I needed to be a little more inconspicuous if I was going to do this right. "Oh yeah, I'm fine. Something just struck me as humorous, that's all."

Everyone's thoughts were flying around the table. I felt all the tension and decided the only way I was going to know what was going on was to hear their thoughts. They were not going to tell me willingly. Rick seemed a little out of sorts. I knew it had more to do with something other than being out in public, but I couldn't put my finger on it. I watched him fidget. Something was bothering him.

I looked at him; he looked at me and smiled a little. "What's up with you today?" I asked.

"Nothing. Just a little cranky I guess. Must not be getting enough meditation in."

I gently crept into his thought center and listened, my Richard was more than just cranky. He was worried and I wanted to know why. I put a little piece of tape over my human side, hushing it. I knew I shouldn't be snooping in his thoughts uninvited but that was the only way I was going to find out what was bothering him. He was having a discussion with Sandy.

⟡

I can't believe we let those two in our group. We have been so cautious over the years. Damn. I don't want her out of our sight tomorrow at this party. I wish she wasn't even going. I don't like it, Sandy, not one bit. You know as well as I do, Thomas will be there with his entire clan. Do you realize what could happen? I don't think we could get there in enough time if Thomas decided to attack her. I don't know what he's playing at. You just can't trust that clan. She doesn't realize it yet, and I don't want her hurt. Thomas probably wasn't trying hard last night to make her fall to him; he was playing her. Steven will never forgive himself if anything happens. Sandy you have got to stay close.

I'll be as close as I can sweetheart. I'm scared too. I don't think she fully understands what could happen. You will do the right thing with Ted and Becky. You four have been charged with keeping her safe, and you will. Stop beating yourself up. One mistake, that's all.

That's all it will take, Sandy, just one mistake!

As I sat there listening to them Madalyn's thoughts came whizzing pass me, she was crying to Steven.

Steven, please, I am so scared and I hurt. You two are so close. The hunt is so far away. I feel our bond slipping away the closer you two get. I've asked Brad for his blessing. I've asked him to talk to Bree. He says he can't ask that of her. The two of you care for her so deeply I fear I will lose you both. I truly hurt, Steven.

Steven's thoughts were firm and straight to the point. *Madalyn, I told you our bond would hold. I'll not let you hurt, I promise. You can make it until the hunt. You have to understand I love Bree. She is my mate and Brad is yours. I will not ask her to make a concession. I don't want to lose her. I won't lose her. I need her in my life, Madalyn. You have to understand that.*

Why can't you spend just one night with me? If Sandy or Gina wanted a night with you, you wouldn't hesitate. Why can't you do that for me?

Right now, I would – I've just gotten Bree back in my life. I don't want to be with anyone else right now!

☙

Billy was talking with Brad as I took a stroll through his mind. I safely settled myself in a corner and listened to his conversation.

You seem more relaxed today, Billy said.

I heard Rick's voice now, *Mind if I join in?*

Not at all, I was just telling Brad he seems more relaxed.

Yeah, I've noticed that too, Rick snickered.

Well, I am! I can't begin to tell you how happy I am now to have someone like Bree to lead with. She completely fills that missing link in our family. But let me tell you, sitting here with her this close – DAMN it's hard. There is just something about her presence that pulls at you. There is this...energy that surrounds her when you're with her...man! It hit me hard. I mean, I was fine until yesterday, but after we consummated that bond. DAMN! I knew we would all be close to her but nobody told me how close. It's like...I'm whole now. She is a complete part of me. There is such a sweet, softness to her. She just folds and melts into your arms. You want to protect her from everything. You may think you're in control, but damn, you don't even realize she's controlling you and leading you where she wants you. You don't mind being led, because in the end she has all your senses pinging off the wall. I mean I've been with mortals before, but holy shit, not like her. You guys just be prepared that's all I can say. No wonder Steven is so happy. I will say he is one damn fucking lucky man. I really don't know what has come over Maddie though. She knew when she joined us about Bree. She knew the four of us would all be connected to her and she knew Bree belonged to Steven. Sandy and Gina don't seem to have any problems.

Sandy's fine with all of this. In fact she told me that last night when we woke from our rest. She told me she felt such a surge of love from Bree when she pulled her pain away. She had never felt that love from anyone before. Sandy said she actually felt Bree's warmth and love for her flow through her. I think that's the bond these women will have with her.

Well, Gina's always felt it. She bonded to Bree a long time ago really.

You guys just wait, you think you love her now, but mark my words...you just wait. Steven is one very lucky man.

Yes, I am and don't you guys forget it. Steven laughed. Damn I love her.

Well, barge right on in Steven, laughed Billy. We were just thinking how lucky you are.

Damn, Steven, you should have warned me. I never knew it could be that good.

Now Brad, why would I want to ruin it for you? And now you have just ruined it for these two! Steven laughed.

It's good to be back in the saddle again, isn't it? Billy teased.

You don't know the half of it. Did I mention how much I love this woman?

Yes you did, many, many times. So quit rubbing it in, Rick said.

Are you going to be okay until the solstice, Brad? Steven laughed.

Have to be; I promised her that. Dumbest thing I ever did.

Tell me about it. I lived it for thirteen fucking years. Every time I saw her in that moron's arms. His hands all over her; well fuck, their hands on her. Those pricks! Damn, if they ever touch her again...

Calm down, we'll keep them away, Billy said.

Well, we have another problem. There are three more that belong to her and we have no idea who they are! We have to be very selective from now on as to who comes into this clan, Brad said.

Yeah, but we don't even know if they have to belong to our clan. The prophecy wasn't real clear on that. The only clue was seven companions in her court and she will know their hue, Rick stated.

Well I don't want her to be familiar with anyone outside this clan, so they had better be willing to join, Steven said.

We need to rethink our rules, Brad said. *New members coming in will have to understand she is off limits to them. So you three are going to have to be very selective. You three are going to have to make our rules known up front! I'm sure many will want to be in our clan now; knowing we have a Chosen One. Steven you had better prepare her on that and Steven — you are going to have to tell her the whole prophecy. We can't keep letting little bits out at a time.*

We've told her everything except for that, I'll tell her when we get home. It was hard enough trying to calm her fears in Yellowstone.

Well, I'm content to take my time. When she's ready, she'll let me know, Rick said confidently.

You're content, bullshit! Steven laughed.

Steven, that hurt, Rick laughed back. *I'm a very patient man!*

Patient my ass! If I were you, I wouldn't wait too long. She just might get comfortable with the status quo, Billy advised. *Then where will you be?*

Well, Bill, what about you? You're just as much in our family. You're on her court. When are you going to tell her? Rick teased.

I have no idea. Wonder how she will react when I tell her Gina and I want to join the clan? She says she considers us part of the clan, but I haven't mentioned we want to turn. We'll cross that bridge when we get there.

Well, Bill, you are going to have to tell Bree everything, and I mean everything. Don't let her find out you aren't related on her own, Brad warned.

I know, I know, but Steven's right - let me tell her when we get her home. Not here and not now. We've screwed her head up enough with what we've told her so far. Let her come to terms with that first.

Just give me fair warning when you do tell her. She is going to come unglued and I want to be ready for it. And please, just let me know when you tell her you want to spend time with her. We all may want to leave town, Steven laughed.

ᴄ∕ᴓ

I sat there dumbfounded. This could not be happening! What were the Elders thinking? Odessa and I were going to have a long conversation – she could count on that! I wanted it all on the table and now.

My mind was spitting questions out that I couldn't answer and I was getting tired of finding everything out this way. Seven for God's sake! What did he mean Billy and I weren't related? I asked Billy that! He said we were Campbell's, he said we were related. Didn't he? I was so busy yelling at myself, I was missing the conversation. My human thoughts were busy beating up on my Magical side. I couldn't let my facial expression give away what I was doing. When I had gained control again, Steven was asking something else. Great! What did I miss?

❧

You two that sure you want to give up your race for ours? Yeah, we do. Hell, we're always with you. Why not join you? Not the kids though, we want them to come of age first. Let them decide if they want to join and when. Gina wants to make sure she doesn't want any more babies. Don't worry guys. I'll give you all fair warning before I tell her anything.

❧

My mind was still in a state of chaos, I felt the panic start low in my stomach. I had to keep control. I couldn't let them know I was snooping and listening to their conversations. But the panic was taking hold. *Damn, Bree what were you thinking? You knew you shouldn't have done that!*

I left their conversation and sat there numb. I wanted to cry, I wanted to yell at them and make them tell me everything. I knew they wouldn't though. They still had too much fear I would walk away. Maybe I should. Maybe I should just get up and run, and keep running. Don't look back. Run away from Steven and Brad and Rick, and damn it yes, even my own family.

Aubrey, Odessa whispered in my mind. *Please, don't run away. The Elders knew what they were doing. You are strong child. You have been told everything except this, and I should have told you. It was my place to tell you, but I didn't; and for that I am sorry. Your world needs you child. You will find a way to deal with this.*

I don't want seven lovers Odessa. I don't. I'm drawing the line here and now! I have accepted my clan and their ways. I

423

have...damn, what was the word he used...consummated my bond to Brad. I love Steven with all my being. I have accepted I will spend time with Rick. Billy though – I can't do that Odessa. I just can't. I will take no others; this is all I can deal with! I saw myself in the darkness of my mind crying.

Chosen One, who said they had to be your lovers? They are companions to your court. That's all. They are seven very special people to you. The four you see before you, they are your family, and you have accepted your clan's ways. If these others are not of your clan – then you choose how they serve. You choose how you accept them. You are the Queen – it is your right.

I don't have to...be with the others?

Not if they are not of your family. You are the Queen. Aubrey, dry your eyes and listen to the women of your clan. They love you dearly my child. They will give you the strength to get beyond this. Our world is so different than anything you can imagine. Listen to them.

I knew the only way I was going to know what was going on was by listening to their thoughts. I had to steady my nerves; I had to be careful. I couldn't let them know I was listening.

ↄ

Madalyn, what's the matter with you? Why are you so pissed at Bree? Gina asked.

Because, Brad loves her, Steven loves her; hell they all love her. Why aren't you two pissed?

Because we love her. We knew what it meant to get Bree back, so did you. Brad told you all about her. You accepted all of it Madalyn. You knew Steven belonged to her. This was the way it was supposed to be when she came of age. Now you can either help her through all of this or sit there and sulk. But you will be doing that all by yourself, Gina announced.

I'm ecstatic she has finally come into our lives, and you should be too. Brad will not stand for your treatment of her and if you continue and cause Steven to take her away you will have to deal with us. Do you understand that Maddie? Sandy scolded. *I haven't had a chance to tell you guys, but when she drew my pain away, man. She replaced it with a warm feeling of love. She asked nothing from me but gave me everything. I have never felt that kind of warmth from anyone – not even my own mother. It was as if she was there to protect me and care for me. I believed her when she said she would not let anyone harm me.*

I felt that same sensation when she was just a child. She and I bonded quickly. And the bond she has with Bill, well, he would die for her.

I don't want her love, Madalyn spewed.

Then that is your loss and I feel sorry for you, because she will give it to you without any strings attached. She is in our family now, and you will need to accept that. I strongly suggest you get your head on straight or Brad may adjust it for you, Gina said.

I can't wait for her to be with Rick, I told him that. I told him how special she made me feel and I could only guess how he will feel. He has always loved her and for them to bond... well, he will be a very lucky man!

You have got to be kidding me. You act like she is our savior. She is nothing more that a mere human. She can't possibly be able to push all this...love at you!

Get your head out of your ass – she is much more than a mere human and I will not allow you to treat her badly. I'm warning you now, Madalyn – I will defend her if I need to.

Gina spoke her words with such force even I had to take note!

I really need to be there for her when Bill tells her they aren't related. God, it's going to hit her hard. And then when she realizes she isn't related to anyone in her family, I can only imagine the loss she will feel, Gina said.

What about the seven? I'm sure when she learns about that she will fall to pieces – I might just enjoy that! Madalyn laughed.

I pity you Madalyn. I never thought I would hear myself say that, but I really pity you. You are missing so much. We'll be there to help her through this; I only hope you are too, Sandy thought to her.

Are you threatening me?

I don't need to threaten you. Steven will take care of that!

I sat back and started looking around; looking for a distant point I could focus on. I kept swallowing to keep the tears inside my eyes.

I told you they love you, Odessa whispered. *Put your concerns out of your mind child.*

๛

"Bree, are you okay?" Steven was asking me.

Am I okay? What a question to ask. No, I'm not okay. I'm really not; but you won't understand. I had stopped listening to them or so I thought, but my off switch must have been broken because I heard their thoughts anyway.

I can't get in; she's locked me out. You try, Madalyn, Sandy pushed.

No good. Steven you're connected to her better than us, you give it a shot. Her comment was harsher to him than she intended.

Nope. It's locked tighter than a drum. Brad, Bill, can either of you get in? Steven asked.

Not at all! Damn I hate it when she does this. Steven, you need to talk to her about it. She isn't supposed to block her mind from you or me, Brad said.

Well, Brad, what would you have me do? She is a very stubborn little thing. You're her leader, you tell her.

Right, like she'll listen to me. You're her mate; she's supposed to listen to you!

Yeah, right. I'll let you know when that happens!

"Steven, I'm fine." I figured I had better say something to keep them from getting into a fight. The waiter came back with our drinks and brought me the Pirates Smash cranberry cocktail. "Just in case you change your mind. Are we ready to order now?"

I gave it back. "I won't, so please take it back. I didn't ask for it; I don't want it." I didn't smile as I spoke to the waiter. *Now is not the time to be pressing me buddy!*

We gave our food order to him and he started to leave. "Excuse me, you forgot your drink," I said forcefully. Rick handed him the drink.

⁂

I needed to get away from this table so I let my mind wander through the restaurant all the way to the back.

I found a small table straight back from where we were sitting. Two women were talking. They were Traditionals, so I thought it might be a good idea to *listen* in on their conversation.

⁂

427

"Honestly, Sylvia. What does he see in her? Stupid human." Sylvia sat with her hands folded on the tabletop. She was a petite brunette; her hair was short and cut in a style that feathered to her face. She had thick bangs that came just to her eyebrows. Her eyes were brown and her lips were thin.

"Rebecca, trust me; Steven will be yours. He'll bed you tomorrow just like he used to."

*Rebecca, huh, I wonder...*my mind observed her, matching us up. That must be the one Steven was always with. Surprisingly she reminded me of me. Her hair was short and fine. She wore it feathered into her face with full bangs, no part down the middle. *She must blow it dry like I do.* Her lips were full, pouty lips. She wore lipstick, but I thought that was because she was so pale. If she were not a Traditional, I was sure she wouldn't need lipstick. She had a pale olive tint to her skin. My skin had an olive tint; she wore makeup and I didn't. Her eyes were brown and I could tell she was short, just like me. *Hmmm, I wonder if that's why Steven picked her.*

"Just look at them. It makes me sick. What does he see in her? He never would commit to me. I so miss his arms. Oh Sylvia, he knew just how to make me tingle. God, he was so good. If I had the nerve, I would walk over to that table and straddle his lap. Oh, I'd give him something to remember. When she's dead, I will be there. You just wait and see," Rebecca said.

"Calm yourself sister. If the whole clan was here, I'd tell you to do just that; but they aren't so calm your motor. She's strong. Thomas said she was. She holds a soft spot in his heart. Thomas has grown weak, and Esmeralda has noticed. He could have ended her life many times, but he has not fulfilled his commitment to Esmeralda and she's losing patience with him."

"How do you know this; and why do you speak of her by name?" Rebecca asked. She looked around making sure their conversation couldn't be overheard and I giggled in my thoughts.

"I have had many conversations with Esmeralda. We have become close over the years. She has taken me into her confidence. Do you think it is possible Aubrey could be weaving a spell over the men in her life to get them to do her bidding?" Sylvia questioned.

"A spell? Oh come on now, she's a mortal. She hasn't transformed yet," Rebecca scoffed making air quotes.

"I agree, but can you explain why then Thomas and his clan have not ended her life?" Sylvia questioned.

Because I have an 'energy' about me! Don't you know anything? I mused in my thoughts.

"Sylvia, he's a man for God's sake. They don't always think with their brains. She's a challenge to him, something he can't have. If it were easy, she would have been dead a long time ago," Rebecca laughed.

See, she knows, my pettiness was breaking through.

"So you think because Thomas would love to bed her, he would risk Esmeralda's anger? I don't think Thomas is that stupid," Sylvia quipped. "I do know he wanted her the other night."

Yeah well, according to my clan they all do. So get in line! I was becoming just a wee bit pissed.

"Best sex we've had in a while," Sylvia moaned. "Thomas hasn't spoken to me about his plans. But look, if we can get her to drink the drink that Nick always gave her, we could speed this along. Thomas doesn't need to know anything about it. Nick is kind of sweet on me. I can get it from him, and then we can slip it into her drink. Once Thomas starts with her, she will fall to him. There would be no way she could resist him. Steven will be so mad at her, hell - he'll throw her away. And there you will be ready to pick up the pieces. Her whole clan will think she's tainted. Someone from another clan will have claimed her, and they won't want anything to do with her. I want to be on the winning side, Becca. Esmeralda has shown me her vision of our world and I want to be there to enjoy it. You can console Steven and then he will be yours forever, because she won't be alive!" she firmly stated.

"I don't know Sylvia. What if we get caught? I don't want to have Thomas angry at me."

"Thomas," Sylvia laughed, "Esmeralda is going to replace him. Did you not hear me? She is losing patience with him. She has someone else in mind. She introduced me to him. Oh Becca, he was so handsome and the powers he had. Esmeralda doesn't think Thomas has the stomach for this anymore so..." she let her thoughts trail off. "Oh such powers this new male holds." Sylvia inhaled deeply at her thoughts. "Yes, I want to be on the winning side. And if you help me, you will be there too."

"I don't know, Sylvia. Thomas is not someone to toy with. He will not let us live if we betray him," Rebecca warned.

"You aren't listening to me. Esmeralda will have Thomas' entire clan killed," Sylvia roared.

❧

I snapped back to my table and inhaled deeply.

"Okay, Bree, out with it," Steven said. He had a smile on his face.

I was just about to say, 'What' when our food arrived. "Oh good; I'm starved." The waiter placed everyone's order in front of them. I took a french fry, looked at Steven, and smiled as I bit down on the fry.

Steven sat there with his arms crossed, trying to look stern, and said, "I'm waiting."

I looked around the table and everyone was looking at me. "Am I in trouble?"

"That all depends on what you have been doing, Squirt," Rick said, just a little amused. His arm was over Sandy's shoulder and she had her arms crossed looking at me sternly. I looked over at Brad, Madalyn, Billy, and Gina. They had the same expression on their faces.

"Did I miss something?" Trying to sound innocent; which, in my mind I was.

"Bree, what, or should I ask who, have you been listening to?" Steven asked; and I couldn't help but see the laugh lines near his eyes.

"Steven, I'm not listening to anyone at this table," I said as I popped the rest of the french fry into my mouth. They weren't convinced.

"Okay, I'll give you the run down," as I took a bite of my hamburger. "You see that little old man over there? Well he was salivating over his waitress' breasts." Rick, Steven, Billy, and Brad checked out the waitress and agreed. "Well, the woman with him was looking at the young busboy and she wanted to get him between the sheets." Madalyn, Gina, and Sandy looked around. "No guys not that one, that one."

I nodded in the direction of a young college student, whose shirt and pants were hugging his body outlining all of his attributes. He knew he was hot, but he wasn't smug about it. I think he enjoyed turning these women on. "Well, she does have good taste; I'll give her that," Sandy said. Madalyn, Gina, and I agreed.

"Who else?" Steven asked.

I took a small bite of my hamburger and looked at him. "Steven, did you know Rebecca is sitting in the back of the room, and she has a good view of this table?"

"No."

"Well, she is and she does; and I must say she doesn't like me much."

Rick laughed, "Oh gees, Bree, ya think? You have just taken her main squeeze out of commission for good. Of course she hates you."

"That being said so eloquently; did her main squeeze realize she is in Thomas' clan?"

He sat up a little straighter. "No, I didn't know that. Did any of you? Wonder when that happened?"

"Yeah, well, evidently, they, her and her friend Sylvia back there, are making their own plans." I repeated everything I had heard.

"Okay, I'm putting my foot down, you aren't going to the party," Steven said flatly. "I'll take you shopping instead. I promised to take you shopping, and that was interrupted; so it's settled."

"Steven you're taking me shopping today; you don't need to take me shopping again," I reminded him.

"You're not going. Understand? It's settled." He was getting angry.

"It's settled. Just like that?" I looked at him.

"Yeah, just like that. I don't want you there; I think I said it very clearly." His voice was very stern.

"No, I don't understand. You need to understand, no, you all need to understand; I will be there. I need to do this," I pushed back.

"Why? Explain why you need to do this. Convince me," he demanded.

I didn't back down from his demand. "Steven, I can't keep hiding away. The problems will not go away because I'm not there. It will only fuel the flames that I am timid. By doing that you make me more vulnerable to attack. They will think me an easy target, and that will put more stress on my clan. I'll make a deal with you."

"Bree, you can deal all you want. You aren't going."

"I'll make a deal with you," I laid my hand on his arm and continued, "I promise not to talk to Thomas. I promise to only dance with my clan. I promise I will not drink the drink that will be offered to me or any other drink unless it comes from my clan. Would you accept that? Steven, I do keep my promises."

"I know you keep your promises, Bree; I just don't want you to go!" His thumb tapped the table.

"I have to go, Steven. I can't keep hiding away. I know it's hard, but I have to do this. That's why I'm here," I said firmly.

Steven was talking with the others. I could tell, but I didn't want to listen; which probably wasn't a wise move on my part. I knew they were trying to think of a way to get me to stay away from the party. "You promise not to be out of our sight the entire time?" His thumb was thumping on the table. Slow rhythmic taps; he watched me, watched my body language. Tap, tap, tap. His arm was around my shoulders; that thumb, tapping as well. Both thumbs tapped in unison. *Tap, tap, tap; mind torture by thumbs*, I laughed to myself.

"I will stick to you like glue."

"What do you think you will accomplish at this party? Are you going there looking for a fight?"

"No, Steven. If I wanted a fight I would have had that a long time ago and it wouldn't be with Thomas. The Council needs to understand whom they are dealing with. Right now, they think of me as a child, a mortal, someone they can snap their fingers against and I will be gone. You think of me as a child, a mortal, and you think I am in over my head. You all think that; but I'm not. I know exactly what I am doing and I know what needs to be done. They need to see and understand I have no fear of them. If this is too dangerous for you, then I don't think you want to know the rest of the things I'm going to have to do."

Steven relented, "I still don't like it, but I will agree as long as you keep your promise. If you renege, we leave. Deal?"

"Deal; now will you guys please eat?" I looked at everyone and took a bite of my hamburger.

"Bree, you do know it's rude to listen to other peoples thoughts?" Sandy asked.

I chewed my food slowly as I looked at her. Very calmly I answered her, "Yes, but you keep trying to listen to mine. Oh, cut me some slack, Sandy. I'm new at this and I have to practice. Now if you want me to practice on the seven of you, I can."

"No," the unified answer came from them all. I grinned at their response.

❦

Everyone continued talking and laughing. The waiter came and refilled our drinks. Steven told everyone we were going to a show tonight. By the time he was finished with our nightly lineup, everyone was going with us.

I started getting very warm; my headache had returned. I closed my eyes and the room started spinning. I knew this feeling and my panic started to grow. It was a feeling I'd had many times from Nick. I started rubbing my temples.

"Bree, are you okay?" Sandy asked. "You look a little pale."

I put my head on Steven's shoulder and closed my eyes. No good, this was a big dose, lots of little black dots started to appear. I put my head in my hands. The room was spinning faster now.

"Oh shit! Bree, what's wrong?" Steven took my hands away from my face. I was very flushed. I tried desperately to focus, but couldn't. His voice was getting farther away. My ears were ringing and I couldn't stop it.

"Oh God, not again. Steven, it was in the food. He's done it again. This one's much stronger; my head really hurts." I was completely white by this time.

"Brad, take her to the room. Rick, Bill, you're with me," was all I heard and I passed out.

CHAPTER 31

When consciousness came back to me, I was on my bed and Brad was the only one with me. I tried to focus and the harder I tried the worse it got. I felt sick to my stomach and knew I had to get to the bathroom, but couldn't communicate that to him.

"Bree," his voice was soft, "do you feel sick?" I nodded, I thought.

"Bathroom." My voice was weak, it didn't even sound like me.

"Okay, up you go." He helped me to the bathroom, but the sick just wouldn't come. I did what I had done many times before, stuck my finger down my throat, and was able to purge the contents from my stomach. This was more violent than all the other times and I was finally able to ask him to leave the bathroom.

"I'm not going anywhere," Brad said as he rubbed my back.

"Please, I really don't want you in here." Tears were running down my cheeks, I truly didn't want to be seen in this state. So many times I had faced this by myself. Having someone else witness this somehow made it worse, if that was even possible.

"No," Brad's voice was firm. He put a cool cloth on my neck. "Better?"

Another violent round came, and then the dry heaves. My head was pounding and my face was white and sweaty. Eventually, I was able to lean back against him. I took the cloth and pressed it to my face. He went to pick me up. "No, I can walk."

"Bree, let me help you," he demanded as he helped me stand.

My legs were like rubber; I couldn't get them to move. "Okay, maybe not." I leaned against him. "Could I go to the sink?"

"Why?"

"I have to get this taste out of my mouth; I can still taste it." I was fighting hard against the tears. *Damn you Nick,* I thought. *Damn you.*

"Okay," he fixed my toothbrush and helped hold me steady. "Bree, was it this bad all the time?"

I took a deep breath. I wanted this behind me. I was embarrassed for being sick around him, and I really didn't want everyone to know how stupid I had been to stay with someone who would do this. "No, this was by far the worst."

I ran the toothbrush over my teeth, brushed my tongue, which gagged me. "Okay that was stupid." I waited for the spasm to stop, and then rinsed my mouth. I tried splashing water on my face, just trying to focus. Brad grabbed another washcloth and soaked it in cold water, then wiped my face with it. Color was starting to come back.

I leaned against him and started to cry. "I hate this; I really hate this. I should have known when the waiter couldn't get me to take that damn drink they would have tried something else. I wasn't paying attention. None of us were paying any attention. And why should we have to? It has to stop now, Bradley." Then the shaking began. My body wouldn't calm itself and I felt what control I had escaping. I felt the panic return as I held on to him, desperately trying to calm the fear of what always came next with Nick.

"What would you have me do, Bree? Tell me and I will do it." He held me close to him not understanding my panic. He gently rubbed my back and swayed ever so slowly, as he tried desperately to calm me.

"Let me talk to Madalyn," I tried to stand up straight and just focus, but my eyes were not cooperating. "Oh dear, I think I better lay down." The room was spinning faster. The tighter I closed my eyes the more little black dots appeared. I was afraid of passing out again. *That's when Nick always came at me.*

"Does your head still hurt?" He kissed me gently on the forehead. "You're burning up, Bree."

"I know. Every time I close my eyes the room spins too." I held onto him. I needed to keep talking; I couldn't stop for fear I would just drop. "Where is everyone anyway?

"I left Gina and Sandy with Madalyn at the table trying to calm her down. Rick, Bill, and Steven went to look for the waiter."

"They won't find him, he's long gone. Brad, I need to lie down. I don't want to fall asleep though; maybe if I sit up in the living room, maybe some coffee." I tucked my arms into him and he held me as my tears kept coming. "Damn it; I hate this feeling." The panic was winning and I struggled hard to keep it concealed.

"Bree, you don't need coffee on your stomach now. How about some water? Maybe some ginger ale, but let's not do coffee. I promise I won't let you fall asleep, at least not for a while anyway. How often did this happen to you?" He kept talking to me as he maneuvered me toward the sofa.

"I don't want to remember it. Please," I cried, "I don't want to relive this." It was all too much. I thought I could deal with it, but I couldn't. "Enough times to last me forever. To remember everything else that went with it is just too much right now. I'm amazed I could ever have a relationship with anyone else; now to have two males bonded to me. I don't know if I'm strong enough anymore."

All those memories of Nick's assaults started rushing forth to the front of my mind. "Oh, damn Bradley. I can feel his hands all over me. I hate it. He was so mean, I hate it." I was struggling to stand; I was slapping at the air trying to get Nick off me. "It always hurt, I just feel so dirty inside, disgusting. Please make it stop."

"Okay...it's okay, Bree, he's not here. He'll never touch you again. We promised you that." He grabbed my shoulders firmly and made me focus on him. "This is me; Brad. Nick is not here." He pulled me close to him, and tried to ease the pain he couldn't see or feel. "Shhh, don't think that way, please. None of us will ever be mean with you or rough; you need to believe that. We will always be tender.

You have nothing to be ashamed of. He did this to you; you didn't ask for it." He raised my chin up and gently kissed me on the lips. "We need you, Bree. Steven and I both need you; our clan needs you."

"It's so hard to understand this need, Bradley."

"Let me get you a glass of water." I held onto him. "Bree, I'll be right in there, he's not here." His voice was firm; he held my face to look at him again. "He's not here; he'll never touch you again. Okay?" he whispered. I tried to focus on him. "Now, let's sit you down and I'll get you something to drink." He pried my hands loose from him, kissed them as he sat me on the sofa.

"I don't want to ever eat again." I curled up. I heard a soft tap on the door, and Brad opened it as he passed. I could hear soft murmuring, and then Madalyn came and sat on the floor in front of me.

"Bree, I'm so sorry. I drew everyone's attention off you. Steven is furious at me; Brad isn't happy either. I can't explain what, for the life of me, has happened. I am so in love with Brad, but I feel so threatened by you and what you and Steven share. I guess for so long it had always been just them and me. I had their attention and affection. Now I see you with Steven; and how much he adores you. Then you become our clan leader with my husband, my mate; my head is spinning out of control. You have both of their affections now, and I'm in the middle. Please forgive me."

"Are you here alone? I'd look, but my head may fall off my shoulders," I said.

"She's alone, Bree; I called her here. Do you want me to leave?"

"No," I blurted out, the fear rising again. "I'm sorry. No Bradley, I don't want you to leave. Would you please call Steven?" I tried to regain some semblance of calm. How was I going to live through this? I was not that strong.

Odessa came into my mind. *Yes, Bree, you are. They are just now understanding your pain, child. They knew what happened but they didn't understand your pain until now. Brad will tell the males of your clan. You needn't relive it again. Rest child, you have another pain to cure.*

Madalyn was crying now. Steven came and sat on the end of the sofa. Rick, Sandy, Billy, and Gina arrived. The clan was now together. They all felt the need to be close again, to close ranks, and soothe away the pain. I could feel all the worry in the room. Maybe if I handled this correctly they would begin to understand my strength, they would begin to relax a little. I needed them to trust my judgment.

"Madalyn, Steven isn't mad at you; neither is Bradley. I'm not mad at you either. Tell me what you need Madalyn, to make you comfortable. I promise; you will have Steven to yourself during the hunt. I understand the bond you two share; and I understand the need for you to renew that bond. I know the rituals you will go through. I know my place and my commitment to the clan and I will live up to my end, I promise. I will not contact Steven during your time together. I made that promise to Steven and to Bradley. I'm making that promise to you as well. What more can I do?"

She sat there quietly, fidgeting. "Madalyn, I have a very bad headache, and I have neither the strength nor the energy to read your mind. You're going to have to talk to me."

She looked at Brad, then at Steven. "Brad, you know I adore you, and Bree, I adore you as much; but I need one night with Steven, please. I can't explain the pain inside of me; but it is stabbing me terribly. It burns as I have never felt it before. I have tried everything to make it stop. I honestly do not think I will be able to contain myself much longer. I have never felt such pain or agony at what I am asking of you two."

℘

I watched her; she sat like a caged animal ready to leap at anything that startled her. I used what energy I had to speak to Odessa; *Essie's spell has found its target.*

Odessa agreed with me. *They know the predicament you are in and she is trying to drive a wedge into your clan. The spell would break with her one night request, but they hope it breaks you as well.*

What should I do? I asked her.

It is your choice. Give in to her request and ease her agony, but break you, or hold Steven to his promise and lose her, and have Steven feel the guilt.

Can't you think of a third?

Try to break the spell. Bree, you can do this. You have the power within you to do this. I just don't know if you have the strength; and that may have been their intent all along. Do you feel strong enough? Hold her close and pull the spell Esmeralda created out of her, and into you. You will have to go deep into yourself, Bree, to find the strength you need. I am worried for you on this one, my child.

I had to look deep into my heart to make my decision. Madalyn had not given me the warmest welcome into this clan, but I couldn't let anything happen to her. I couldn't stand the hurt my Bradley would feel or the pain I would carry knowing I could have helped her and didn't. This was the perfect time to prove to her, to all of them, I could handle this life. Maybe it was the perfect time to prove it to myself as well.

"I will not be beaten by them." My mind made my choice for me. It too was tired of all the drama. My human side and my Magical side seemed to have come to terms with one another. I just wondered how long that peace would last.

"Beaten by whom, Bree?" Steven asked.

"Esmeralda." I saw her face in the center of my mind. I remembered her words as she mixed her potions. *You will not win Essie; I'm so much stronger than you. You should begin to fear me.*

Then her face was gone. A small flicker of a flame replaced it, there in the darkness of my mind. I felt its protection. I felt the tiniest breeze cool my face and I drew my strength from it. I heard my Shaman's voice as he spoke words of comfort to me and danced his tribal dance. I saw my valley in Yellowstone and I watched the river flow and I felt the blood racing through my own body. I felt my strength and knew what I needed to do and exactly how I needed to do it.

I held my head as I tried to sit; Madalyn assisted me. I felt a shock as she touched me causing me to jump; the tension was racing through her. Her body was in overdrive. I knew this was not of her doing. I secretly wondered if her jealousy of me was adding to the strength of the spell.

I propped myself up on my elbow and held my head, my hand pressed against my temple. I closed my eyes so the tears would stay inside; they were not accommodating me. Small dots danced in my vision adding to my dizziness.

"Bree, I have put a heavy burden on you and for that I am truly sorry. I will not ask it again; I will deal with this." I watched her tears fall down her cheeks and raised my finger to touch one. I rubbed the salty moisture between my fingers but saw no sparks of color, no touch of energy. My senses felt nothing from her. *Essie's spell is a strong one Odessa.*

"Madalyn, hush; please don't cry. This isn't your doing. They are using you to get to me. They know our predicament, and are using it against me. They know when you two bond, they know the rituals you have, and they think they know me. I will not have my clan used as puppets to get to me."

"Bree, what do you need us to do?" Steven asked. He moved close to me, I could feel his vibration; it soothed me. "Brad, I really don't like her skin tone. She's too pale, and her body is very warm." He laid my head against his chest.

"Steven I can't give her anything yet. She needs to rest. She was able to empty her stomach; but no telling how much is in her system. I don't know what they gave her. She's just going to have to tough it out. We'll just have to watch her."

"Madalyn," I said very quietly, pushing away from Steven, "I need you to come and sit very close to me. Right here in front." I opened my eyes; I still couldn't focus. "I am going to try to lift the spell."

"Bree, you really shouldn't do this. It can wait until you have rested. Madalyn will be fine until then," Steven said.

"I'm going to have to agree with Steven. You really don't look so good, Bree," Madalyn said.

I felt Brad's hand on my forehead, then my neck. He took my pulse. "Bree, you need to rest, lay back. Steven, pick her up and let's get her to bed now." The others all sat watching; I could feel the tension in the room. Gina and Sandy were still upset with Madalyn. I could feel my men's worry.

I raised my hands, "I appreciate what you are telling me; however, Madalyn, you need this done now. Tomorrow will be too late."

Billy spoke up, "Bree, can Gina and I help you? We can add to your strength."

"No, Billy. Thank you, but I have to do this by myself."

Madalyn sat in front of me, my eyes still out of focus. My head ached and I was very warm. I cupped her face in my hands and rested our foreheads against each other. Then I spoke softly, and the melody played in our heads.

Hear me demons of the dark; I pull this spell from her heart.

Go back to where the words were spawn.

Your pain I feel; your heart does break. Your pain is real; your lust is not.

My strength I give, to break the spell. The life you live, in my heart it dwells.

The stone and the pendant I wore warmed against my chest, and that soothed me. They gave me strength. I repeated the verses three times to myself. We swayed to the melody only Madalyn and I could hear. The wood flute played a sad melody and the tears ran hot down my cheeks, but Madalyn's tension eased. I felt all of her fear, all of her tension, come into my body, and I hurt, the pain was intense; all of my joints burned. I thought I was on fire, I thought my body would combust from the heat it was generating. Instinctively my body tried to free me from all that was entering me. I held tight to Madalyn. I could not give in to my need to rid myself of the pain.

Several long minutes had passed and Madalyn's breathing started returning to normal. I had successfully pulled the spell from her into myself, and I released her. I raised my hands to my temples and pressed. Steven's arms were around me holding me against his chest. I felt his tone for me and it soothed me. "Steven, can we please lay down for a while?" I asked weakly. "Madalyn will be fine now. I just need to rest for a while." I was shaking from the torment that was running rampant through my body. I tried desperately to curl up into a tight ball to stop it.

Steven picked me up and laid me on the bed. Brad examined me. I remember seeing the concern in his eyes as he pulled his face close to mine. He tried to get me to drink some water. I drank a little then curled back into my ball of protection again. "Steven, call me if she gets any worse. She needs to rest now. She'll recover, but if anything changes, call me. She needs fluids too. Her body temperature is very hot; I don't want her to dehydrate. I'll stop by later to check in on you."

I heard Steven, "Madalyn, you're sure you're okay. You don't hurt anymore?"

"No, Steven I feel fine now. She took my pain away; I felt it leave. The melody, did you hear it?"

"No, we didn't hear anything. All we saw was her holding your head and the two of you swaying. She was crying and finally you were smiling."

"That was such a sad melody. I hurt when I heard it, but it carried my pain to her. I didn't hear the words to the spell though. I can't believe how good I feel. Brad let's go; we'll come back later. Steven, she needs you now."

I heard no jealousy in her voice. Maybe her anger at me was part of the spell.

I heard Billy and felt his worry, "We'll go see what we can find out. We'll be in touch. Rest Half Pint."

I heard the bedroom door close. I felt the bed move; a blanket was laid over me and Steven was by my side, unfolding me out of the fetal position I was in. "Lay your head on my chest." He continued to hold me, stroking my head. The vibration felt good against my temple. I was able to slow my breathing and close my eyes. The room started to spin, and I reached out to grab anything to steady myself. Steven took my hand in his. "Just hold me Princess, just hold on to me." Slowly the spinning came to a rest. I wrapped my arms around him and was able to sleep.

I slept for a short while; when I woke, the room was dark. Steven was still there; the vibration in his chest was still strong. "How do you feel?" he asked.

I gingerly moved my head; I raised myself up on my elbow. "Better; my head doesn't hurt any more. I don't feel as hot. How are you doing?"

"I'm fine. Feel like talking?"

I really didn't want to talk about everything. I was feeling better, and I didn't want to remember what had just happened. However, he needed to understand it. "Sure," I said slowly. "What do you want to know?"

"What happened? How did you know what needed to be done for Madalyn?"

"I told you earlier, I have the memories, the knowledge. It has been buried deep in my mind. It's surfacing and I just know things."

He continued to stroke my arm as he spoke with me. It was almost hypnotic the way he did it. "Bree, Brad told me what you spoke about. I am so sorry you experienced that. It never should have happened. I will never be rough with you or mean; I will never make you feel that hurt. None of us will."

"I don't feel that way when we love, Steven. You make me feel so special. I just hate the feeling I have inside me, it's as if I'm dirty and no amount of washing will take it away. Oh, how could you love me so much after everything another man has done?"

"He is not a man, Bree, just a monster. What they did was wrong, and it should never have happened to you. You are my Princess; and nothing will ever change that. They will never touch you again, my angel. Never! Everyone is asking about you, can I tell them you're awake?"

"Do you want to?"

"Are you sure you're feeling better?"

"Yes, tired, but better," I answered.

He rolled over and kissed me very tenderly. "I'll tell them later. I want to be with you by myself for just a little longer. Just the two of us."

CHAPTER 32

I fell back asleep in Steven's arms after we made love. I remembered how gentle Steven had been with me before we were separated, but now the gentleness and tenderness was well beyond that. Steven had his china doll back in his arms; he was tenderly gluing my pieces back together. He tried desperately to remove any scars I still carried. I knew Brad would be just as gentle.

I slept for another hour, finally stirring. I placed my hand on Steven's neck. "Steven, you need your Drink, and I would like to take a hot shower. My joints are so sore. God, is that what you two go through?"

"I think you got the jest of it, yeah. Sorry, I never wanted you to hurt."

"Well, I don't think I want to feel that again, that's for sure; and I don't want you to hurt like that either. I want you to tell me when you do. Understand? I'll not let that happen to you." I tried stretching as I sat up.

He started laughing, "Oh my little Bree, trying to take all the problems on your shoulders. I love you; now go take your shower. Are you hungry?"

I was hungry but I most certainly didn't want to eat from that restaurant. "Well, yes, but not from there."

"We'll go some place new; I'll let everyone know they can come by." Steven pulled me to my feet and kissed my forehead. "Go take your shower before I change my mind about calling them."

༅

Twenty minutes later, I came into the living area of my suite. Rick and Sandy were sitting on the sofa.

"Hi, guys," I said, still rubbing my neck and shoulders.

"Hey Squirt, Steven said you were feeling better and you were hungry. Sure you want to try that again?" He laughed as he and Sandy came to greet me. Sandy gave me a kiss on the cheek and Rick leaned in and kissed my lips, then winked and smiled. I smiled back at him.

"Damn, Bree, I thought I was going to have to come and get you out of the shower. Did you fall back asleep?" Steven teased.

"No, silly. I can't believe how sore I am." Steven started to rub my shoulders. "Oh, Lordie, you could keep that up all night."

"Why don't you spend a few hours at the spa? Let them work the kinks out," Steven offered.

"Sounds good to me. Where's everyone?" I moved to sit on the arm of the love seat next to Rick as Steven went toward the bedroom.

"They'll be here shortly. I'm going to go take a shower; that is if Bree left any hot water," Steven said.

"Big hotel, Steven. I'm sure there's plenty."

I nudged Rick's shoulder. "How's it going with Becky and Ted?"

"Still working on them, Squirt. Can't really tell you anything just yet."

"Can't or won't?"

"Both," Rick smiled as he put his arm around me. "Our contact hasn't gotten all the info yet. When we have pieced it all together I promise I will tell you, but until then," he looked at me and became serious, "hush. Understand? You're not to badger Bill, Steven or me on this. Just cool your jets, sister. We'll tell you when we're ready. Now seriously, are you feeling okay from today?" He pressed his hand against my head. "Okay, you're not burning up at least."

"Rick, I'm fine; really, I'm fine. We'll go to the party; I'll see the Council on Friday and we go back to normal on Saturday. So when can I come visit?"

"Squirt, you can visit anytime you want. So you're that sure about the party and Friday?"

"Yes, Rick, I'm that sure." There was another tap on the door, I got up and started to move toward the door. Rick took my arm and moved me back to the sofa. "Stay put, I'll get the door," and I sat back down next to Sandy.

❧

Brad, Madalyn, Gina, and Billy had arrived, arms filled with bags of food and I could smell the Italian. Sandy and I jumped up from the sofa and went to see just what we had to eat. Sandy greeted Brad with a smile and a kiss.

Madalyn came up to me and hugged me very tightly. "I can't begin to thank you enough for what you did. I haven't felt this good in a very long time. Are you feeling better?"

"Yes, I'm fine. I'm sorry you had to go through that because of me."

"Nonsense, I think it has even made the bond between us stronger somehow." The tension in her voice was gone. Maybe it was all tied together.

Brad came to me. He didn't seem sure how he should greet me, whether he should kiss me on the cheek or the lips. He had always been sure of what to do, but now he was at a loss and I didn't like that. So I rose on my tiptoes and kissed him tenderly on the lips and put his hand on my chest. *Please, don't be this way Bradley. I need you to be strong and decisive. You may greet me any way you like.*

Brad took my hand and was walking with me to the dinning area, "I thought it might be best to eat in for a change."

☙

Rick stood close to Gina; she allowed him to touch her tummy, and he smiled as he felt the little one kick. I could hear their thoughts as if they were right next to me. *Just a few more weeks, huh? Then how long?* Rick asked.

Not that long, Rick. Why, miss me?

Yeah, I do actually. Does that surprise you?

No, not really. We do have fun, don't we? Now, what's really bothering you? Gina asked.

Oh, you think you know me so well. Nothing is bothering me.

Rick, talk to Bree. She will not deny you once she understands completely. I know Bree cares for you greatly. I have watched you two teasing one another. Why do you keep the pain inside you?

Bree has more healing to do. Tonight proved that. I just want to kill those motherfuckers. When the time is right, I will ask, but not yet. I can still hold her and that will have to do for now, Rick said.

You don't give her enough credit. Bree is very strong; she'll not let this happen again. You know you will never be able to make love to her as you do us. You understand that, right? Gina looked to make sure he understood her comment.

That's not how I want to love her; she is too soft for that. I find it amazing, this one little person, he laughed, *could cause me to feel this way*.

She is shy. She will not speak to us about her time with any of you. That will piss Madalyn off. Sandy treats her like her little sister. She's bonded to Bree now. She won't mind you spending time with her. Hell, she'll get Steven then. I know that will piss Madalyn off, Gina laughed.

You enjoy pissing Madalyn off? Why Gina, a side of you I have not seen.

I'm just as protective of Bree as you are. She's new to this life and Madalyn will take advantage of her. Then again, Bree just might show her a thing or two if she gets mad enough. Bill said Bree wants to handle Madalyn's problems, but I will be watchful. Madalyn can be a bitch when she wants.

What about Bill? Do you think he will ever ask her to spend time with him? Rick asked.

Ah, that will be interesting. Bill does love her. Oh my, yes he does, and he is one of her companions the prophecy spoke of. She giggled. *So are you Richard*, she smiled at him and gave him a little nudge. *Do you know who the others are yet?*

No idea.

Well, maybe with some tender coaxing I can persuade Bill, but we shall see. It is important the prophecy is adhered to. For her clan to protect her - you males must be familiar to her. Poor Brad, I don't think even he thought it would be this difficult. He was always so in control until she came along. Now he doesn't know which end is up.

You are actually enjoying this, aren't you? Rick laughed.

Oh Rick, you have no idea how much. It's about time someone led you four around by the noses instead of you four always leading us. Yes, I do so much enjoy Bree.

☙

I kissed Billy and Gina on the cheek. "What's all this?"

Steven walked into the room. "Whoa, do I smell Italian?"

"Hey, Steven," Billy called. "Bree, I thought I would treat you tonight to your favorite Italian restaurant from home. I see your feeling better," he smiled. "Ready for the party and Friday?"

"Yep, all ready," I said as I took the Italian subs out of the bag. "God I love you for this." Billy brought me my favorite; a hot ham, salami, and provolone cheese sub, with just the right amount of garlic, lettuce, and tomato. Heaven. The aroma was making my mouth water.

Sandy handed everyone plates from the little kitchen area. We gathered in the living room and I settled on the floor in front of Steven to eat my sandwich. I smiled at their comments as they ate theirs.

Rick finally finished his, "Bree, I would have to agree. That was the best damn sub I have tasted in a long while. Sandy, we have to remember to eat there when we come to visit."

Sandy was enjoying hers as well; a small moan escaped as she said, "My God, this is good. Bill, I could kiss you for this. Bree, take me home with you; I'll live there."

Billy got up to get everyone some more wine. "Yeah, that's one of our favorites, right Half Pint? We try to eat there at least once a month. The restaurant is in one of those strip malls. It's small, but damn they do make good Italian food. Hey Bree, the message light is lit on your phone."

I looked up at that, momentarily forgetting about my sandwich. My face betrayed my calm manner, "Okay, I'll get it in a few. Probably Mom." I knew it wasn't; I continued with my sandwich.

"Bree, I just saw your mother a little bit ago. She knew we were coming tonight. If she had a message for you I'm sure she would have given it to us to give to you," Gina offered, watching me out of the corner of her eye.

"Maybe she forgot; she generally calls me. It's usually nothing important; she likes to hear my voice every so often. Probably didn't want to bother you." Gina could always tell when I was hiding something. I saw her look at Billy. Yes, I'm sure she'd told him I was hiding something.

Bree, Steven thought to me, *you okay?* He wasn't looking at me, not wanting Madalyn and Sandy to notice his concern over my hesitation.

Sure, I'm fine. Why? I said, trying to go back to making love to my sandwich. I couldn't do it. I got up and took the message. I knew it would be the voice I had become familiar with. Warning me, giving me short little messages that I needed to put together. I picked up the receiver and pressed #7 on the dial, got the familiar you have 1 message, and then it began.

457

"*Bree,*" the voice was soft and calm. "*You need to embrace your role in your clan. Your enemies knew where you went; they were the ones responsible for the attack. You made the right choice this evening. Madalyn would surely have been dead by the morning. The pain would have driven her mad; she would have ended her existence. She will be fine now. The spell has been broken. They know the pain you are feeling and it makes them happy. You must do better at hiding your emotions if you are going to survive. I have not yet discovered how they know these things. Keep your movements close to you, the less known the better. Hurting you has aroused their appetites. More pain will come. The stones are yours. You have one; there are more. Know your sisters love you, and our fate rests on your shoulders. Tomorrow will be very dangerous for you. Do not allow her to take you.*"

That was the end of the message. I pressed 3 to erase the message, hung up the phone and went back to my sandwich. I made the mistake of looking at Brad. I smiled, "Just the front desk letting me know my dry cleaning's ready," was the only thing that came to mind. If I had said it was my mother, they surely would have asked her.

"You sent clothes out to be dry cleaned? Pretty long message for that." Brad wasn't buying it.

"Yes, Bradley I did; and now they are ready." I sat back on the floor in front of Steven and continued eating my sandwich as if nothing was wrong, but Brad had other ideas.

Bree, don't hide things from me. Do you understand? We are on your side in this you know.

Yes, Bradley I know this. But please, now is not the time.

"So, what's new with everyone?" I asked changing the subject.

"Well, to be honest Half Pint, we can't stay. Gina really needs her rest, and you should probably get yours too."

"Oh Billy, I'm fine. I would like to stay. Besides, we can help Rick and Sandy with our problem children. Steven needs to stay with Bree and Brad can't be around them."

"Yeah, Sandy and I need to round up our two problems," his voice was serious. "We told them we would meet them for a drink later. Maybe while we're getting more information out of them we can get some college stories from Becky." He looked at me and winked.

"You'll never get my secrets out of her," I promised as I raised an eyebrow to him.

"No, probably not." He gave me a smile telling me he probably already knew most of my stories anyway.

Steven patted the cushion next to him on the sofa. "Bree, come sit next to me."

I turned to look at him. "Why?" I was sure he was going to question me about the phone call.

"Because I want you to." He looked at me and I knew this wasn't going to be pleasant.

I sat next to him and he put his arm around me, his hand resting on my shoulder. "Okay, what?" I asked. I braced myself for the lecture I was sure was coming my way. The room got quiet, which made me a little nervous.

Rick finally spoke, "Bree, we're concerned about the next couple of days. Somehow, your enemies know your moves. It has Bill and me concerned. You are taking risks we feel you don't, or should I say, shouldn't take. Remember the umbrella I spoke to you about? Well, you're doing it again." His soft blue eyes pierced my soul. I couldn't take my eyes off his, but then Sandy spoke.

"Look what happened in Yellowstone; look what happened to you right here." Sandy spoke her words with such concern for me; her face showed me her worry.

"You two need to relax and go meet Ted and Becky for that drink," I said. I should have known Steven gave in way too easily at lunch. I should have listened to their thoughts. At least then I would know what my little clan was planning. I had a sinking feeling I wasn't going to the party.

"What are you thinking, Bree?" Rick asked, watching my eyes. Evidentially, he was getting better at reading my actions. He paid way too much attention to details. I let my gaze stay on Rick for a while. "Did Ted and Becky know we went to Yellowstone?" I asked.

"No, they knew we were gone for a while, but they didn't know the location," Rick said.

"Can you be tracked when you travel?" I looked at Brad.

"Yes, if they know when we leave it is possible to be followed. But we all left from our rooms, so I really think that was unlikely," Brad answered.

"We're just concerned about the coming days, Bree. We're just not comfortable with the party," Sandy said as she looked at everyone. She took a deep breath before she continued. She wasn't comfortable talking to me in the manner she was getting ready to speak to me, but she continued anyway. She stood and started to pace, "Thomas isn't someone to play with. You insulted him last night and he will be ready for you tomorrow. What is to prevent him from just killing you at the party? His clan is strong and they will all be there with him. There will be nothing we could do, and I am truly afraid of losing you." She stopped pacing, put her hands on her hips and faced me; waiting for me to, I guess, yell at her. But I did not intend to do that. If I wanted them to be open with me, I had to give them the room to state their feelings without fear of my reprisal.

"Bree, we are asking you to rethink the party. We love you too much and it would kill me if anything happened to you. Isn't there any other way you can show your strength? Must you really go to this party? I know you are strong. I have seen your growth over the past few days, and I will say, I am very impressed. Isn't that enough? You don't have to prove anything to us. We have accepted you as our leader and we would all give our lives to protect you; but please reconsider this path you are going to venture down tomorrow." Rick's eyes stayed with me; he never looked away as he made his plea. His thoughts quickly kissed my mind; *I just can't lose you Bree. I just can't, not again.*

I looked at both of them and smiled. Calmly I answered, "I appreciate your thoughts, and I will consider them. I'm glad I don't need to prove myself to you; but I still need to prove myself to others. Thomas isn't going to strike at the party. I really need you all to understand." I leaned into Steven; he kissed the top of my head. "He is being sent to see my strength. I do not have the luxury of only worrying about my clan. I have two families, two worlds, to consider. I have to weigh all the pros and cons, to make the right decisions. Some of my decisions are not going to be what you want to hear." I looked at all of them, "but they are necessary for my other family, and for our worlds. I don't want you worrying any more on this tonight. Why don't you all go have that drink with our problem children? Steven, Brad, Madalyn and I can go to the show and then we will meet you later," I smiled.

"Yeah, sounds good. And Bree, on the way back maybe you can pick up your dry cleaning," Steven smiled.

"Perhaps."

CHAPTER 33

Thursday Morning – Party Time!

"Good morning, sunshine," Steven whispered, trying to stir me awake.

I couldn't suppress my smile and my happiness at seeing him. "Morning." I stretched and wrapped my arms around him a little tighter.

He rolled on top of me, giving me little kisses. "Are you awake now? We have a full day today, missy. Let's get started. But first, Bree, what about your dry-cleaning? You conveniently forgot to pick it up last night; and Bree; this is a very fancy hotel. They deliver dry cleaning. So, you want to tell me about the phone call?"

"Oh, yeah, about that," I moved to get up.

He smiled, "You're not going anywhere so just get comfortable. Now, what about the phone call?"

"Steven, are you trying new tactics on me now?" His smile answered that question; and I knew from the set of his eyes, it was time to come clean. "Okay, keep an open mind. It wasn't the first time I got a call."

I couldn't remember ever seeing someone get mad that quickly! Steven was clearly angry; his eyes penetrated mine, the twinkle in them vanished, his smile hardened. "Bree, damn it! When are you going to let me in? Why do you continue to keep me at arms length on this?"

"Steven, I didn't tell you because, well, there really wasn't anything to tell. I got the first call on Sunday; it was very short. She just told me, "My sisters love me very much and their fates rest on my shoulders." I received a few more like that, but I actually thought they were prank calls; so I really didn't pay any attention to them until the day we were going to go to Yellowstone. When you were in the shower I noticed the message light, so I checked it."

"So why didn't you mention it then?" he asked.

"Steven, I had just been made aware of all of this. My mind was being flooded with all these memories of us, of what I am to do. Dang Steven, cut me a little slack here. Do you want to hear the rest?"

"Yes, Bree, continue," Steven's tone was angry, but his eyes were beginning to soften.

"She gave me a warning telling me we should not go there, to Yellowstone. She said strong protection was needed, to give you my blood. And before the call ended, I was reminded to take the stone. The last call I got was more detailed." I relayed to Steven her message. "The only stone I received while I have been here was delivered to my room, and I wasn't even here. There was a note saying it was a healing stone and that I always needed to keep it with me. I think it has helped enhance my healing powers since I am not a sorceress just yet. This particular stone has a warm feeling. I can feel its heat. Does that make sense to you?"

"Yeah, it does. But why didn't you mention this earlier?" I knew from my earlier dreams that my clan was aware of more than they were letting on. Hell, they were aware of a whole lot more than they were letting on, but they played this game well. They weren't going to tell me they knew; they were waiting on me to tell them. They were all still unaware of Odessa though, and I didn't think I wanted to be this close to him when I told him about her!

"When, Steven? When would you have liked me to tell you? In between the time I learned that you and Madalyn share a bond? Or how about after I learned I was now a leader in our clan? Or maybe after I had spent my time with Brad, or, I know, maybe after I was drugged? Which time? Tell me when we have really had ten minutes to ourselves?" I was frustrated now. His face softened and I continued, "Like I said, I didn't think there was really anything to tell and besides," I hesitated, "I didn't want to worry you. It's a beautiful necklace though. It's a deep red teardrop shaped stone with black veins of onyx running through it. It's set in sterling silver and hangs from a long sterling silver chain. You've seen me wear it. Well, maybe you haven't; but anyway, if you let me up I'll get it and show it to you." I batted my eyes at him to see if he would give in. He didn't.

"That's okay, you can show me later. Go on with your story." He smiled and gave me a quick kiss.

"There's really not much else to tell. I've told you about all the calls, the messages. I have no idea who this person is, or how they know me. Do you have any ideas?" I asked, wondering if he would tell me what he knew.

"No, Bree, I have no idea who is calling you."

"Well, I guess I could also tell you about the voice I hear if you like."

Steven groaned, "Bree, what voices are you hearing?" He placed his thumb and index finger to the bridge of his nose and pressed a little.

"Voice Steven, singular. Just one voice; her name is Odessa. She's been guiding me." I gave him a quick smile. "Okay, let me explain this," I rose on my elbow, "You remember the night I found out I was going to transform into a powerful sorceress?" I made air quotes. "Yeah, well that was the first night I heard her. She's been explaining things to me; letting me know what I can do with my mind. Everything has always been in there; she's just helping me bring it out. She was the one that helped me understand the phone call about your hunting trip. That's why I asked for the three vials; that's why I poured it into your Drinks. I understand the power of my blood more than any of you. Odessa and my mystery phone voice understand the power of my blood more than you guys do. She's helping me with things you guys can't because you didn't even know they were there. Am I making any sense to you?" I wrinkled my forehead and was looking at him to see if he understood me. I let my fingers rub across his arms, as I waited for him to answer me.

"That's it; I have nothing left to tell. Now you can let Brad know everything I told you. If he and Madalyn would like to come down now, we can all discuss this." I reached my arms around his neck and pulled him to my lips. I kissed him softly and smiled. "I'm sure you have some questions. Why don't you just call everyone here? Let's get this out in the open now." I kissed him again. "May I get up now?"

He suppressed his smile. "Bree, what am I going to do with you?" I shot a thought into his mind of us a little earlier. "Okay, I do like that thought, but let's get through this right now. Will you please let me know these things? Damn, I just want to get you home where I can keep you safe. Go get dressed; we'll go get something to eat. I made an appointment for you at the Spa; Sandy and Madalyn are going with you. We'll discuss this all later, but for now let's get the soreness out of you." Before I moved, I placed my hand on his chest, just to ensure my vibration was still there. "Princess," he said softly, "you've nothing to worry about, I love you very much. Go get dressed." He kissed me before he would release me.

❦

Steven had made a three-hour spa appointment for me and I was back in the room by one o'clock feeling like a new person. Everyone was there and I knew Steven had already filled the men of my clan in on our conversation this morning. I knew they had spent the majority of the morning planning for tonight. Damn, I would be so happy when this was all over and we could go home. I smiled to myself at that thought. Steven and I could go home. I did like the sound of that.

They all greeted me, with Brad being the last. There was not a hint of indecision. I knew he was a little upset with me but I received a very warm vampire kiss from him and he himself placed his hand on my breast. He got the response he was looking for; I felt my tone in him as well. He took his place next to Madalyn and I stood next to Steven.

467

"Do any of you have any questions about the messages I have received? Brad, I'm quite sure you do, so ask them please. Rick now is the time for you to ask as well," I said.

"I've no questions now, Bree. Just please tell us when you get these calls. We understand the stress you are under for both clan and family. All we want to do is help. There is no reason for you to carry any of these burdens by yourself," Brad said.

Okay, this was new. Something was up. These three don't give in that easily. "What do you know of the other Chosen One's on the Council? Is Esmeralda a Chosen One, or did she gain power by default?" I asked.

"I really don't know anything of them. They are seldom seen. As for Esmeralda, no, she is not a Chosen One. She has one powerful House, I think. She gained power through family. She has been seen with Thomas occasionally; I think they are more lovers than mates. His mistress as you called it. Not too sure how that plays in his clan. It's generally never done like that. It's okay to love within the clan; but to go outside, not such a good idea," Brad offered off-handedly.

Room service came and Steven handed me my plate. "Bree, this is from our special number; you've nothing to worry about. Just eat." They poured their Drink and Brad poured me a tall glass of iced tea. "Where are our other two members?" I looked at Rick and Sandy.

"Meditating," Sandy offered. "We had them out very late last night. Rick wants them relaxed for the party tonight. They will be there, Bree, as prospective members of our clan. They understand they will be representing our group and are looking forward to it.

"Anything from your informant?" I raised my eyebrows to Rick causing a smile to come to this his lips.

"Nothing yet. I told you I would tell you, and I will. Patience grasshopper," he laughed.

"Fine," I said a little irritated. I was getting tired again. The sun was coming through the windows; the room was warm, my tummy was full and I was relaxed. Rick turned on some soft music. I could feel the tension ease in my clan and that made me happy. Rick and Steven were talking about a trip we all needed to take when this was over. Rick's voice was low and deep and Steven's was very soothing. I struggled to pay attention. I soon gave up, curled up next to Steven on the love seat, and fell asleep, listening to the muffled voices of my clan.

Chapter 34

I found myself in the passage; I heard their voices and hurried toward the sound. The smell of damp earth was strong; the air was much cooler than the last time I visited. They stood at the table; the clay bottle was in view. Esmeralda stroked the smooth surface and smiled her pleasure as she spoke to her servant.

"My Lady, she will be at the party tonight. What are your wishes?"

"My wishes are simple now, Thomas. I want her dead. I want her family powerless." She was not pleased. "Things have changed and time is short, Thomas." The clay bottle shook.

"My Lady, she has proven to be a challenge. What do you need of me tonight?"

"How can a simple mortal be a challenge to you, my dear? Will your clan be strong tonight?" She caressed her lips with her tongue as her finger circled the opening of the bottle. The clay bottle shook. She smiled.

"Yes, my Lady, my entire clan will be there."

"Can you end this tonight?" She turned to him and smiled. She placed her hand delicately at his jawline and gently stroked. He stood straight.

"Yes, my Lady, if that is your wish. I thought you wanted to wait until Friday?" Thomas answered.

"I did, but as I said, things have changed. Is there a problem?" She smiled, trying to read the tension in him.

"No, if that is your wish, then I will comply." He kept his answers short.

"Your plan should be simple; a simple scratch will suffice Thomas. That is all that is needed. One simple scratch," Esmeralda reminded him.

"It is never simple, my Lady."

"You were close the other night; you held her hand, Thomas. You pulled her close to you as you went into her mind. Your lips were so close, Thomas. Take her again tonight. One tiny scratch, that's all it will take," Esmeralda coaxed.

"Do you think that wise? Her entire family will be at the function. Her grandmother and cousins will cut my clan into pieces," Thomas said.

"Ah, yes, her grandmother; such the meddling old woman. Just as meddling as my mother, I will enjoy seeing her family brought down," Esmeralda hissed.

"Why Essie, you never spoke of your mother. Does she still live?" Thomas gave her a sexy grin; one he knew she could not resist.

"In a manner of speaking the old bat does live." Esmeralda smiled back at him. "If the opportunity presents itself, then yes, I want you to finish her tonight along with her clan. Bring her body to me first before your clan feasts upon her. None will be left to oppose me. My power will grow. Your status will grow; you and your clan will be feared." She ran her fingers over his lips and he kissed the tips of her fingers. "You may leave now, Thomas. I have no further need of you tonight." Her attention went back to the bottle.

"As you wish; if the opportunity presents itself, my Lady."

"Thomas."

"Yes, my Lady." His body language told me he wanted to leave.

"Do not disappoint me tonight."

"Yes, my Lady," and he left the chamber.

Esmeralda returned her attention to the clay bottle. She bent close. As she stroked the smooth surface, she whispered to it, "Soon, my master. Very soon you will be whole." The bottle shook.

Chapter 35

I finally woke; I was lying in bed alone. The room was quiet and dark, but Steven was there. I could feel him in the room. I opened my eyes but laid very still, I didn't think he was aware I was awake. He sat in the sitting area of the bedroom with his feet up on the ottoman. His head was resting on the back of the chair; his fingers were interlaced and resting on his chest. His eyes were closed. I didn't understand why he was sitting in the chair. Why wasn't he here in bed with me? Why did I not wake when he moved me from the living room to the bedroom? Then it hit me. My own clan, no, surely not. Damn, well, there's only one-way to find out.

I crept into Steven's thoughts. He was meditating; his mind was going over a conversation he'd had with Brad not that long ago. The memories were still fresh in his mind.

No Brad, she's not awake yet. She may sleep through the party. I know she was very tired and with the sedative you gave, plus the massage. Hell, she may sleep the rest of the night.

Not too sure I want to be here in the morning, I'll tell you that much. She is going to be extremely peeved.

Steven, sorry to put you in this predicament; but with all this new information we just couldn't let her go to the party. No one was aware the Guardians were helping her; she is progressing too fast. Her enemies will be pressed to act soon; we'll not give them the opportunity. I don't care if we have to hide her away until she transforms, they'll not get the chance to touch her. Bill, Stanley and Ryan understand; Millie is the only one not in agreement. She thinks Bree should be there; sometimes Millie can be trying. I do agree; she is going to be extremely upset. I'm glad you're there and not me, Brad laughed.

Shit, thanks Brad. Knew I could count on you. She'll get over it; I can usually calm her down. We could always take her to the mountains; she would like it there.

Yeah, I agree, she would like the mountains. Keep me posted.

Trust me; you'll be the second to know when she wakes, Steven warned.

ભ

My own clan did to me what Nick had done to me. Drugged me to get me to do what they wanted. Albeit, my clan didn't hurt me or rape me, but just the same they took my choice away. Think again Steven and Brad, my anger is off the scale!

Odessa, can you hear me?

Yes, Bree, I can hear you and I can feel your anger. Temper your mind. You can still go to the party; let your mind roam and listen. You forget in your anger what you are capable of. Let Steven know you are awake. I fear making you stay here this evening was a mistake. You need to be ready; you will need to act soon. Bree, they do love you so much. Don't be too harsh.

Odessa, you don't drug the one you love. You just don't do that.

Theirs was not to hurt you Bree, but to protect you, Odessa reminded.

And what of tomorrow, Odessa? Will they drug me then too? Will they hide me for fear I will be taken? I know my path; they need to know this. I have another family to consider, another race. What of them? Oh, I'm sorry Mom and Dad but my clan now comes first, or sorry Magicals and mortals, can't help just yet; my clan thinks it's too dangerous? My mind's hands were waving wildly as I tried to explain my thoughts.

I understand your anger Bree. Temper it; you need to focus now. Odessa said sternly, motherly.

I stirred in the bed, and did what I normally would do and reached for Steven. He was quickly by my side. "You're awake, sunshine. Did you sleep well?" His voice was calm, and that angered me more.

"Yes, thank you. You can let Brad know I'm awake. Next time maybe he should make the sedative a little stronger." I pulled away from him and moved to the other side of the bed to get up. Steven was quicker. He was on that side and took my arms. "Bree, I know you're angry; but we didn't want you to go tonight. It is far too dangerous for you. Not tonight. You can be mad and pout as much as you want; but I will not allow you to go."

"You have no idea just how angry I am. You go to the party. I won't go, I would prefer to be alone."

"Bree, you don't mean that; you're just mad right now."

"Yes, Steven, I do." I couldn't hold the tears back; and I told him how it made me feel to have my own ability to choose taken from me. I could tell from the look in his eyes they hadn't thought of that. For all of their combined intellect, common sense was not a factor. They all knew what was best to take care of 'little Bree'. They would make the decisions for me. I turned from him and went to the bathroom, closing the door hard.

I heard the light tap on the door. "Bree, we didn't think about how you would feel; we were more concerned for your safety. Don't be this way, come back, and let's talk." His fist pounded the bathroom door. He was becoming just as angry as I was.

"I don't want to talk now. Please go to your precious party, and join your clan. They will need you there tonight." Then I turned the shower on.

I finished dressing and went to the living room, flipped on the TV, and retrieved the bottle of wine from the refrigerator. I poured myself a large glass of it.

Bree, don't miss the party because you are mad. Open your mind; your clan will learn much tonight. You will be called upon very soon. Know the players, understand the stakes; open your mind, Odessa instructed.

I wanted to be mad; I needed to feel mad. However, she was correct; I needed to listen. I needed to be ready. "Okay, let's see what I see." I turned some soft music on and sat in the chair, took a drink of my wine and let myself relax. I saw myself walking into the ballroom. Everyone was there except Thomas. He and his clan hadn't yet arrived. I could see Steven talking with Brad and Rick. Madalyn and Sandy were there as well. I could see the worry on their faces. Steven's jaw was set; his arms were crossed over his chest. He was resolved in his decision to keep me away from the party. He had relayed my reaction to them.

"Brad, she's very mad and maybe a little hurt. I didn't even think she would feel like that. How could she think we could hurt her like they did? She'll just have to get over it. Our decision was the correct one. Damn this woman can be so stubborn. Does she not realize how much danger she has put herself in?" I could tell from his facial expression he was just as mad at himself. He too felt the whirlpool sucking any control we thought we had down the drain.

"Don't worry Steven. Yes, she's mad; but she'll come around. We may get the cold shoulder from her, but she knows we did this for her own good. Once this is all over tonight, she'll be fine. Besides our contact said we needed to keep her away this evening; Thomas may not even be here tonight. She needs her rest for tomorrow. She has to understand that. I will not apologize for this; nor will any of you. Sometimes she needs to let us take care of things," Brad said, trying his best to convince them.

Well, Bradley, I will put my dream up against your contact.

"You don't think she's mad enough to leave do you?" Sandy asked. She was twisting a napkin around her fingers; clearly, she was upset. After all, she had asked me to reconsider my actions too.

Billy was close behind her; he wrapped his arms around her waist, comforting her. "Don't worry Sandy; Bree will be with you for a long time. Oh, yeah, she's mad right now; but I know her. She'll get over it in no time. Then all will be back to normal. Just give her some space." He tried his best to reassure her, and maybe himself.

"I don't know Bill," Steven said, "she told me to leave and she meant it. This is going to take a little more than a few hours for her to get happy again. I'm not going to give her too much space, just out of self-preservation," he laughed. "Ya know, I think we will be doing a lot of apologizing to this little individual. No matter; I don't care if I have to tie her down, she will listen to me."

"Ah, Steven, stop worrying. We'll go with you when this is all over. She can't hit us all at once. We'll make it right. I don't mind apologizing again. Really, whatever it takes," he smiled, which caused me to smile. *Oh Richard, you are going to be a fun one, I can tell.*

I continued through the room, watching and listening. I came upon two male witches. It looked like both were drinking whiskey. "Did you hear the gems are missing?" asked one of the men. He looked to be about fifty. His hair was sandy brown and cut short; he smoked a pipe and wore glasses, he had a full bushy beard. I had never seen him before; but I knew not to trust him.

"Gerald, she's furious. How could they lose all five? Bunch of morons." He gave a low laugh; I sensed he was pleased Esmeralda was unhappy. "Why does she keep that clan of vampires anyway? He must be damn good." His hair was gray, his eyes smiled, his manner was calm.

"She's not happy, Fredrick; she's pissed as hell someone stole them. They are sure someone in the castle did it. She's powerful enough without them, but with them there is no way that Campbell gal can stand up to her," Gerald said. "I don't understand why she cohorts with the vamps either. Bunch of bloodsuckers. Dirty bloodsuckers; that's all they are."

Fredrick took a drink of his whiskey. His eyes scanned the room before he spoke, "Speaking of the Campbell gal, where is she? Thought she was going to be here. Huh, her clan is here," he laughed. "Can you believe that, a witch living with vampires? That's as bad as Esmeralda. Vampires must wet these witches' appetites." A smiled creased his lips. He looked away not wanting his friend to notice, then he continued, "They are so beneath her, and even her family cohorts with them and those werewolves," Fredrick said.

"I heard that Campbell gal has two mates in that clan. How disgusting. That family isn't the only one socializing with that kind. Haven't you been watching the Smiths, the Van-Heusen's? More Houses are growing with those that want to socialize with the lowers. Esmeralda has to gain control; we have to get the old standards back. She must set the example though and get rid of her own clan! Put these animals in their places. Witches are always on top; everyone knows this," Gerald finished. He took a long drink of his whiskey; his face grimaced from the sting of the drink. "Don't even know what the Elves are thinking," he continued, swirling the drink left in his glass. He was unhappy; this was not the world he wanted. He thirsted for war, dominance over others, clearly, this individual would be happy with everyone else's misery. "Well, let's fix one thing first, then we can turn our attention to all the others. Get rid of the Campbell gal; that's a start. Let's start making plans to start more wars. Damn this sitting and waiting shit is for the birds," Gerald spat.

"Esmeralda keeps her clan to do her dirty work, Gerald; that's all. Well…I'm sure she has them for other reasons as well," he laughed and took a drink.

"Esmeralda needs to put things right. We can't have inter-relations with the humans. They are too weak minded. We could enslave them; make them do our bidding. But marry them? Never." Fredrick motioned with his chin and lowered his voice, "Did you hear about the Robertson's daughter being caught while eloping with a mortal? That little girl will be punished; you mark my words. Esmeralda has promised to punish any Magical that marries a human. That'll put those self-righteous bastards in their places. We should be able to do away with these families, get back to the way it was," Fredrick said.

"Robertson's? Really? Damn, she is an attractive little thing; I'd hate to see her waste away in the dungeons. Maybe I can make a deal?" Gerald smiled wickedly, his hand scratched at his beard under his chin. He continued scanning the room. "The Campbell gal must have chickened out; left her clan to take the fall. Smart girl; tomorrow it will all be over for her though. There is no way she is walking out of here. Thomas should be here shortly, and then the fireworks will begin. He'll make quick work of her clan. Patience Fredrick, you need to learn patience. Good things come to those that wait." They both broke out in laughter.

I continued through the room and came upon a small group. From the looks of them, they were a mixture of vampires, werewolves and a few fairies.

"She's not coming. Why isn't she coming? Doesn't she understand how important this is? Tomorrow will not go well," she said while biting her nails. Her complexion was very fair; her hair was golden, her eyes blue, her eyebrows arched. I could only assume she was a fairy; I'd never meet one before.

"Harry said Bree was a strong one. She'll be here. Harry said she'd be here," said one of her companions as he strained his neck to see through the crowd, obviously a werewolf to know Harry. His body didn't have as much hair as Harry's. He was young, lightly tanned, and blond. He had a beautiful smile and bright green eyes.

I wanted to listen to their conversation a little longer but my trip through the hall was interrupted by a disturbance at the front. Thomas had arrived. He entered the hall without a care in the world. His arrogance was overwhelming. His cloak billowed as he walked straight up to my clan. My clan stood with their arms across their chests, the men in front, the women behind. My other cousins came up close to support them. Damn this wasn't good. I could see the headlines in the papers in the morning, 'Blood Bath in Vegas'. Thomas' clan was large, at least twenty, if not more. My clan was small but they had many friends; I just wasn't sure if they would all help in the end.

"Bradley," he tipped his head. "Where is your lovely Bree? I had so hoped to hold her hand again this evening," Thomas smiled wide. He knew I wasn't there; he knew I wasn't coming. "She isn't as strong as you had hoped, is she? No matter, tomorrow she will be mine. How does that make you feel, Steven? There will not be anything you can do about it," Thomas said as he examined his fingernails, then looked at Steven and smiled. It wasn't a mean smile; I detected a note of relief; but relief from what?

Thomas opened his arms wide and turned to let everyone hear him, "You have all lost. You who want to break from the old traditions, you who want to accept the lesser. We go back to the old ways; you have lost. I told you we would win." His voice had venom in it. He was close to Sandy as he said, "We will claim this world as ours. It will be cleansed of the weak."

Thomas looked into Sandy's face. "I have something of yours," backing up a little as he spoke, fanning his arms to show his prize. "You wanted to grow your clan with these," he laughed. "I have them, they will be mine, and we will make quick work of them as we will make quick work of you my dear." Thomas had his clan behind him now. There was Sylvia and Rebecca. Sylvia placed her arm on Thomas' and whispered in his ear.

Thomas smiled, "Ah, Steven, you are welcome to join my clan; Rebecca would love to have you as her mate. Think about it, won't you? I could spare you."

I heard her scream; I turned toward the disturbance. One of Thomas' clan had Becky; he was walking toward the head of the group. His talons were ready to strike; another clansman had Ted. My thoughts became urgent. *Dang! Just what are they playing at?* It was time for me to act now. *Had I been totally wrong in my assumptions?*

Bree, don't forget the stone and the pendant, Odessa reminded.

I ran to the bedroom, got them both, and put them around my neck. I grabbed my shoes and room key and ran out the door. I was frantically pressing the button to the elevator, hopping on one foot to the other as I put on my shoes. *Why didn't I do this earlier?* The elevator wasn't coming. I nervously kept punching the button. *Damn, if only I could fold space.* Finally, the doors opened. I continued viewing the party. They were still talking. "I can make it, just keep talking," I begged. "Don't stop, don't stop," I continued to beg the elevator. The elevator gods heard my pleas and the elevator went straight down to the main floor; I bolted out the door and ran toward the hall. Gathering my composure, my pace slowed.

Hear me my strength; please be with me. I will be called to do much and I have not transformed. I need your help this night. I felt the gentleness of the air circulating around me and I felt its strength. Just as I had imagined, my three favorite people were at the door. I continued forward.

"Hello, Bree," Nick stepped in front of me. "Can't let you go in there just now, buttercup. Thomas is making his point. You're too late, can't help your friends now. Why don't you let us show you a good time? I've missed you." Nick blew me a kiss and started laughing.

"Oh, Nick, not tonight dear. You have a headache." My mind threw him into the doors to the hall, slamming him into them hard. Nick slid down the door and laid flat on his back. For good measure I picked him up and slammed him against them again, and again he slid down and laid flat on the floor. I opened the doors with my mind. Everyone turned to see what brought about the noise. As the crowd parted, Thomas was at the front looking at me. Brad, Steven, and Rick were in my view as well. Their faces concealed their worry. I smiled and walked forward, "Damn that felt good."

Jared and Fred started toward me. I just looked at them and took their feet out from under them, slamming them hard to the floor with my mind. "Floor's just a little slippery. Watch yourselves; wouldn't want you to get hurt." I wanted to stay and slam them into things a little longer, but I needed to focus my attention on what was happening inside. I would deal with them later; I knew I would have my revenge. I continued forward and I stepped hard on Nick as I passed, then walked straight to Thomas. His clansmen still held Becky and Ted.

"Let them go, Thomas," I said as I approached.

"What do I get if I do Bree?" He smiled and I watched his eyes view my body. *You do look very inviting, my dear.* His eyes washed over me.

I smiled at his comment. I must have looked threatening standing there in my blue jeans, Converse tennis shoes, and my Denver Bronco's football jersey. Yes, I was sure I struck fear in them all.

"Your clan can walk out of here for one. Yeah, I know, what can this little mortal girl be talking about? You must be having a good laugh. You're what, twenty strong?" I looked around the room and turned back to him, "And yet I am just one person."

He laughed a deep laugh, but I could read the tension. He hid it well; but I heard it. My eyes narrowed on him. "Thomas, it has been a long week for me. I have had a lot thrown at me in the past few days. I'm tired and you are starting to get on my nerves. I'll ask nicely again; release them."

The confidence I had in my abilities was showing and he sensed them. I was not the scared little human he had thought he was up against. He was facing a potentially powerful sorceress. I hadn't transformed but I was able to do things none of them had expected.

"Thomas my patience is wearing thin. You don't know me well. I am not a very happy person right now; don't press your luck."

Thomas nodded to the clansman holding Ted; he released him. "No, please keep me. Let Becky go; you can't harm her."

I turned to him. "Theodore, move to the others. Becky will not be harmed. Do it now," I could see the dark creature with him as he moved to stand by Sandy. The DC licked toward her as she put her arm around him. I would need to end this here with him. I would not let it touch Sandy. I glanced at Brad and Steven. My emotions were under control; there was nothing for them to read. Their faces remained silent and no thoughts came to me. We would be speaking later.

I looked back at Thomas. "You have one more of my family, release her."

"Again, I ask you Little One. What do I get for doing that?" He smiled at me and I felt violated by his eyes.

I raised my hand to him, "Thomas please, no more. I am through playing games with Esmeralda. I will show you my strength and you may take that information back to her. You can't mesmerize me Thomas; I can't fall to you or any other vampire. She knows this. I am not weak. Let me show you." I violently grabbed Sylvia with my mind and brought her to her knees. I dragged her over to my side. People in the crowd started whispering, "She's human, yet she grabbed her and moved her without the use of her hands."

I heard someone else squeal in delight, "Oh they do put on a good Halloween show!"

Oh dear Lord, they think this is a show. I smiled at Thomas. I could tell several of his clansmen were getting nervous. "Release my clan member."

"Potential clan member," he reminded me.

"Nonetheless, release her." I pressed a little harder on Sylvia's throat. Thomas watched my eyes, looking for any sign of stress. He found none. I was effortlessly controlling the situation.

"Thomas your want for her is strong. I will release her unharmed; all you need to do is release my clan member." I let up just enough for Sylvia to make a plea, "Thomas, please," then I clamped down again and smiled sweetly to Thomas.

"Bree, you will not harm her. You do not have that in you," Thomas smiled.

"You will be surprised to know what I am capable of Thomas; do not press me."

I grabbed Rebecca just as violently, brought her to her knees, and brought her to my other side. "My patience with you has ended, Thomas." I acted very quickly with my mind and struck at the clansman holding Becky. I struck with enough force to send him flying into the crowd. His hand was burnt from my flash of anger. Becky was free. "Becky, please move over by Rick and Steven." I turned to glare at the clansman standing next to her. "Don't give me a reason," I said and he moved out of the way. Becky moved to Ted. I turned slowly and with my mind moved her to Rick and Steven. "Evidentially you did not hear me; I said Rick and Steven."

I turned back to Thomas and thought to him. *Your want is strong for these two; quench your thirst, and dip into their well. I will not spread my legs for you; you will never dip into mine. I will show you just how strong I am this evening, watch and learn.* I made Sylvia and Rebecca stand and threw them into him, maybe a little harder than I needed to.

I turned and walked back toward the clansman I injured. I stood in front of him and held out my hand. He didn't move. I looked back at Thomas then turned back to the clansman. "Ask your leader for his permission, and then give me your hand." He looked at Thomas, and Thomas nodded. He stood and extended his burnt hand to me. I blew gently on it and it immediately started to heal. I looked at him. "Next time keep your hands to yourself."

I walked slowly to the front and thought to my men and Thomas and Greg, *I will ask this just once, please trust me on what I am about to do.* They all looked at one another. *Thomas,* I continued, *please tell the men of your clan to remain calm, not to attack. Keep all of the women out of this conversation, and I do mean all. I will not hurt your clan; however, you may be six short when I am finished.*

My eyes fixed on the dark creature; I could see it envelope the six new members of Thomas' clan. It noticed my gaze, it watched me as I spoke, "You need to leave them; they are not what you want. Go back to your master."

No one saw what I spoke to; but they heard the cries of the ones the DC enveloped as it inflicted more pain on them. They fell to their knees and hugged their sides. I knew they felt the cold fingers; I knew it was squeezing their hearts and lungs.

I watched with sympathy as they lay on the floor, then said to the dark creature, "I will ask again for you to release them; go to your master." The dark did not move. I closed my eyes and summoned the wind. I guided a strong gust directly at them. The wind forced them down flat on the floor and pushed the dark away from them, back toward its master.

The dark made itself known and heard with its haunting whine, "You will die; you can not win. We will walk the earth once more. Your time is short Chosen One. Hear our warning." Then the DC was gone.

I turned my attention back toward Sandy and Ted. The creature was still with Ted; it still licked at Sandy. I needed to remove her as quickly as I could before I struck out at Ted. I thought to my grandmother, *Gran, please, very quickly remove Sandy from Ted's side. Please do it now.*

My grandmother did not hesitate, as I knew she wouldn't. Sandy disappeared and reappeared next to Gran. Ted was immediately alerted to me. His eyes watched me as a smile came to his lips. He realized I could see his friend hugging him and caressing him. Giving him as much love a mother would give her child.

The crowd was silent. I could feel the tension in my clan, in Thomas' clan, in my family. I was surprised no one had screamed when they saw the dark from those that stayed motionless on the floor, too afraid to move. Maybe they thought it part of the party too.

"Aubrey, I'm impressed," Ted laughed.

His confidence in his abilities was impressive; I'd give him that. My clan was alerted, as was Thomas' clan.

"Gentlemen," Ted continued, "you can't harm me. I have a protective shield around me. Relax. Your time will soon come, gentlemen, but today is not the day. Our alliances grow as the darkness grows. The dark was correct, your time is short Chosen One," he tipped his head toward me. "Enjoy yourself while you can," then he disappeared.

I walked slowly back to Thomas and spoke as I came nearer to him. "You have your information; take it back to your mistress. Let Esmeralda know her spell didn't work, the opportunity didn't present itself, and that my mind is strong. It will be an open forum tomorrow; my families will be there. Let Esmeralda know I will not go with her tomorrow; I will return home with my families. My clan is strong and my family will not fall. Tell Essie that for me, won't you? And Thomas, you have nothing to be ashamed of this evening. Essie didn't listen to you and you didn't understand my strength; but you do now." I tipped my head at him and smiled.

He smiled back and thought to me, *Aubrey our clans need to meet. We need to discuss these events.*

Thomas, you will need to speak with Bradley but I agree - we do need to discuss these events.

Aubrey, do not underestimate my want for you.

Thomas, accept my friendship, for that is all I can give you. Then I said aloud to keep up the pretense, "Do not attempt to harm my clan again; I promise I will strike *you* down the next time." My smile was cold, but he understood what I was doing - trying to save face for him and his clan.

Thomas and his entire clan left the ballroom. I watched as a few of his men picked up the three unconscious heaps I left at the entrance.

I turned to face my clan; I said nothing. I turned to leave the hall and was met by a large group of people. They were smiling; people were clapping and cheering, talking with one another, pressing in on me and into my space, my zone. I didn't become defensive. I didn't feel the need to back away from them. That was a good feeling for a change. There was no panic in my muscles; I had control for once and I did so enjoy that feeling. The music started again. Several reached to take my hand. Instantly Rick and Steven were on either side of me. I looked up at them, and then reached to take the hands that were offered. A very attractive looking young man asked if he could have a dance with me. I smiled and asked him his name. "Justin, my Lady; I am from the House of Boyd's."

"I will remember your House name," then I asked if he would accept a rain check on the dance. I had business to attend to now.

"Certainly, my Lady." Justin tipped his head then smiled at me; I returned his smile.

I was making my way from the room, when a very distinguished looking gentleman walked up to me. Steven introduced me to him, "Bree, this is Señor Hernandez of the Spanish Cult."

Señor Hernandez clicked his heels together and bowed at the waist. He took my hand, raised it to his lips, and kissed it. I could feel the strength of his heart as he held my hand. His words were true; he hid nothing from my mind. His hair and dark eyes added to his strong features. He wore his hair over his ears, but as he bowed to me, I saw the pointed tips. I then realized I was speaking with one of the leaders of the Elves. "Ms. Campbell, let me be the first to tell you the Spanish Cult will stand by you when you have transformed. We pledge to you and your clan, protection. You need only to ask. Protect her well Steven; I fear many will want to mate with her. She is very strong." He bowed again and left.

Rick and Steven remained at my side. The two gentlemen, Gerald and Fredrick, I had overheard earlier made their way to speak to me, eager to shake my hand. Billy and the rest of my clan had joined my side as these two stood before me. I did not offer my hand to them, but I stood politely as they babbled their support. I said nothing as they continued. Billy made the introductions to me letting me know they were advisors to the Council. I was not impressed and still did not move to shake their hands.

"Is there something that displeases you, my Lady?" asked Gerald.

"Yes, you displease me greatly. Inform your Council we will not revert to the old ways. You have chosen your side. Do not embarrass yourselves further by trying to get on mine." They looked at one another, tipped their heads to me, and left.

I looked at Rick and Steven, and then turned to the rest of my clan, "The child is going back to her room now. Goodnight." I started to turn to leave.

"Bree, stay. You are here now; the threat is gone. Please stay and enjoy the evening," Brad said.

"I prefer the quiet of my room. That was where you wanted me to be, that is where I will be," I said back to him and I turned and left.

ॐ

"Okay, you know when I said she would get over this in no time? I was wrong. We are so deep on her shit list; we may never see the end of this. I don't even think an

493

apology will work," Billy said, as he gave Steven and Rick an 'oh shit!' look.

"I'll talk with her," Steven said as he started for the door knowing Billy was right.

"I know it's not my place to speak," said Becky. Her voice was sad, still trying to figure out what just happened to her life. All those years she had spent with Ted; all those years she had thought he loved her. Her anger would come, but right now, she was numb. "If I were you I would let her work this out on her own. She'll speak with you, but I saw her eyes. Somehow, you guys have really hurt her feelings. Oh, she's mad, make no mistake about that. I've seen that look before. Give her a night to be on her own. If you can't see your way to a whole night, then give her a few hours."

Brad looked at Becky. "I will give her ten minutes to throw her tantrum, and then I will speak with her. We will not give her a night, not this time," he said confidently.

"Your funeral, chief."

"I've been to it before."

❧

I thought a message to my grandmother and asked her to send a bottle of bourbon to my room. I was tired of wine and wanted something a little stronger to work through this anger. I hadn't been able to make things appear out of thin air yet. It was waiting for me with a note when I got to my room.

My child, they had your best interests at heart; I know they weren't thinking of how you would respond. Steven is so scared to lose you and now you have Brad who is just as scared. Do not be too harsh with them. Finding two loves in one lifetime is indeed very precious. Get your anger out and establish your ground rules, then kiss and make up. Do not let a day go by that you do not forgive each other. Remember we are all human in one form or another.

Love,
Gran

"Ah damn it." I was all set to be royally peeved and now this. I opened the bottle, added ice to a glass and poured myself a drink. I noticed the light on my phone; I had a message. "Gees, I wonder who?" I listened to the message as I drank.

You have made a strong statement. Many are pleased. She is not. The dark has been exposed; this was not her wish. Tomorrow you will meet her; do not let your resolve weaken. I have left a package for you on your dresser. Wear them tomorrow along with the necklace. Your place is strong on the Council. We love you, our sister.

The message ended; I didn't erase it. I finished my drink, poured another, and went into the bedroom to get the package. Inside were two sterling silver bracelets; each had a large amber stone. They were quite striking. I took a long drink as I looked at the bracelets. I slipped them on my wrists. They were heavy but they felt right on my wrists. Then I felt the healing stone in my necklace. The stone was warm, and the bracelets were warm. I took all three off and went back into the living room. When I arrived back in the living room, Brad had appeared.

I walked to the bar and poured myself another full glass; I was starting to get generous with the alcohol. I had never been able to get drunk; my blood kept me from finding that buzz. I could get light headed but never drunk; but the burn it gave my throat helped keep the painful lump away.

"Can I offer you anything?" I asked. Brad raised his Drink in answer to my question. "What part of 'Goodnight' did you not understand?"

Brad took a drink of his Drink and continued to leave his eyes on me. He remained silent. I knew what he was doing and it wasn't going to work. I drank my drink and continued to watch him. I poured myself another large glass and sat on the love seat. Brad sat in the chair, drinking his Drink, and remained silent. I finished mine, set the glass down, and started toward the bedroom when he finally spoke. "Where do you think you are going now, Bree?"

I turned to him. "Well, you can speak. Amazing. I'm going to bed Bradley, by myself, to bed. Goodnight, I will see you in the morning."

"No, Bree, you are not. You will come back here and speak with me. You and I will not part tonight mad at one another and you will not remain mad at Steven. We made the wrong choice tonight. We made a mistake. We misjudged. We were wrong. Is that what you needed to hear? Given all the same information, I would do it again in a heartbeat. We care that much for you. Steven cares that much for you, and damn it Bree, I care that much for you." He sat there looking at me.

"You drugged me, Bradley." I stood rigid at the bedroom door. "I had no control over my own being. I had no choice in the matter. People I thought loved me drugged me. You and Steven are not treating me as a partner. You are both treating me as the little human who knows nothing. Well I have news for both of you; I know plenty, I can do plenty. Did you not see that this evening? When will you seven listen to me?"

He got up from his chair and came to me. I crossed my arms over my chest. "Bradley, please, keep your distance; I need to be angry at you right now. I do not want your apology," my voice softened.

Brad wasn't listening to my plea. He wrapped his arms around me and pulled me to him. "I will not give you an apology; I love you too much to see you hurt." His kiss was cool and intense. With one arm around my waist he held me tight until I relaxed in his arms, his other hand tenderly held my neck. I returned his kiss, struggling with my mind over the feelings I was experiencing. My emotions were back at odds with each other.

"Bradley, we can't do this," I said softly to him.

"Shhh, yes we can," came his reply. His embrace was strong, and he pressed his lips to me again. He laid me on the sofa and pressed into me. "I love you Bree. Damn, I so do love you."

His kisses were intense and I responded softly to him, calming him. "Bradley, please, this is not the time for this." His embrace softened. "I do love you, but this is not our time. You will wait until the solstice. You told Steven you could wait, and you made a promise to me. You will keep your word." I felt his chest, searching for my tone. It was there and that made me smile. Brad laid his hand on my breast feeling my heartbeat; he was satisfied.

He was on his side, stroking my cheek. "I am sorry we did that to you this evening. It was my decision. Please don't be mad," Brad said as he calmed his emotions.

I did my best to compose myself. "Apologizing again, Bradley?" I smiled and kissed him softly on the lips. My eyes searched his face; I waited on his smile, which came very quickly from him.

"I do so love you, Bree. Never doubt that."

"I don't doubt it. Bradley, call the others, we need to have a clan meeting. We need to set the ground rules. If I am going to lead with you then we need to have an understanding. I need to talk with Steven. I need to forgive him; I can feel his heart all the way up here." I kissed Brad softly again on the lips. "What came over you by the way? My goodness."

He started laughing, "My dear, I have found when you are angry with me, it excites me. You stand your ground with me and I love it. Can you not see your way to release me from my promise?" He saw me grin. "Yes, maybe you will weaken," he teased. "Steven was right, you are a handful, and I do like that." He kissed my hand.

I gave a small sigh. "I'll remember to keep my anger at you to a minimum. Will you please call them? We shall see about your promise." I went to the bathroom to compose myself. The cool water on my face felt wonderful. I brushed my hair and brushed my teeth. I let out a small moan, "Oh, Steven where are you?"

There was a light tapping sound and I smiled. I opened the door and there stood Steven. His eyes were soft as he looked at me. "Are you still mad at me? I am sorry, I just want you safe. I didn't stop to think how that would make you feel. I would never hurt you or take advantage of you in that state. Nor would I let anyone else. But Bree, I would do that again if need be just to keep you safe."

"I know you wouldn't hurt me, and I'm sorry I reacted like I did." I rose on my tiptoes, leaned in and kissed him. "Let's get this meeting over with; I need time alone with you. Tomorrow is coming quickly and I need to be with you. You give me more strength than you realize, and I fear I am in desperate need of it now."

"You do realize Brad is hurting," he gave me a naughty grin.

I smiled back just as naughty, "Steven, he has a mate and she can ease his pain. He will not die from his. I admit he may be uncomfortable, but that won't kill him. His desire for me will cool, once the newness has worn off."

"No, Bree, it will never cool. His passion for you will always be great. My passion for you will be immeasurable. You will need your rest." He laughed and hugged me tightly. "I will see you get enough rest."

CHAPTER 36

We went back to the living room. There were a few new faces in our group. One was my cousin Stanley and his friend Dirk, plus two females and another male I had never seen before. I could only assume some planning was going to take place.

I walked around to each of my clan and ran my hand along their jugulars. Then I whispered in Billy's ear and several pitchers of their special Drink appeared, along with a variety of different foods. "Help yourselves to the food. I didn't see any of you eating at the party." I kissed Billy on the cheek and offered him a glass of whiskey. I looked at Stanley, "Stanley what can I offer you...bourbon, whiskey? What can I offer your friends?"

"Bourbon, will be fine, Sweet Pea and my friends will have the Drink of your clan," Stanley smiled back at me.

I poured their Drink, and gave them out. Then sat on the arm of the love seat next to Steven. I looked up and Rick was watching me. *What's wrong, Little One?*

I've a lot to sort through, that's all.

Let us help you, please. Tell us what your path is, he pleaded.

There are too many present for that now. Later, I promise.

My thoughts went to Brad. *Did Thomas make his request to you?*

Yes, he did. You surprise me sometimes Aubrey. Thomas and several of his clan are waiting for me to call them. Do you see any more of the dark creatures? Does Becky have any clinging to her?

No, Becky never did. Ted, for whatever reason, kept it from her. She was unaware and now she is very scared. You can't turn her away now. Ted will surely kill her.

That is not my decision. But I can tell you the other three males of your clan wish her gone and gone now.

Please, you can't turn her away now. We can find another solution. Please talk with them, I pleaded with him.

He didn't answer me, but he spoke to everyone, "We need to have a short meeting. I would like the females to leave. Stanley, Dirk, and Andrew you are welcome to stay."

"Does Bree get to stay?" Madalyn questioned. I could tell by the way she sat, her hands folded tightly in her lap that her frustration with me was growing again.

"Yes, Madalyn, she will stay. This concerns her," Brad said firmly and without another word all the women left.

"Thomas has requested an audience with us again. They are waiting on my answer. I suggest we meet with them. However, does anyone have any questions before they arrive?" Brad asked.

"Yeah, I do," said Rick. "Bree, what brought you downstairs this evening?" He looked at me, and I felt him tapping on the door to my thoughts. I looked at him and gave him entrance to my mind. *Time for you to let me know how much you have grown my little lady. If I am going to protect your pretty little ass you better show me what you got.*

I smiled at him and slowly closed the door to my thoughts. As I started to answer his question, I got up and poured myself another drink. Then I picked up a pitcher and started going around the room to pour more of their Drink into their glasses as I spoke. "Well, as Brad put it earlier, I was up here throwing my tantrum," I smiled at him and he grinned. "I got bored and decided to venture downstairs to join the party. I heard your conversations, then heard others, then saw Thomas and heard his threats. I heard Becky's scream and I left here and came there.

Nick, Fred, and Jared were standing guard at the doors, as I somehow knew they would be." I looked at Steven, "Sorry, I couldn't resist throwing them around. It felt great!" I smiled and he smiled back at me.

"I knew if I didn't come down there, Thomas would have hurt them. He had to save face with Esmeralda; so to protect his clan something bad would have happened. It wasn't his intent, but it would have happened. Then every one of you would have gotten involved and I just couldn't sit by and let it happen. I knew he had no control over me; I knew he had no strength over me. I was still very mad at all of you." I poured Stanley another glass of bourbon; he looked at me and gave me one of his sweet grins, I smiled back at him. "I knew tonight was important, but my clan

503

seemed to have different ideas." I poured Billy another glass of whiskey.

Billy took my hand. "Bree, I was aware what they were planning and I bought into it as well."

"Yeah, I know, I heard. What am I to do with you, my sweet William?" I shook my head as I grinned. "When will you all listen to me?" I nudged him, "Billy, ya got to let me grow up."

"No, I don't," he whispered.

"Anyway, where was I? I had a thought, oh yeah. The dark was all over Ted; I had Sandy too close to him. He was keeping the DC with him, but I decided at that moment I wanted him away from my clan. I wanted it away from those in Thomas' clan. Not for Thomas' sake but for theirs. They were nothing but pawns in Esmeralda's plan and they didn't have a choice. So now I have given their choice back to them. I gave Thomas the information he needed to take back to Esmeralda. End of story."

"DC?" Stanley had a skeptical look on his face.

"Bree has named the dark shadow – dark creatures," Rick advised him. "Bree, you said for him to tell her the spell didn't work. You also said she didn't listen to him. Earlier, the first time you met Thomas, you told him you saw the jar. What did you mean by all of that?" Rick looked at me; damn he paid attention all to well.

"Yeah, I did say that." I shrugged my shoulders. "Don't know; it just came out." Brad and Steven pressed the bridge of their noses; I could tell they were upset again, they knew I wasn't telling all that I knew.

"Bree, your strength is growing; it will be more difficult to protect you now," Stanley said. He looked at Rick,

Steven, and Billy. "I will have someone outside her door at all times, *even* with you in here, and someone in the room with her when you aren't around. We'll make new arrangements at home. Looks like we need to go back to the day and night surveillance."

"I'll be with her at night Stanley, she will be fine then. If I am gone, then one of the male members of the clan will be with her. Let your men rest at night," Steven said.

"Are you sure? It's no problem to watch the house. We're used to it," Dirk offered. Just a little hopeful Steven would change his mind.

"Yeah, we're sure Dirk," Rick laughed.

"Stanley, how long have you been watching me?" My eyes narrowed on him.

"How old are you again?" he asked with a grin. "You have been watched your entire life, Sweet Pea. Get used to it. We will continue to watch over you, so save the speech. I'm not Bill, I won't melt," he laughed. "Even when you transform, you should consider my men over the Red Guard. The Red Guard's allegiance is questionable at best."

"Bree, how long have you been able to use your mind like that?" Rick asked.

"For a while now and the madder I am the stronger it is. I can control it; I know just the right amount of pressure to apply. This one was by far the best experiment I have had to see how many I could control at one time. I didn't even feel spent. I don't know how many I could have controlled; hope we never need to find out."

"Any more questions, gentlemen?" Brad asked.

"None that won't keep until after we've met with Thomas," Rick said.

"Very well," Brad spoke. Then a few minutes later Thomas, and seven of his clan, arrived in my suite.

Thomas tipped his head to Brad. "Thank you for allowing us entry; we will not abuse it. You have my word."

"Your word," Dirk scoffed.

"Dirk, manners. The clan has accepted this meeting; let's hear them out," Stanley spoke.

Thomas was not daunted by Dirk's remark, nor was Greg. However, I could sense the unrest within the rest of Thomas' group. Thomas made sure he'd brought the correct number with him. His clan and mine were matched man for man. Obviously, I was not even considered a threat. I decided not to join in on this discussion. I would observe; I would probably gain more insight that way into how the clans work with one another. I offered them all a Drink, which they all accepted and I watched them as they drank it very quickly and I poured them all another.

With a swish of his hand, Billy made several comfortable chairs appear. "Have a seat, gentlemen - it may be a long night."

"It has been brought to my attention, Aubrey had a," he looked at me, then Steven, "problem earlier," he paused, "that was not our doing," Thomas spoke. "I was going to send a messenger earlier with that knowledge. However, under the circumstances I thought it best I convey that message personally."

"You had no hand in this?" Stanley asked.

"None," Greg replied. He kept his eyes on Stanley.

"Any idea of who might have done this?" Stanley asked.

"It was not done by our hands," was all Greg would say.

Rick began, "You may want to look deeper into your clan; I think you may find others working against you."

"My men are loyal, Rick; they know the score," Thomas replied.

"I wasn't referring to your men, Thomas," Rick said, watching Thomas' clansmen.

Thomas sat a little straighter, eyed Rick with suspicion. "Exactly to whom are you referring? Are you accusing my females? Unlike your clan, we do not involve them in our business. They have no need in knowing."

"A conversation was overheard that I think you might be interested in," Rick answered.

"A conversation, and who heard this conversation?" Thomas asked; his men stiffened behind him.

"In the restaurant yesterday, where Bree had her problem. Two females of your clan were overheard planning. They wanted to prove themselves to your mistress," Rick offered.

"What was heard, Rick?" Greg asked.

Rick relayed the conversation to them. When he had finished, Greg spoke, "So you want us to believe our lead female and her companion are joining with Esmeralda?" He laughed, "Rick, come on. Sylvia, she is too timid, and Rebecca, hardly. Who heard this talk?"

"I did," I said - so much for not getting involved.

The room became very quiet. Everyone was looking at me now. I had remained quiet long enough; they had forgotten I was even present.

"You heard them?" Greg repeated.

"Yes, Greg, I heard them. What Rick has told you is the truth. Thomas, your clan has been compromised. You have fallen out of favor with Esmeralda and Sylvia's lust for power has compromised you."

"Aubrey, Sylvia is a weak female, and Rebecca is even weaker. I find this all very hard to believe," Thomas spoke.

"Believe what you like; I have no reason to lie to you. Sylvia's lust for power is strong. She wants to be on the winning side. Esmeralda was impressed enough with Sylvia to introduce her to your potential replacement. You have lost your leader, your mate, to this lust. The saying, "power corrupts" crosses both our worlds," I said.

"You have every reason to lie to us," one of Thomas' clansmen said, immediately wishing he hadn't from the look Greg threw to him.

I laughed, "Thomas, if you had wanted me dead, I would have died a long time ago; but that was not your charge."

"How do you know what my charge is? How did you hear this conversation; and why the hell did your clan not heed the warning and keep you away this evening?" Thomas demanded.

"Your warning!" Stanley yelled, "We received no warning from you."

"Did your contact not tell you she must not attend?" Greg asked.

"He did, and we did try to keep her here. However, Bree had other ideas," Brad said quietly.

"Yes, I did. I told you all earlier I needed to show the Council I had no fear of them; but all of you are so worried I have a death wish. I have no such wish. I have told you repeatedly I cannot fall to a vampire; there is no power in your eyes to me. Esmeralda knows this. She just wants to know how strong I am, how much I have grown. Now I have given her that information. I have shown you her dark creatures."

Thomas nodded at me. "Thank you for removing my problem. We didn't speak of it as you had suggested. Now I can claim no knowledge of their penetration into my clan. We will dispose of the new members soon."

"NO!" I said, much to everyone's surprise. "Thomas, you took them in, you have a responsibility to them. They were duped into this, just as you were. You can't simply dispose of them because you don't want to be bothered by them."

"They are not your concern," the same clansman spoke.

Greg was quick to admonish him, "Stinson, that's enough. When your opinion is asked for you may offer it. Until then hold your tongue."

"Bree," Steven spoke quietly, "Becky will not be allowed to stay with us either. It is far too dangerous for you. I will not allow it, Brad will not allow it; nor will the rest of the male members of your clan. She will have to take her chances on the outside; we can't offer her protection. She knows this."

I couldn't believe my ears. Even my own clan was ready to throw an innocent person away because it would make their life a little harder. I looked at Brad and he spoke to me, *Bree, if you want her protected, make yourself heard.*

I immediately looked back at them all, "I can't believe I am hearing this. Rick, do you feel the same way as Steven? Billy?"

"Yeah, Half Pint, we do. The danger is too great. Ted will be back with more of your enemies. He can't leave her alive; she knows too much. Or at least he thinks she does."

"So, we just open the doors and throw her out? Leave her vulnerable to his attack, which you know will be swift. Just like that?" I stood and went to stand by the window, then turned to Thomas and his clan. "Thomas, you would dispose of six innocent lives because you don't wish to be bothered? Six innocent lives who pose no threat to you? It's that easy for you?"

Steven spoke, "Bree, you don't understand. You're looking at this with emotions, female emotions I might add."

"This is why we don't allow females to partake in our meetings," Sean spoke.

Greg started to say something, but I raised my hand to silence him. "You are correct Steven. I am looking at it with emotion, human emotion, because it is what I still am. If I remember correctly, you went looking for them. You did it for me, but now the tables have turned. You didn't see the dark until I came along. By me protecting my clan from it, I have put her in danger; and we will not leave her vulnerable. Stanley, you will have your men watch over her until other arrangements can be made. I am protected by my clan and my family, I will be fine."

"No can do, Sweet Pea. I am charged with your protection," Stanley said firmly. "We can manage both; I will place four men with her but the rest will be assigned to you. End of discussion."

"Stanley, who has charged you with my protection?" I asked a little confused. I looked at Brad, his smile widened.

"Your clan," he smiled, "and Gran. And frankly, I'm more afraid of her than I am of your clan," he laughed. That seemed to lighten the mood. My clan and Thomas' had to agree they were equally afraid of Gran. Stanley continued, "That little old woman has too many old friends and I don't mind telling you they play very dirty. So if it's all the same to you, Sweet Pea, I'll take my orders from her and your clan. Once you have transformed, then I will take orders from you," he said and sat there looking at me with a satisfied grin on his face.

"Stanley, I can offer you a few of our men to help...protect Becky, I mean. I'm sure you will not accept our offer to help protect Bree," Greg offered.

"I appreciate the offer; but seeing the blood boil here in this room, it may not be wise to mix our groups. I think we can handle it until the clan comes up with a solution." Stanley gave a slight tip of his head to Greg.

"Thomas, please do not think I have forgotten about your six members. You allowed them entry; they deserve your protection now. You may be surprised with them," I said.

"I doubt that Aubrey. Once you removed the..."

"DC," I offered. "I couldn't think of anything else to call them. They are not a true life form; just something Esmeralda has conjured up to do her bidding. DC – dark creature."

He smiled at my explanation, Greg chuckled, and the rest of his clan had an amused look on their faces. "Once you removed the...DC, they were very timid, nervous, and weak. I can't have that in the males of my clan," he said.

"Well, I suppose if I had just regained control of my faculties and realized I was in your clan, not remembering how the hell I got there, I too might be a little timid, nervous and weak," I countered. "I'm not asking you to put them on the front lines, or to give away clan secrets; I am asking you not to dispose of them like they were the trash." It was then I noticed the clansman I had injured at the party. I motioned to him with a nod of my chin, "How's the hand?"

That surprised him; he looked at Greg, then Rick. Greg gave permission for him to answer my question. "It's fine, My La," he noticed Greg shaking his head, "Aubrey." He was a little unsure whether he should use my proper name or not. I smiled at him then looked out the window.

The quiet had returned to the room. It was starting to make me uncomfortable. I knew Thomas had other questions and I guessed I needed to give him permission to ask.

"Thomas, you and your clan are now in great danger. Sylvia and Rebecca do not know you now know about them. Use that to your advantage. I'm sure you have heard the saying, 'keep your friends close and your enemies' closer.' I suggest you do that. Do not show your hand yet. Esmeralda is not ready to implement her plans. If she were, she would have done it some time ago. I told you she would begin to panic once she realized how strong I had become as a human. She is still gathering her forces. She does not have enough of the Council on her side. She needs more races to join with her. Once she has gained enough members, she will show her strength. She needs to show she is powerful, and then she will strike." I looked back out the window. "Thomas, you have something on your mind, ask it."

Thomas readied himself for the question he had. He exhaled and ran his hand over his face, not wanting to appear out of control to his clan or mine. He asked his question, "Aubrey, you seem to know things, about me, about Esmeralda. How? You know the pet name I call her? It relaxes her. You seem to know things about my missions. You know what she seeks and you give me that information, all the while keeping my cover? Why?"

I continued to look out the window. Everyone was watching me; they wanted answers and I wasn't ready to give them. I knew these two clans would need to work together if we were to succeed. But I wasn't ready to tell them I needed to destroy the clay bottle that held the demon. I needed to destroy the gateways and the cosmic portals that tore through the delicate fabric that bound our worlds together. That was how the demons entered our world. Once I had secured those portals, then I needed to seek out other demons that lingered here, waiting on their time to tempt the leaders of both our worlds to the darker side. That was my path, besides guiding my world. The weight was heavy on my shoulders. I had never asked for this. It was mine to do and I would not walk away from it, but I was not ready to talk about it either.

"Thomas, just know, I know much; and I see and hear a lot." I smiled. "What I do know, these two clans," I pointed at each group, "will need to work together in the future. And that future is getting closer. I'm sorry to be so vague, but I'm still trying to understand all of this. You have been here longer than you should. She will be looking for your report. Good luck Thomas. The more you walk in your path, the riskier it becomes. I hope your true master knows this."

He smiled at me and with a nod of his head. Then they disappeared.

The tension in the room was thick and it too was weighing very heavy on me. I felt the pressure on my chest and I didn't like that feeling. The quiet remained. I looked at the clock expecting it to be late but it was only ten-thirty. I wanted to stop talking about all of this and I wanted my clan to relax. I wanted Steven to hold me in his arms and keep me safely there forever. The mountains were sounding better with each passing thought I had. "Billy, where's Gina?"

"I made her go to bed. She wanted to be here, says she feels great. She was pretty proud of you this evening, Half Pint."

"Well, I was thinking maybe we should all go dancing or for drinks. It's only ten-thirty. I want to be in bed by one-thirty, so what do you say about getting rid of some of this nervous energy? What do you think Bradley? You think these guys could use some down time? Billy, do you think Gina might want to come down and sit with us? I'll bet she's not asleep."

"I'll bet she's not either, Half Pint."

"Come on. All of you have such long faces," I nudged Steven. "Smile, take me dancing, Steven. Tomorrow will come soon enough."

"Bree, we really should discuss this," Stanley said.

"No more tonight. Tomorrow, after I meet with the Council; then you can all plan your strategies. But for the remainder of the night I want my clan to relax. I want you to relax. Let your minds relax, nothing will happen to me tonight," I said.

"Yeah I'm up for dancing. You Steven? Bill, I know I could use a stress reliever," Rick said.

"Stanley, please, you and your friends are welcome to join us. Come on, cousin, I hardly get to spend any time with you. Look, you can protect me there. I'll even let you take a drink of every drink I get so they don't slip something into it again," I smiled. "Come dancing with us."

"Oh, all right. We'll go secure a spot. Andrew why don't you go and get Tina and Kristin; we'll meet you there." They disappeared.

Steven got close to me, held my hand, and very calmly said, "You are not to be close to Becky at all tonight. Do you understand what I am saying? Not at all."

"Yes, I understand you Steven. We'll think of something, maybe another clan. Maybe she'll have to hide away for a while." I kissed him. "Now, let's go dancing for heaven's sake."

CHAPTER 37

Everyone had arrived by the time Steven and I had gotten there. Billy had ordered our drinks. Brad and Madalyn were heading to the dance floor. Rick was already dancing with Becky and Sandy was dancing with Stanley. Dirk and Andrew were dancing with Tina and Kristin, I could only assume. I was sure I would be introduced to them when they got back to the table.

"So, Gina, have you decided on a name yet?" I asked as Steven and I sat down.

"Yes, I have decided on the name Todd." She looked at Billy.

"Todd, didn't you have a boyfriend named Todd?" Billy asked. He winked at me so I knew he was needling her as he passed us our drinks. "I'll not have one of my boys named after one of your boyfriends."

"I like the name Todd, reminds me of a little fox. That's a good name. How about you Steven, do you like the name

Todd? Todd Campbell. Sounds strong." I smiled at Billy and took a drink of my wine.

"Bree, it does not sound strong," Billy retorted.

"Does too." I stuck my tongue out at him.

"Oh, now that was real adult of you; and you expect me to let you grow up! Steven, as Stanley observed, you do have your hands full with this one. I relinquish her to your care." He smiled at me, but I knew he would never relinquish my care to anyone. He would always be in my life.

Rick and Becky returned to the table. Becky sat very quietly; I could only assume Rick had informed her of the clan's decision. I couldn't stand it. I thought of something to distract myself. "So Billy, I'm curious. You said earlier that you were with me at college on some occasions at parties and in my classes. I have racked my brain and I gotta say, I got nothin."

"Okay, let's see. Do you remember the time, Becky you were there as well. You girls went to a party and were doing whiskey shots? It was another dumb ass little game you used to play Bree." His voice was stern but his eyes smiled.

I looked at him and squinted, lips pursed as I thought hard, trying to recall those days. "Billy I went to a few of those parties. You're going to have to narrow it down just a little more. What year?"

"Junior year, second semester."

Everyone had returned back to the table and Sandy was full of laughs. "Bree," as she sat next to Rick, "Stanley is a very good dancer."

"It's one of the many talents of the Campbell family," I informed her. Rick quickly filled everyone in on our current conversation.

"Were you by yourself or did you have your cohorts in crime with you?" I pointed to everyone.

"Yes, my cohorts were with me, as well as Gina, for my protection," he laughed.

"Huh, now how was Gina protecting you? Was Madalyn and Sandy with you?"

"Because some of your girlfriends were, let's just say, excessively friendly. Madalyn was but Sandy wasn't."

"I'll say," said Steven

"Well, Steven, if I remember correctly you did have a big problem with one that night," Rick said.

"Damn straight, talk about octopus," Steven laughed.

I turned to look at him, "And that bothered you?" I was a little shocked.

"Bree, unfortunately, Steven wasn't your date that night," Billy snickered.

"Oh man! Those damn parties you went to," Stanley said shaking his head. "Man, I thought Gran was going to skin me alive letting you do half the shit you did."

I looked at Stanley and smiled, "Sorry to put you through so much trouble, but that was part of being in college." Then I turned back to Billy, "Huh, okay. I have to assume you all looked different so I wouldn't recognize you."

"That would be a good assumption," Billy teased.

"Okay," I eyed him wryly. "I remember two frat parties where we were doing whiskey shots, so I need a little more info to know which one you're talking about."

"You were doing shots with this one little skinny guy," Billy offered. He made a face when he told me this.

"Oh my gosh! I know which one you're talking about," Becky shouted. "Shit, I did it again. I'm sorry Rick."

He leaned over and put his arm around her. "S'okay kid, I have given up on it tonight. Just don't try to hug her."

With the green light Becky started, "Bree you remember? Jeanine was so hot on that kid. Gosh, what was his name? Ah! Jake. She knew you could drink them under the table and she really didn't want him drunk so we put 7-up and peppermint in a bottle and we told him it was peppermint schnapps. Anyway," she continued telling the story; Billy sat there with a little grin on his face watching me. I wasn't sure why; I must have done something at this party, but I couldn't think what it was.

"We set up twenty-five shot glasses a piece for each of you. Bree's were filled with whiskey. Those boys didn't trust us to fill the glasses, so they did. And we didn't trust them to fill Jake's, so we did, and we substituted the 7-up for the alcohol. Anyway, each would take a drink, then turn the shot glass upside down. You had to down the shot; you couldn't sip it, and Bree was real good at it. Huh, I understand now why you never got drunk; but at the time, I was impressed. Anyway, long story short, Bree and Jake finished all twenty-five and he was the champ. Didn't he take Jeanine out after that?"

"Yeah, they got married a few years back. I don't think she ever told him about that though. And you guys were there because..." I asked.

"To keep an eye on you. You know how stupid that was drinking whiskey shots with a group of frat boys? We needed to give Stanley and his crew time off; you were running them ragged. Since you couldn't date Steven anymore, we had to improvise."

"Oh come on Bree; don't you remember?" Becky's memory was becoming a problem because I was remembering and I thought I was going to be embarrassed very soon. "Jackie was drunk and she was all over that guy. He was very polite; I think he even took her back to the dorm. She was very impressed with him I must say. Remember? For the longest time she kept looking for him at all those parties we went to. He was such a dream, she kept saying."

The light switch came on and Billy's smile widened. "Shit, which one of you was Buddy?"

"That was his name!" Becky shouted. "Buddy. Oh my, she was so impressed with him."

Steven raised his hand. "That would be me. She latched on to me as soon as I came in the room."

"Oh poor baby!" I teased, patting his cheeks. "I might have known; always the gentleman. I am so sorry you had to do that. Jackie was wild at times."

"Ya think? Damn woman, my life was in jeopardy," Steven laughed.

I sat there looking at Billy; he smiled. I kept thinking about that night because I sensed Billy wanted me to remember something. Since Becky was given a green light to talk, she didn't let it pass. She had jumped onto one of our many escapades.

Billy smiled and Rick thought into my mind, *keep thinking about it, Squirt. It'll come to you.*

My God, what did I do that night and how did Rick and Billy know what I did? I wasn't drunk because I didn't ever get drunk, so I knew I didn't do anything that embarrassing. Jackie had 'Buddy' take her home; I wondered if I should ask Steven about that night. Jeanine went with Jake, and Becky went with a fellow named, what was his name, think, think, think, Gary, yeah. What did I do? My eyes widened and I looked at Billy, then at Rick; they both had big smiles. "Oh fuck."

Steven and Brad both looked at me. I immediately blocked my mind. Sandy chuckled, "Bree, such language. What on earth brought that out?"

"Sorry, didn't mean to say that out loud." I took a big drink of my wine.

Steven and Brad continued watching me. My mind was blocked from them and I was content to leave it that way. I'd take the punishment from them later. I knew my face was turning red and Billy was enjoying himself. Billy was with Gina and Brad was with Madalyn. That just left Rick. Oh damn, oh damn, damn, damn. I cloaked my mind and Rick's. *That was you?*

Calm yourself, Little One. You've nothing to be embarrassed about. I rather enjoyed it; and yes you have a pretty ass, nice and firm.

Oh my God, oh my God. My eyes widened as I tried to remember that night. Think, think, did we have sex that night? No, no, I know we didn't. Well, I'm sure we didn't. No, no, I know I didn't. Why was it so foggy? I couldn't remember all the pieces. Why couldn't I remember those damn pieces? Where the hell was that file?

I tried to focus in on what Becky was talking about, trying to calm the thoughts running through my mind. I smiled at Steven and then thought to him *you've not allowed her to speak for far too long!* That caused him to smile.

"Bree, I haven't had a dance yet," Rick said. I jumped; I hadn't been expecting that. He came around before it registered with me. He extended his hand to me and I accepted it.

❧

Of course, another slow dance was playing. I was beginning to think that was the only thing they played here.

"The look on your face was priceless, Little One. You needn't worry; Steven is well aware of what happened."

"What? What the hell do you mean he is aware? Do you guys tell each other everything?"

"Yeah, we do actually. Well, most things anyway," Rick said.

"I will never get used to this," I moaned.

"Yes, Little One, you will. I've kept that memory tucked away. It's special and I cherish it. You were so much fun. We went to breakfast. Do you remember that?"

"Vaguely. I really just met you and went to breakfast with you? Man - that is just not like me."

"Well, we did. Even though you didn't know us, your mind did. You knew you were safe. We didn't want you left there after your friends started leaving with those boys. Steven took octopus lady home, and well, you'll need to ask him about that. I took you back to your dorm; you drove but I needed to make sure you got there. We sat in your car talking for the longest time. Even in college, you didn't sleep much. I walked you to your dorm room. Becky had left you a message on the note board on your door. She said she'd be back in the morning and she was sorry. I knew what she meant, but you didn't know I knew."

I pulled back to look at him, he continued. "I knew she meant she wouldn't be there, and that you would most likely stay up all night because of the sounds you would hear. So

523

I invited myself into your room. We talked some more, laughed a lot. It got a little awkward, so I thought what the hell. What could one little kiss hurt? Well, let me tell you something, you have the softest damn lips I have ever been fortunate enough to lay my lips on. That was one damn good kiss. Well, one kiss led to another and before too long we were on the bed, having a pretty good time."

"Oh, my God." I could feel my face warming again. "I had no idea it was you."

"Of course you didn't; that was the whole point.

"I really did that? That is so unlike me."

"Yes, you did," he laughed. "I can be very persuasive. Anyway, we stopped before we really connected; but that was tough. Damn was that tough. Steven, you'll love this, Steven popped into my mind asking me what the hell I thought I was doing. It was all Brad could do to control him. I told you I had to leave, but that I would be back. And damn, I wished I had been able to come back. You looked so inviting lying there. I just wanted to love you so badly that night." He kissed the top of my head. "Oh, and just so you are aware, guys do tell guys things. But we aren't stupid enough to tell girls. So Madalyn, Gina and Sandy know nothing of this."

"Thanks for the heads up."

"You're welcome. I really did have a good time that night. You are very special to me Bree; please don't ever forget that." He held me softly to his chest and raised my hand to his lips, giving it a soft kiss. "Let me tell you something, if I had been able to make love to you that night, well, let's just say Steven is like my little brother. Anybody else, I would have moved heaven and earth to be with you."

"You know this do you?" I laughed.

"Oh yes, Bree, I know that." His arms held me just a little tighter. "You want to tell me about the cryptic message up in your room?" he asked as another song started. "I'm taking advantage of my time with you, so spill it sister."

I shook my head and laughed, "Rick, you don't have to find a reason to dance with me, ya know."

"I know, but I enjoy holding you close. Come on, I don't get to bond to you the way Brad and Steven do. The least you could do is let me hold you."

"Ya should have taken your shot when I was in college then," I teased.

"Yeah, maybe I should have. Now back to the question."

"I've started having my dreams again."

"What dreams? We've never known you were having dreams," he said pulling me back so he could look at me.

I gave a soft sigh, *when will I learn.* "Look, if I'm going to have to disclose all my inner secrets, then let's all go back and talk. I don't want to have to tell you, and then tell Steven, then Brad, then Billy. It's just easier to tell you all at once and get it over with. Steven and Brad are going to be mad either way; but in my own defense, they just started a day or two ago and you guys put me to sleep before I could tell you. Oh wait, I probably should have mentioned it to Steven when he had me pinned to the bed."

"Excuse me?" he smiled.

"Did I give ya a good picture there, Ricky?" I laughed. "Just hold me now and dance."

"Oh my God, this is going to be an interesting ride." Rick gave a sexy laugh, "Yes, Little One, I am going to enjoy being with you again."

The dance ended and we went back to the table. I knew Rick had already mentioned the dreams to everyone; their looks gave that away. We all left to go back to my room. Dirk and Andrew walked with Steven and me. I wanted Steven to transport us to our room, but he said the walk would do us good. When we got to the room, I told him I forgot my key so he would have to fold space to get us inside. He smiled and knocked on the door. Brad answered.

Steven couldn't contain his laughter any longer, "I know you Princess; you pay too close attention to things. You will learn to travel once you have transformed; I'll teach you then." Brad's grin showed his agreement. "Now get yourself in there and explain." For good measure, he swatted me on the butt.

❧

Everyone stood with their arms folded and serious looks on their faces. That caused me to laugh, "I'm sorry, by now you should know that doesn't work on me; but since everyone is asking so nicely, I'll tell you about the dreams." I made a spooky motion with my hands as I walked to the chair. My three male clan members and Billy, Stanley, Dirk and Andrew stood in front of the entertainment center, arms still folded, watching me. None of the women were present.

"Okay, Bree, out with it. All of it. It's time you told us what you know," Brad said sternly.

I was uncomfortable talking in front of Stanley and his men. Steven noticed my hesitation.

"Bree, Dirk and Andrew and their mates will be joining our clan, so you can talk freely in front of them."

Just like that?

Yes, dear, just like that.

❧

The room remained very quiet. This was going to be bad! "Okay, for starters I've never told anyone of the dreams. When I was little, I really only had pieces. They would come and go and I never could make any sense out of them. As I got older, they would come to me when Mom and Dad came back from out of town. All I remember of those was a dark passageway. It was carved out of the stone. Ground water would trickle down the walls in places. It smelt damp. I could smell it; even after I woke up, I could still smell the dampness. Sometimes, my clothes would be muddy and wet. I could hear voices, but I never could get close enough to make out what was being said."

"Besides being damp, was it cold?" Steven asked.

"No, never cold. Cool maybe, but I wouldn't say cold. I knew I was underground, deep underground."

"Your clothes were muddy and damp? I guess it is possible you transported yourself there. How though? That's interesting," Stanley said. "Do you remember traveling at all?"

"No, I was just there. I would be in bed, asleep. Well, as much as I slept anyway. One minute I was there and the next I would wake up in bed," I answered.

"You said it was dark. How did you find your way; could you see?" Rick asked.

"I felt my way at first. Then the more the dream came to me, I could see in the dark. I saw the light I needed to go to, but I could never get there. Then they just stopped. I would say they stopped around the time Steven went away."

"When did they start back?" Steven asked.

"When I came here, after the night we bowled. They weren't dreams really. Just the pieces and parts flashing through my mind, and then I slept. The big dream," I widened with my arms, "came the night I found all of this stuff out."

"When you say, 'BIG', what happened? Were you able to walk the passage?" Billy asked.

"Yeah, I walked the passage; my mind told me to remember the passage. I needed to know that route. I kept walking and I heard them. I saw her, just her, but I heard his laugh. I was in the shadows and watched them; well her anyway. He wasn't in bodily form." I wrinkled my forehead trying to figure out how to explain this next part. Do I just tell them I watched the bodiless laugh make love to her? I wasn't sure if I was comfortable explaining this to them. Do I just form the picture in my mind and let them view it? I laughed aloud not meaning to, but I did. I didn't think I could do the explanation justice anyway.

"Bree, why are you laughing? Was he saying something funny?" Dirk asked. My mind was blocked; so I knew they weren't seeing my inner turmoil. If Sandy were here, I knew she would love this scenario.

"No, no, he wasn't telling her a joke. The laugh was making love to her, or she was making love to herself with its help. Oh hell. Here, I'll just show you." I decided to let them in my mind to see what I had seen. They saw the room, her, heard the laugh and watched the entire scene play out before their eyes. Then I closed my mind when they left the chamber.

"Whoa, way to go Thomas," Andrew said and I immediately blushed causing Steven and Brad to laugh. "Bree, how do you know you weren't just dreaming this?"

I was a little taken aback by that. I blinked. "I will agree I have a very good imagination, but that was a little beyond even me. Besides, I'd never meet Esmeralda and Thomas before this dream. That was how I knew them. I was surprised no one asked me how I knew their names; but I guess with everything that happened, it slipped under your radar." I smiled to Rick; he didn't smile back.

"So after they left the chamber Bree, what did you do? And please save us all time, I know you didn't just turn around and walk away," said Brad finally.

"No, Bradley, I did not." I met his gaze but didn't try to read his thoughts. I was sure he was going to let me know them soon enough. "You're not going to like it."

"I'm sure we aren't Bree," Brad said.

"I walked along the table and looked at the jar, the clay jar she corked before she let Thomas in the room. It shook as I came near. I spoke to it. I knew it. My line had put it there. It knew my strength. I told it that it would never be made whole again. I told it I would destroy it. I touched the bottle with one finger and it shook. I told it I was still human but my magic was strong and when I transform I will be beyond its measure and that it would be no more. That is my path." I looked at them. "My path alone; you will not be able to help me do this," I said to each of them.

"Then what, Bree?" Steven asked.

"Then I left the chamber, the way I came. I walked back down the passage; my mind told me I needed to know this place. It was important; no, it *is* important. I don't know why. I passed four cells and my mind showed me the atrocities that happened there, that still happen there, and my mind told me to remember. I needed to end it. That too is my path."

"Do you know where this place is, Bree?" asked Stanley.

"No. I tried to continue on the passage, but the phone rang our wake up and I woke up."

"Bree, is this the only dream you've had?" Billy asked.

"No, I've had a couple more after I met Thomas. Same chamber, just her and Thomas though. It didn't last as long. He was telling her I knew this place, I knew more than she realized. She didn't believe him. She did a spell, the one she focused on Madalyn. She was hoping that would break me, us, all of us. She got her answer tonight. When they left the chamber, I didn't bother with looking around again. I needed to see the entrance. I needed to know where this place was. My mind kept telling me this was very important, but I don't know why."

"Did you find the entrance?" asked Stanley.

"Yeah, but it didn't do me any good. It's just a hole in the side of a mountain. I don't know where. The odd thing is, I feel as if I have been there before; but I can't place it."

I sat there looking at them, trying to decide if I should tell them about the other dreams.

"What Bree? What else do you need to say?" Brad asked.

"There were other dreams. They had nothing to do with Thomas or Esmeralda though, so it's not all that important."

"Let us be the judge of that. What were they about?" Brad asked.

"There was one just of Ry and three other people. He was concerned. They were his friends from the Council,

I think. They sat in a library and they just re-discussed everything he told us."

"Is that all they spoke about?" Billy asked.

I looked at him and I thought about the conversations I had heard. "Yeah, nothing else of consequence really. Their faces were blurry; Ry was the only voice I recognized."

"Bree, you said there were other dreams, meaning more than one. What were the others?" Rick asked.

I exhaled and looked at Rick. He wasn't smiling; none of them were. They were in their serious mode now. I told them about all the other dreams. I told them what I knew of Zamora. I even told them about the dark I had seen and watched in Yellowstone.

"Bree, make our job easier. What is your path?" Rick asked. His eyes begged to enter my mind but I denied him entry. My solider, my protector, my Hercules was making his plea to me to bring them into my confidence and I finally relented. I exhaled, I knew they weren't going to stop until I told them, but I also knew they would never allow me to do what I must do.

I kept my eyes on Steven as I spoke to them all. "You won't like it. If you know it, you will not let me finish what I was meant to do."

"Tell us Bree. You owe it to your clan; you owe it to me. What terrible path have you been born into?" Steven asked. He came and sat before me, his eyes stayed with mine. He took my hands in his; he strengthened me with his touch. The energy that passed between us was so very strong. I was comforted by the tiny flashes of energy I saw as Steven ran his thumb over the back of my hand.

"All the Chosen Ones have had the same path in one form or another. Some have succeeded in their quests - others have not. According to Odessa, mine is by far the most dangerous. I need to destroy a clay bottle that holds the demon that Esmeralda protects; the one I touched in her magic chamber. I need to destroy this demon."

"Sounds simple enough," Stanley said.

"That's a start." I smiled and continued, "I need to destroy the gateways that allowed the demons to enter in the first place, and there are so many. The cosmic threads that bind our world with other worlds are so very delicate now. They need to be strengthened and that will be a difficult task, if it can ever be accomplished at all. My sisters will help me with this task, because we are the only ones that can see the portals.

Then I must seek out the other demons that tempt the leaders of both worlds to the darker side and destroy them. They *must* be destroyed and I fear I will never find them all. Many have come to this world. They are so good at tempting the weak; but if we can strengthen the frail cloth that protects our world, we can at least stop other demons from entering. Then my sisters and I must watch and wait for the demons that still exist in this world to show themselves. And they will...show themselves. They thrive on destruction, despair and hate. That's how we will find them. That is my path, besides guiding my world, besides protecting the mortal world from the Magical world and vice versa."

Their eyes widened as I spoke to them. I could tell they were angry, they hadn't known everything that was expected of me. All they had thought was that I would sit on the Council and help guild our world. But that was just a small part I was to play.

"The Elders did not finish their task when they walked the earth. They did what they could; they thought they left this world in stable condition, but the evil entities that entered were very strong. There were enough mortals and Magicals of this world that were weak and the demons feasted upon that weakness. The demons grew in strength, and as my sisters were born, they were not strong enough to defeat them. But they were able to keep them at bay. The Elders misjudged the strength the Chosen Ones that came before me needed. Chosen Ones are born when the threat to this world is at its greatest." I smiled at Bradley, "You should take comfort in the fact that this is why they have been born so infrequently."

"I find no comfort in knowing you are in harms way, Precious," Brad spoke softly.

"The Chosen Ones have the knowledge, the strength and the wisdom of all our races to ensure the course is corrected. We are stronger than any that walk this world." I smiled at Rick and winked, "In magic only, not in bodily strength."

"I know what you meant, Little One," he smiled back at me.

"My magic is stronger than all my sisters before me. That is why I can do what I can do now, even though I have yet to transform. I will strengthen those Chosen Ones that still live and want to help me in my quest. I can't force them to do anything; and there are those that will not be willing to go this path. My birth was a long time in coming and the threat grew more dangerous. I needed my human emotions, my compassion; they needed to be strong. Therefore, you see, there's a reason for my stubbornness. I cooked a little longer than most," I smiled. "The threat grew more deadly than the Elders had anticipated by the time of my birth. As I have spoken, the fabric that binds our worlds together has weakened and has let too many demons into our world. My sisters before me tried to close them as they opened; but this world was easy prey to those that wish destruction and chaos. You can't help me because you can't see these openings or the demons. The dark that you saw, that was of the demons, Esmeralda's creatures. They must be destroyed too. These are my paths. Now you know."

"How do they expect one person to do all of this?" Billy asked. "This just isn't right, Bree. They are asking too much of you."

They stood there watching me; no one spoke for the longest time. My eyes stayed with Steven and his with mine. "You will not walk this path alone, Princess. I will not allow you to. I said I would never leave you again and I meant that."

"I know that Steven; you give me more strength than you know. However, I can't bond to you until I have transformed. What you and I have now is complete love for one another, but it will be much more when we bond. Then you will strengthen me more than you could possibly imagine."

I looked at Bradley and my smile widened. I saw the worry in his eyes, and I knew I needed to comfort him too. "Don't worry Bradley, I am still bound to you as your Alpha, and I am still the leader of our clan. Nothing will change that."

"Good, cause I was getting a little worried there," Brad smiled and Rick slapped him on the back and laughed with him.

"My enemies are many now, but we have many followers. I have told you Thomas is not your enemy. Believe me on that, there will come a day when you will need his help and he will need ours. Esmeralda is his mistress for now because he needs her to be, but she is not his master. Do not betray his path."

"What do you need of us, Bree? We have sworn to protect you and we will. Do we take our orders from you now?" Stanley asked.

"I am going to ask you all to continue like you were before. I have not transformed yet, so take your orders from my clan and from our grandmother. I need my clan to continue to treat me as you have - nothing special. I do not want our enemies to become aware things have changed, because in reality things have not changed. I have not transformed."

"We have so much planning to do. I will meet with my team leaders, and Brad, I'll send you the information so you and the males of your clan can attend. We can formulate our plans then," Stanley said.

"Stanley, promise me you will protect Becky until other arrangements can be made," I pleaded.

"I told you I would and I meant it. Now leave the security details to me, Sweet Pea," Stanley answered. Then he, Dirk, and Andrew left.

I turned to my clan. "It has been a very long night; I want you all to go and meditate. I am not giving Steven permission to go out and play with you," I laughed. "I want each of you in your rooms and resting. Not at the bar, not worrying. Resting. Am I making myself clear?"

"Bree," Brad started and I cut him off.

"Bradley, I have told you and our clan everything. I promise you I have. You have not meditated in a long while. None of you have; and Billy, you need your sleep. Please, tomorrow will come and go and then we can all go home. I want you fresh in the morning, and if I have another dream I will tell you. You have my promise."

"Bree, if I could find a way to tie you up and stuff you in a box until this is all over I would," Brad finished. He pressed the bridge of his nose and exhaled.

I looked at him and smiled, "A box will not hold me, Bradley. My time is now, my path starts now." I got up and moved close to him. "Please Bradley, you are tired. Rick and Billy and Steven are tired." I held his face in my hands. My thumbs gently rubbed the dark circles under his eyes. "One night's meditation will not interfere with the events that are going to unfold tomorrow. Rest with Madalyn - hold her in your arms and rest. Please do this for me," I begged him. I saw the moisture in his eyes build and he closed them tight before he spoke.

"Very well." He softened, "One night can't hurt; I'll see you in the morning." He smiled at me and gave me a sweet kiss then left.

Very pleased with myself, I looked at Billy. His face was drawn and he too was very tired. "Sweet William, you need your sleep. Kiss Gina goodnight for me and we will see you in the morning." I tenderly kissed his cheek and he pulled me into a tight embrace. "Billy, I am going to be just fine; it's you and this lot I worry about."

"They ask too much of you my sweet angel, entirely too much," Billy said, then kissed me on the cheek and left.

I looked at Rick; he had finally sat on the sofa. He looked utterly exhausted. "Okay, enough. You need your rest too." I took Steven's hand and stood with him. Rick didn't move. Steven nudged me forward and I went and sat with him. "Rick, what's wrong?"

"Bree, how are you going to do all of this by yourself? Bill is right, they do ask too much of you."

"Rick," I started and I took his hand in mind, "I'm not doing this by myself. I have my clan with me. We will take one piece at a time, one day at a time; and we will complete this task. I told you we would all be together for a very long time and I meant that. Believe me, I wouldn't dream of going this alone. There are things that I must do, but I will have my clan behind me all the way. It truly warms my heart to know you and Sandy care for me so much, but I really do need you to go and get your rest. The future will come soon enough. Go to bed; I will see you in the morning. You're very tired and I need you to rest." I smiled and winked. It took him a minute but then he smiled back.

"See you in the morning, Squirt." Rick gave me a sweet kiss on the lips, and was gone.

"Steven, come sit by me." I patted the cushion next to me.

Steven gave me his best smile, "Nah, really don't want to sit, Bree."

"You don't? You don't have any questions, problems? I don't need to sooth your ruffled feathers, or make special promises, or anything?" I smiled.

He took me by the hand and pulled me to him, "Nope, that is not what needs soothing." He nudged me toward the bedroom, turning off the lights as we went.

CHAPTER 38

I slept extremely well with Steven lying next to me. His tone was strong the rest of the night and I really needed it; because as I knew it would, the dream came. I was in the passage again, walking toward the chamber. They were there, as I knew they would be.

"I can't explain it, my Lady. She moved them without the use of her hands; she blew on his burn and healed it. She is still human. How can she do these things?" Thomas was angry with Esmeralda. He was distant with her; he kept his arms to his side. I saw no hint of his desire for her as I had seen in my previous dreams.

"She will come with us tomorrow, my love. We will bring her here, to the cell. She will stay there until she transforms or dies. Without her family she will die. You may take her if it pleases you." Esmeralda watched for his reaction. He gave none. She continued with her plan, "I will take her blood daily, she will weaken. When she dies I will cut her heart out." She raised the dagger on the table and smiled as she admired the sharp blade. "Her heart should be warm for our master. Her soul will linger long enough for me to capture it. Then our master will be whole again and we shall rule. You may then destroy her lovers and her families. None can remain; do you understand this Thomas? None."

"She knows this chamber, she has seen this room. She has told me, she knew of the spell. She knew of what we spoke about. Could she know your Black Magic as well?" Thomas asked, but did not listen to her answer. He was paying more attention to the room and the shadows. Did he sense me there? Was he trying to warn me?

"Nonsense Thomas, she is playing you. She reads too many books and she is using them. She knows nothing of this chamber."

They left the chamber and I walked back down the passage toward the opening. It was dark but I could feel the fresh air coming in through the opening. I knew I wouldn't be able to see, not at night. I reached the opening, and then I felt the hot air coming from deep within the chamber toward me. I ran out the opening and pressed myself hard against the mountain wall as the wind violently bellowed through the opening. It smelt of death, and earth. I heard the screams, and then all was quiet. I knew something bad would happen here.

ରୀ

I woke at six-thirty, Steven was still meditating; I had been correct, he'd needed this time. I let my mind wander to my other clan members. I found Becky in her room, lying on the bed. Her eyes were open and I saw her tears. I stayed and watched. She finally blinked, wiped her tears, and closed her eyes. I needed to talk to her, but right now I needed my clan. I found Billy and Gina still asleep, Billy resting a protective arm over Gina's belly. I didn't want to linger so I quietly moved on. Rick and Sandy were lying comfortably together; Rick's forearm was over his eyes. Sandy was lying on her side, her back up against him. Again, I crept out of their space. Next, I found Bradley and Madalyn. Madalyn was lying on her back next to Brad. Her eyes were closed and she was in deep meditation; I could tell by her breathing. Brad, not so much. I watched him; his eyes flickered and then he opened them.

∽

Good morning, Bradley, I kissed his mind.

Morning Precious. How long have you been watching me?

Not long, I was just checking on you. Did you rest well?

Well, enough. How about you Precious, did you sleep well?

I did. I had another dream; I'll tell you about it later. Steven still out?

Yes, he's a very tired boy, I giggled to him.

Bree, you are so wicked sometimes. Tell me about your dream, my sweet. We have time. Everyone is still meditating.

Bradley, there will be enough time for all of that. Let's just spend some quiet time together for a change. Do you like to golf?

Golf? What brought that up?

Well, you're a doctor and I haven't had time to find everything out about my clan. So I thought I would ask. Now, do you play golf? I asked again.

No, Precious, I do not play golf. I do play tennis occasionally with Steven or racquetball with Rick, but no golf. We all get together and shoot some hoops. We do play baseball, and occasionally, when we have enough friends around, we play football.

Bradley, why have you changed my nickname?

Because, you are precious to me. Breekins was this kid I used to know; she's grown into a very beautiful young woman. Stubborn, but beautiful.

What's it like living in Chicago?

Cold in the winter and humid in the summer, and it is entirely too far away from my clan.

I'm going to go shower now; I'll see you soon.

Can I watch?

No, your time will come. I kissed his mind goodbye and went to shower, leaving Steven tucked in bed to finish his meditation.

CHAPTER 39

Friday Morning

By eight o'clock, everyone was back in our room. As I watched them all talking, my mind started remembering my first night here when I had met Steven at the reception, our dinner together. All of that seemed so long ago, but it had only been seven days. Seven days and so much had happened.

I'd be happy when this day was over. I so much wanted to go home with Steven. I sat on the sofa very quietly listening to them.

Billy kept a watchful eye on me. "Bree, are you hungry? When did you eat last?"

I had to think about that. "Yesterday, when I got back from the spa. Yeah, I guess I am hungry."

"Bree, you really need to do a better job of taking care of yourself. We can't have you fainting in front of the Council." Billy snapped his fingers and a banquet of French toast, pancakes, bacon, sausages, hash browns, scrambled eggs, biscuits and gravy, several carafes of orange juice and coffee, and my clan's special Drink appeared. I really didn't realize how hungry I was until I smelled the food. Billy came up to me and took my hand. "Come on, Half Pint. Damn, how can you expect me to let you grow up if you keep forgetting to eat? Stop worrying about today. I won't let anyone take you."

"Billy, you misread my quietness. I'm not worried, not in the least."

Odessa came into my mind. *You are prepared Bree. You know this; they are just worried.*

I know I'm prepared, and yes my clan is worried; but after today their hearts will settle and we can get on with the business at hand, I said.

It's hard for them. They have been so long without you; they fear the loss, Odessa said.

I know, but I'm not going anywhere.

You and I know this; after today they will know it too. Understand this Aubrey; if I did not think you could handle what will happen to you at this meeting, I would encourage you to leave. You can do far more than you realize. Trust your mind; trust your heart.

We all ate breakfast and then everyone went to change. Brad told them he wanted them all back here in an hour. Then he teased Sandy, "Think you can handle that amount of time?"

"I have it down to an art. Thank you, Bradley darling," she teased back.

❧

Steven was standing in front of the mirror tying his tie when I came into the bedroom. I gave him a sexy little grin,

"You do clean up well." He was dressed in a sharp black tic-weave suit and crisp white shirt with a black silk tie - the lawyer side of him showing. "Tell me...did you actually pack that suit and bring it here?" I laughed; he smiled.

"No, after Ryan told us you were to go before the Council I went home and got it."

I dressed comfortably, dark blue Dockers, white oxford shirt and vest. I was not there to impress anyone. I stood in front of the mirror and selected the jewelry I wanted to wear. I put my pendant under my shirt and left the healing stone necklace out for Esmeralda to see, then donned the bracelets. Just a little touch of perfume and out the bedroom door we went.

Every member of my clan was there. Rick and Brad were dressed similar to Steven; Madalyn was dressed in a tan three-quarter cropped jacket and a black chiffon skirt. Sandy wore a long tweed skirt with matching three-quarter jacket. Becky wore black Dockers and a white v-cut sweater.

Madalyn looked at me, "Bree wouldn't you prefer to wear a dress? We can run you home; it won't take but a minute."

"Ah, that would be a 'no'. This is who I am. You need to understand that. They need to understand that. I'm not here to impress anyone and I'm not changing to suit anyone. Sorry."

I poured their Drink and started taking them around. "What's up with you guys?"

"Nervous I guess," said Brad. "I think we all have a bad case."

"Is that your professional opinion?" I smiled at him.

"Yes, it is," he stated flatly.

"Bree, I have a question," Becky said.

Rick shot her a look, but she held her ground. "I know I'm not supposed to speak to her, but this has been nagging at me since last night. I gotta ask Rick, I gotta know."

"Well, you gotta go through me. Understand?" he countered. "Now, ask your question."

She turned back to me, undaunted by his retort. "What did you mean when you said you had to assume they all looked different so you wouldn't recognize them? You knew these guys for a long time, you knew about them right?"

"What, that they were Magicals, vampires. That stuff?"

"Yeah. Hell Bree, you were going to become a Sorceress. Why couldn't you recognize them? If we were such great friends, why didn't you tell me about this life?"

"Becky, I didn't know any of this until just the other day. I didn't know any of this growing up. I wasn't supposed to until after I turned twenty-five."

"So, you knew nothing. Nothing at all?"

"That's what I'm telling you. When this meeting is over I'll have someone explain it all to you." I thought to Rick, *Obviously, Ted wasn't straight with her.*

The phone rang, and I answered it. It was Ryan, they had moved the time to noon. "Okay, Ry, I'll let them know. See you then." I put the phone down and turned to see all eyes on me. "What?"

"We're just nervous. How are you holding up?" Steven asked as he wrapped his arms around me. His chin resting on the top of my head

"I'm fine, a little nervous too. But I'm not nervous for the same reasons as you guys. I'm sure of the outcome today."

"Well, then why are you nervous?" Madalyn asked.

"She doesn't like crowds?" Becky said. "She hates large groups, always has. I remember if she was late to class, she wouldn't go in."

"I thought you knew that," I said looking at Steven.

"Yeah, I knew that. Good Lord, you're nervous over that? Bree, for crying out loud, of all the things to be nervous about, that should be the least of your worries," Steven said shaking his head. "You surprise me sometimes, Princess. You can use your mind in ways I have never seen done before by someone who is not yet Magical, and you worry about people looking at you, getting into your space."

"Yeah, don't even mention people getting into her space," Becky said as she made a face and used air quotes.

"Okay enough. You can all talk about my phobias later. Right now, you need to go downstairs and take your seat. Ryan's probably pacing by now. You're messing with his schedule."

I started toward the door as Becky said, "You'll do fine in there today, Bree; so stop worrying. They can't hold a candle to you."

Steven came into my mind as Brad and Madalyn passed by me. Brad gave me a quick kiss and a smile. *Don't worry; we'll keep an eye on her.*

Rick leaned in and gave me a kiss on the cheek. "Come on Sandy let's get a move on."

Steven wrapped my arm around his as we walked to the elevator, just as he had when he took me to dinner on my first evening here. *Just keep smiling. They can't resist your smile; I couldn't. We've got a lot to do when we get home.*

We do? I knew he was trying to keep my mind free of thoughts of the upcoming event.

Yeah, we have to go furniture shopping. Remember? We haven't discussed that ye. What style do you like? I don't think you're a frilly kind of girl; I'm guessing more earth tones. I remember your bedroom.

Rick pressed the elevator button.

No, I don't want flower patterns or light fabrics. I prefer leathers, and wood. Dark rich colors. The sofa has to be deep enough so we can lie next to each other comfortably. Plus, I want it comfortable for you; and I don't think you like frilly stuff either.

Just so you know, both Sandy and Madalyn's furniture is like that. Brad and Rick have the entertainment areas of their houses, but the rest of their house is decorated that way. It's all pretty girly. He laughed, *they don't care for it; but hey, they love their mates.*

The elevator arrived. I entered first and moved to the side. Steven immediately pulled me toward the back of the elevator. Everyone stood in front of me. I started laughing as they all turned to face the front. "Good thing I'm not claustrophobic."

"Hmmm, Bree," Becky started.

"Not a word, Becky; not a word."

Steven continued to talk with me. *I'm surprised that's the type of furniture you want. You don't have that now.*

I looked at him. He was correct, but I didn't know how he knew. He had never been to my house. Nick liked the Victorian style of furniture, but to me that was the most uncomfortable stuff in the world. My living room looked more like an old-fashioned parlor. The furniture was cream colored. The sofa was long, but not wide. Not something you wanted to curl up in on a rainy winter day. Each seat section had a deep tufted medallion on the back. Each piece of furniture was edged in decorative maple wood, and rested on ornately carved feet raising them off the floor. The walls were painted very light lavender, with shear cream white window coverings. Victorian artwork adorned the walls. The room left me very cold and I hated it. It wasn't a comfortable room and I spent little time there. That was Nick's taste, his room.

The master bedroom wasn't as bad, although I hadn't slept in that room for sometime. When he'd had that room decorated, it had been done in a Renaissance style; and for the most part it wasn't too bad. I liked the earth tone of the walls and the hardwood floors.

The dinning room was another one of Nick's projects; we rarely ate in there. No, the furnishings in my house were cold and I didn't care for it; but I hadn't had a say in how it was decorated. Nick liked that style of furniture, so that's what we got.

How do you know what my house looks like? When were you there? I asked.

Honestly? Well, I did come with Bill a few times. You never saw me, but he brought me along. You always stayed in your kitchen; we sat at the nook every visit. I like the kitchen the best. Well, there and the guest bedroom. I like the way you decorated them.

I did like the guest bedroom. That's where I had slept since Nick left. The bed was large, with dark hardwood posts. It sat high off the floor; the mattress was thick and soft. The plush bed coverings were all in warm browns, hunter greens, and gold tones; several pillows lay on the bed. There were hardwood floors and warm colors were painted on the walls.

The bathroom connected to the room always gave me the feeling I was walking into a cave. The walls looked like stone, giving you the feeling it was carved right out of bedrock. The sink was a large basin set in rock. The bathroom had a large walk-in grotto shower that you stepped down into with dark stone walls and large rough inset openings carved into the walls to hold soap, shampoo, or anything else you needed while you showered. The far end had a stone bench. There were three showerheads in the ceiling. I always felt like I was standing in the rain when I took my shower. At least until I turned on the water jets that sprayed from the sides, then I felt like I was in a car wash! I had no idea what I had been thinking when I'd designed that! The lighting could be soft or bright depending on your mood. A small panel next to the shower controlled everything.

I had a large farmhouse style kitchen, which really went with the house. When you entered from the back door off the deck, you entered the mudroom and laundry room. This was a good-sized room. I had places for coats and shoes, a washbasin, cabinets for garden tools. Quite a bit of storage space. There was a front-loading washer and dryer, in red of course, built in ironing board, which I never used unless I was really pressed to, and a large folding counter. At the end of the room was a door leading to the garage, and an opening that led into the pantry, which led into the kitchen.

The breakfast nook had a kitchen table with six chairs. I did like the nook. It had huge bay windows that overlooked the back deck. I could sit there and see all the way to the woods behind my house. Along the side wall from the nook was my cooking area. The granite counter tops, with speckled browns and gold chips, were clear of any utensils. I hated clutter so everything had to be in a drawer or a cabinet. There was a large stainless steel gourmet gas stove. Double ovens were next to the stove. My cabinets were a lighter green giving the room a sassy appeal. A large copper double sink was in the middle of the counter and in front of the kitchen window that looked out over my flower garden. More counter tops and cabinets ended with a large French door stainless steel refrigerator set into the wall. A large work island was in the middle of the kitchen opposite the kitchen sink with a breakfast bar attached.

Well, we need to get rid of all of that furniture and have the whole house painted. I laughed, *Dang Steven, maybe it would be easier just to get rid of it and start new.*

Nah, we know someone who does this. We'll tell them what we want and they will do it all. Probably take about two weeks. I've already been talking to them so they will have some ideas for us when we get home. You have plenty of bedrooms, so we'll have them done for each of our family members. You know they will be over quite a bit.

Well, here's an idea. Why don't we just build a compound? One large compound; we can each have our own home and still be connected, I laughed.

Don't laugh, it's been suggested.

We arrived at the large ballroom that had been rearranged to accommodate the event that was about to take place. Each of my clan members gave me a hug and a kiss. Becky asked for permission, but Rick and Steven denied it. She didn't protest; she smiled and wished me luck, then went to take her seat at the front.

Steven was still with me. He didn't want to release my hand, but time was growing short. "Steven, it will be fine. Now kiss me, and go take your seat," I said.

"You'll be in my heart the entire time. Be watchful." He pulled me to him and kissed me hard, then reluctantly left.

I turned to Ryan, "Bree, are you okay?"

"Ryan," I smiled, "of course I am. I'm nervous, but I'm ready. Let's go."

Chapter 40

Friday Noon – The Council Meeting

We needed to wait until the appropriate time before we made our entrance. That gave Ry enough time to talk with me to let me know what I could expect.

"Bree, when we go in you will stand in the middle of the room. The Council members will be seated at a long table in front of you. If you get scared or nervous, just look at me. I'll be off to your left a little way down the table. We will not be able to communicate with you and you will not be able to communicate with us. Do you understand that? You will not be able to gain access into anyone's mind, and they will know if you try. Their punishment will be swift. They could strike you down where you stand if you try; so please, Bree, don't. They will be able to search your mind though and they can inflict pain if you resist. So don't resist," Ryan pleaded.

We stood at the entrance, Ryan didn't move. "Ry, come on. Let's get this over with," and I pushed the door open.

The room was packed. I walked down the isle. Chairs filled the spaces on each side, ten rows deep and maybe fifty chairs in a row. My family and clan sat in a section all to themselves in the front off to the right facing me. My parents, aunt and uncle and my grandmother along with Billy and the men of my clan were in the front row. The women of my clan sat behind them. My mother gave me a quick smile, and I smiled back. I knew my clan was unhappy with my parents for what they had agreed to. I couldn't be. I'd tried, but I just couldn't bring myself to be mad. I saw Steven, his face was stone silent. He was trying to remain in control, so I gave him a quick smile.

Odessa came into my head; *Close your mind now Bree, close it quickly.* I did as she instructed.

Ryan walked me to the front of the room and I saw the chair. He stopped beside it. He glanced up at the members seated at the table and glanced back at me. He wanted to tell me something. I saw the fear in his eyes, he was absolutely terrified. I've never known my cousin Ryan to show any fear.

"Co-Council Ryan, please take your seat," a bodiless voice sounded from somewhere along the table.

He glanced at my families. He turned back to me. His hands shook as he took me by my shoulders to draw me to him for a kiss on the cheek. And then he left me standing by the chair. As Ryan walked to his seat at the table, he snapped his fingers and was dressed in black robes with a green sash.

I stood beside the chair. It was an ordinary high back wooden chair with arms. The seat, back and arms of the chair were covered in heavy black fabric. Symbols were carved into the wood with various crystals and colored stones used to adorn the carvings. The chair looked very heavy and I knew I couldn't pick it up.

Do not sit in the chair, Bree, Odessa said. I didn't sit in it, but I did lean against it.

Somewhere along the table in front of me, a gavel banged loudly. "The Council will come to order," and then it struck again.

An elderly man walked up and stood in front of the table. He was wearing a black robe with a red sash. He was tall, his hair was gray, his eyes were warm, but his smile was smug. "Before we begin we have a little business to handle. The Council calls before us the Robertson family." Several hushed voices went through the room. A middle-aged man and woman rose from their seats in the crowd. "Is your daughter with you?"

"Yes," replied the man. He was scared; I could hear it in his voice.

"Have her stand please," the elderly man commanded. I knew I didn't like this man in the red sash. Nope, I didn't like him at all.

A young girl, who couldn't have been more than eighteen, rose from her seat. Her father tried to shield her, but the man in the red sash commanded him to step aside.

"You will not protect her; she has broken the rules and punishment must be made. Are you Janet Robertson?"

"I am. What is my crime, sir?" Janet spoke with as much attitude as she dared.

"You will wait until you have been addressed by the Council. Do not speak again. Come here to the front and sit before us."

Odessa came into my head. *This Council member's name is Nelson. He is rude, unfriendly, and mean spirited. Do not trust him. Janet's crime was falling in love with a human. Your cousin, Stanley, is in love with a human. The Council will destroy this family, any family, to make a point. Stanley fears the same fate awaits him if he is found out. This is something you need to change when you are on the Council, and they do not want it changed.*

Ah, this is the young girl they spoke about at the party, isn't it? Will they really send her to the dungeons just for this?

Yes, she will be forgotten and she will die there. She mustn't sit in the chair, Bree.

What will happen to the boy?

He will have an accident and he too will die.

Just for falling in love with a Magical? I can't let this happen.

Odessa gave me a sweet chuckle. *Your test begins. I am here. Keep your mind closed. The power is yours.*

The young girl moved away from her parents. I could read her fear; her mother was crying. Her father hugged her tight. "You will move here now," the red sashed man commanded.

I watched her walk toward me and the chair. She knew to be afraid of the chair; and she didn't want to sit there.

"Sit!" he commanded.

"Do not sit in the chair, Janet," I said as I reached to take her arm and gently pulled her to stand beside me. "Stand here by me," I stood between her and the chair. She didn't know what to do and I was making it up as I went. If this went badly, we were in a pickle.

"You dare speak out of turn to the Council? You have not been addressed. You will remain silent or I will strike you down." His face was starting to redden with anger.

"Nelson, we both know that is not going to happen." I was very calm. This took him by surprise. He was wondering how I knew his name. Evidentially, my guardians had dealt with these Council members before. This was an advantage I had, and they didn't know. Several more hushed voices from behind me were heard. Janet moved closer to me.

Nelson figured it was time to bring me into his party. "Are you Aubrey Marie Campbell?"

"I am," my voice was strong.

"Please sit."

"Thank you but I prefer to stand." I heard the voices murmuring behind me.

"What did you say?"

"I said, thank you, but I prefer to stand."

He eyed me warily. "Why is that?"

"It is what I prefer," I said; my eyes stayed fixed on him.

"Very well," he tipped his head.

You're doing fine, Bree.

He walked back and forth in front of the table. He was taken a little off guard. How dare this human tell him what she preferred? I watched him move back and forth. My eyes did not move from him. I felt the shoves he made as he tried to enter my mind. He pushed with his thoughts, but the doors to my mind stayed closed to him. He shoved harder, but my mind's doors held.

"Her mind is blocked. Who has blocked her?" He looked at the crowd; no one spoke. He looked at my families but could tell they were not blocking my mind. "I demand to know who has blocked this human's mind from me."

I raised a finger. "That would be me," I said. More voices rose from behind. I could feel my families tensing now. Ryan stared at me with one of those 'What the hell are you doing, girl?' kind of looks.

"Co-Council Ryan, did you inform your cousin of the etiquette of the Council?"

"Yes, he did," I answered before Ry had a chance. "That's just the stubborn side of me. I have issues with people taking trips through my mind. It's rude."

"You? You are still human. You cannot possibly block me. Why is it you try?" Now, he was curious. Still mad, but curious.

"It is my mind and they are my thoughts. You have no rights to them, Nelson. Obviously, I can and I have blocked you from them even though I am still human."

"I have every right to them. You are here because we so demand it. You will unblock your mind and let me in."

Am I pushing too much, Odessa?

You are doing fine.

"No Nelson, you do not have any rights to them; I won't unblock my mind. You are correct; I am here because of your demand, but I will not be subjected to your search."

He decided on another approach, "Why do you try to protect this girl? Do you know her?"

"No, can't say that I do. What terrible crime could she have committed to make you send her away from her family?"

"She fell in love with a human and that is strictly forbidden. Section 5; paragraph 1 of the Race Code states none from the Magical world are allowed to marry anyone from the mortal world. There will be no mixing of the mortal and Magical races. We have been very lenient with those from the Magical world socializing with the mortal world. These two were going to elope when they were caught. Now she will be punished. We do not want our race tainted by the weak. We will set an example with her. She will pay for her crime; five years imprisonment is the sentence."

"Wow, Nelson, that's a little harsh don't ya think?" I turned to Janet and whispered, "Was he worth it?"

She smiled and her eyes widened, "Oh, yeah, big time."

I smiled and nodded my head as I thought of Steven. More low voices broke out and another bang of the gavel sounded. "Order, we will have order."

"Maybe we should imprison you along with her. Your attitude will not be tolerated. You should fear me, my dear. I hold that power over you."

I looked at him for a long minute. My silence made him nervous, not to mention my family and clan. Finally I said, "No Nelson, you hold no power over me and I do not fear you. I am starting to tire of you and your condescending manner."

"Why do you feel you can speak to me in this manner? Do you know who I am? You are nobody. You haven't become a witch yet; you are nobody." His anger was showing, his shoulders rose and fell with his hard breaths.

I knew I was pushing my boundaries, but I was not going to be timid. Not now, too much was riding on this meeting. They were going to learn quickly, I was not going to be bullied into submission.

"Well then, if I am a 'nobody', why am I here?"

"Guards," he yelled. "Take this young girl to the dungeons and return. Aubrey will be joining her soon."

I looked toward the two guards that were moving in our direction. *Odessa, do you know their names?*

Walter and Justin.

"I'm sorry, Walter and Justin; you will not be taking Janet today." They stopped, confused on whom to listen to apparently. I turned back to Nelson. Your ruling is harsh and will not stand. She has committed no crime. She's eighteen and in love. Where is the crime in that? Because he is human? Do you not think their love can't be just as strong as a Magical? What right do you have to judge?"

"She broke the rules. She must be punished. I will not stand here and banter with you. I am not required to answer your questions." He raised his hand and pointed his wand toward her; I moved in front of her.

"I would think twice before you do that, Nelson." I felt my mother tense. The sensation of that was strong, but I did not acknowledge it. I continued to stand my ground in front of him. My eyes were fixed on him but I was aware of everyone in the hall. Where they stood or sat. Where their hands were, and who was thinking of picking up their wand to help. I looked down the table to another Council member in black robes, no sash. The name Rodney came to my mind so I went with it. "Rodney, I would leave my wand where it is, if I were you." My eyes moved back to Nelson. Our chess match continued.

Nelson smiled, "Yes, I heard how you were able to handle those vampires. Several at a time, wasn't it?" He laughed, "My dear, they do not possess the magic I do. You are young; you haven't even been schooled in casting. I am not afraid of you. Watch and learn."

A red flash came at us, one from Nelson's wand and the other from Rodney's. I raised my hands to them and caught their spells. I blew gently on my hands and opened them. Two white doves appeared and flew to the ceiling. I looked back at Nelson with a smile on my lips. "You are correct; I haven't been schooled in casting." My mind grabbed their wands from their hands; I let them hang in the middle of the room. Voices became louder from behind me. The gavel pounded on the table, the voices quieted.

When the hall had quieted enough, I continued with my warning, "Do not ever raise your wand to me again. Your rule is stupid and should be rethought." I snapped the wands in two. "And I am not *your* 'dear'."

The room was very quiet now! I stood in a relaxed manner and remained still; my eyes focused on Nelson. His cheeks were turning a flush red, his hands stiffly at his side. Low muffled voices started in the back of the room, growing louder as the seconds passed. The gavel struck again, calling order to the room.

"Well, Aubrey that was impressive," said a portly white haired woman sitting behind Nelson. How is it you can do these things? Do you know how hard it is to break a wand?"

"The magic runs deep in my soul. It always has; I was just unaware, Elsa."

"You think our ruling is too harsh? Why do you feel this way child? You are new to this life. How can you speak of something you know nothing about?"

"Yes, I am new to this life. However, even I can see the injustice in this law. It was not meant to be this way. Your Council has lost its vision. You are here to guide, not dictate. The Elders have shown me this. Your ways must change. You have no right imposing your will on the mortal world. The Elders wanted to coexist with them. Their realm is not as weak as you might think. Imposing your will on them will only strengthen them; and it will be our downfall. The Elders have seen this. Why have you lost your way?"

Murmuring started at the mention of the Elders, "You have spoken with the Elders? You have met them?" she asked.

"Their knowledge is buried deep in me as it has been with all the Chosen Ones. I have the knowledge when it is needed and I have their guidance. I do not need to see them in body to know it is true. The dark has gained control in this Council; I am here to change that course. Only those of the dark need fear me," I said.

"You are a danger to us then?"

"As I said, I am a danger only to the dark. They will not succeed in their desires."

"What changes would you make once you sit the Council?"

"Without seeing all the laws the Council has imposed I can't comment on that. However, this one at hand would be a good place to start. Why do you fear a union between a Magical and a mortal? What harm could possibly come from that?"

"What if the union dissolved? The mortals would know of our world. What then?" Elsa asked.

I smiled at her. "Elsa, many mortals already believe in this world. Why do you not see that? It has not dissolved our world. Guidelines could be put in place to handle these problems. Memories, events could be altered. It has happened before. Your ideas were not thought through. The Council is leading by fear, causing races to fracture. Guidelines must be followed; on that I can agree. However, those guidelines should be fair and just. Our world would follow those rules if given the chance; but this Council has chosen to dictate."

"Why go to all the bother? Is it not easier just to keep with our own kind?" Elsa asked.

"That is what the Council is here for, to go to the bother of guiding our world. The Council has lost its way. True leaders do not lead by causing their charges to fear them. Your Council is off balance. I do not see a good representative of our races. Where are the gnomes, the giants, and the werewolves? Do they not have a voice?"

"Aubrey, you are very young and very naive."

"I can agree I am young in body, but my mind is old with the knowledge. You know this to be true. Think back to your childhood, Elsa. These rules were not in place at the time, yet you have survived."

She sat there watching me for a few minutes. A tiny smile formed on her lips, then quickly faded. She needed to keep her composure. She cleared her throat, 'Nelson, please, take your seat. You do not intimidate her. Aubrey, continue to stand if you like. We will not take the girl; she may join her family." She waved her hand at Janet, motioning for her to take her seat back with her family. "We will review the guidelines set forth by this Council and when you transform and sit on the Council, we will then pass judgment. Until then, she is free to be with her family. But Aubrey, be mindful. If you do not transform the ruling will stand."

"What of the boy?" I asked.

"Aubrey, do not push your luck here," Elsa said.

"The boy has committed no crime. Why should your hands punish him? What rights do any of you have to do that?"

Elsa looked at me the way my grandmother did when she didn't want to argue a point with me. She exhaled as she said, "No harm will come to the boy. I command it so."

"Thank you, Elsa," I smiled. She looked down and started to shuffle papers, but I saw that tiny smile line her lips. Janet hugged me and went to sit with her family.

Odessa spoke to me, *Very good, Aubrey.*

Can I trust her?

Yes, child. She is one you can trust.

Another woman spoke, "Aubrey, do you know why we have asked you here?"

I looked in the direction of the voice. "Yes, it has to do with my transforming. You want to know where I am in the process. You want to ask me questions. You want to see for yourselves if I am weak or strong. You want to have me stay with the Council so you can **help** me through the process." She noticed my emphases on the word "help" and tipped her head.

"I have not transformed. It is up to you to decide if I am weak or strong. I can only tell you I am strong; you must decide that for yourselves. If you want to ask me questions, then ask. I will answer truthfully. On that you have my promise." I stood straight with my hands behind my back. Not stiff, but I stood as tall as my five foot, three inches would allow.

"Do you know the stories about your transforming?" she asked.

Odessa, do I call her by her name or should I just say ma'am?

Her name is Karol, and yes you may call her by her name. But remain polite. And before you ask, no, she can't be trusted. Not now nor when you sit the Council.

"Yes, Karol, I have heard them."

Karol shifted in her chair. "Then you know you will die when you transform?"

"I may die," I corrected her. "Yes, I know this."

Voices rose again behind me. The gavel hit the table. "Order, order, we must have quiet or you will be asked to leave."

Karol continued, "You will need to come with us so we can see you through the process, as you put it earlier. I agree; the little show you just put on was impressive. However, Elsa is correct; you are very young and naive. We have a place for you. You will be made comfortable until you either transform or you die - which ever." She waved her hand showing me she didn't care one way or the other.

"I thank you for the kind offer, but I will not come with you."

The hall grew very quiet. I remained calm and waited for her reply. She took a deep breath; her face was reddening. She started to remind me of an elderly schoolteacher who had lost control of her class and the only way she could get their attention was to yell. I could see a little spit spray as she spoke. "You dare to stand before us, you simple human, and tell us what you will and will not do?"

"Yes, I do," my voice remained strong. I did not move from my pose.

You're doing fine, Bree.

Several people in the crowd clapped. The gavel struck again. "I will give you my final warning; any more outburst and we will go behind closed doors."

My head turned toward the sound of the gavel "Behind closed doors or in front of opened ones, I will not go with you, sir."

"You do not have a choice. I am not as forgiving as my good Co-Council Elsa. Should you continue this show of disrespect you will feel my anger," Karol said. She seemed to be chewing on her cheek. Evidentially, she was unaccustomed to being told no.

Steady Bree, you know you have a choice. Don't let her bait you. Be firm with your response but be in control.

"I beg to differ with you Karol. Everyone has a choice and I will not let mine be taken from me. All my life, others have decided what would be best. I was not given a choice. I am now in control of my life and I do have a choice. My enemies dictated to my family how I must live. My family followed their directions; there was no choice. My enemies preyed upon parents that loved their daughter and only wanted her safe. My enemies took their choice away; my enemies took my choice away. They will never take it again," I said firmly but politely.

Then we heard a soft laugh, and Esmeralda made her entrance. A soft white fog appeared, swirling gently with the light breeze. She slowly materialized in the middle of the fog. Her form was translucent at first, becoming solid as the fog and breeze cleared.

When I could finally see her, she was indeed very beautiful. She looked just as she had in my dreams only she wore white robes with a gold sash. She was tall and slender. Her hair was long, thick and strawberry blond. Her eyes were a beautiful shade of violet. Her skin was slightly tanned. She stood poised behind her chair at the table. With a simple wave of her hand, her chair moved out allowing her to sit and then gently slide back into her place. Thomas appeared behind her. He looked at me, but remained uncommitted to a greeting.

"My Lady, welcome," said Nelson salivating. She acknowledged him with a smile and a slight dip of her head.

"Tell me," she began. "Where are we in this little show?" She looked at me. "Did I hear correctly? Aubrey does not wish to stay with us? Come now, my dear, this cannot be." She smiled. I envisioned her as a snake coiling to strike.

Before Nelson could answer her, I answered for myself. "Yes, you heard correctly, Esmeralda. I will not go with you." I smiled and the snake curled a little tighter.

"You need to address her in the proper manner," Nelson spewed.

Stand your ground, Bree, Odessa said to me.

"I showed no disrespect. Is her name not Esmeralda?"

"You will address her as 'my Lady' when she requests you to speak," Nelson bellowed.

"No, Nelson. I will address her by her rightful name. I am not her servant. That is a title she has imposed. I will not use it."

Esmeralda raised her hand and Nelson grew silent. "She will learn our ways Nelson, when she transforms. We have no worries here. Bree, may I call you Bree? I hear that is what your friends call you."

"Yes, my *friends* do call me Bree."

She looked at me. It took her a moment to process my words. I saw the hint of anger light her eyes. She drew a cleansing breath to calm herself before she spoke again, "Tell me Bree, how do you know us by name? You have never met us before today, yet you know us. Have you been schooled by your family, your," she gave a smug laugh, "clan?"

"Oh I know you all; I have seen all of you. I do know you Essie." I used Thomas' pet name for her. I saw the unsettlement in her face register. She looked at Thomas, as he stood rigid behind her. I smiled again, "Yes, Essie, I know his name for you."

More hushed sounds came from behind me. I didn't want to look at Steven, but I did go into our special place. *Steven, I love you.* I whispered it so softly. Out of the corner of my eye I saw him shift.

Esmeralda rose from her chair in a commanding form. "You will come with us, Bree. We can take care of you better than anyone. We have the best doctors to help you through this difficult time." She started to walk behind the table. Thomas stood back giving her room to pass. "I am told your body is warming. That can be most uncomfortable. And your headaches, they are painful aren't they? Our doctors will help with the pain. No, you must come with us." She stopped behind Karol and continued to smile at me.

I folded my hands in front of me. A smile came to my lips as I thought about the last headache I'd had and how Steven's tone soothed it away. "Again, I appreciate the offer, but I will stay with my own doctor thank you. I know he has my best interest at heart."

"You have a doctor? Ah, yes Bradley. Yes, he is very good. But Bree, he is not your kind, our kind." She spoke in a mocking whisper then continued walking behind the table, heading in Nelson's direction. She gestured her hands toward me, "We are the Chosen Ones, you are a Chosen One," she continued to walk back toward Thomas. "You need to have the best doctors available. What does he know of witches? Vampires can be very unpredictable. Even the most restrained ones could slip up." Her hand rose up to Thomas and he kissed it gently. "Where would you be then, Bree? Their bite doesn't always kill a normal human; but Bree darling, you are not a normal human. Their bite will kill you," she laughed. "You would have no such fear from our doctors. They have studied the transformation process and are the best equipped to handle your situation. And Bree, they don't bite."

"Well, Esmeralda, you are correct, *I* am a Chosen One and my doctor hasn't bitten me yet. I think I'll take my chances with him. No, I will stay with my doctor and I will stay in my own home. I will not go with you, Esmeralda."

"Your clan's ways are strange to you, are they not? Our ways are strange. Tell me how are you handling this? It was not your wish, was it, to have two strong men attracted to you? I am told the human side of you is strong."

"Only two, Essie? The prophecy spoke of seven," I smiled. "It is an adjustment, I'll not lie, but I do so love a challenge. I will adjust Essie, you needn't worry yourself."

Very good Bree, Odessa smiled her comment to my mind.

Her friendly posture turned angry; she squared her shoulders toward me. "I wish to know where you are in the process," her voice was hard. "You will have blood drawn here in front of us all, by our doctors, to see how green you really are," she commanded.

Her smile was wicked. If she thought they were getting near me with a needle, she had another thing coming. "I will submit to your test, here in front of everyone. However, my doctor will draw my blood, not yours. I have had enough of your meddling in my health," I stated firmly.

"Is your doctor prepared to take your blood? I am sure he will need to go get his supplies. That will take time and our doctors are ready now," Esmeralda said.

"He never goes anywhere without his medical bag," I smiled at her, then looked at Bradley and winked. "Would you like him to begin?"

She inhaled deeply. Anger showed in her violet eyes, but she kept her smile and hissed her words through her clenched teeth, "Yes, I would. Come out here to the front Bradley." Esmeralda continued to look for weakness in my armor. "Do you need to sit, Bree? I understand you have a problem with needles."

"No, standing is fine." Brad's eyes looked straight into mine. I smiled to him and went into his mind. *Hello, Bradley. Don't worry I have everyone blocked.*

Hello, love. You're doing fine. Are you going to be able to do this without sitting?

We'll soon see, won't we? How are you holding up?

Brad had my arm pinned against his side with his arm locked around it. *We're doing just fine. Don't look and breathe through your nose, Bree. Here's the stick.* I felt the pressure of the vial going into place. *All done. Put your finger on the cotton. You did just fine. The solstice is not that far off; keep that in mind.* He bent my arm up.

You do have a way about you, Bradley.

Best bedside manner this side of Chicago. Still thinking about my promise? So, you know about the seven then?

Yes, Bradley, I know about them.

One of Esmeralda's doctors rolled a table forward with a microscope on it. He needed to verify Brad's findings. He touched the vial and commented on the warmth that came from the small amount of blood in it. He watched as Brad put a few drops on a slide and slid it onto the microscope viewer. A projection went on the wall. Brad and the other doctor, who was starting to look very familiar to me, spoke quietly to one another.

"Bree let me introduce one of my doctors to you. This is Doctor John Craig. He is the leading expert in these transformations."

Doctor John nodded at me, then turned back to face the front and spoke. "As you can see, my Lady and Council, her red and white cells are being boosted by the green and purple cells." He took his laser pointer and indicated the cells he was speaking about. "These cells are making her change. The numbers of the green and purple have increased considerably since her last test. Her doctor just confirmed this to me. I am estimating another seven to eight months before she transforms."

I had hoped for the nine months Brad had given me earlier. Brad reached into his bag and brought out the bottle of clear liquid. He dropped three drops in. A darker shade of green than the last time rose from it. Brad and Doctor John spoke softly to themselves.

"My Lady and Council, Aubrey's doctor has confirmed to me the shade is three times darker than the first."

Esmeralda nodded to imply she understood; I knew she didn't have a clue what the levels of green meant. Karol brought the question to the forefront. "Exactly doctor, what do these levels imply?"

I spoke before he had a chance to, "It will tell you how powerful I will be once I transform." Brad and Doctor John turned to me. I smiled; they smiled back.

"She is correct, my Lady and Council. From what her doctor has told me she should balance out somewhere between thirteen and seventeen times the shade." The doctor noticed the confused looks on members of the council. "Meaning, she will be very, very powerful."

I thought to them both as they were packing up the equipment, *Thank you doctor. If I didn't have a bull's eye on me before, I certainly do now.*

He thought back to us. *Keep her safe. A lot is riding on you, my dear.*

I thought I recognized you. I never got the chance to thank you. Brad left to go sit with our clan.

Doctor John smiled, *Good luck, my dear.*

"It is settled, Bree; you will come with us. We will guide you through the process. As you can see, my doctors are just as good as yours. Have her room made ready..."

"Esmeralda, I will not go with you."

Esmeralda stood still. I was getting the distinct feeling *many* people on this Council were not used to anyone defying them.

Elsa spoke, "It is clear she is her parents' child. Warren was always the stubborn one. Martha, I don't know how you do it." That remark brought a little laughter from the crowd as I looked at my mother and father. Mom gave one of those 'Oh, Elsa' slaps in the air. It was probably a joke they shared from a long time ago. "I think we can work around this. Don't you, Esmeralda?"

That's a good sign for you Bree. She called her by her name; she is standing by you, Odessa said.

"I agree with Co-Council Elsa," said the Spaniard. He gave me a slight tip of his head. I smiled back. "I do not see any problem with the child staying with her family until she transforms." Several others agreed, nodding their heads. By the look of things, it appeared over half the Council was pulling to my side. Ryan would have to give me a progress report later.

A small man toward the end of the table spoke, "My House will protect her as she sleeps; she will fear nothing during her restful hours from dusk to dawn. She needs to be allowed to gain her strength so she can succeed during the transformation." He looked at Thomas, "Wherever she sleeps, she will be protected." Thomas nodded, as he understood I was off limits from attacks during the night when he was at his strongest. The small man looked at me and said, "I wish you well, my dear." I could tell he was a short man from his height in the chair. His hair was black, his eyes were dark and his skin was quite pale, causing the circles under his eyes to be a little more pronounced. He had hollow cheeks, thinned lips, and a very straight pointed nose.

Odessa spoke to me, *that was Steven's ancestor, Count Wentworth. He is very powerful and does not like Esmeralda at all. I think you have won a soft spot in his heart.*

I went into Thomas' mind very cautiously, *my Lady, we may have to let her transform. By bringing her here to the Council, you have strengthened her. I told you this would happen; you should have listened. We will have to be very careful.*

I heard Esmeralda's words of warning to him. *Do not lose your resolve, Thomas. I can replace you! I have spoken with others that could do this! She must not live. Gather what you need, be sure of your path. I want her dead. I want **you** to bring me her dead body and I will watch your clan feast. If you can't do this, I will find those that can.* I heard her gasp in her thoughts she as she suddenly saw the gems! *Damn her, she is wearing my jewels. How did she get them? I want to know who is aiding this, this creature. I want the Chosen Ones at the castle questioned thoroughly. Do you understand?*

Esmeralda regained her composure quickly. She reminded the Council, "She may not transform. Have you forgotten this? The transformation may indeed kill her; that is why she needs to be with our doctors. If we do not have her in our care, how will we know what progress her change is making? No, she must come with us." Her composure was starting to fade as she saw she wasn't gain-ing much support. I could see the fear creeping in. Soon she would panic and that would make her very dangerous. I continued to listen to their thoughts. *Damn her, the support I have cultivated these many years is waning. They fall for her young face. She must not survive. Do you understand? Even if she succeeds in transforming, we will end her life.*

"Esmeralda," I said and Nelson bellowed, "You will wait until she has spoken to you before you speak!"

"Esmeralda," I began again. "My doctor will keep your doctor posted on my progress. He can be present during the test, or my doctor, Steven and I will come to you. It doesn't matter to me where the tests are done. When I transform, trust me Esmeralda, you will know. Should the transformation go badly, I would prefer to be with the ones who love me instead of surrounded by doctors I do not know. No Esmeralda, I will not go with you."

Thomas thought to her, *my Lady, we can still get her blood when she dies. If we do not get the chance to kill her here, I will simply go there. Her blood is what I want most; my clan will feast on her flesh. You will remain strong until she dies; then there will be none to ever replace you, as she is the last. Let her go to her family, we will watch her closely. You will appear merciful in the Council's eyes. She is surely doomed to die; the seers have seen it.*

Esmeralda nodded as she listened to his thoughts. When he had finished conveying his thoughts to her, he chanced a glance at me. *You are in great danger Aubrey. I can only do so much; you must do the rest.* Then he stood back behind her and kept his hand on her shoulder.

I didn't show any recognition of his remarks.

"Bree, if I agree to allow you to go home to your family, what reassurance do I have your family will be truthful when you die?" Esmeralda smiled a cold smile.

"Esmeralda, if I should die, I will give you my body, and I will instruct my family to honor my wishes. You will have your proof. You may send one of your minions to collect it. After my family has said their goodbyes, it will be yours. When I transform," I paused for effect, "you will know."

She took a moment before she spoke. She calculated her words carefully. "Bree you have our," she spread her hands wide meaning the Council, "blessing to go home to die or transform, if it is to be. If you transform, I will welcome you to the Council. You may sit on my right side as we rule our world."

Okay, Bree, you may now let her know that you know you will be more powerful. You will gain many here and probably add to her paranoia, Odessa laughed.

"No, Esmeralda. When I transform, and I will transform, my sisters will sit beside me as it was written long ago. I will wear the white robes with the golden sash. My Houses are stronger than yours and when the Fourth bonds, I will stand far above you. My powers will be greater. I will guild, not rule our world. Others will have a say, as it is their world too. You have been asleep at the lead. There are problems that need addressing I am told. They will be addressed. I will return once I have transformed." I dipped my head slightly, turned and started to walk out of the room.

Esmeralda slammed her hand down hard on the table. Clearly, she had lost her composure. "I have not dismissed you."

I turned slowly back to face her, and smiled. "Esmeralda, you have mistakenly thought I am your servant; I am not. I do not need to be given permission to leave a room like a child. You have work to do. I suggest you get to it." I turned and left the room.

CHAPTER 41

When All Is Said and Done

I made it to the hall before I allowed myself to breathe. I realized we hadn't arranged a meeting place for when it was over. I contacted Steven with my thoughts, *Steven where shall I meet you?*

"Turn around, I'm right behind you."

I wheeled around so fast I almost fell over. He caught me and I jumped into his arms. I needed to hold him; I needed his lips on mine so desperately. Steven held me in his arms. We had a few minutes to ourselves before everyone started filing out of the room and our lips were locked in a heated kiss. My arms were around his neck. I just couldn't let him go; I was only concentrating on him.

Then I heard them all. My parents were the first and Steven reluctantly put me down. I stood with him behind me, his arms still around my waist. My parents stood in front of me; they seemed to have aged in the past week. I saw the pain and worry in their eyes. They needed to talk with me, to try to make me understand. My mother fought to hold her tears, but she wasn't having much success. My father kept his arm around her. Billy, Brad, and Rick stood back. The anger was still in their eyes. My aunt and uncle stood with my parents. They were there to help explain the events that had unfolded in my life, if I was willing to listen. My heart softened as I looked into all their eyes. I understood they had done the best they could. They did not understand the strength I had, but maybe I wouldn't have had that strength if my life went down another path.

Odessa spoke in my mind. *They are hurting child. Soften your touch. You are their only child and they desperately love you. They never meant to cause you pain. Comfort them child. Show them your strength.*

"Bree, please forgive us; we are so sorry we put you through this. We completely understand if you hate us, but please know we did what we did because we wanted to keep you safe." My father's hands trembled as he wiped the tears from his eyes. He had old eyes now. The stress this must have put on them was taking its toll. My father was a tall man, big and strong, but he was crumbling in front of me and I could not bear that. "We were so old when we had you. You are our pride and joy and we couldn't let anyone take you away from us. At times, I know our judgment was clouded. We made many mistakes. You couldn't hate us anymore than we already hate ourselves. We only ask you give us a chance to make it up to you." His voice cracked as he held back his pain, his tears. My mother stood by him. Her face was pale; her lips quivered as the tears fell from her eyes. She let my father do the talking. I knew she wanted to speak, but her voice would not obey.

"Dad, Mom, please, what happened, happened. We can't change the past or what led to it, but we can change the future. Our energy needs to be focused on that. I don't have time to think of the past. I love you both and could never hate you. Did you not hear me in there? Your choice, as much as mine, was taken from you. Your fear clouded your judgment. I promise you, I will never let that happen again. You must understand I am strong now, much stronger then they had ever imagined. I don't want to remember the past. It's gone. I want to move forward, with Steven."

Steven's arms slipped away from my waist as I held my arms out to my mother for her hug. My father threw his arms around both of us, and I let their tears fall. I could hear my Uncle Donald talking with Steven, making his amends to him and to my clan. My grandmother came up and patted my father on the back and he moved away.

My mother released me and whispered, "I need to hug my new son-in-law." She and my father went to talk with Steven and my grandmother moved in to talk with me.

"Bree, listen to Odessa. She can guide you far better than I ever could. Listen to her child, your path is very dangerous now." She kissed me and went to join my parents, and I watched as Steven was being smothered by my mother's kisses.

Ryan and Kim came up behind me. "Bree, I had no idea they brought the chair for you to sit in. Damn, I'm sorry."

I looked at him a little confused, "Why, what was wrong with the chair?"

Ryan shook his head in disbelief, "Okay, we really need to do a better job at this. The chair has many functions. It can inflict great pain; make you vanish to where ever the

Council sends you. I have even witnessed people being consumed by flames. It's a terrible device. No one knows where it came from; but the Council does use it, and they have been using it a lot. There is no rhyme or reason to the punishment it gives. Some say it has a mind of its own," Ryan said.

"Well, Ry, then it's a good thing I didn't sit in it," I laughed. "Ry, you need to start a list and put the chair and this mortal-Magical falling in love law on the top. You and I will be spending time together once I transform, but I want to get married first." I smiled at them, "I need to go rescue Steven."

I walked over to the crowd around Steven and my clan. Steven pulled me in close to him, his arms around my waist, I faced my father, "Dad, how much longer until my divorce is final?"

"Maybe another month or two. Why?" he asked.

Steven rested his chin on my head and smiled at him, "Why do you think Warren?"

"Ah, yes, I'll see if I can't speed the process up."

"If we killed them you wouldn't have to wait," Rick said as he came up and took me in his arms for a big hug. "Finally, I thought I would never get to hold you." He buried his head against my neck giving me a sweet kiss. His tone for me was just as strong.

"Now, Richard, there will be no killing," I said as I hugged him back.

Billy was next, "Damn, can't wait to get home and get things back to normal with you, Half Pint. Little Timmy's been asking for his favorite Auntie Bree."

"I miss him too."

He finally put me down and Madalyn and Brad came up behind me. Brad swung me around and pulled me close as he thought to me. *Our family is whole now. Damn, I love you, Bree.*

My clan was going to need a long rest after this.

The Robertson's made their way through the crowd toward me. Mrs. Robertson reached for my hand; I had Rick and Steven by my side immediately. I looked at her and smiled. Her smile widened as I extended my hand for her to shake. "We can't thank you enough for what you did in there. You don't know us from a hole in the ground, but you stood up for her when we couldn't do anything. Bless you. Your parents raised you right. We will be praying for you. You boys keep her safe."

Then Janet said her thanks. She smiled at Steven and Rick, I shook my head and laughed, "Sorry, Janet, they are spoken for."

Count Wentworth was moving toward us. His bodyguards moved the crowds out of his way as he walked up to me and took my hand. "My dear, that was truly fun to watch. I wish you the best of luck. Steven, please, my dear boy, you must bring this lovely creature for a visit once her transformation has transpired. I look forward to spending more time with you, my dear." He kissed my hand and licked his lips. "Sweet, you taste very sweet," he smiled, winked and left.

Next came Señor Hernandez; he took my hand and kissed it. "Aubrey, my dear sweet child, I wish the best for you. As I promised, you stood your ground and we will stand with you. Guard her well, Steven." He dipped his head to Steven and Rick, and left.

I looked at Steven, "Well at least he didn't comment on my taste. Where are Brad and Madalyn?"

"Over there, Squirt. Why?"

"I just want to know where everyone is that's all. It's time for us to go home and rest. Where does Becky need to be?"

"That's something we need to discuss," Rick said.

"Let's keep the status quo for now. Let's put her up in an apartment. After we have rested we will tackle this problem," I said.

"Very well Princess. Stanley will watch over her; but I want this resolved quickly."

"Okay, you guys are in charge."

Rick pulled back, "Steven quick; I think they've taken Bree and given us this short little shit who listens!"

I smiled at him, "After everyone has rested, I'd like for us to get back together. Plus my mother will be expecting everyone for Thanksgiving." I could feel Rick and Steven tense. "Enough you two." I wrapped my arms through theirs and started walking toward Brad and Madalyn. "We have a lot to be thankful for, so it won't be that bad."

"What are you talking about, getting back together? Are you going somewhere we don't know about, Squirt?" Rick asked, a little tension in his voice.

I put my hand in his and turned to him, "I'm sending you home to rest. Gee Rick, you and Sandy need your time together. Brad and Madalyn need their time. Besides, Steven wants to redo the house. So everyone can come and see it when it's finished."

"Don't worry Rick, I'll have her call daily," Steven laughed.

Madalyn and Brad were talking with a group of people I didn't know. Billy and Gina were there as well. Sandy joined us as we made our way to the group. "Steven, do you know those people they're speaking with?"

"Yeah, 'fraid so. They want to join our clan."

"And?"

"And we don't know if we want them or not. We're still thinking about it."

"What's wrong with them?"

"Bree," Steven started.

"I'm sure you and Rick will do what's right," I finished.

They stopped again and looked at me. "Come on you two," I laughed as I pulled them along. We walked up to the group and Brad moved to my side, replacing Rick. "So Bradley, what's up?"

"Just talking a little business here. Why?"

"Can I talk to you for a minute?" I kissed Steven, "Be right back," and took Brad's hand and led him off to the side.

౼

"It's time for you and Madalyn to go home and rest." I was fixing the collar on his shirt. Brad started to protest, and I raised my finger to his lips. "Please Bradley, enough. I am fine. I am going home. I'm sending Rick and Sandy home, and you and Madalyn need time to yourselves. You need to rest. Madalyn needs to feel secure with you. Please do this for me. We all need a rest. One week. That's all I'm asking, then we will all get back together."

"Bree, we...oh damn...I am used to seeing you daily now. A week will feel like an eternity."

"Bradley, take Madalyn home. You can call us every day if that helps. I don't know, maybe Steven and I will drop by. We'll see. Now go," and I reached to give him a tender kiss on the lips.

We rejoined Steven and the others; Brad collected Madalyn and they left. Dirk and Andrew joined the group replacing the four that wanted to join our clan. I noticed the conversation had turned serious, not what I wanted to hear. As I joined the group, they quieted as Steven put his arm around me. I knew that sound and frankly, I had had just about enough of all the secrecy. "What's up?" I asked knowing I wasn't going to get a straight answer.

"Nothing Squirt, just talking with Dirk and Andrew," Rick supplied and gave me a smile.

"Uh-huh...whatcha talking about?" I batted my eyes at him. He knew I wasn't buying it; but being the good sport he was, he smiled back.

"Nothing Squirt, absolutely nothing." He thought to me, *I can be an ass sometimes, little missy.*

"Sometimes?" I whispered back.

Dirk was a very good-looking guy. He and Stanley were good friends, but I had never really met him before last night. He had a head full of curly thick black hair; his skin was tanned, he was stocky. He wore dark Dockers, a white shirt, brown tie and a hunter green vest. He had a beautiful smile; brown eyes and a couple days beard growth on his face. I liked him. I had no idea why, I just knew I could trust him.

Andrew was skinny, tall, and somewhat nervous. He had short wavy blonde hair, blue eyes, and a fair complexion.

He was dressed similarly to Dirk. I didn't dislike him; but I just didn't feel as comfortable with him.

I smiled at them, and then went for a little walk through their minds. As I entered Dirk's, he was talking with Andrew and Billy. My own cousin should know better by now, but I listened anyway. *Bill, Thomas has been seriously tasked to kill her. She is royally pissed. Frankly, I'm surprised she didn't try to strike her down right in front of everyone. Your cousin sure has some balls for a girl.*

Yeah, she's a pistol that's for sure. She goes off half-cocked sometimes, but hey, I love her. What can I say? We'll just have to increase the protection, any idea on his plans?

None, I can tell you they will use humans as often as they can. Thomas is more afraid of Count Wentworth, than he is of Esmeralda. The Count has a soft spot for your cousin, and he knows it. He's not going to cross him, not at any cost. We'll keep our contact on the inside and let you know of any changes. All we can tell you now is to keep a sharp eye out. She's in more danger than I think your cousin realizes, Dirk said.

Nothing new was gleaned from this so I started to move through the hall to see if I could pick anything up. All I noticed were happy people, and then I found one of Thomas' clansmen. It was the one I had injured, so I knew Thomas was close. I kept searching as I kept listening to my own group. Then I found him.

Bree, I know you can hear me. We should talk - just you and me. He sent his thoughts out to me.

I hear you Thomas; you know I can't meet with you alone. Steven will not allow that and I will not lie to him. Speak to me now. What is it we need to discuss?

Your life for one. I will stay close to Esmeralda; I will do what I can. Learn as much as you can about Black Magic, my dear. Esmeralda is extremely knowledgeable in this area. She has been waiting on you a very long time.

Why are you taking a chance telling me this, Thomas? Your mistress will be most upset to learn you have warned me.

What can I say Aubrey? You fascinate me. You aren't afraid of me; but Bree, you really should be. I am very dangerous. Steven knows, Rick knows, Brad knows. My dear, your entire clan knows I am dangerous. Everyone but you. In the end, you will know it too.

I'll keep that in mind, Thomas. By the way, I really don't think you are as dangerous as you want everyone to believe; but I will play along. There is more to your story than that.

I have told Esmeralda I can't do anything for a few months. I need time to put a plan together, so, have some fun. Maybe by then we can think of something to stop her.

You know she will replace you because you were unable to make me fall. I fear I have put you in jeopardy, and I am sorry for that. Your replacement will fail too though. Be aware Thomas, you play a dangerous game.

You fear for me, huh? Could I have made an impression on you, my dear? Thank you for your concern; I'll keep that in mind. Oh, and Bree, you do taste very sweet.

I looked at him, and watched him run his tongue over his teeth and smile. *So I've been told Thomas; so I've been told.* I turned my attention back to my clan. I whispered in Rick's ear that it was time for them to go home. It was time for life to get back to normal. He thought to me, *you are still safe in my special place.*

I know. We'll see you soon. Then I gently kissed his ear. I turned to Steven, got right up in his face, and smiled. "Talk business later, I want to go home now," then kissed him. He wrapped his arms around my waist. "Your wish, my Princess, is my command. Talk to you guys later." I waved good-bye to Billy and Gina. "See you later." With Steven's arms around me, we vanished.

Made in the USA